Hawkmaiden

*A **Spellmonger** Cadet Novel #1*

By Terry Mancour

All rights reserved.

ISBN:1535050853
ISBN-13:9781535050852

Dedicated with love and affection

to my darling daughter,

Morrigan Laine Mancour

Author's Forward

I started writing the fantasy series known as the **Spellmonger** series even before my kids were born. Writing good, compelling, and adult fantasy was my goal. As the **Spellmonger** novels have progressed, so has my life; I now have three children who, alas, would likely love to read my stuff, but there are too many naughty bits.

The Cadet novels, the first of which you now read, are my answer to this. It's hard finding "Young Adult" fantasy that doesn't treat either the issues of youth or the imagined realities of a fantasy world without feeling trite, patronizing, and fluffy.

Hawkmaiden isn't fluffy. But it isn't brutal, either. It isn't an adult novel, but it doesn't talk down to its reader. Only time and the market will determine whether or not it's popular, but my goal was a fun, challenging read that requires kids to look up words they don't know, because that's how children educate themselves.

Please enjoy the book. You may always write the author at tmancour@gmail.com, and I particularly encourage you to do so if you're a kid who liked this book – or if you didn't. Tell me why, either way. I love hearing from my readers, and your feedback is important to how I write things in the future.

Because that's how writers educate themselves.

Terry Mancour,

January 22, 2015

TERRY MANCOUR

The Falcon's Call!

From the moment Dara of Westwood spied the Silver Headed Raptor nesting in Rundeval Peak, the precocious redheaded twelve-year-old girl was enchanted. The youngest daughter of the Master of the Wood lived in ramshackle Westwood Hall, in the independently-minded Westwood estate of Sevendor. Her determination to capture a baby falcon and train it wasn't hampered by the fact that Dara had never climbed a mountain, had never been trained in falconry, or even remotely had permission from her father to do it. Dara wanted the falcon . . . and the only thing in her way was the mountain, an angry mother falcon, and her own fears.

But the daring climb up Rundeval and actually capturing the fledgling falcon is just the beginning of her troubles. Actually learning falconry and training the willful bird is a responsibility she had barely considered. Worse, there is trouble afoot in the domain: a new lord has come to rule over Sevendor and all of her people, replacing the corrupt old Sir Erantal. While everyone welcomes the change, the new lord is a wizard: a magelord, the first of his kind in four hundred years: Lord Minalan the Spellmonger. And he's not alone. He's brought thousands of oddly-dressed Wilderlanders with him, families escaping the wars in the west . . . and settling in Sevendor.

Within weeks of holding his first court as lord of Sevendor, the wizard's magic begins to cause problems. Magelord Minalan turns Sevendor Castle, the entire mountain of Rundeval, and a good portion of the Westwood –including Dara's home – into enchanted white stone when a spell goes unexpectedly awry one fateful night. As a result, Dara learns that she, too, may become a mage someday. Soon after she discovers that she can see through her falcon's eyes and share her thoughts, the talents of a beastmaster, opening up a brilliant new world for her.

The folk of the valley have enough to eat for the first time in a generation, there are wizards all over Sevendor, and the castle glows with a magic light at night. The fortunes of the Westwood estate rise. But the Magelord finds foes as well as friends in Sevendor.

Though prosperity flows from the Magelord's benevolent rule, the changes are frightening to some who have lost power since the Magelord came. Outside the Westwood, the other natives of the domain are upset by their magical lord and his strange new people, and there are whispers of rebellion. And outside of the domain, the neighboring lords, urged on by sinister forces, conspire to plunge Sevendor into war – with Dara and her family along with it!

What can one girl and her falcon do? When the Magelord leaves on business and his enemies close in on her home, Dara discovers she may hold the answer to saving them all! The fate of the entire domain rests with Dara of Westwood, the girl they'll call the Hawkmaiden!

CONTENTS

1	The Eyrie On The Ridge	2
2	The Cottage In The Nutwood	22
3	Stealing Rope	40
4	Rundeval	56
5	Frightful	76
6	Training	95
7	Sevendor Castle	117
8	The Blizzard	138
9	Wizards Of Sevendor	157
10	Market Day	180
11	To Arms!	210
12	Under Siege	230
13	Sevendor At War	249
14	The Magical Corps	267
15	The Lifting Of The Siege	286
16	The Spellmonger's Trial	309
17	The Witchstone	335

Uwarri Hills → Sevendor Vale
                              ‿
                            valley
   Narasi lords from — east + south

p.11   Westwood   400 acre estate behind jagged
                       chasm that protected them
                       "the great manor" on a cliff
                                    hall

p.14 [Kamen] Dara's father = { Yeoman
                                { Master of the Westwood
              Mother, Gessi — died in childbirth of Dara
                        ⇓   6 children
        ┌ Leska ♀
        ├ Linta ♀   p.28
        ├ ▓▓▓▓▓▓▓▓▓▓▓▓▓▓▓▓▓
        ├ ▓sta
        ├ Kyre ♂
        └ (Dara) Lenodara

p.6 — Uncle Keram   — Aunt Anira
       p.26 — app. tied — under the castle falconer b 4 the domain d'd hards

p.25   Kamen's [uncle Keshin] had been Master of the Wood
                    ↓ son   { climbed Rundeval
         cousin → Kilmer   { Peak when
                                       { Keram was a child

p.22
P
- Westwood manor's central fireplace
 = The Flame — burning continuously for hundreds of years

Chapter One

The Eyrie On The Ridge

"It's *beautiful!*" Lenodara said, barely able to speak above a whisper as she watched the magnificent hawk soar across the sky. It was massive, she could tell, even without anything around it for scale. And the way it soared through the air was majestic . . .

"It's deadly," her oldest brother informed her in a low voice. Kyre was five and a half years older than Dara (as everyone but her Aunt Anira called her), but unlike her other siblings (or her father, Anira, her cousins, or just about every other resident of sprawling Westwood Hall) Kyre never acted as if she were still a baby. He treated his youngest, twelve-year-old sister like an adult. That was just how Kyre was: mature and thoughtful. He pulled himself up the giant spruce tree limb by limb, barely disturbing the needles of the spruce as he climbed, until he had found her perch.

"It's a Silver Hooded Raptor," he continued, authoritatively, after studying the bird with his dark eyes a few moments. "They're the king of the birds-of-prey in the Uwarri ridges. They can see a mouse take a leak six miles away, Uncle Keram says."

Their favorite uncle would know . . . in his youth their father's younger brother had been apprenticed as a falconer at Sevendor Castle, briefly. "Lords pay real gold for them – they're supposed to be the best hunters in the world."

"They can be trained?" Dara asked, not taking her eyes from the bird as it soared majestically above. "To hunt?"

"If you have the nerve," Kyre chuckled, indulgently. "And the time. It requires a lot of patience and conditioning to train a bird to hunt. Keram has done it, though not with a raptor," he added. "From what I hear, they're too hard to manage, much less capture."

"It's a beautiful hawk!" she sighed, watching its graceful wings against the perfect, cloudless blue sky.

"It's not a hawk, it's a falcon," corrected Kyre, shifting his weight on the branch to get a better view. "Hawks kill with their claws, usually, and are larger than falcons, who use their beaks mostly. *Usually*," he emphasized. "The Silver Hooded Raptor is one of the largest falcons. Larger than many hawks. They nest on the highest peaks, in the most inaccessible spots in these mountains. That one must be new – I don't remember that eyrie on Rundeval's peak from last year," he added thoughtfully.

If a Westwoodman didn't remember a beast or bird in his wood, he wasn't worth the name, Dara knew. The Westwood was the largest of Sevendor's seven Yeomanries – manors and estates organized for production – and its economy depended upon the forest that gave the manor its name. And while Kyre wasn't the most experienced woodsman in the manor, he was more woodwise than many men twice his age.

Of course he looked half-wooden himself. His dark hair and eyes and his dusky complexion told him out as a Westwoodman as much as his thick leather vest over his woolen tunic. The Westwoodmen stood apart from any other people in Sevendor Vale. None of the Sevendori from the other yeomanries were nearly so dark as the men of the Westwood, though they toiled in the fields under the sun.

She, in contrast, had pale skin, red hair, and freckles that seemed to multiply every time she found herself in front of a looking glass. It was a rarer combination in their little land, but considered lucky – the birth of the "fire-haired" was seen as a blessing from Briga.

Her late mother Gessi had been similarly "Flame-kissed", and had borne six children before she died bearing Dara, twelve years before – *"flame spreads quickly!"* was a Westwood proverb associated with the many children red-haired folk were reputed to have, and Gessi bore out the saying. Fertility wasn't the only talent associated with red hair, however. Many of her flame-haired ancestors were rumored to have possessed second sight or other gifts from the gods. Westwood Hall had more than a few figures of legend the Flame had touched.

But to Dara's knowledge she hadn't shown any signs of greatness in her twelve years of life. In fact, to most of the folk of Westwood Hall, Dara was a pure nuisance. She was known among her kin for being impetuous and unrealistic, a dreamer. She had no idea how such an unfair opinion of her had developed.

"How can I *get* one?" Dara asked, her eyes following the bird carefully.

"You *can't*," her brother said with a chuckle. "When I say they nest in the highest peaks, I wasn't kidding. Look, that one is nesting . . . at the crest of Rundeval!" he said, as the raptor landed on the tallest peak on the next ridge. "No one's climbed Rundeval in twenty years. Not to the peak. Not even Father or Uncle Keram. I'd start with something a little more manageable anyway, if you want to learn falconry, Little Bird. Perhaps a kestrel or a goshawk. Or an owl."

"I don't *want* an owl," Dara insisted. "I want a Silver Hooded Raptor. I want *that* Raptor, Kyre, I want it! I want *that* one!" she said, as the bird wheeled perfectly over the wood, slowing down so quickly she wondered how it stayed in the air.

"You can't just go capturing a full-grown falcon to train," her brother said, chuckling at her enthusiasm. "It doesn't work that way. Adult birds are too wild. You have to get a nestling in the autumn, before they take flight, and train it from before it's got its full fledgling wings. *That's* a full-grown bird."

"Then I'll get a hatchling," she decided. "If they can be trained to hunt . . ."

"You're dreaming again, Little Bird," Kyre laughed, as he started to descend the tree. She almost took exception at the nickname she'd borne since youth, but not against Kyre. She adored her oldest brother. "You'd need wings of your own to get to that nest. Look at it. *No one* climbs Rundeval. That's why the Westwood stops at that ridge."

"It's not impassable," she reminded him. "People have climbed it before!"

"No, but the high pass isn't easy. I've been two-thirds of the way up, and it was hard as Anira's biscuits. And from the pass you'd have to . . . wait, why am I even *telling* you this?"

"Because I'm curious," she urged. "And you *love* me. And if anyone could get up there, Kyre, *you* could. Now tell me, once you got to the pass . . .?"

"Once you got to the pass you'd have to make your way west, over those rocks, and then do a vertical climb up . . . hells, from here I'd say it was at least sixty, seventy feet – and that's only got you partway there."

"And then what would I have to do?"

"I have no idea," he admitted. "I've never been as far, myself. *Why* do you want to train a falcon, Dara?"

"Why wouldn't I?" she asked, noting exactly where the bird

had landed and committing it to memory. "I mean, falconry is a noble sport. If I could get Uncle Keram to teach me how, then I'd have a trade . . . and I wouldn't have to worry about growing up so much."

Her Uncle Keram was her favorite, perhaps because after her mother died, her father had been nearly heartbroken. Keram and Anira had only three children of their own, before the midwives told them sadly that they would have no more. So as a baby they had served as surrogate parents while her father worked through his grief. Dara shared a very close relationship with her uncle as a result. Less so, with her stern Aunt Anira.

That was part of the problem. Aunt Anira felt she should be preparing to go courting, at her age. As a daughter of the Master of the Westwood, her aunt constantly reminded her, she would be highly prized among the folk of the vale. That prospect frightened Dara. She had only given up playing with dolls last year. She was not ready to even think about such things as husbands and children. Her reluctance to consider the matter had been the cause of much friction between herself and her foster mother.

"Don't worry, Father isn't ready to marry you off just yet, Little Bird," he laughed, guessing her thoughts.

"No, but he *could*," she reminded him. "Just ask Aunt Anira. He did it to Leska!" Leska was their eldest sister, and had been married to a boy from Gurisham the year before. She had always been eager to trade the Westwood for life in a village, and when she had met a husky farmer lad at market she had quickly persuaded their father to make the arrangements.

"Yes, but Leska was eighteen, not twelve, and she loved the boy, and she was *Leska* . . . can you really see her doing well in the Westwood? She's been pestering Father to find her a husband since she was fourteen. She *should* be near

Mother's kin, and be a farmer's wife. Far, *far* away from here," he added. Leska had not been the easiest older sister to get along with.

Dara couldn't help giggling. "Yes, I can see your point. At least you never had to share a room with her! But if I knew falconry," she reasoned, "then Father wouldn't even have a reason to consider it."

"Not unless you wanted to," agreed Kyre. "If you had a real trade, you could forestall it awhile, at least. You know, you might not mind being wed, one day . . . in fact, you're about the only girl I know who *isn't* consumed by the idea."

"The thought of being chained to some peasant oaf in Sevendor or Genly . . . it makes me consider taking holy orders," she confessed.

"Father would never marry you against your will," Kyre assured her. "Nor me, for that matter. And I hear he's had offers," he added, slyly. As heir to the yeomanry, *of course* Kyre had had offers. It only made sense. But the idea of her oldest brother married off to some girl she didn't even know made Dara angry for some reason. "But I don't—"

"KYRE!" came a shout from across the fields, interrupting their lazy discussion. The spruce they were in was on the edge of the Westwood Hall compound, just by the hedge that shielded the main yard from the woods, proper. From this spot, if you climbed the big spruce high enough, you could see both the grand stone Hall as well as see over the rocky ridge that separated the Westwood from Sevendor Castle. A good place to daydream, and a popular place for Dara and her siblings.

The shout was loud, male, and alarmed. Dara wondered what was happening. It was a good three hundred yards to the manor house, but when the brass bell that hung from the peak of the barn started ringing that only meant trouble, she knew, if it wasn't the three bells that signaled mealtime.

She and Kyre looked at each other for a split second before moving.

Kyre dropped from his perch soundlessly and was sprinting across the meadow like a hare. Dara followed more slowly, more clumsily, and with more trepidation. She didn't want to slip and add more drama to whatever it was that was unfolding. That was the *emergency* bell, she realized, the one suspended from the watchtower. Not the dinner bell.

In fact, she noted as she landed on her hands and feet, the rest of the manor was already headed in to the Hall from the shops, sheds, and yards of the settlement as fast as they could. She pushed her legs to follow her swift-footed brother through the gateway and into the outer yard and found her older cousin Larvan standing there, holding his bow and quiver and looking grim.

Holding *two* bows, she realized. He handed the other one to Kyre with just a hint of deference – Kyre was younger than Larvan, but he was the Master of the Wood's heir, as his silver wolf's head ring designated, destined to inherit his father's important office and the manor in his time.

"It's a man from the *castle*," Larvan said, distastefully. "He's on the other side of the ravine. He's demanding that your father deliver his *proper* tribute."

"And Father . . .?"

Larvan smiled mirthlessly. "He is not inclined to make that delivery," he said, simply.

Dara's heart sank. That could mean fighting. And fighting could mean killing.

"It's been brewing for a while," Larvan said, as they

walked back to the manor. Kyre strapped on his quiver and took a short sword from his cousin to set beside it on his belt, before he strung his bow. "Sir Erantal has sent three men to demand tribute this year. Father has sent two of them back empty-handed."

That was news to Dara – she hadn't been aware of the visits. Then again, most manor business was conducted around the Flame, and she was rarely involved in those matters, being twelve, female, and precociously curious.

"Why only two?" she asked, dumbly. The boys looked at her.

"The third seems to have . . . tripped and fallen into the ravine," Larvan said, quietly. "It's a shame. Everyone knows how *treacherous* that bridge can be."

Dara realized he was being sarcastic . . . and that the third representative from the castle had never returned from his duty. That made her feel a little ill. She knew her Father had to do such things, to protect the Westwood from the knight-in-residence at the castle, but this was the first time she had heard of him actually having someone . . . *killed.* It sent a chill up her spine.

"Aren't we *supposed* to pay tribute to the castle?" she asked, trying not to sound stupid. If it had been one of her other, more obnoxious cousins that might have been a risk, but Larvan had always been nice to her.

"Aye, and they are supposed to guard the people and ensure their welfare . . . and old Sir Erantal hasn't done a thing when folk are starving in the castle's own village." Kyre sounded disgusted. "The harvest was poor this year, and he took more than his share."

"But how does that concern the Westwood?" she asked.

"Simple: he wants more. From everyone. But if we allow

Sir Erantal to run roughshod over his own people without protest, he'll soon do it to us, too," explained Larvan.

"Besides, your father hates the sight of the man. Says he's not fit to be the lord of winesops, much less a proper lord."

That was a frequent topic of conversation around the Flame, she knew, though she had never dared participate in it.

Sir Erantal was holding the domain in the name of the Duke. Theoretically, the Duke was their lord . . . but Sir Erantal was who the Duke had hired to run the domain until it was given away or sold or inherited or bequeathed to a proper lord. At which point, her Uncle Keram had said, cynically, they'd likely hire someone just as bad as Sir Erantal to run the place as castellan.

"There are three or four of them, this time," Larvan informed his cousin as they strode resolutely toward the manor hall. "Armed and armored," he added, grimly as they rounded the corner and strode into the yard. Dara followed behind, because no one had told her not to, yet.

"That's not good," frowned her brother. Dara was just about to say something similar, when Kyre suddenly turned to her. "Dara, get up to your room," he ordered. "I doubt it will come to fighting, but if it does . . . well, you'll get the best view from your window," he pointed out.

It was a blatant ploy to keep her out of trouble, she knew... but she also knew that if Kyre thought she might be in the way, she should probably stay out of the way.

"Be careful! Flame guide you!" she urged, as she watched them walk through the courtyard toward the bridge yard. Kyre turned around and gave her a confident smile.

"Don't worry," he dismissed, "when they see how many archers are on this side of the ravine, they're going to reconsider crossing that bridge."

She nodded, but she didn't stop worrying. It was happening again.

The Westwoodmen had always been outsiders in Sevendor Vale, though they had been here in the Westwood since before it *was* Sevendor Vale.

When the first Narasi lords from the east and south had come to the Uwarri hills, the Westwoodmen had been there for centuries, already, behind the jagged chasm that protected their four hundred-acre estate. Their customs and manner of speech were different from the Narasi folk who had settled to farm grain in the more arable regions of the valley. The rest of the Vale's villages and hamlets were wary of the manor's odd folk and that suspicion was mutual... despite two centuries or more of occasional intermarriage.

The key to the Westwood's ability to maintain its independence, as Dara's father had lectured her family often enough, was the position of its holding. The great manor hall was situated on a rocky outcropping facing a cliff over a forty-foot deep (deeper, in some places, it was said), twenty-foot wide (and much wider, at the northern end) chasm that split the rocky woodlands in the western end of the valley from the rest.

The ravine spanned the entire western end of the vale. The land behind it was higher than the rest of the vale, and remained thickly wooded while the rest of the domain was slowly but surely deforested. The Westwoodmen did not farm, as the other Sevendori did, apart from a few vegetable gardens. They hunted, gathered, fished, trapped, tanned leather and cultivated the forest for lumber, trading their products to the farmers of Sevendor for grain. But the ravine kept them forever apart from the folk who farmed the lands beyond it.

The bridge that connected the Westwood with the rest of

Sevendor was narrow, a moveable contraption of wood and rope, without rail or rest. It was designed to present the flanks of whoever crossed it to the archery of the Westwoodmen. And, of course, should the Master of the Wood order his men to retract the bridge it would be extremely difficult to cross if anyone stood in arms at the Hall.

So when Sir Erantal sent men from Sevendor Castle to treat with the Master, they were not doing so from a position of strength. Dara hurried up the stairs to her loft, high in the older part of the manor hall, which faced out over the chasm. From where she was she could see the bridgehead very clearly with her sharp eyes . . . and the men standing upon it.

Lord Erantal's men were mail-clad men-at-arms, and Dara's heart raced when she saw their deadly-looking longswords at their sides. Soldiers. But these were no knights – Sir Erantal was the only knight in Sevendor and he was hardly the picture of chivalry. These were hired swords, men barely better than bandits, who had taken Erantal's coin for the job of squeezing more tribute from the folk of the Vale from the castle garrison.

One of the four wore a full helmet, as opposed to the iron pots the others wore. He also wore a faded yellow baldric over his shoulder. That meant he was some sort of castle official, Dara suspected. The man looked strong but brutish, and he surveyed her home with a sneer of contempt that raised her ire the moment she saw it

Dara may not have fit in with the rest of her extended family, but *no one* had a right to wear an expression like that when they looked at ancient and distinguished Westwood Hall. This was her home, and had been her family's home for centuries. The fact that she felt like a changeling the Tree Folk had dropped off here most of the time did not lessen her loyalty to her little land.

Dara leaned out the window as far as she was able, in order to overhear the conversation . . . or see the combat, if it came to that. She devoutly wished that it wouldn't – she could not bear the thought of any of her kin getting hurt. But the haughty way the castle reeve addressed her uncle – like a common villein! – made her angry.

The castle's men were on the small landing just on the other side of the bridge. They were strutting impatiently back and forth, having called to the watcher (her sleepy cousin Kapi) to release the small ten-foot section of drawbridge, so that he and his men might cross. Kapi had told them that none could enter without permission of the Master of the Wood, and he would fetch him.

When her Uncle Keram showed up, instead, the reeve insulted him and demanded entry. Her uncle slowly repeated that none could enter without the leave of the Master, and they grew even more impatient . . . but five or six of the Westwoodmen had quietly found positions behind the wall that screened the chasm from the manor, and more were taking positions as they arrived. Each bore a long hunting bow, and each was proficient with its use.
Westwoodmen can shoot, ran another popular proverb.

All Westwood children, boys and girls, learned to shoot. Even Dara. Dara had never been particularly good at it, but she knew how to nock and draw and loose an arrow. She had proven better with an old hunting arbalest [crossbow] her Uncle Laris had lying around in his woodshop, something he'd used to shoot squirrels and racquiels with as a boy. Dara "borrowed" it to practice with last year and never quite returned it. She had never killed an animal with it – the thought made her a little ill – but she had become proficient with the small darts and pebbles it shot over the last year.

The young men of the Westwood, on the other hand, hunted for their living. They were adept archers and had practiced specifically repelling potential invaders at the bridge their entire lives. When the reeve tried to cross the span without leave, and began making threats, Dara's Uncle Keram raised his fist. The Westwoodmen all stood up from behind their screens and boulders, their bows drawn and arrows nocked.

The castle folk seemed to calm down a bit after that, Dara noted.

We might be villeins, in their eyes, but dead by a villein's arrow is still dead! she thought with satisfaction, as the castle men realized their danger. Of course that wasn't technically true, either. The Westwoodmen were freemen, masters of their own fates. They weren't serfs or peasants. Of course, to most lords anyone who wasn't a lord might as well be a serf or peasant, she knew.

More of the manor's men came out, the younger ones who had been at their chores and the older ones who had been in the tanning or curing sheds, until there were almost two dozen dark-haired Westwoodmen preparing to volley against the castle men. That's when Dara's father, Kamen, Master of the Wood, finally came out of the manor house.

To Dara's dismay, she saw he was wearing his armor. That was a bad sign. She'd never seen her father don his armor, which usually hung from a rack at the north end of the Hall, to speak to a visitor on the bridge before.

"What's all this?" he asked loudly, motioning for the boy pulling the brass bell to stop the noise.

"A summons!" the reeve called. "Are you Kamen, Yeoman of the Westwood?"

"If you were a proper castellan, you'd know that answer," grunted her father. His armor was a thick bear hide vest sewn with dozens of thick iron plates, but he bore it as if it was made of cotton. He was wearing his longsword, too, as his rank permitted him. The other Westwoodmen near the bridgehead who bore swords lacked the rank to bear them, she knew, unless the domain was at war and under siege, but there was not much anyone at the castle could do about that. "But I am Kamen, the Master of the Wood. What business have you with the Westwood?"

"Your estate is in arrears of its lawful tribute by nearly two years!" the reeve bellowed over the chasm. "Sir Erantal will have his rightful payment!"

"Sir Erantal already takes too much of my money at that pathetic excuse for a market," barked her father. "We sent forty cords of firewood to the castle this year, as is custom." Her father had complained that half of the wood would be sold to Erantal's profit, while Sevendor Castle stood cold and drafty all winter, but that wasn't his business. The Westwood had done its duty.

"You owe money rents for two years," the man repeated, his voice echoing slightly in the chasm. "That comes to seventeen ounces of silver!"

"I'll not pay rent on land that was my blood's for centuries. We're Westwoodmen, not villeins!"

"Then call it a tax," the reeve shouted. "But you will pay it!"

"Sevendor is the *Duke's* land," Kamen reminded the man. "He has not levied any taxes, else it would have been published and posted, as the law requires!"

"A *fee* then!" the reeve called, exasperated.

"A fee? A fee for *what?*" demanded Kamen. "What service has the Westwood asked of the castle? We keep to ourselves, save market days, and then we pay our proper fees like the rest!"

"Pay your damn taxes to your proper lord!" bellowed the reeve, losing control of his anger.

"I'm not inclined to," Kamen said, his jaw set resolutely. "Sir Erantal is a drunken fool surrounded by thugs. He's no proper lord at all. He wants the coin for wine, not pay, and we all know it. He can kiss my hairy arse!"

"Brave words from a man with a crevasse guarding him!" sneered the reeve.

"Aye," Kamen agreed. "And even braver with my lads ready to *fill you with holes*. I know my rights and the rights of my folk. Sir Erantal has no right to demand more than his proper tribute, which is paid in meat and firewood at Yule. Well, *we* keep his frontiers clear, and *we* police his forest. He can squeeze the Genly peasants if he wants better than ale to keep him warm this winter!"

"I dare you to come over here and say that, churl!"

Kamen chuckled. "I've beaten younger and stronger men than you. I'm doing you and your heirs a favor by not crossing."

"Come within the reach of my sword and see how brave you are!" the reeve snarled, drawing his horseman's blade. Dara was not much judge of such things, but even she could see it was old and a bit rusty.

Kamen smiled, and with the alacrity of a much younger man he sprang across the bridge to the edge of the gap . . . then leapt onto the ropes beyond the pulled-up span, one foot perched on each thick twisted line. He drew his own sword, a war sword that had been in the family for generations, a gift from one of the real lords of Sevendor for faithful service long ago. It had no trace of rust on its blade.

"If you've reason to doubt my courage," Kamen called, brandishing his sword as he straddled the gap, his feet balancing on the ropes, "then see to your own. If you're so keen to test it, crawl out here with me and we'll settle the matter!"

The challenge made the reeve blanche. One of his fellows behind him even laughed at his predicament: after challenging Kamen's valor, he now had to prove his own or lose honor.

"What trick is this, old man?" the reeve called back, after a moment of hesitation. "I come out here and take an arrow in my gut?"

"I'll have the lads drop their bows," agreed Kamen, adjusting his precarious footing slightly. Dara held her breath. "Then we'll see if you can dance in the air with a Westwoodman!"

The reeve hesitated again, then spat and sheathed his sword. "I didn't come here to fight a crazy old man. I came here to get Sir Erantal's money!"

"Then I suppose you'll be disappointed on both counts," laughed Kamen. "For you'll have that silver only when I'm at the bottom of that chasm!"

The defiance in his voice made Dara proud of her father. Seeing him standing alone on the narrow bridge, his ancient sword ready to defend his home, made her want to run out and fight herself.

But the castle men were not interested in testing their agility today. They looked at her father skeptically, and one by one they prepared to leave. The Westwoodmen had enough grace not to cheer, but there were some murmurs from the west side of the gap. Enough to anger one of the castle men, who suddenly drew his blade and struck at the rope bridge.

The thick twist of hemp was too thick to yield to a single

sword blow. But the damage was done. The moment his sword struck the rope, a bowstring twanged and the man grew an arrow out of his thigh. Worse, the shock of the blow had thrown Kamen off balance on his perch. His knees wobbled and he dropped his sword behind him as he struggled to right himself. When he could not, he tried to move both feet to one side, but slipped.

For an endless moment Dara thought she was going to watch her father plummet to his death. But his strong hands grasped at the rope and scrambled for purchase. Another rope became entangled in one leg as he slipped again. While it kept him from falling, there was a sharp crack that Dara could hear from her window.

Before she could remember to breathe, her uncle – and her brothers, she saw – had leapt to assist her floundering father. Another few bowstrings twanged and the castle men began to retreat. With great relief watched as her brother and her uncle pulled her father up onto the rope bridge. He was alive!

Alive but hurt, she saw. His face contorted in pain, and he clutched at his leg. His two rescuers began examining the damaged limb immediately, and before the castle men had cleared the bridge her Aunt Anira and her sister Linta had burst into the courtyard, screaming in alarm.

He's all right, you idiots! Dara thought as she watched her sister wail ineffectively. *Apart from that leg, that is . . . don't they know how close they came to a real fight? How close Father came to . . . to . . .*

Dara found herself running down the narrow stairs before she realized what she was doing, then ran across the stone-flagged yard to join the growing knot of people tending her father. She stopped short of plunging in and adding her useless hands to the chaos. Her brother and Uncle Keram were already fashioning a splint, and someone was preparing their mantle to be used as a stretcher to bear him inside.

"Broken," her uncle pronounced, "but a clean break. We'll set it inside, near the Flame, and he'll be walking again in a few weeks," he promised them all. There was a hint of worry in his voice, only because he knew that broken limbs sometimes had other complications. But she trusted her uncle's judgment. He'd seen plenty of such wounds before, in the field.

"If he had fallen," Kyre, her brother said, his eyes flashing dangerously, "if he had fallen I would have—"

"Enough of that talk!" demanded their father, as he was lifted onto the stretcher. "They'll be back in a few days, and there will be more of them. We'll be ready. No one goes to market, this week or the next. We keep the bridge up. And we don't do anything to rile them further."

"But, Father—" Kyre began, angrily.

"*I* am Master in this hall, and by the Flame I have spoken!" he said, sternly. "We have to think about the whole manor, boy, and everyone in it. Always. Starting a fight with the castle folk is foolish."

"But Father, they started it! And we could take them!" Kyre pleaded. "We have *twice* as many men as they, and—"

"And that would make us *rebels*," Kamen finished. "And thus would we be hung. We will not pay what we do not owe. But we will not call down the Duke's wrath on us for rebellion, either."

"The Duke has no idea he even owns Sevendor!" challenged Kyre, defiantly.

"And you would bring us to his attention through word of *rebellion?* By the Flame, hopefully you will gain wisdom before you become Master of the Wood in your own right," her father said with a grunt as he was hoisted into the air on the stretcher. "This will blow over," he called out to everyone in the yard. "With winter coming, old Sir Erantal just wants to stock his larder at our expense. He's not looking for a fight – else he would have fought for Brestal, when the Warbird took it," he finished. "Now, everyone *back to work!*"

There was a nervous chuckle among the manor folk at that remark. It was Kamen's most common refrain, and it helped assure everyone that he really *was* all right. But the tension from the confrontation still hung in the air, Dara could feel, and her friends and relatives kept looking at each other nervously.

Dara tried to take a deep breath and relax, herself. She felt her Uncle Keram's hand on her shoulder, as the others followed the stretcher inside. Keram didn't say anything, he just gave her a meaningful look. She returned it . . . until her eye caught something above his head.

One of the raptors from the mountain was diving gracefully into the chasm, intent on some prey it had spotted. Dara watched, entranced, as the graceful bird struck at some rodent it had sighted below. She followed the bird's path eagerly with her eyes until it was out of sight. Her uncle was still clutching her shoulder, but she barely felt it.

"So beautiful," she breathed. The tension from the fight was gone, for her, swept away by the whisper of deadly wings.

"Are you well, Dara?" Uncle Keram asked, concerned. She could almost feel the falcon's savage triumph as it tore into its prey. Dara realized that she was quivering.

"I'm fine, Uncle," she said, taking a deep breath. "Just . . . excited."

"I'm not certain the Hall can stand an excited Dara," Keram – called "the Crafty" for his adept management of the estate at her father's direction — chuckled, quietly. "Why don't you go fetch the healing bag for me? Setting that bone is going to be tricky. Then go down to the herb house and get willow bark and poppy oil. With that and some spirits, I think my brother will be fine." He still sounded worried, Dara realized. If her father was incapacitated, it would fall to Keram to lead the Westwood until he was well. And that was his older brother he was about to tend.

"Right away, Uncle!" Dara called, as she ran to do as he bid. She felt guilty for focusing on the hawk when her father was hurt, but as she ran to the herb house behind the manor, she knew she couldn't help it. The raptor had captured her imagination in a way nothing else had.

She *had* to have one, she knew, no matter what it took to get it.

Chapter Two

The Cottage In The Nutwood

The oldest part of Westwood Hall was the actual hall, a large square stone room which was dominated by the great round stone fireplace in its center, where the Flame lived. The fireplace structure was four feet tall and ten feet wide, with three grand pillars of rock supporting the massive stone chimney above it. The Flame was built, family legend had it, when the Westwoodmen first arrived at the Westwood, centuries ago. Everything else in the manor had been built after and around that central fireplace. The Flame was, literally, at the center of the Westwood's existence.

Supposedly the Flame had been burning continuously for hundreds of years, constantly tended by her family, but Dara somehow doubted that. It just seemed impractical. But the reverence her family displayed for the fire was profound, bordering on religious. That made them very odd to the rest of the Vale, who worshipped the proper Narasi gods when the monks and priestesses made their circuits through Sevendor. To them, fire was just *fire*.

But a Westwoodman swore his most sacred oaths by the Flame, bore witness to the most important ceremonies, and he would not willingly lie in its light. Her people were wedded by the Flame, and when they died their funerals and wakes were held in its presence. Babies were named in the light of the Flame, and promises made there had to be kept.

The great fireplace was where the meals of the house

were served, where the family gathered to eat and socialize. The Flame was where the Hallfolk gathered to talk and drink and share stories, where anyone from the various cottages and homes of the Westwood could find warmth, comfort, a mug and a pipe. The hall around it was scattered with benches and chairs, while chests containing the estate's more valuable property lined the walls.

There were other fireplaces in the house, in the kitchen and in the additions to the hall that had been made over the years, but there was only one Flame. It represented the goddess Briga, the Westwoodmen told outsiders, because the Narasi fire goddess was something the people of the Vale understood. But the Flame was more than a shrine. It was the living heart of Westwood Hall, the light in the darkness, the heat against the cold.

Everyone had a role in keeping the Flame burning, from the time they were children. The youngest were taught to guard it and bank it, while older children were tasked with cleaning the ashes away and feeding the flame. After adolescence, girls usually tended the flame until they married, while boys were responsible for supplying the great stack of hardwoods kept on the north wall. The Flame was eternally hungry, and it was the duty of the Westwood boys to feed it.

Dara had taken her turn, in due course, and had spent plenty of time simply staring into the Flame. Now those chores were given to younger children. But when Kamen was brought inside to have his leg set, bound and bandaged, he rested and recuperated near the Flame, instead of his small room. It was considered beneficial to healing.

Though Dara was now thankfully exempt from tending the fire, she and her siblings each took turns sitting with their father near the Flame to keep the normally-active man company for the next few days. Kamen was a robust Master of the Wood, and was used to spending his time ranging the forests or overseeing the various enterprises that supported the estate. As the manor's Yeoman, he was responsible for fulfilling the castle's requirements.

Now that he was injured, however, Uncle Keram had to take over seeing to the day-to-day operations of the estate. While he was fully capable of doing so, Kamen started complaining about things almost immediately. The forced inactivity soon had him irritated with nearly everyone in the Hall. After two days sitting next to the Flame with the youngest of the Hall, Kamen looked like he was ready to eat a basket of kittens.

His youngest daughter proved to be one of the few people that did not invite his ire. Dara did her best to be entertaining, even singing to him in her disturbingly uneven voice. She tended and cared for him, to keep him from verbally abusing her Aunt Anira and other members of the family, but she quickly grew weary of the chore.

That's when she remembered the falcon's nest on the peak of Rundeval, and the rumors that her father had once scaled the summit. Dara suddenly realized she actually had something to talk to the cranky old bear about. She could not come right out and ask him if she could go after the fledgling – he would refuse, of course, on the grounds that it was far too dangerous.

But she could solicit information just by showing interest, Dara figured. She'd noticed that her father loved to talk about his exploits in his youth, back before he'd met and married her mother. In fact, most men she knew did. If she asked him the right questions, he would never know what she was planning.

She began, innocently enough, when she brought him his afternoon tea. She gingerly stepped around his splinted leg, shaking her head as she handed him his great earthenware mug.

"Poor Father! It's hard to believe that broken leg once climbed to the top of the peak of Rundeval," she said, with just the right amount of sass to her voice.

Kamen warmed, patting the broken leg fondly.

"Oh, aye, they've carried me from one end of Sevendor to the other," he agreed. "And when I was a lad, they carried me all the way to the top of the mountain. It was glorious," he recalled. "It was my cousin Kilmer, and his father Keshin, who was Master of the Wood at the time. We went all the way to Rundeval's peak. It took hours."

"You scaled the entire cliff?" she asked in wonder. The raptor's nest was three-quarters of the way up the steep slope of dark gray basalt mountain.

"Scaled it? Nay, Little Bird. We went the long way around, the trail up the south side of the mountain. It's steep, but we only had to scale the last forty, fifty feet to get to the peak. Why, my legs were ready to give out as it was – I can't imagine scaling the entire front face!" he laughed.

Dara's face fell at the news, but she recovered before Kamen noticed. If even her powerful father had not considered scaling the cliff, how could *she* possibly think to do it?

"But surely you *could* have, when you were younger?"

"Younger . . . and had wings," he snorted. "By the Flame, girl, the back ascent was difficult enough. Barely a handhold to speak of, the last twenty feet. There's no more than a knob of rock the size of a hogshead atop the thing to keep you from sliding down the slope, and there are briars and needlebush everywhere. It was a test of our manhood, scaling that mountain. It fought back. I could have hurt myself far worse than *this*," he said, gesturing to the large wooden splint on his leg. "The mountain is no picnic site, Dara," he said, seriously.

"Just promise me that if you go up again someday that you'll take me!" she said, with just a little too much girlish enthusiasm. She couldn't let him forbid her to go, not in front of the Flame. That would end her plan before it was begun. But if she tried to get him to promise, he might back off telling her not to go, she reasoned.

"Now, Dara, I'm not a young man, anymore," he sighed. "I'll never scale that mountain again."

"But *if* you do—!" she pleaded.

"*If* I do . . . and gods alone know what would possess me to undertake such a fool stunt . . . but *if* the notion does take me, then *yes*, I will consider bringing you along," he conceded.

"Oh, *thank you*, Father!" she said, kissing his head with relief. *That had been close.* If he had made her promise not to try to scale the cliff in front of the Flame, she would have been compelled to obey. This way, *he* was the one who felt compelled to consider taking her, if he went. Someday, maybe.

Dara was not inclined to wait. She didn't have much more time before the fledglings she knew were in that nest would learn to fly on their own and that would be too late to train them, from what her Uncle Keram said.

She had been haunting his steps, too, as he made the rounds from the curing sheds to the wood yard to the nuttery, asking him a thousand questions about falcons and hawks.

He apprenticed under the castle falconer, briefly, as a youth, before the domain had changed hands. Then the new tenant lord, who had a love of boar hunting, had the mews, dismantled and turned into a kennel. But for a year and a half her uncle learned about hunting birds. Dara asked him everything she could think of, without annoying him. And while he thought he was merely entertaining her, he was helping his niece assemble a list of the equipment she'd need.

She considered all that Kamen and her Uncle Keram had said, that night, and the more she thought about it, the more she realized that there *had* to be a way.

At some point, she realized that she had committed herself to actually trying. She *would* find a way to scale that cliff, or die trying. That night her dreams were filled with wings and shadows, and in the morning she barely felt as if she had slept. But she already had the beginnings of a plan.

If she wanted to succeed, she knew, she would have to be organized about it. And there were no half-measures involved. She was not just breaking the rules and risking punishment, she understood, she was *endangering her life*. No one in the Hall would be agreeable with that, regardless of how obnoxious she thought she was. It seemed insane to even consider such a stupid, *stupid* course of action.

But the idea of such a magnificent bird perched on her arm was just too enticing.

After helping serve her father his breakfast and gather laundry for the week, Dara dashed off to the tall spruce tree she and Kyre had perched on a few days earlier. Scaling it was easy, she proved, going up the smooth bark of the tree with the alacrity of a raccoon. She found her familiar perch, the one that offered the best view of the cliff overhead.

She studied the bare rock face for hours, imagining every way she could possibly ascend to the cliff. Some routes she estimated brought her hundreds of feet in the air . . . but in the end, all of them met the sheer vertical face of the cliff, where handholds and resting points ceased altogether. The best route she'd envisioned to the nest still left her eighty or ninety feet shy.

There was no way to do it, she could see. No matter how badly she wanted it to be so, there was no *possible* way the cliff face could be scaled. The raptor mother had found an impregnable site for her nest. There was no way any predator could sneak up on the vulnerable nest from below.

Frustrated, Dara climbed down out of the tree and cast herself into the loamy ground below it. She seethed with frustration over having the chicks so near to her – near enough that she could almost imagine seeing them, if she squinted really hard. The clouds in the sky floated by serenely as the mother falcon mocked her with her beautiful flight over the vale.

Dara watched the raptor fly for a while, until she could imagine what it was like to fly so vividly it alarmed her. She shook her head to clear it, and then saw the mountain peak again, upside down from her perspective on the ground.

If only I could fly to the nest, Dara teased herself. *Perhaps if I made wings, I could just descend from the sky . . . once that mountain peak moved out of the way . . . and light right* there, *on that cliff. And then you and I would be together, little chick,* she promised.

Come get me! she imagined the baby falcon was calling to her, in her mind.

But even as she thought it, she knew it was pointless. The idea that she could find a way to steal away a fledgling, and then raise it and train it to hunt – all without her family or anyone else at the Hall knowing – was laughable, she knew.

She was just being Dara the Dumb, as her big sister Linta called her sometimes when she asked too many questions.

Dreaming impossible dreams far too big for a redheaded oddity of twelve. This was no different than when she had tried to build her own castle, out behind the tanning sheds. She'd gotten the help of several enterprising children who agreed that having their own castle would be the best way to guard against bad old Sir Erantal's men. Together they had built a tiny hut out of stone that had collapsed the first time someone put weight on it.

Dara the Dumb, she scolded herself. *You can't scale an impossible cliff, so now you dream of flying there yourself . . . because you'll never reach that nest from below!*

Then something occurred to her, and she opened her eyes. They fixed on the very top of the peak, which seemed upside down, from her perspective. In the light she could make out the nest perfectly where it sat near the top of the mountain . . . only fifty or sixty feet below the peak.

With stunning clarity, she realized . . . *she could reach the nest from the top of the mountain!*

The more she studied it, the more it looked possible. Indeed, the slope above the nest was not nearly so steep as right below it, and the ragged eastern side seemed to have handholds and rests aplenty . . . yet before she could reach that point, she would have to rappel down a rope . . . three or four hundred feet above the hard black rock below.

She wasn't certain that there was anything to anchor such a rope to until she remembered Kamen discussing his own ascent, and the "*knob the size of a hogshead*" that was at the peak of Rundeval.

The very idea made her dizzy, and she wondered for a moment if perhaps she was crazed, as some had whispered. *What sane girl wanted to risk her life for the sake of a pet? A pet that she couldn't even be sure she could keep alive?* From what Uncle Keram told her, many fledglings died in captivity. She could be risking her life for a dead bird, she realized.

No, another part of herself reasoned, *you are risking your life for the chance at a live bird. A great hunter. A master of the winds.*

When she thought about it like that, there was really no question.

She was going to get herself that bird.

* * *

The next few days were busy. There were a lot of chores to do to prepare the Hall for winter and not all of them were pleasant. While her slight size spared her from the laborious task of washing laundry in the huge kettle over a fire in the courtyard with her sister and cousins, her Aunt Anira (who had stepped into the role of her mother since the day Dara was born) always seemed to find other things for her to do. Sure enough, Aunt Anira had a special assignment for her at the breakfast announcements.

This time, however, the task was not too objectionable. Anira had thoughtfully given Dara a job suitable to her size, skill and ingenuity: repairing the nutwood cottages.

There was a row of the tiny cottages against the far northeastern edge of the manor, up against the wood proper. Unlike the cots near the center of the estate, where young families lived in a small hamlet behind the manor hall, these cottages were reserved for the elderly. Pensioners who had served the estate faithfully but were too old and frail for regular work. In other villages and manors, the old people were nearly cast aside after their productive years were behind them.

But not in the Westwood. The Master took care of all.

The Westwoodmen worked for the estate even in their dotage. The pensioners' cots were close to a large stand of pecan and hazelnut trees intermixed with a few walnuts, cultivated over the decades as part of the manor's economy. In the autumn the pensioners did the tedious but necessary work of gathering up the fallen nuts for the estate, and in return the manor provided for them for the rest of the year. Every month each cot was delivered a bag of flour, another of barley, and usually a little meat and some vegetables. That was in addition to the little gardens the pensioners grew, the nuts they gleaned, and the gifts they received from the younger residents of the manor. A few even still hunted.

The cottages were very small, no more than fifteen feet on a side, constructed of sturdy poles and wattle-and-daub, with a thick lining of dried mosses to keep out the chill. The roofs were thatched with stiff ferns that kept the rain out better than the river reeds the people of the Vale used. A tiny fireplace with a clay chimney hugged the back wall of each cottage, allowing a fire sufficient to heat the cozy room, and two small windows permitted light inside, when the wooden shutters and leather curtains were thrown open. The cottages were large enough for a bed, a small trestle table, a cistern, and a chest or two for their belongings and stores. Most hung herbs and dried meat from the poles in their ceilings, and a few had hung ragged tapestries or trophies from their youth on the walls.

The cottage of one of the pensioners, Widow Ama, needed to be cleaned and repaired after the old occupant had quietly passed on in her sleep at the end of last summer. Anira thought that the work was well within Dara's capabilities. It was the Master of the Wood's duty to look after those who had spent their lives caring for the estate, and she was the Master's daughter.

The pensioners' cottages were a peaceful place, Dara decided as she walked down the trail into the nutwoods, but it was also a kind of sad place. This is where people came to await death, she realized. Her grandmother had lived here, she recalled, until she'd passed away. As she waved to Old Kam, the grizzled and lame forester who lived in the second cot, she realized that he, too, was awaiting death out here in the nutwood.

Widow Ama had lived out here for three years, Dara remembered, as she neared the remote little cot. It was dark and empty, of course – Ama had been burned weeks ago, in a quiet little ceremony. She had been one of the vale folk who had married into the Westwood, and for forty years, Aunt Anira had told her, Ama had been one of the hardest-working women in the manor. While her husband ranged and toiled in the tanning sheds, she had been a stalwart of the manor hamlet, raising four children to adulthood in the process.

When her aging husband did not return from a hunting expedition deep in the mountains, she had taken to grief. A few months later she had offered to move out of the large home she'd raised her family in and go live in serenity amongst the pensioners. The Master of the Wood had agreed, and she'd spent the last few years of her life in this tiny home.

Her grown children had already removed her personal affects, those small things of sentimental value, but few Westwoodmen accumulated anything akin to the Vale folk's ideas of wealth. Unlike the agrarian manors in Sevendor, in the Westwood folk contributed their work to the Hall, and the Hall supported them from birth to death. The wealth the community created, such as it was, got invested back into the welfare of the entire estate. Her father may have been Master of the Hall, but apart from that he lived as much like the common folk of the Westwood as anyone. He'd even ceded the large bedchamber he'd shared with his wife to his brother, when becoming a widower made it feel too large and empty. No one had much in the way of personal wealth in the Westwood.

As a result, although the Westwoodmen were poor, by outside standards, their standards of living were much higher. The Westwoodmen never went hungry, with the wealth of the forest to feed them. They never were cold, with the Flame to warm them and the Wood to feed it. Their purses might be empty, but their bellies were full and they slept safely at night, without fear from their neighbors. That was security few in Sevendor could boast.

What was left of Widow Ama's cottage needed to be cleaned and cleared, and made ready for the next tenant. She could think of no one in the manor who might be considering such a move, off the top of her head, but Anira was not the sort to let the place sit abandoned.

The narrow door to the tiny cottage was propped shut with a rock to keep the forest creatures out – raccoons and racquiels would delight in finding no one at home. Two old clay pots, their usefulness for other purposes doomed by cracks or holes in them, contained flowers now dead in the cool autumn.

Dara pushed aside the rock and opened the creaking door. The mustiness of the room, tinged with the lingering scent of death, nearly overwhelmed her, but once the cottage aired out it wasn't so bad. She opened the shutters to both tiny windows to help that process. That also allowed enough light inside the dark little room to see the extent of the task before her.

It was bad . . . but not nearly as bad as it could have been. The few belongings left behind by the widow's family had been carelessly left scattered across the room, much of it piled on the table in no particular fashion. The fireplace was bursting with ashes, and the hard dirt floor of the house was littered with debris. Widow Ama had not been a fussy housekeeper in the last few years, Dara noted.

She began by cleaning the ashes from the fireplace – a task every Westwood child knew by heart – and kindling a small fire. The chimney needed to be cleaned, she noted, but it was clear enough for the moment. Once she'd laid the fire and added tinder, it only took a few seconds to strike it into life with the flint and striker left behind.

Soon the tiny little flame was crackling and dancing, adding just enough heat to the air to burn away the chill and just enough light to make Dara's task look impressively daunting. With a sigh, she got to work, after warming her hands in front of the flame.

It didn't take long to put the few remaining possessions out of the way. The old clay chamberpot she tucked under the bed, the battered teakettle she returned to the fireplace, and assembling the Widow's few spoons and knife in her cup was simple. She removed the larger pieces of trash from the floor and piled it all outside the door for later disposal.

She'd noticed a musty smell that she tracked to the leaky clay cistern. Built into the wall next to the fireplace, the clay tub held four or five gallons of rainwater . . . but a leak had rotted out the pole under it, which had allowed a hole to open in the roof.

With a critical eye Dara assessed the damage. The entire pole would have to be replaced, she decided, which would be a bit of a job. Until then, a piece of leather or oilcloth could be used to stop the leak, but until it was replaced the cottage would not be respectfully usable – certainly not up to her aunt's standards.

Worse, the constant dribble of water had eroded the clay of the wall. That would have to be patched, too, Dara decided. She made note of it, and continued cleaning.

Unlike her older sister, Linta, who could not go ten heartbeats without speaking, sometimes, Dara did not mind the quiet and solitude of the remote cottage. Indeed, she reveled in it. Things were always so busy around the Hall, with someone always telling her what to do or where to be, but here, in the quiet of the nutwoods, Dara was perfectly comfortable. She even hummed – poorly off-key – as she swept the bare floor clean of the remaining trash and dust with an ancient besom.

That's when she realized she wasn't alone. *She felt eyes on her.*

She glanced up quickly to the door, just in time to see a tiny furry head duck out of the way.

"Hello?" she called. "Are you visiting?"

She went to investigate, and saw a furry ringed tail disappear around the corner of the cottage. She froze. In a moment, a tiny black nose peeked around the corner, followed by two little eyes in a bandit's mask.

"Hello, little raccoon!" she smiled. This close to the manor she hadn't been worried about one of the predators of the forest sneaking up on her, but it was always a possibility. "Aren't you supposed to be a night walker?" she asked the furry little animal, as it tentatively stepped toward her and chittered.

He seemed to be questioning her.

Perhaps, she reasoned, he had been an acquaintance of Widow Ama. Elders often doted on pets, and the pensioners frequently kept a cat or small dog for company, but perhaps the widow had made animal friends in the wood, instead of supporting them on her meager allowance.

"She's gone, now," Dara explained to the raccoon, who chattered again. "She's . . . she's *passed on*," Dara said, not knowing just how one explained the concept of death and the afterlife to a raccoon. "Were you a friend of hers?"

The raccoon ignored the question when it spied the pile of garbage. Not seeing Dara as a threat, it walked right up to the pile and began sorting through it with his clever paws, sniffing every piece with interest.

"Try not to make too much of a mess," she cautioned. "But take what you like. How many days have you been by here without seeing anyone, I wonder?" she asked, aloud. The raccoon, for all its friendliness, had no answer for that.

Dara brushed dirt off her hands, realizing that the sun was already beginning to set behind the ridge. No wonder the creature was out and about – she'd been so busy she'd forgotten the time. It was near to dusk. The manor's dinner bell began pealing in the distance, emphasizing the lateness of the day.

"Time to go!" she said, returning inside to bank the fire, and gather up a few things to take back to the manor hall. She had a mental list of things that she'd need to make the place homey – most could be gotten from the manor's store rooms. But it would take a while, she knew. Especially with that broken pole and the hole in the wall.

In fact . . . this place would likely be empty all winter long, Dara realized. The perfect place to, say, *train a baby falcon*, she reasoned.

With a growing sense of excitement, she closed up the cottage against the weather, departing the same time as the raccoon, who had gathered an armload of old apple cores and chicken bones. "See you tomorrow!" she called, happily, as she propped the door closed again with the rock.

She had her mews. Once she captured the bird, she had a safe, private place to train it.

* * *

Dinner was already being served by the time she ran back to the manor, venison stew with plenty of potatoes and beans, with cornbread. There were close to forty people in the hall around the Flame when she arrived. Her sister Linta grudgingly spooned her out a bowl before she found a trestle near her father's chair, his wounded leg propped up on a stool in front of him.

"Where have you been, Dara?" he called to her, concerned. "Not to see some boy, I hope?" he teased.

Dara blushed but ignored the teasing. "I was down in the nutwood," she explained. "Anira sent me to the pensioners' cots. Widow Ama's cottage. It's a terrible mess."

"Is it, now?" he asked, absently.

"Yes, it has a leaky cistern and a hole in the roof. I can patch it enough to get through the winter," she proposed, "and with some help I can repair it. But the place needs a *lot* of work," she said, warningly. "Maybe I'm not the one who should be—"

"It sounds like you have things well enough in hand," Anira said, suspiciously, from behind her. "I'll not pull someone off of more productive work so you can go play in the forest, Lenodara. You just keep at it until it's done!"

Dara did her best to look appalled. "But Aunt Anira! That will take *weeks!* Do you have any idea how much of a mess it is? The fireplace is cracked, the bed is rickety and needs to be replaced, the shutters have holes in them, the floor is filthy and needs to be completely stripped and re-done, the plaster inside is—"

"That is quite enough, young lady!" her aunt said, with fire in her voice. "I don't care if you have to be in the nutwoods every moment of your day for weeks, you will scrub and repair that cot until it's fit for someone to live in. The Flame knows poor Widow Ama was fading, these last few years, and I've no doubt her place needs repair – those sons of hers barely went to visit her, the poor dear.

"But it's the manor's responsibility to see it repaired, and repaired properly. You can take what you need from stores, and you can recruit help as you need to, but I want to have that cottage ready to live in by Yule. Do you understand me, young lady?"

"Yes, Aunt Anira," Dara said, meekly, as she bent over her stew.

So I have my mews secured, she thought to herself, as she ate in silence, pretending to be feeling chastised. *No one will want to go out there, not for weeks. And now I have the perfect excuse to be out there.*

She thought about all the details of her plan, including the other things she'd need. She'd paid close attention to her Uncle Keram's stories about falconry, and she had a pretty fair idea of what equipment she would have to assemble.

Jesses were no problem – she could get leather straps from the tanning shed and cut them to fit. She could make a perch out of wood, she knew, or borrow something from the long storage shed, where the broken furniture was kept. Constructing a hood or blind would be more difficult. The little leather "helmet" that fitted over a bird's head to keep it docile was a very specialized thing. She knew it was made of leather, but she had little idea how to make one. The journey up the mountain would be tough, but most of the gear she could scrounge up easily enough: gloves from the workroom, her boots, a basket she could take from the storeroom to get the bird down, once she got it. That was the easy part.

In the end she dismissed the problem for a later day. It seemed silly worrying about gear for a falcon she didn't even have yet.

Now that she had a mews, the next step was to capture the fledgling. That was the dangerous part, too – well, that and getting caught. She wasn't certain which she feared most, plummeting to her death from a mountaintop or getting caught doing something she knew full well her father would object to.

Yet she had to try. The very thought of the powerful raptor in flight sent shivers down her spine. She would have to move soon, too, she knew, else the fledglings would fly, and all her hopes would be dashed.

The hard part, she realized, was going to be finding over a *hundred feet* of rope. That was her next task, she decided as she finished the bowl. She had to have rope.

Chapter Three

Stealing Rope

Rope. Dara needed rope. A *lot* of rope.

She measured the distance by eye several times, calculating in her head just how much rope she would need to get up the back side of the peak, and then to descend the front side to the cliff. She kept coming up with a hundred and twenty feet, minimum, that she would need to get the job done.

The problem was that there just wasn't rope of that size lying around the manor.

The Westwoodmen were familiar with rope. The bridge that connected their estate with the rest of Sevendor was secured by giant ropes the size of her leg, specially made of hemp, cotton, and blackberry, woven in a pattern developed to support the great weight of the bridge.

But that rope was far too thick for Dara's purpose. More, it would have been ridiculously heavy, impossible for a girl of her size to carry up a mountain, she knew. There had to be another answer. The next morning, when Dara arose and went to the storeroom to collect supplies for her chores at the nutwoods cot, she discovered two coils of rope in the dusty room, each a disappointing twenty feet.

Dara took them anyway, as well as a broom, a mop, a

bucket, some rags, a pair of gloves, some tapers, a trowel, a hammer, a sheet of oilcloth, some beeswax, three thick iron nails, a pot of sticky clay, another of tar, and an old moth-eaten sheet destined for the rag bin. She packed it all in a wheelbarrow, then stopped by the kitchen to wheedle some food from her aunt to take with her for lunch.

She did her best to look despondent and reluctant, when she reported to her Aunt Anira before she went. Dara loved her aunt like a mother – she was, in truth, the only mother Dara had ever known – but she seemed to constantly suspect Dara of being "up to something" whether it was climbing trees or throwing rocks into the chasm. The reluctant act worked, however. Anira gave her a wedge of cheese and a small loaf, and added a few small sausages as an afterthought, all the while insisting that the work would go faster if she kept focused on it.

"You be sure to do a thorough job," she warned, waving a spoon in her face. "No shirking. This will be a good task for you. You'll be expected to keep your own home, someday. Best you learn what that entails."

Dara looked properly dejected, until she left the kitchen. She placed her lunch basket in the wheelbarrow and then took it down the trail toward the nutwood . . . and near to the harness shed.

If there was any place that could be concealing rope, it would be the harness shed, she reasoned. The manor only kept a half-dozen horses, mostly ronceys that could be used either as beasts of burden or ridden to range the frontiers on this side of the bridge.

Horses disliked going over the rope bridge and standing over the crevasse, so they rarely made the trip. Westwoodmen preferred to walk. The Westwood landscape was not well-suited to horses, due to the rugged nature of the land, but the few they had were kept in the stable near the cow byre. The harness shed, where saddles, bridles, blankets and such were kept, was next to the small stable.

Dara let herself in as casually as she could, not even looking around to see if anyone was watching. That would just arouse suspicion, she knew.

Instead she walked in, boldly, and then began searching the rich-smelling shed for rope. After pushing past the hanging bits and bridles, past the saddles hanging from the walls of the close little shed, she finally discovered a peg in the back upon which were three coils of supple line, as thick as her thumb, in neat forty-foot coils.

Dara knew at once that if she tried removing all three coils at once, someone would see her and start asking questions. Instead she contented herself with taking just one of the ropes, concealing it in the wheelbarrow under the oilcloth.

The trip down to the pensioners' cottages seemed to take forever, and the old wheelbarrow she borrowed seemed to have a mind of its own. It kept trying to steer itself off of the path, forcing Dara to wrestle it back. It was slow going, and she didn't arrive until midmorning, covered with sweat and exhausted.

And you think you're going to climb a mountain? she challenged herself. *You're going to have to be tougher than that – stronger than that – if you want that bird!*

Once she caught her breath, she was filled with new resolve, despite her weariness. She opened up the cottage, kindled a fire, and got to work.

She didn't want to accomplish *too* much – she had to stretch this chore out, if she was to have use of the place for as long as she needed it. She tucked her precious coils of rope under the bed, for now, and unloaded the other supplies into the cottage. She did take the time to fit the oilcloth tarp over the hole near the cistern – it looked like it might rain soon – and tied it down well. She also heated up the pot of pitch on the fire, once it was hot enough, and smeared enough on the leak in the cistern to seal it.

Satisfied that she had accomplished at least some work, she turned her attention to her real purpose. She sorted out the cleaning supplies from the climbing supplies and began assembling everything she thought she might need on her expedition. By noon, when she halted for lunch, she felt as if she had nearly everything but the rest of the rope.

She spent most of the rest of the afternoon climbing trees around the cottage, choosing the hardest ones. Dara had been a confirmed tree-climber for years, enjoying a reputation for daring among her fellow children long past the time when most girls gave up such pursuits for those more refined. But Dara was far more active than that, and saw her sisters' and cousins' interest in such things as needlework, marriage, and gossip as supremely boring.

She ascended one tree after another, refusing to rest between attempts as she tried to build her strength and endurance up. It was exhausting, and when she did take a break for water and rest, the only chore she felt at all ready to do was pull the dead flowers out of the planters by the door before she collapsed on the rickety old bed for a rest.

Then the bed collapsed under her.

Despite the pain and sudden jarring, Dara stared at the dusty ceiling of the cottage and laughed hysterically.

*   *   *

When she returned to Westwood Hall, comfortably before dinner, she apparently looked exhausted, too, according to her Aunt Anira. After assuring her it was merely from her labors, and not a sign that she was getting ill, she was surprisingly approving, and even slipped Dara one of the tiny cakes that were to be served for dinner.

She told everyone over dinner how Widow Ama's bed had collapsed, and complained how long it would take to repair or replace it, just to emphasize how she was really unhappy with her chore . . . and she received the expected number of chastisements for her laziness. Ordinarily that would bother her, but each one ensured that she would be able to use the cottage without the danger of folks wandering by. After enduring a lecture from her father on the importance of hard work, she reluctantly promised she would stick with it . . . no matter how long it took.

The next morning, she arose early and left just before breakfast was served, wheedling a tin of porridge and some things for lunch from her aunt before she left, suggesting she wanted to get an early start. While the rest of the household was eating she slipped back into the harness shed and took the second coil of rope. All day that day she practiced tying the ropes together in one long line, then testing her knots against her weight as she dangled from a tree limb.

Dara was actually good at knots – good enough that her aunt had frequently told her she had no idea why her needlework was so poor. She paid attention when her brothers were tying them, preparing snares and traps for the Westwood. While she was not adept, her nimble fingers knew enough to keep the ropes from slipping.

At lunch she spent an hour working on the cottage, removing the broken bed outside and sweeping the dirt floor smooth. She would bring fresh dried ferns from the herb house tomorrow, she decided.

The bed was ruined. It had been old when Widow Ama had taken residence in the cot, and while the headboard was solid enough; the rest of the bed was warped, cracked, and uneven. Once she decided that it wasn't salvageable, she used her hammer to bust it apart.

The footboard, she discovered, would make a decent perch, for now. Even if its legs were in no condition to support it, turned on its side the piece was the right height and thickness for a perch, Dara decided. She placed it in one corner of the cottage and piled the rest of the debris with the other garbage outside (cleanly picked through by her raccoon friend, she noted).

The headboard went into the wheelbarrow, so that it could be used in a new bed. That would take her cousin Keru a few weeks to put together in the woodshop, she knew with satisfaction. Which would extend the time before the cottage was ready even more. Dara had no idea how long she would need the privacy for training, but every day was precious.

Once she stowed her stolen ropes in the cottage, she headed home again, propping the door shut and leaving the last of her lunch for the raccoon. She was exhausted, after her days of hard exercise. She skipped dinner and went to bed early, earning a look of concern from her aunt.

It rained all day the next day, which forced Dara to actually work on the cottage instead of preparing for her climb. She decided against bringing the dried ferns (no sense transporting them in the rain) and focused on re-mudding the wattle-and-daub inside the house. She noted with satisfaction that her patch over the hole in the roof seemed to be working splendidly. Not a drop was coming through, now. And the cistern was holding water without leaking.

But there was only so much she could accomplish inside the cottage. Eventually she ran out of easy tasks to do, and she found herself idle, staring out the window. The rain and the forced inactivity also gave Dara time to think.

Am I really going to do this? she asked herself as she watched the raindrops collect on the side of the window. She had been thinking about the Silver Hooded Raptor's majestic flight all morning, imagining herself with wings flying nearby. *Am I really going to risk my life, risk my poor behind if I get caught, just for this little bird? Or is this just the stupidest little girl idea I've ever had, and I'm too stubborn to admit it?*

She was overcome with doubt, for a while, and seriously considered giving up on her plan entirely. The idea of a twelve-year old girl who hadn't even flowered yet doing something as preposterously dangerous as climbing a mountain was laughable enough. Even if she didn't die, what would she do if she actually succeeded? A falcon wasn't like tending a baby rabbit abandoned by her mother, or taking care of goats or chickens. Raptors were *predators*, and everything she'd heard her uncle say about the process of turning one into a trained hunter sounded complicated and daunting.

Dara struggled with the question all afternoon as she cleaned and tidied the cottage in the downpour, until it turned into a drizzle. She took a brief break to pull on her heavy cloak and go dig up some sassafras root from near the springhouse down the trail, so that she might make some tea – she should have brought some from the hall, she chastised herself. But *the Forest and the Flame would provide for the Westwoodmen*, as the old saying went.

While she was digging into the dirt with her knife, she heard a screech from overhead. A hawk – not one of the big silver-headed raptors she coveted, but a common redtail – had taken the respite in the rain to hunt. It dove and plucked some unfortunate rodent from a small meadow nearby; its delicate and deadly grace was irresistibly captivating.

That's as good as a sign from the gods, Dara told herself, fervently, as she walked back to the cottage. *How could it not be? I want that bird,* she decided. *I want that bird more than I want* anything.

With her doubt resolved, Dara prepared for the journey ahead. Rain or no rain, she couldn't waste any more time. She had to make the attempt soon. Autumn was coming, and any fledglings in the nest on Rundeval would be empty, if she did not get there.

The rain held for another day, and Dara begged off visiting the cottage in favor of shadowing her Uncle Keram again, as he made the Master's rounds in her father's stead. Dara stopped only briefly to discuss the need for a new bed with her cousin Keru, who acted as the manor's woodwright when his father wasn't around. He gladly accepted the headboard and promised the completed project in four weeks. Then it was back to Uncle Keram to pick up whatever morsels of falconry he was willing to impart.

Getting her uncle to talk about falconry was easy enough – she just mentioned the redtail hawk, and asked innocently if they were good hunting birds, and that was enough to set him off about how poorly they hunted, compared to larger and more majestic birds.

"Good bird for a beginner," her uncle acknowledged, reluctantly, "but they'll never take anything bigger than a hare. A squire's bird," he said, disdainfully. "Pretty enough, but hardly worth the time and effort to train them. But that's where most falconers begin training their first birds. Red tails and kestrels."

That got him talking about the arduous process of training a hawk, and with a few leading questions Dara got him to explain the entire process of capturing and training a hawk, from his memories as a youth. She learned again the importance of the hood, the jesses, and the bells.

Bells. Dara had forgotten *bells*. As her uncle reminded her, bells were essential to attach to the legs of the bird, so the falconer might find the bird in the wild.

With a sinking feeling, Dara realized she'd have to find bells from somewhere. That was not going to be easy. Such dainties were rare in the Westwood.

Her uncle explained the difference between taking a fledgling bird – an *eyas*, she learned the falconers called them – and an adolescent bird still learning to hunt. He went through the long, three-month process of acclimatizing the bird to humans and imprinting on the falconer specifically. How you had to keep the bird constantly fed and dependent upon you, how you had to teach it how to fly from block to glove and back again, how you had to hack it out in the outdoors, and a dozen other vital elements of falconry.

Dara absorbed every word with special care. It seemed far too easy to accidentally kill a bird, she realized, when her uncle began speaking about the importance of supplements to aid in casting. Dara only had the vaguest idea what casting was, and had no idea what she should supplement the bird's food with to aid it. Asking such a question might draw suspicions, though, and Dara was adept enough at social relations to know when she was pushing the boundaries of an ordinary twelve-year old's curiosity. Satisfied she had enough knowledge to begin with, at least, she began putting together the final elements of her scheme.

Dara needn't have worried about anyone figuring out she was up to something, however, as that night's dinner conversation was filled with news from market.

Though Kamen had forbidden the regular market party from the Westwood going to the market in Sevendor Village, he had sent one of her uncles, his two boys and Kyre to the market to pick up a few essential supplies . . . and to listen to the gossip about the castle. Shooting a castle soldier, however brutish, was not the sort of thing a commoner could get away with, but apparently Sir Erantal was not bent on revenge, yet. Indeed, the gossip was about his latest dalliance with the wives of one of his Yeoman, Ylvine of Southridge Hold, and the scandal it had caused.

Dara's matronly aunt looked properly indignant – no doubt the thought of fat old Sir Erantal trying to pay her court revolted her. And while Kamen had no wish to be known as a rebel, having the lord of the domain trying to sport with his sister-in-law or wife would have brought every Westwoodman down on the old castle in a swarm. Such a thought was repellant to the traditional Westwoodmen, and the fact that the folk of Southridge Hold weren't up in arms over the affair only confirmed in their minds the degenerate state of the Vale folk in general.

Dara was entertained by the gossip, but her mind was elsewhere. She approached her Aunt Anira quietly after the meal with the next stage of her plan.

"Anira, there's so much work to do at the nutwood cot," she began, dejectedly. "The rain has really put me behind. I might have to stay over, a few nights, to get it done."

"If that's what needs to happen," her aunt said, absently. "I do hope you're getting something accomplished, and not just playing in the forest."

"Anira!" Dara protested, holding out her hands. After days of climbing, working with rope, and even actually cleaning they were rough, torn, and calloused. "Does this *look* like I've been gathering wildflowers and dreaming of handsome knights?"

Anira snorted. "Clearly not. Very well, just take extra bedding, and keep the fire going. I don't want you to catch a cold," she warned. "Those cots are sturdy, but they can get draughty."

"Thank you, Anira," Dara said, rolling her eyes. "I'll try not to die of anything horrible until the job is done."

"That would be best," her aunt replied, already on to another task and not paying attention to what Dara said. As much as she resented it other times, in this one instance she had to admit the lack of careful attention was a good thing.

That night she packed the rest of the things she thought she would need, both for the climb and staying at the cottage for a few days.

And, a morbid part of her reasoned, if she did plummet to her death from the top of the mountain, it would save her family the time and trouble of clearing out her room afterwards.

As an afterthought she grabbed her little crossbow. The arbalest was good for little other than hunting birds or rodents, or shooting rotten apples off of fences, but it might be helpful if a wolf or bear showed up unexpectedly, as was like to happen this close to the deep wood. Her brother Kyre, who was learning the ranger's craft, had often said a sharp pain to the nose would drive off most predators. The bear he'd killed last autumn proved he knew his woodcraft.

She took it all in the wheelbarrow the next morning before breakfast and she liberally raided the kitchen for supplies before she left. Oats, bread, cured bacon, some sausage, half a small wheel of cheese, salt, and a few other things to keep her going. A last stop at the harness shed to fetch the last coil of rope and she was half a mile down the trail when the breakfast bell rang.

Dara barely worked on the cottage that day, beyond setting up a bit of a kitchen and preparing a bed on the floor. After that she just kept practicing her knots, laying out the long, long lengths of rope, and climbing trees using her gloves.

She was in the process of descending one large tree when she realized she wasn't alone. And it wasn't a curious raccoon who awaited her at the foot of the tree, either.

"Hullo!" she heard a young voice say. "That's about the highest I've ever seen anyone climb a tree!"

Her heart pounding, Dara got close enough to recognize that her visitor was a child – a boy, she realized, not much younger than herself. She felt relieved. At first she thought she had been caught by her aunt, her uncle, or even her brother. Just a kid, she told herself. Nothing to worry about.

Dara dropped the last ten feet and landed nimbly, without injury, on the soft loam under the tree. "I've gone higher," she boasted, brushing off her gloves. "But that's the highest tree around here, so I thought I'd give it a try."

"I'm Kalen," the boy said, suddenly. He was maybe ten, and stood no higher than Dara's shoulders. He had light hair – a certain sign one of his parents had likely come from the Vale – and a runny nose. "I come to bring some beans and biscuits to my gran – he's Old Kori, two cots up."

Dara knew of Old Kori. He'd been a great hunter, once, and had sired many children, but the toothless old man had been living in the nutwood for as long as Dara could remember. "I'm Dara," she mentioned. "Lenodara, actually, but only my aunt calls me that."

"*Lenodara?*" the boy said, his eyes growing wide. "You're . . . you're the *Master of the Wood's* daughter!"

"One of them," she admitted. "The lesser one. I'm the one they don't like talking about. Not the tall one," she said, referencing Leska. "And not the pretty one," she grumbled. For as long as she could remember, she had heard how pretty her older sister Linta was, and how well she would wed someday. No one had said as much of Dara.

Kalen blinked. "What do you mean? You're *plenty* pretty! And no girl I know can climb a tree like that!"

He had such earnest admiration for the skill that Dara was forced to laugh. "Thanks! No one's ever called me 'plenty pretty' before. Or complimented my tree climbing. Quite the opposite," she chuckled.

"So what is a lord's daughter doing down here in the nutwood, climbing trees?"

"The Master of the Wood is no lord," she corrected. "He's just the yeoman of the forest. Sir Erantal is lord in Sevendor. And I'm supposed to be getting this cot in shape," she said, nodding toward the little hut.

"Old Widow Ama's place," Kalen nodded, sagely. "I remember her. She died."

He said it in such a matter-of-fact way, Dara was surprised. "Yes, you're right," she admitted. "She was very old. And she had a good, full life. I'll be spending a few days down here, getting it repaired and re-stocked."

The kid didn't seem concerned. "Can I help?"

"The tree climbing or the cleaning?"

"The cleaning," he said, quickly. He glanced warily up at the fifty-foot spruce tree. "I'm not so good at the climbing."

She laughed and invited the boy inside. Kalen proved to be very smart, and well-behaved, though she suspected that being in the company of her father's daughter had much to do with his good behavior. He was a curious boy, and immediately asked about the lack of bed, the smear of tar on the cistern, the empty planters by the door, and the ropes.

She had very good explanations for everything but the ropes.

"I've got a project I'm working on," she said, hesitantly. "It's kind of complicated and . . . well, if you wouldn't mind not mentioning the ropes to anyone . . ."

"Then you'll command me to help you fix the cottage?" he asked, brightly. "Otherwise I have to gather nuts." He did not make the task sound appealing.

"Command you? More like ask you. And I won't need you much, but there are a few things that having a second pair of hands to help with might be good." The advantages of having a confederate immediately presented itself to Dara's mind . . . but then so did the disadvantages. Security, for one. "But you mustn't mention more than you are helping me. To anyone. No need to get specific about what we're doing. Can I trust you to do that?"

"Sure," the boy answered with a shrug. "No one ever asks me about anything, anyway. I've got two brothers and a sister. All older," he said, making a face. "I barely even get to speak, at home."

Dara, being the youngest, could sympathize. "All right, then, Kalen, I'm going to start on the floor, sometime tomorrow. Let's take a look at what kind of horrible task is ahead of us."

She took the boy inside and poured him a cup of tea, apologizing for the lack of honey. Kalen looked startled and mentioned he'd never tasted honey. Dara kicked herself, inside her head. The folk of the Westwood weren't poor, exactly, but such luxuries that did come into the manor were usually reserved for the manor house. Only at Yule and at special occasions did delicacies such as honey trickle down to the working folk who lived in the hamlet outside. Apparently that hadn't happened in Kalen's short memory.

They went on to discuss just how good he was at digging holes, and the boy assured her he was both proficient and enthusiastic at the task. Dara had designs on crafting a kind of awning over the doorway to the cot, and explained to Kalen where she needed the holes dug, and how deep.

"Then we'll get to the floor. It's woefully uneven," she pointed out, "and it's dry as dust. It *is* dust. I think if I add some clay to it, sprinkle it with water and pack it down, I can level it out a bit with a log and make it more sturdy. That way it won't get this rut in the center, where Widow Alma must have walked back and forth."

"And ferns," Kalen reminded, "you need new ferns!"

"I've got them, already," she said, glancing upward where the bundle of dried leaves was safely out of the damp. "I was going to start laying them, when I noticed the floor . . . and noticed the wet spot in front of the door. So an awning and a resurfaced floor, and then the roof, and this cot will be ready to live in again before you know it!"

Kalen was enthusiastic about the work, and even insisted on shaking Dara's hand like his father did to seal a bargain. The little boy marched back down the road an hour before twilight, proud of his rising station in the world.

Dara liked the boy. He was smart, and clever, and his eyes saw a lot. He was also inquisitive – a trait Dara had herself in abundance.

But as the light outdoors faded and Dara was forced to go inside and light a taper, she realized that she really couldn't use Kalen's sudden appearance as an excuse to wait on going up the mountain. As much of a risk to her secrecy as he might be, she simply couldn't wait any longer. She'd climbed that tall spruce partially because she wanted to see as much of the horizon as she could . . . and the sky portended clear weather in the morning, if the lore she remembered was correct.

She would not have many more days before the eyases left the nest, and were lost to the wild forever. If she wanted one, she would have to go soon.

Not soon, she realized, as she counted off the items she needed – and acquired. She had to go *tomorrow*. Before first light. There was no telling how long she could keep up her various ruses and avoid interception by someone in authority who figured out she was "up to something". Once she had the bird, no one could stop her, she reasoned.

But until she had the bird in her hand, she was just a little girl dreaming and playing, not a novice apprentice falconer. She had to commit.

I'm going to do it, she realized, as she prepared to go to sleep early on a bed of ferns and blankets. *I'm really going to go after that beautiful bird.*

Or die trying, another part of her whispered, forebodingly, before she fell asleep.

Chapter Four

Rundeval

There was a thick mist in the air when Dara woke in the early hours of the morning. It was still dark, just before dawn. The night was still, as the nocturnal creatures began to rest and the earliest birds of morning started their first songs. She had to stir the fire to life enough to light a taper, then fed the flame just enough to boil water for tea.

She stared into the fire while she sleepily watched the pot. For no real reason, she found herself praying.

Flame, guide my hands and feet. May your sacred light see me safely to the top of the mountain and back again, oh Living Flame, my quest complete. To be thorough – or just desperate – she added the Vale folk's rendition of the prayer, personified the way the pure Narasi liked to do:

By the flame that burneth bright,

My life in trust to thee tonight;

Lady Briga, light my way,

Inspire my thoughts and deeds this day!

Dara wasn't ordinarily a particularly religious girl – the Westwoodmens' rites were simple and sublime and didn't require temples or shrines other than the Flame – but when she considered that this might be her last day alive, she didn't see the harm in invoking the anthropomorphic version of her people's patroness. The Flame was merely an incarnation of Briga . . . or was Briga an incarnation of the Flame?

She mused on that metaphysical question over breakfast. When she had washed her face and drank a cup of tea, she assembled her gear into the bag she had brought along for the purpose.

Including the carefully-coiled ropes she packed a bit of lunch, the three long iron nails she'd taken from storage, the hammer, her gloves, a few small bandages (just in case), a water bottle, a knife, and the basket. She fastened a long loop to the basket so it could either dangle at her side or be shortened and allowed to hang around her neck, next to her chest.

She set out just as the sky began to pale in the east, her feet taking her to the far side of the Westwood by a circuitous route she knew would not allow her to encounter anyone, unless it was a ranger returning from walking the frontiers, as was their duty. In that case, she had reasoned, she could claim that she was searching for mushrooms in the early morn.

Although why a girl needed over a hundred feet of stout rope to harvest mushrooms, she hadn't quite worked out yet.

It took an hour for her to make it to the path that led up the south side of the mountain. Dara took a deep breath and steeled herself for the ascent when she came to the boulder that marked the end of the regular path and the beginning of the mountain trail. The first part of the journey was only arduous in that it was long, and every step took her a little higher in elevation. The trail wound all over the western and southern slope of the mountain until, at the far eastern side of the southern slope, the path grew much narrower, and much rockier.

From then on, Dara was sweating. She was a strong girl well used to hard work, but the path was harder, more a staircase of rock with occasional patches of dirt than a proper trail.

At a small clearing about half way up the eastern slope Dara rested and drank some water. The climb was a lot harder than she'd anticipated, she realized. She felt like she'd been hiking all day, yet the sun had yet to peek over the far eastern ridge. Dara gave herself until the bright orb made an appearance, which also illuminated the trail helpfully. But she also realized she needed more leverage if she was going to make it up the increasingly steep trail.

She found a hickory sapling not too far off the trail, and she used her knife to score it enough to break it off. It was tough work, but the difficulty she had in breaking the sapling loose gave testament to its strength, and Dara needed that strength. Once she'd trimmed off the branches and topped the sapling off, the result was a pole just over an inch thick and five feet long. A perfect walking stick, for a girl her size.

Dara continued up the trail. It was decidedly harder, after that lovely little clearing. And much steeper. The trail went from being less stair-like and more ladder-like, as she had to employ her hands more to pull herself up.

A brief respite offered by a hundred-yard long game trail gave Dara some hope that the worst was behind her . . . until she came to the far western side of the mountain. She realized she was already three-quarters of the way up, and she could even see the peak, from a few vantage points. But when she reached the end of the game trail, she had to ascend a much, much steeper grade. Nearly straight up. It was a daunting task, but Dara rested a bit and then tore into it. She had come this far up the mountain, she reasoned. She didn't see the point of coming back down without a bird.

It was light enough to see clearly, now, and the mountain-top swarmed with life around her as she climbed. Every tree she grasped for leverage seemed to have a bird or three in it, or a swarm of late autumn tid-gnats, and once she disturbed a sleepy old racquiel who was not happy with her trespassing through his neighborhood.

And all around her the mountain was alive with birds. This time of year, when the leaves were changing, there were armies of the things around the Westwood. And first thing in the morning, they were all hungry for the night insects that had been lazy getting home.

A perfect time for a mother Raptor to feed, Dara reasoned.

Redoubling her efforts, she persisted at the climb until she came to the bottom of the final cliff face. A small ledge gave her a little room – a *very* little room – to rest herself for a few moments on one of the last few tufts of grass and shrubbery before the mountain turned to dark rock.

Dara eyed the cliff nervously as she drank a few more swallows from her bottle. It was almost gone, and she was barely at the top. It didn't look so bad, she reasoned. It was a bit smooth, but the grade wasn't *that* impossible, she decided. In fact, the peak was less than fifty feet away, from where she sat.

The ropes that had been such a burden on her shoulders the entire way up she piled into a long coil, before fastening one end to her body, tying a kind of harness around her waist and shoulders. Donning her gloves and leaving her mantle behind, she began the last ascent. She began searching for a good place to anchor the rope to, and almost at once she learned why the last fifty feet to the peak were so bad.

There were scant handholds, and the face of the rock was smooth and hard. She hadn't climbed ten feet before she realized that there simply *weren't* any more handholds, nor anything she could secure her rope to. Not where she could reach them. She tried to hammer a nail into a crack in the hard basalt, but the crack was too thin and the rock was too hard. Nor could she swing the hammer at an angle that might drive it in. She bent the iron of the precious nail in the attempt, and nearly lost it.

She was frustrated when ten minutes of maneuvering and repositioning herself yielded no better result; she was stuck. Had she been a foot taller, or if she could get even one toe purchased on the rock, she could lift herself up to the next round of handholds above. But try as she might, there was just no way forward. She studied the matter long and hard before she gave up. She could see the handhold, tantalizingly close, but there was no way to get there.

That's when she spied a scraggly shrub, a type she wasn't familiar with, lodged in a crack far above her head, just shy of Rundeval's summit. If only she could get a line up there and get solid purchase, she could use it as leverage and nearly walk up the rest of the cliff.

But that tiny tree was at least twenty feet above her. She couldn't throw the heavy rope – or even the lighter coil she'd brought – that far. Not even if it was weighted.

Her little arbalest, on the other hand, could throw a bolt *thrice* that distance, she realized.

Dara started envisioning the plan, using her tiny crossbow to propel a bolt over the tree. If she aimed at a rock above it, she figured, and hit it at the right angle then deflecting the bolt back down on the other side of the tree shouldn't be too difficult.

Of course, how to attach the rope to the bolt was beyond her.

Frustrated, irritated, but unbeaten, Dara descended the mountain after reaching her limits, leaving the rope and much of her other gear up there. She wasn't finished, not by any stretch. She merely needed to regroup and approach the problem again, better prepared.

It took just over half the time coming down the mountain as it had climbing it, so Dara was well on her way back to the nutwood by lunchtime. While discouraged and disappointed, she had a plan, and she had not died in the attempt.

Yet.

She stopped by Westwood Hall on her way. Even though she had brought her lunch, someone was baking something wonderful smelling, and Dara's nose led her inside. She managed to cajole two meat pies from her old Aunt Lini, who baked for the Hall.

While she was there, her sister Lista came in. Dara froze. She very much wanted to avoid her big sister. She delighted in getting her in trouble in some misguided idea that Dara was devious, just as their brother Kobb delighted in teasing them both.

Lista was nearly old enough to be wed, now, and she had taken her father's restrictions on market day visits with little grace. Traditionally, if a maid did not fancy any of the Westwood lads she had grown up with, the place to find a husband was Sevendor Village market – or even farther afield, if there was no decent man who showed interest at market.

But with market days winding to a close for the winter, her sister was going mad with anxiety over the lack of social opportunities. A pretty Westwood girl had attracted the attention of prosperous young farmers at market before. Lista was determined to put herself in a position to be so noticed.

Yet Dara understood the danger of allowing her to roam into the Vale, right now, even if she didn't. The Castle men were always leering at the village girls, no matter how plain they were, and a fair one would attract their attention like crumbs did geese. And Lista was more beautiful than their older sister, sure to attract the leers of Sir Erantal's lackeys. While they usually didn't bother the Westwood women much, on account of the manor's militancy, that didn't stop the occasional harassment.

Worse, if nasty old Sir Erantal spied her and took a fancy to her, there was little the Westwood could do about it, save rise in rebellion. And rise they would, she knew; if the old knight made unreasonable demands for tribute *and* sported with a Westwoodwoman – the Master of the Wood's daughter, no less – then the honor of the Hall would demand an uprising. There would be bloodshed, all over her sister's desire to kiss boys.

Lista was in a fine fit today, Dara saw. A pretty decorative belt she'd been given by their mother's late sister on her flowering wasn't fitting anymore, thanks to Lista's widening hips. It was made of copper, a kind of pretty chain design of interlinked pieces that fit around her sister's waist.

Or, at least, they used to. And that was the problem.

"I don't know *how* I'm going to wear this now!" Lista complained to Aunt Lini, mostly because she couldn't go anywhere while taking pies out of the oven. Anira wouldn't have done anything but scold her and send her away, but their oldest aunt was more sympathetic. Lista stalked behind her while she worked, the older woman giving only the most meager responses to the teenager's ranting. "It fit fine when I tried it on two moons ago, but when I put it on this morning the catch wouldn't fit!"

"Oh, by the Flame, that *is* a pickle," Lini clucked. "Your mother intended that for you, Flame keep her warm, and it does so suit your figure."

"It *did*," Lista emphasized, shaking the tingling belt under her aunt's nose. "It did look incredible! Now it won't fit! What can I do? Wear it as a necklace?" she snorted.

Even Dara, whose sense of femininity was dulled, according to her sisters and aunts, could tell that the belt would work poorly as such an adornment. But she noticed something else when her sister shook it.

Bells. Tiny silver bells, each no bigger than her pinkie fingernail. *Dozens* of them.

"I can fix it," she said, before her sister could begin her next wave of ranting.

"What?" she snapped. "Where did *you* come from, Little Bird? And what happened to you? Flame and smoke, you look like you fell into a pit!"

"I've been working on a cot in the nutwood," Dara reminded her. "The opportunities for a cleansing bath have been scant," she said, sarcastically. "It's hard work."

"So?"

"So . . . I can fix your belt. Make it fits your . . . larger hips," she said, trying not to be insulting.

"There's *nothing wrong* with my hips!" her sister screeched.

"I didn't say there was," Dara replied, evenly, sipping a cup of hydromel she'd grabbed when her aunt wasn't looking. "Clearly, the belt is at fault. I'm offering to fix it for you."

"How are you going to do that?" Lista demanded, arrogantly.

"I'm *good* with that sort of thing," Dara reminded her, calmly suppressing the urge to yank her sister's dark hair so hard her head would snap back. "That's why I'm fixing the cot. But if I string a leather thong on the back side of the belt, then the pretty part will be all that anyone sees. Plenty of belts like that have leather closures."

"So I'll look like I tied my belt on with string!" she snorted, angrily.

"No, I'll put a bead or something on the end, make it real feminine," promised Dara. "Flame, I'll even shine it up for you."

Lista eyed Dara suspiciously. "Why? Why would you help me?"

Dara snorted back. "To get you to shut up about your 'broken' belt and your . . . *hips*."

Dara watched in fascination as her sister decided whether she wanted Dara's help more than she wanted to be mad at her. Finally, Lista thrust the belt at her. "Fine! See what you can do with it! And at least I *have* hips!" she said, demonstrating the fact with emphasis as she left the kitchen.

"That girl," her aunt said, shaking her head. "If she isn't wed soon, she's going to tear the whole hall down around us."

"Promise me," Dara asked her kind Aunt Lini, when she

was certain her sister was safely out of earshot, "that if I ever get that bad, you'll hit me in the head when I'm not looking? And throw my body in the chasm?"

"I'll remind you that you gave me permission of that, don't think I won't!" her old aunt chuckled. "She's too much like your mother, that one: stubborn and opinionated, and dead sure she's always right. You're natured more like me, and your father, for that matter," Lini observed. "You have a good head between your ears, girl, and the Flame's own touch on top of it," she said, mussing her already messy red hair. "But you can't remain a girl forever. All too soon your life will revolve around *your* . . . hips," she snorted, looking down at her own. They were broad and full, testimony to the five stout cousins of Dara's that she'd birthed, now all grown with children of their own.

"Remember, do it when I'm not looking," reminded Dara, as she left with a kiss and the belt and pies in hand. "It will be more compassionate if I don't see it coming."

Dara stopped by the tanning shed long enough to explain to her cousin who was working that post what she wanted to do with her sister's belt, and after she got permission she was given the run of the shed. She'd proven far more adept at leatherwork than needlecraft, much to Anira's dismay. Her male cousins didn't mind indulging the crafty girl in her interests, either.

Finding a bit of leather among the piles and piles of the stuff was easy, and in a few moments she had turned a thick deerskin thong into a decorative knot that complemented the copper pattern. She tied another on the other side, threading it through the inadequate clasp and fastening it with a simple slip-knot that wouldn't come undone . . . particularly past her sister's hips.

Fixing the belt was easy. Prying two of the tiny silver bells off of the piece was much harder. Dara had to use a sharp iron leather tool to pry apart the wires that held them in place to get them loose, but soon she had two of the precious things in her hand. Tiny silver bells, perfect for attracting the attention of a husky peasant lad . . . or that of a falconer, to locate her falcon in the wild.

She replaced the two missing bells with two more knots of the same leather she'd used in the clasp. It tied the design together, she decided, and hid the fact that two of the bells were missing. She doubted her sister would ever notice their absence.

While she was letting the copper sit in salt and vinegar for a few moments to shine it, Dara pilfered several other small scraps she thought would be useful in her pursuit of falconry: one to make a hood, another two for soft jesses, yet another for a lure.

Then, while she was rummaging around for a knife, she spied the three thick spools of waxed thread.

It was heavy woolen thread, coated with beeswax and spun to a fineness that made it useful in stitching together leather garments, places where using tougher (and uglier) sinew just wouldn't do. Dara realized that each spool contained at least thirty or forty feet of thread . . . tough, strong thread that wouldn't break under a load. She even unwound one of the rolls and pulled a single strand as hard as she could. She wasn't able to break it.

Strong enough to tie to an iron crossbow bolt, then, she decided. The spool ended up in her basket with the belt and leather.

Lastly she stopped by the toolshed to borrow a spade – a narrow-bladed iron spade, not a blunt wooden one. The Westwoodmen had accumulated many such tools over the years. They were essential for keeping trails clear and such, and there were always three or four sitting around. Dara grabbed one and slung it over her shoulder, her basket dangling from it, before she headed back to the cottage.

It seemed like she had been awake all day, but it was only a little past noon. Her body ached, her hands were scratched and bruised despite her thick leather gloves, and her feet were numb with use. As she approached the little cottage she felt like breaking into a sprint, but her feet would not let her. She settled for stumbling into the tiny house and collapsing on her bedroll on the floor, leaving her carefully-gathered supplies scattered. She fell into a quick, shallow sleep, not waking until late afternoon.

The nap had done her well, she decided. She stretched and wiped the sleep from her eyes before dealing with the fire. It had gone out in her absence. She used the cold hearth as an excuse to clean it before she set and rekindled another. She put both meat pies on the stove-plate atop the fireplace and boiled more water for tea.

Before the tea boiled she heard Kalen's young voice approaching, a tidy sack of pecans at his side.

"Spent all morning gathering nuts," he said, sourly, "and listening to how hard things were when gran was a kid."

"They all talk like that," Dara grinned. "They can't help it. I'm sure we'll talk about how horrible our childhoods were, too, when we get old."

"Speak for yourself," Kalen shrugged. "I'm enjoying it, so far."

The fair-haired boy probably *was* enjoying it – the children of the Westwood did not have to start laboring in the fields when they were seven or eight, as the Vale folk did. They began to get chores around that time, but childhood was cherished in the wood in ways it was not in the rest of Sevendor. Children were especially valued in the light of the Flame, it was said, and children's laughter was said to be a wholesome and healthful thing.

All too soon, she realized, Kalen would turn from boy to man, and it would be him grabbing a bow and facing off with the Castle men. Perhaps when her brother Kyre became Master of the Wood in his father's place. Perhaps before then, if the conflict with the castle men continued to grow.

That thought sobered Dara. She didn't like the idea of her playmates growing up just to die in some stupid battle. There were more important things to do.

"Let's start with the hole digging," she suggested, handing him the shovel. "I need two dug, here and here," she said, drawing out the spots in the dirt in front of the cot with a knife. "About a foot deep, maybe a foot and a half— "

"How much is a foot?" the boy asked, curious. "My foot or your foot?"

"Huh? Oh, just do it so that your foot can fit in it up to your knee," she suggested. "That should be deep enough. I'm going to cut a few poles while you do that. It might take me awhile. I'm better at climbing trees than chopping them down," she added, remembering the tough time she'd had with the hickory sapling.

She grabbed her little hunting crossbow and quiver, along with the twine and the cot's small hatchet before she went deeper into the nutwood, to where the nut trees gave way to hardwoods and evergreens. She found a secluded clearing between two big oak trees and sat down.

She spent half an hour figuring out the best way to tie the waxed thread to the small iron dart, and then began practicing. Dara quickly learned that she had to pay-out the line in a loose coil before she shot the bolt, else the resistance on the string would slow and eventually stop the tiny arrow.

But soon she discovered that paying out too much line was just as bad. As small as it was, the bow of the arbalest was powerful, a laminate of hickory and yew. She found a branch of one of the oaks about as high up as the shrub she was trying to reach, and she spent almost an hour figuring out how to allow just enough line to reach the branch, but not so much as to overshoot it.

Then she was stuck with another problem: how to allow the dart enough slack to lower it back down to within her reach, after she had slung it over the tiny tree. She hit upon the idea of re-tying the dart so that an additional six feet of line easily fell from the dart's lowest point. It shouldn't be that difficult to make at least one shot clean enough to recapture the dart and the end of the string.

When she was satisfied she could make the shot properly, she put the weapon away and got out the axe. It didn't take her long to find a few cedar saplings that were fated to become doorposts. After chopping through the trunks and trimming the tops and branches off, she had two seven-foot lengths and several five-foot or shorter lengths.

Dara chose cedar for its insect-repelling properties. She'd stayed in the cot overnight, now, and she could see there was a definite need for such measures. To that end she bundled up the cedar boughs she'd trimmed and hauled them back to the cottage with the poles. Their fresh scent would eliminate the stale smell the dank cottage still suffered.

When she got back, Kalen was just finishing the second hole. Both were approximately where she had wanted them, and although one was bigger than the other by four inches the boy had done an admirable job.

"We'll put pebbles and water in them tonight," she explained, when she stopped his work and praised it. "That will settle it to the bottom, after a day or so. Then we can put the poles up, back-fill it with clay and more rocks, and then once it settles properly we can lash header pole overhead, and then run the ridgepoles back to the cot. Then we'll do the roof and maybe even walls. That would give the place a nice, cozy little place to hang a mantle and store the firewood, before you got into the house. That will save the floor and keep the inner room warmer."

"You sure do know a lot about building," Kalen said, shaking his head in admiration.

"I just pay attention to stuff," she shrugged. "It's not that hard. Honestly, I don't know why no one has done it sooner."

After a hard afternoon of hole-digging, Kalen was all too happy to devour one of the meat pies, pronouncing it much better than the ones his sister made. Dara sent him home after that, an hour or more before dusk, and cautioned him to wait a day or so before returning, so that the poles would settle. She wanted some peace to think about the next part of her plan, go back over her failed attempt, and figure out if she was forgetting anything.

She packed her supplies that night after a meager dinner of sausage and potatoes, and even prepared the water for tea the next morning. Then she stared at the fire for an hour from her bedroll before finally drifting off to sleep . . . and dreamt of rocks and wings.

Once again she roused herself before dawn the next day, though it was far more of a struggle to get herself out of her cozy bedroll than it had been the day before. Her muscles complained bitterly as she heated her tea and prepared herself. She began by trimming the hickory stave she'd cut with the hatchet, to make it more useful in climbing. Then she filled two water bottles and packed a lunch. She was off on the trail before the sky even began to get pale, and was already climbing up into the mountain path by the time she heard the first stirrings of life from the manor in the distance.

She tarried at the first clearing on the eastern side to watch the sun rise again. Gone were the morbid thoughts that it might be her last; Dara was determined to be successful. She continued scrambling up the trail through the mists that clung to the tree line, and without pausing she began the steep ascent before the sun had cleared the distant ridge.

It was like she was in a dream, as she approached the narrow ledge where she had left her ropes and other equipment. In a daze she got her cold fingers to cock the crossbow, and though her first shot went wide and had to be retrieved by pulling the thread back, the second arced perfectly over the sturdy little tree. The length of waxed string caught and then plummeted, weighted by the iron bolt, and the dangling length suspended from the dart was within inches of Dara's fingers.

Eagerly she gathered the end of the line, and then slowly pulled it taught. Then she tied the end of the much stronger – and heavier – rope she'd brought, and began to slowly, gently pull the rope up the side of the cliff.

Her breath caught a few times, as the rope seemed to pull more and more heavily on the thread, and then again when the knot between the two struggled to go over the summit of the tree. But she started breathing more easily when the heavy rope began to descend again. Soon she had both ends of it in her hands.

Tentatively, she pulled on it, then let her full weight lean on it, while she was safely over the ledge. The rope and the tree held stoutly. Grinning to herself, Dara made ready for the last climb to the summit.

It was hard work, even with the assistance and security of the rope. When she reached the point that had stopped her before, she was able to walk up a few steps, her weight entirely on the line, until she found another handhold. But six feet beyond that she hit another smooth patch, and she had to trust the rope again.

Then she was over a particularly difficult scramble, and ready to face the next one, but there weren't any more. The grade leveled out somewhat, and Dara climbed the last few yards by herself.

Then she was on top of the mountain, at the very peak of Rundeval, the entire valley of Sevendor spread out before her.

To the left, the western enclave of the Westwood seemed so small, compared to the rest of the valley, though the Westwoodmen's mandate extended as far into the interior of the mountains as a man could range. To the north she saw the distant and distinctive mound of Matten's Helm; it was beautiful, with the autumnal foliage arrayed at its base.

Directly below her, at the base of the north face of the mountain, was Sevendor Castle, a dark and hulking mass of stone that represented everything oppressive to Dara. She wondered if she could throw a rock from the summit and manage to hit Sir Erantal as he relieved himself for the morning.

Of course she knew that was silly. She was here to get a bird, not take petty revenge. She began to fasten the end of the rope on the "knob of rock no bigger than a hogshead" that her father had spoken of, when she finally had a chance to look down – *really* look down – and appreciate just how high up she was.

I'm above the falcon's nest, she observed to herself. *I am above the birds. And it's a long, long way down. With a very dreary ending awaiting her at the bottom.*

For a few moments fear overtook her, and she almost started back down the way she came without her prize. But despite the fear of falling, the fear of failure was even greater. In the end Dara's need for the falcon's eyas won out over her fear of losing her own life.

When she was certain that her ropes were secure, her equipment in place, and her basket tied firmly to her chest, Dara whispered one last prayer to the Flame, took a deep breath to calm herself, and took her first step over the ridge and down the sheer wall of black stone that was the north face of the mountain.

Chapter Five

Frightful

Moments after Dara began her journey, she knew it was a terrible mistake.

The first few moments weren't too bad, as Rundeval's summit arced gracefully down away from the ridge . . . but after that, every step she took pushed her farther and farther away from safety. The face of the cliff was smooth, with few handholds. Without a rope, Dara would never have had a chance.

As it was, she slipped and found herself almost dangling several times on the way down. She had wrapped a long portion of her line around herself, and tied the end securely around her waist and shoulders so that if her hands let go she would not fall automatically, but one crazy step after another turned her adventure into a harsh lesson in gravity and friction. Her fingers were soon scraped and bleeding, as she paid out the hempen rope one painful hand at a time. The gloves she'd brought had smooth leather palms which made the rope slip too easily, and she had to abandon them to her belt before she'd descended twenty feet.

But after the first scrambling descent, there was a gentle knob in the cliff that gave just enough support so that she could lean against it and catch her breath.

Dara was exhausted after just a few scant yards. Her arms ached with effort, her legs – which were tender from all the climbing she'd done – were protesting painfully to her after the effort she'd put them to climbing down. But she'd made it this far, she recognized proudly. She'd made it too far to easily turn back now. The nest was only another few dozen feet down over the side, she reminded herself encouragingly.

Then she looked down.

Vertigo struck her as she saw with unobstructed clarity the long, long way down the face of Rundeval. The bottom of the cliff seemed so far away, yet she seemed to be able to see every little detail of the rocks that promised to punish her slightest misstep below. The distance was terrifying, and the reminder of the price of one mistake was just too potent; Dara made herself look elsewhere. Otherwise, she realized, she wouldn't be able to make her hands and feet do anything, she was so frightened.

Sevendor Castle's hulking dark mass was the next easiest thing for her bewildered eyes to focus upon. It seemed laughably small from up here, a square stone keep the same color of the mountain's dark stone with some additional towers, all of which were in a shabby state of repair. The shingled rooftop of the castle's hall and round refuge tower had patches and holes she could see from here. She couldn't imagine her people trying to defend themselves against enemies behind that wreck. Old Sir Erantal had a lot to answer for in the Duke's service, Dara told herself in an effort to distract her mind from the terrible danger she'd brought on herself. She could almost imagine how the neglected old pile of stones must smell.

When she'd calmed her fear and took stock of her situation, she realized that she had to force herself to go on. Dara glanced over the side of the knob and saw the falcon's nest below. Another twenty feet, perhaps thirty, and she'd be there. She could see the wide tangle of brush and twigs that made up the nest . . . and she could see three distinct bobbing shapes below.

And no mother bird. She must be out hunting for breakfast, Dara decided. *No better time to capture one of the fledglings, then.*

Taking a deep breath Dara grasped the rope tightly and took a step down, backwards, into nothingness. The knob overhung just enough to make finding a foothold maddeningly difficult. First with one foot, then the other, Dara probed the cliff below her until finally her left toe found purchase . . . if she stretched her legs out as far as she could. It wasn't much, but it gave her just enough purchase to descend another few inches, where she repeated the process with her other foot.

Her mind sang a frantic monolog the entire time.

One more inch, just one more inch, please . . . oh, there! Almost at that pretty bird, I'm almost . . . almost there . . . Flame, this rope is hurting my hands! Maybe I should put the gloves back on? Certainly for the climb back up, if I can even get back up . . . there! Now just lower yourself carefully down and flex that knee carefully . . . Yikes! Slipped! Oh, ashes and cinders this hurts! What was I thinking? Flame, my elbow hurts now! Have to keep going, though, must keep going, every inch brings me closer, just . . . have to get my toe . . . right there . . . am I going to slip? No? Am I sure? No? Oh, Flame, what do I do now . . . maybe just . . . a little to the right . . . but ---AHHHHHHHH!

Dara yelped as her foot slipped and she felt the mountain slap her in the face and chest. She fell rapidly, her hands madly scrambling for any kind of purchase. She fell six feet, scraping her chin badly and biting her tongue, when her left toe unexpectedly found a shallow concavity she was able to use to stop her descent. The rope above her was taught with the tension of her weight, still, but almost two inches of her left foot kept her from falling. That was enough.

Checking her rope carefully before she proceeded, Dara pushed herself toward the right, again, until she found another toe hold that didn't quite stretch her legs out like a dressed hen ready for stuffing. Both feet, she realized, had solid rock under her and for a few precious moments she wasn't in imminent danger of a plummet to her doom. She hugged the cliff and panted, letting her legs bear her weight for a few moments while her arms rested.

The position also gave her just enough room to look back and down over her shoulder at the nest below.

There wasn't as much as a hint of a toehold from where she was down the fifteen feet left to the narrow ledge where the nest awaited her. Below her boots the cliff cut sharply back inwards, only a few feet . . . but a few feet might as well be miles away. The slope picked back up below the nest, but the mother falcon had cleverly chosen a hard-to-reach spot for her nest. From the ground the difference had seemed so small. Now that she was here "small" might just

mean "impossible".

Or at least "risky", she decided.

There was one thing she could do, she realized, as she investigated moving strongly to either the left or right, and then decided against it. As narrow as the cliff was, at its widest point there was a space over four feet wide and nearly flat, in front of the nest. She could just pay out the rope enough to drop straight down into that very, *very* narrow space and hope she didn't fall over the cliff in the process.

It was a calculated effort. She'd fallen farther from trees, before, and had landed without problems in spaces far smaller than the one below her, she reasoned. But then she hadn't been worried about plunging over any cliffs, either. She debated with herself for what seemed like forever, and nearly quit the effort when she considered her chances of falling.

But then she looked at her bloodied, scraped hands. The sweat was starting to make them sting even more than they already hurt. If she gave up now, then she'd injured her poor hands for nothing.

Taking another deep breath, Dara pushed herself gently out and let the rope pay out through her hands as gravity pulled her quickly down. She had a few seconds of abject terror as the winds themselves were the only thing between her and death . . . and then she felt her feet hit the rocky ledge so hard her knees flew up and clacked her jaws together.

But she was alive. She clung to the stone and panted, delighting in the sensation of solid ground. She laughed.

She'd made it to the ledge. She noted with satisfaction that she was over a foot away from certain doom, almost two feet. *Plenty* of room.

When she'd caught her breath again, she carefully rolled over and surveyed the nearby nest. It was huge, nearly four feet wide at the center, and deep. Dara pulled herself over to the habitat on her bruised and complaining knees and elbows, until she was staring down at three sets of beady little eyes and three beaks. The fledglings were just starting to lose their baby plumage and grow real feathers. They still looked half like plucked chicks.

Then they all stared back at her and began angrily squawking at her.

They must think I'm a predator, she realized. *I'm certainly not their mother. Best be on my way with what I came for before she returns,* Dara reasoned.

She looked at the trio of eyases and tried to remember everything her Uncle Keram had told her. After a few moments of thoughtful consideration, Dara chose the chick in the rear, the largest of the three. Females tended to be larger at this stage, she remembered him saying, and females were superior hunters to males. They had to be, to feed this many hungry beaks.

"Hello, beautiful," Dara breathed as she reached her bloody hands out to pick up the chick. The bird was not cooperative – indeed, the moment her fingers came in range the angry chick viciously pecked at her until she cried out.

"Flame! You are a frightful beast, aren't you?" swore Dara, sucking on her fingertips before making another approach. The chick fluffed its wings defiantly and took another strike at Dara's fingers, but the girl persisted until she could feel the warm, feathery little bundle madly scrambling between her hands, her siblings now attacking Dara's wrists in defense of their sister.

"Ow! Flame! Ow! Ash and cinders! Ow!" she cried as she tried to get the chick in the basket she'd brought. She earned one final, deep scratch on her left wrist for her trouble before she was able to close the basket and fasten it tightly with string.

Dara took a few breaths and examined the remaining chicks before she left. She couldn't properly tell their sex, at this age, but they seemed confused by the amount of room that they suddenly had. Nor were they happy about it; their screeching and squawking had risen in pitch and shrillness in their alarm at the "attack" on their home.

At least they'll get more to eat without . . . without their frightful big sister around, now, Dara reasoned as she began to prepare herself for the brutal climb ahead of her. Uncle Keram had told her how the smaller nestlings often were neglected in favor of larger, stronger ones. It was Nature's way, he'd said, solemnly, when she'd complained of the unfairness. But without their big sister to compete with, the remaining chicks should both prosper . . . she hoped.

When she had rested sufficiently to attempt the ascent back up the cliff, Dara secured the basket carefully behind her before she began climbing up the only slope that promised even a hint of traction. She also began winding her rope around her waist and re-securing it, every time she collected enough slack to do so. She had no desire to lose an inch of ground her aching arms and back gained for her. She was feeling triumphant, now, the additional weight of the chick on her back giving her extra reason to be cautious as well as exultant. If she could just make it back up to the peak . . .

Dara had climbed no more than ten feet from the nest when disaster struck. She was lifting her left foot painfully into the air, searching for a toehold, when suddenly her right shoulder was struck, hard, by a vicious mass of feathers and claws. Her right shoulder exploded in pain as she felt razor-sharp beak and talons slice into her flesh. Despite herself, she lost purchase on the cliff.

She only fell a few inches, but it was enough to dislodge her from the mountain. Her hands and feet fell away from the stone and for four terrifying seconds she was swinging hundreds of feet in the air over the rocks below with absolutely no control of her body. She was a helpless victim of gravity and momentum. Only the stout rope and her knot-work had saved her from death.

Dara swung out in a lazy arc far, far off her chosen path up the cliffside, before the rope slammed her back into the rock. Her bloody hands scrambled again, but found no purchase. She arced back across the mountain like some terrified pendulum and found her body twisting in the air. With horror she realized that her landing would likely put the basket between her and the mountain, so she frantically twisted around, taking the brunt of the impact on her bleeding shoulder. This time her left hand found just enough rock to grab on to, to keep her from being flung back out into the void.

Her right hand padded the side of the mountain until it, too, discovered a small depression, and she was steady for the moment. It took some searching, but her left toe eventually found another spot, and one that suggested enough resistance to lift herself up a few more inches.

That's when she heard the mother falcon's defiant call. Dara frantically glanced over both shoulders, peering into the sky to try to find the angry bird. She spotted it, almost too late, out of the corner of her eye. She was coming around for another attack, Dara realized. One that might just dislodge her entirely from the mountain.

Dara twisted at the last second, avoiding most of the impact and all of the beak. She merely had to suffer a few seconds of psychotically enraged feathers scrambling against her armpit and neck before it flew off again.

Realizing she didn't have long until she returned for another run, fear inspired Dara to grasp the rope and pull with all her might while pushing with her leg. It was hard . . . but it was enough to allow her to get one knee up on the next tiny ledge. And from there the grade started getting slightly better.

When Dara made it to the gentle knob, and pulled herself over its lip with her elbows, she realized that the absolute worst parts of her adventure were behind her. She crawled five or six more feet up the rope, not even bothering to tie off anymore, until she was no longer dependent on its resistance to hold her.

She was on solid ground now. Unless that falcon knocked her off the mountain, she was safe.

Pulling herself back up to the hogshead-sized knob at the peak was easy, after that ordeal. Still, she did not untie her line from the rock until she was safely on the other side, with her second line secured. Coming down seemed as easy as descending a tree, she laughed at herself, and when she had finally arrived at the little clearing where she had stowed her gear, she felt both exhausted and jubilant.

She had done it. She had captured a falcon.

With exaggerated care she opened the basket and gazed at her new little charge. The bird seemed to be still angry at her – powerfully angry.

"You really are Frightful!" she said, laughing as the pitiful-looking thing glared at her. "I guess I just named you!" She laughed a bit more, but that was a mistake. It pulled on her shoulder where the mother falcon had shredded her tunic. The wound was still bleeding, she realized. She touched it gingerly. Long, but not deep, she decided. It could wait until she got back to the cot.

"Are you hungry, Frightful?" Dara asked, realizing that her abduction had likely interrupted the bird's breakfast.

Frightful didn't respond – but then she hadn't expected it to. Dara closed the basket with a contented sigh and tied it back up. Then she thirstily drank the rest of her water bottle before gathering her things and starting back down the mountain.

It wasn't even midmorning yet.

* * *

As soon as she got back to the nutwood cot, Dara fed

Frightful with tiny shaved scraps of raw meat she'd stolen from the Hall's kitchen. The little falcon ate it greedily, but did not seem grateful to her for supplying it. Indeed, it kept eating until it couldn't eat any more, then tucked its beak under its wing and fell asleep.

Dara waited a little longer, enough time to peel off her bloody tunic with her mangled hands and try to take a closer look at her wounds. They were bad – worse than she'd thought – but they would heal. She would heal. She had survived, she realized . . . not just survived, Dara had succeeded. She had climbed Rundeval's peak and returned with a falcon. Not even her Uncle Keram or her father had done that.

Weakly she drank some water from the cistern, tiredly chewed a small loaf, and fell asleep in the hut.

Young Kalen returned that afternoon, and Dara woke up enough to direct him in the placement of the stout posts, but she felt sick with weariness and pain. She hid her mangled hands under her gloves, and "allowed" the boy the privilege of moving the heavy posts into place. When the dirt was replaced and the poles were reasonably plumb, Dara dismissed the boy early with praise, and told him to return in a few days when the posts had settled to help with the ridgepole.

Then she went back into the cot and collapsed again on her bedroll.

The next few days were hectic. Dara's body was a mess after her struggle, and while her hands had scabbed up fairly quickly, the wound on her bruised shoulder was still painful and seeping blood. It pained her every time she rolled over at night, and she awoke in the morning to find her bedding had adhered to the dried blood on her shoulder. With a sick feeling in her stomach, Dara pulled the cloth out of the wound. It hurt like fire when she did so. She washed out the wound as best she could, then prepared a little food for herself and her new avian charge.

Frightful had stayed in her basket all night long. In the morning, Dara tried to move her to the perching block she had cobbled together out of the old bedframe. While the little bird could perch on the wooden frame, she was clearly uncomfortable and uneasy about the idea, protesting loudly every few moments. In fact, Frightful seemed to chide her nonstop, from the moment Dara awoke until she finally had to close her eyes for a nap in the afternoon.

That evening Dara went hunting. She was not particularly good at it, nor particularly eager to do so, but while she still had a few days' food in her cupboard, it was mostly bread and vegetables and sausage – not fare fit for a growing bird. Falcons needed meat, her Uncle was fond of saying on the subject, the fresher the better. Uncooked meat.

While Dara did not relish the prospect, she knew she had to have some, if she wanted Frightful to survive. Not all fledglings did, once they were captured. Even the best-cared-for nestlings could stop eating or refuse food. So Dara took her small crossbow into the forest and hunted that afternoon.

It didn't take her long to find a family of squirrels nearby. The nutwoods were infested with them, of course; the nut harvest in the autumn was often a race against the nimble creatures for the nuts. Dara patiently took position behind a pine tree and waited for a good shot. Once she found the squirrel she wanted she took aim, held her breath, and pulled on the lever. A moment later the dead squirrel fell out of the tree.

Dara didn't bother with a second. Frightful would make a few days' meals out of this one, she knew, and by that time it would be preferable to find a fresh one. It didn't take her long to skin the corpse outside of the cottage and then slice the raw, tough meat into tiny strips. One by one she fed them to the bird until she was stuffed and lethargic.

"Oh, thank the *Flame*," Dara whispered, as the tiny falcon finally fell asleep. "I'm exhausted again!"

She was actually worse than that. In the middle of the night, Dara awoke with a strange sensation in her head, with the air around her lamentably difficult to breath. She felt hot and cold at the same time. She was sick, she realized. She felt dreadful.

As bad as she felt, she forced herself to get up the next morning and spend an hour just holding Frightful on her chest, staring into her dark little eyes and murmuring to her in a quiet voice. The bird seemed over her anger, at this point – Dara was feeding her, after all – but she was still far from friendly. After an hour of staring at her, however, the little bird was at least not antagonistic. That was a hopeful sign.

Dara felt bad the rest of the day. Her scabby hands were hard to use, and the pain in her shoulder was sharp and regular. Her arms and legs still ached from her efforts and she could barely walk outside to pee in the morning, so stiff were they. But she forced herself to keep going. She trimmed the temporary jesses she'd made for her new bird, two soft leather thongs six inches long that she secured with a gentle knot around Frightful's talons. The falcon was not pleased with her new finery, and spent the rest of the day desperately attacking her own feet. A luncheon of squirrel seemed to mollify her for a while, but she was back at it again afterwards.

Dara slept all day that day, waking in the afternoon with an overpowering thirst. She drank from the cistern until the craving went away, then lurched painfully over to check on Frightful. The little bird seemed fine. Except for glaring hungrily at her. The squirrel was gone, by that point, so Dara wearily picked up her little arbalest and went back out hunting.

The cool breeze felt good on her face, she realized. She'd been so hot in the cottage. She returned to her earlier hunting spot and waited for another foolish squirrel, or perhaps something larger, to wander by. As she watched, her crossbow cocked, her eyes slowly closed, and sleep overtook her as she sat crammed between two trees.

Time passed – how much, Dara didn't realize until she came suddenly awake . . . and twilight was quickly falling. Her arms and legs were stiff from being in that cramped position, and she was amazed that her arbalest hadn't discharged while she slept. Dara pulled herself achingly to her feet, stumbled as her head swam dangerously, and then walked back to the cottage in the dark, empty-handed.

She could see the fire was still lit, by the smoke still

coming out of the squat little chimney over the cottage, which she was grateful for. The air was getting colder with each step, and her hands were almost numb. Considering their sad state that was nearly a relief, but she looked forward to the tiny stove's heat as she stumbled through the door.

"Well, Little Bird," came a familiar voice. "It looks as if you've finally come back to your nest."

Dara was startled by her Uncle Keram, who was seated on the one little stool in the room. Next to her stood young Kalen, who looked at her with eyes downcast in guilt.

"Un-uncle?" Dara asked, confused. "What are you doing here?"

"Looking for you," he replied, clearing his throat. "And about eighty feet of good rope that's missing from the harness shed. I hadn't associated the two missing things until your friend Kalen came to me. It seems he was worried about you, too."

"I'm sorry, Dara!" Kalen said, bitterly. "I just saw you in bed like that, all bloody, and—"

"Enough, lad," Keram said, gently. "You did the right thing. See, I thought she was running off to see a boy, which was reasonable enough. You're at that age," he conceded. "But when you didn't show up for two days straight, your father got worried. I was already trying to figure out where all our rope went when Kalen came to tell me about you being in the nutwood. That was . . . troubling, but at least I knew you hadn't run off with a boy, or some other foolishness."

"Uncle, no!" she protested.

"Well, clearly you didn't," he agreed. "Instead I come down here and find your work nearly complete . . . and all of my rope. And then I spied this precious little creature," he said, nodding to the tiny ball of feathers sitting on the broken bedframe, "and I knew at once what had happened. All of those questions. All of that time you spent asking me about falconry. All of those little errands you started doing. I can't believe it, but . . . Dara, you went and caught yourself a raptor!"

"I'm sorry!" Dara said, tears in her eyes. "I . . . I just . . ."

"Don't apologize, lass," Keram said, affectionately. "She's a fine eyas, no doubt. Kestral? No, too small . . . redtail?"

Dara swallowed dizzily. "Silver Headed Raptor," she whispered, closing her eyes. Her heart was sinking. This was too soon. She watched her uncle's eyes grow wide as he realized just where she had been to collect her prize."

"Dara, you . . . you climbed . . ."

"Rundeval," she nodded. "I went up the south side and lowered myself down from the top. That's why I needed so much rope," she added. "Uh, I'm done with it now, if you need it."

Uncle Keram looked at her in disbelief. "You . . . climbed . . . Rundeval. And then went halfway down the other side. Flame guided you, girl," he said, his face pale with fear. "I thought maybe you'd found a redtail, or maybe a goshawk, here – a really big one – but this eyas is . . . a raptor. A falcon. That you risked your life for!" he finished angrily.

91

"I came back," Dara pointed out, weakly. "But now I have to . . . train her . . ."

"Yes," sighed Uncle Keram. "Yes, I suppose you do. You realize it's likely she won't survive the end of the week, away from her mother? Do you know how many times a falconer loses an eyas? Do you realize what an awesome responsibility this is? It's like having a baby of your own, only one that can peck your eyes out. Hawks are hard enough to train, Dara, but a falcon? A good falconer has to know how to train both, but they usually start with the easy ones!"

"I don't tend to do things the easy way," Dara said, gesturing with her wounded hands.

"Flame knows a truer word was never spoken. But right hungry, she is. You chose well. And I cannot wait to hear about how you went about getting to her . . . without anyone in the manor seeing you do it. That kind of dedication means you'll be a good falconer, I suppose."

"So . . . so I can keep her?" Dara asked, eyes wide and breathless.

"Keep her? No one else could," Keram observed. "And she's too young to survive in the wild on her own. Look, she's already responding to your voice. No, Little Bird, you earned this responsibility. I won't take it away. You will train this bird, now that you've taken it from the wild, and you will train it well. That means every day, just so you know."

"Oh, Uncle Keram! I'm so . . . thank you!" was all she could say through the tears that were suddenly streaming down her face. "I'm so . . ." she added, before she felt her knees give way under her.

She heard both Keram and Kalen shout her name at once, and then her face was pressed into the cool dirt floor of the cottage. The last thing she remembered was the pain on her face and some self-criticism on how dirty the floor was. But how deliciously cool it felt against her skin. Then Dara lost consciousness.

For three more days Dara stayed at the cot in the nutwood. Three days Keram attended her, or if his duties prevented, one of her brothers. Mostly Kyre, of course, but at other times she saw her other brothers. Even Kobb, at one point. The bully even looked worried.

After three days her fever broke, and while her healing hands still ached bitterly, Dara still wasn't well enough to travel back to the manor. Uncle Keram and Kalen had taken turns feeding Frightful while she'd been unconscious, her dreams an unpleasant mix of the top of the mountain, the fear of getting caught, and some terror her mind could not even name, at this point. She woke once when young Kalen was back from fetching water from the spring. Keram cared Frightful, talking to the bird on his broad chest while he watched his niece.

It was decided to allow Dara to convalesce at the cottage, though she had ample visitors. She permitted her worried Aunt Anira to bandage her wounds without fussing at her about her dangerous stunt. Her father even visited, once, hobbling down on his bandaged leg to see the fabled bird and hear her tale of how she got her. He was worried sick, she knew, and relieved to see his youngest daughter on the mend.

Her whole family was excited to see her after the alarm she'd caused, and all of them seemed enraptured with Frightful when they came to visit. She and Frightful were minor celebrities, for a little while, and as the days grew colder there were plenty who made the trek to the nutwood. Eventually Kamen forbade all but family be allowed, so both girl and bird could get some rest.

At the end of a particularly long day, she flexed her fingers and painted them with the ointment her aunt had left before allowing herself to be led to her chamber and dumped into bed. Her baby falcon stared at her on a perch nearby as Kalen administered the bitter tea she was also supposed to drink to help her sleep. The boy had been a huge assistance in her convalescence, and she needed to do something for him. She made a promise to herself to do so, someday.

But now other thoughts were more pressing on her mind. She stared at Frightful as her eyes began to close.

"I *can* be a falconer," she whispered to the pretty bird in the darkness. "Uncle Keram *said* so! I can train you, Frightful," she promised. "And when I'm done, you'll be the most majestic falcon in history."

Chapter Six

Training

After three weeks living in the nutwood cottage, a room was cleared for Dara back at Westwood Hall, in consideration of her new charge. It wasn't much bigger than her old chamber, but it was higher up the squat round tower at the south end of the Hall. It had enough room for her narrow bed, her chest of possessions, and Frightful's block.

Frightful was skittish and nervous about the move. Just as she had started to get used to the small confines of the cottage, she had to re-adjust to the noisy environs of Westwood Hall. Dara's room gave her some measure of privacy, and for two days Dara stayed there with her, coaxing the falcon to fly from glove to block and back again.

Eventually, however, Dara's uncle intervened. After checking Frightful's condition, and the state of her wing feathers, he declared that she should take the bird around the house – hooded, at first – to get her used to the strange sounds and smells of the manor that was to be her new home.

"It's called 'manning' a bird," her uncle explained. "You can never truly tame a bird, the way you do a dog, but you can get it accustomed to the things that would scare away a wild hawk or falcon. Get it used to being around people's voices and smells, dogs and cook fires, horses and chickens and that sort of thing. If a bird isn't properly manned, it will stay skittish and possibly not return to you, if it gets scared off."

That made sense to Dara, and that day she started bringing Frightful down to the hall when it was mostly empty, to get her used to the place. She let her perch on her gloved fist, her jesses clutched tightly in Dara's fingers lest she startle and injure herself flying indoors.

One consequence she hadn't counted on was how many people on the estate still wanted to see the bird she'd risked her life for. Every one of them was openly admiring of the beautiful raptor, though Frightful seemed far less enchanted with her sudden popularity.

She trembled around people, at first, but after the third day she stopped being quite so jumpy and started to relax a bit. That was gratifying – it was nice to be able to carry on a conversation without worrying about your falcon suddenly flying away. The popularity Dara enjoyed wasn't lost on her, either. Her brother and their cousins made her tell the story of how she had climbed the mountain a dozen times, already, even insisting she do it in front of the Flame to avoid any embellishments.

People had changed how they reacted to her, too. Instead of treating her like a scheming brat, they looked at her with a new . . . respect. While what she had done was dangerous and stupid, by all accounts, it had also been uncommonly brave. The falcon on her fist was proof of the deed, and her growing mastery of Frightful's care had caused folks who had teased or belittled her before to look at her in a new light.

Of course, Dara conceded that she, herself, had changed. The teasing games and pranks she'd played on her older siblings seemed so petty, now. Facing death, and achieving something she had worked hard for, gave her new perspective. She heard the whispers. Dara the Brat was gone. They were starting to look at her like a true daughter of the Master of the Wood, near enough nobility, within the confines of the Westwood. It was the difference that honest respect made.

Dara was gratified by the change in perspective, but she was too busy to enjoy it much. The fact of the matter was that she wasn't getting into trouble as much because she was suddenly incredibly mature . . . she wasn't getting into trouble because caring for and training a bird was a day-in, day-out job, and she just didn't have time for anything else. She barely fed and bathed herself, much less plotted to get dirty or put pebbles in her brothers' shoes. Dara had a job, and it was not one she could escape.

She was in the Great Hall, one early winter's day, Frightful on her shoulder for a change, speaking with her uncle about designing and building a proper mews in the spring, when one of her distant cousins – Kraf, she thought – burst into the Hall with incredible news.

"Sir Erantal is gone! He's been replaced by the Duke!" the man barked out, breathlessly.

That set the entire Hall in an uproar so loud that Frightful squawked in protest, and Dara had to put her hood on her to calm her down.

Someone brought Kraf a mug of ale while everyone who

could gathered around him in front of the Flame to hear the specifics.

Kraf had his eye on a girl from Sevendor Village, and with her father's permission he worked for the village headman, Railan the Steady, two days a week for coin toward eventually setting up a household. He had been in the village when a long train of mounted men and wains had rumbled up Sevendor's road to the outside world, right to the gate of the castle. A train headed by the new lord.

After demanding entry, it seemed, the new lord produced the papers that demonstrated his new ownership, and tossed old Sir Erantal out on his ear in a most impolite manner. He hadn't witnessed it, himself, but he had seen the wicked old knight astride a horse, headed out of the vale looking dejected, and the tale of his removal spread like wildfire.

That was news, indeed. Sir Erantal had been the tenant lord of Sevendor since Dara was a baby. He was a figure of little respect and much revilement among his supposed subjects. The pressure the man had brought to bear on the Westwood to increase his profit from the estate had been strong, and only the insular nature and strong defense of the Westwood had allowed them to enjoy what little prosperity they could.

"What of our new lord?" Kamen asked, excited and curious. "Losing Erantal could be a blessing or a curse. The new lord is no tenant?"

"Nay, Master, he is titled," agreed her cousin. "That I know for certain. He was given Sevendor by the Duke for service on the field of battle in the Westlands, it is said."

"Ah! A warrior!" Kamen remarked with admiration, and a little anxiety. "What kind of man is he?"

"I know only that he brought a great retinue, that he is a young man, and that he has a young bride who is expecting their first child."

"That . . . that is interesting. Very interesting," Kamen said, stroking his beard. "Sevendor has a lord and a lady again. That hasn't happened in six generations. Not a properly seated lord."

"But what does it mean, Kamen?" her Aunt Anira asked, worriedly.

"Mean?" he asked, surprised. "It could mean a good many things. The only certainty is that Sir Erantal will not be bothering us again. Beyond that . . ." he shrugged. "A new lord could mean improvements. Or it could mean new fees and taxes. It will depend entirely on what kind of man the new lord is. Of old, our ancestors swore before the Flame to protect and uphold the rightful lord of Sevendor. I've always taken that to mean a man who sees it as his home, not his property. We will have to wait and see what kind of man he is," he repeated to himself, stroking his beard.

"Kraf, take Dalc and Kabe to the village with you tomorrow," Dara's uncle said, suddenly. "Hang around the edges of the village, see what you can make of the situation. Be home by noon, and let us know."

The next day brought even more news – not only was Sir Erantal's departure confirmed, but the new lord had begun cleaning out the dingy old castle the moment he'd set eyes on it. He'd drafted dozens of hands to help from the village, and even as far as Gurisham. Sevendor Village was in an uproar, although it was reported that a cow had been butchered and given to the village folk to sooth them.

The day also brought word of the names of their new lord and lady: Lord Minalan and Lady Alya, both in their early twenties and fair. He was from the Riverlands, the story was told, the ennobled son of a baker; she was a Wilderlands maiden he'd met while on campaign.

"It seems awfully romantic," her sister mused at dinner that night. "If he's a warrior, a man-at-arms who saved a count or something, and got Sevendor as a reward he must be very strong and brave . . . and they say that he's handsome!"

"And married," reminded Aunt Anira. "But he's giving that moldy old castle a proper cleaning. And spent good money doing it. The lord is not who I worry about. It's all these strange-sounding folk he's brought into the Vale."

"And more on the way," assured Kabe, who wasn't a cousin of hers any way Dara could figure it. "Many more. We overheard two of them strange-sounding ones, talking about it. More by Yule, it's said."

"More?" asked Anira suspiciously, her spoon stopped half-way to her mouth. "How *many* more?"

"Many more," repeated Kabe. "They're Wilderlands folk who were driven from their homes by goblins. Lord Minalan is re-settling them in Sevendor." He looked around, anxiously.

"More folk in Sevendor," Kamen said, shaking his head. "Well, the Vale's been scant, Flame knows, since that big war. Took almost three hundred good men, and not a one came back. Before that there were thousands in Sevendor. Twice as many manors. Every field was farmed, at one time."

"That's hard to believe," snorted Dara's Uncle Keram. "Who would want to live here?"

"It's not so bad, compared to some other places," Kamen said, unpersuasively. "I've traveled a bit. There are worse places than Sevendor. A few more folk would be a boon."

"A few more *proper* folk," her aunt insisted. "Not foreigners from . . . from . . . from the Wilderlands, or wherever they are."

"Vale folk are vale folk," Kamen disagreed. "Matters not how many, or how peculiar they speak. More folk means better prices at market."

"More folk means *higher* prices at market," complained her aunt.

"We'll see," Kamen admitted. "Let's see how the new lord treats us on market day. Take a small crew, lead it yourself, Keram. One booth," he cautioned.

"The castle has sent word out for provision," warned Kabe. "Foodstuffs might do better than leather," he proposed.

"A fair point," agreed Kamen. "Take a few hams, some bacon, some eggs, and some nuts. See what prices you get. And find out more about this new lord."

"Oh, he's not just any kind of lord, either," Kabe added, thoughtfully, as he chewed. "I heard one of his men speaking, one of the big knights that rode with them. Called him . . . what was it . . ."

"Knight? Banneret?" quizzed her uncle, curiously.

"*Magelord,*" Kabe's memory finally supplied. "They called him 'magelord.' Uh . . . what's a magelord?"

* * *

In the days that followed, the excitement provided by Frightful was forgotten at Westwood Hall as more and more exciting news came from the Vale concerning their new lord . . . their new magelord.

For that was, it was explained, the title Lord Minalan bore. He was called the Spellmonger, as he had been a humble village spellmonger, and he'd saved an entire domain, it was said, from goblins away in the Wilderlands to the west.

Kamen was puzzled with each new report that came, particularly ones that referenced magic.

"We're to be ruled by a *wizard*, then?" he asked his brother, before supper. "I thought it was forbidden for wizards to hold title and lands?"

"He's new," explained Dara's uncle, while she listened intently to the adult conversation, pretending to inspect her bird's plumage. "And he's powerful. I've never seen the castle look cleaner . . . or old Railan more bitter. He's been told to house folk on the Commons, and in vacant lots in the village, and it looked like he was crapping hot coals when he spoke of it."

"Were many speaking against the new lord?" asked Dara's aunt, wiping her hands as she came in from the kitchen. She was constantly overhearing such conversations. Almost as much as Dara did.

"Not at all," reported her husband. "Most folk were quite glad to see the end of Erantal. And the castle folk are paying in hard coin now, not credit or tokens . . . and buying everything in sight. Every ham and every nut we sold, and for nearly double last market!"

"And he's not doing anything unnatural to the folk?" asked Aunt Anira, skeptically.

"He tore out the stocks, his first night here," her uncle replied to his wife, meaningfully. Aunt Anira's eyes got larger. The stocks were particularly hated as an arbitrary and humiliating punishment, usually reserved for those who offended the castle.

"Perhaps he's not so bad, then," conceded Anira.

"There's more," her uncle continued. "The new castellan is hiring men. Construction, he says, when the wood arrives. He wants tents and shelters all over the commons, before Yule. And at the castle," he added. "Says he'll pay in good coin."

"I've never spent a bad one," chuckled Kamen. "See if you can spare a few lads from shelling and curing for a few days. No telling when this lord's coin will run out. Or when the new taxes will start. Might as well be our sweat as is bought as the Vale folk. We can get some folk in closer, take a careful look at this magelord of ours."

"You don't really expect he'll start turning people into pigs, do you, Father?" Dara asked.

"I don't expect anything except the sun rising and your aunt's ire, Little Bird," Kamen assured her. "But I do intend to be prepared."

"For what?"

"Exactly," nodded her father. "Without eyes inside that castle, we'll never know what's coming at the Westwood."

Dara almost forgot about the excitement outside the wood, she was so intent on training her falcon. She had gotten the pretty bird to fly the length of the hall, now, if the dogs were outside, and Dara had hacked her out in the meadow closest the hall every fair day she could. She was starting to introduce the lure her uncle had fashioned for her, encouraging the falcon to pounce on it as if it were real prey.

It was slow, painstaking work that required constant repetition, and Dara did not naturally have the patience for it. Several times she caught herself comparing her falcon to a miss-bred chicken, when she was obstinate, or suggest she might end up with a chicken's usual destiny in a soup pot.

But Dara knew that this was not a commitment she could shy away from. Frightful was utterly dependent upon her, now. She couldn't be released back into the wild at this point, not and survive the winter. It was already terribly cold out, and had snowed twice. Dara couldn't imagine what life must be like for her nestmates.

So Dara redoubled her efforts, working in the meadow with the falcon and the lure until her hands were cold and her fingers ached.

But the day that Frightful finally pounced on the lure as she dragged it across the cold, dry meadow she was jubilant. She ran all the way back to the manor, the bird flapping its growing wings excitedly at the disturbance. Dara burst into the Hall, looking around for her uncle so she could tell him.

But there was already a stir of excitement at Westwood Hall when she had arrived. Kasten, the woodward in charge of the forest beyond the chasm, in the vale, had returned from his post with word from Lord Minalan: a goodly portion of that wood was to be cleared, to provide lumber for the new construction in the village and castle.

"The new castellan has ordered cured lumber from outside of the domain," the man reported, shaking his head in disbelief. "But he wants to fell twenty acres, at least, if not more." Kasten was clearly upset by the idea. After all, as woodward, it was his duty to protect that forest. All too often the villeins of Sevendor Village and Gurisham Hamlet would try to poach in the forest, or – worse yet – fell trees without leave. It was Kasten's job to police that wood.

But how could he protect the forest from the man who owned it?

"That's the new forest," Kamen reminded the man, soothingly. "It was once croplands, when Sevendor was in its prime. And it lies beyond the chasm. He's well within his right."

"But that will leave but a shard of wood in the vale!" the man protested.

"Then that will make your job easier!" reproved Kamen. "If our lord is importing more people, doubtless he will need the lumber, and it is his for the taking. And he will need more land cleared for crops. It will be a year before it will be dried and cured, anyway, and the sooner he gets it cut the sooner it will be ready."

"But . . . but the magelord isn't waiting," protested Kasten. "He was . . . he was drying, curing, and splitting the wood . . . by *magic*," he finished in a whisper. There was a low murmur in the room as everyone considered the implications. Then, one by one, they turned and looked to the Master of the Wood for guidance. Kamen was drumming his fingers on his wooden cast, looking thoughtful.

"Well, if he's a magelord, then it stands to reason he'd have recourse to magic," Kamen began, quietly. "If he can use it to turn green wood into lumber . . . I'd say that's a handy trick."

"It's unnatural!" Kasten protested.

"*Of course* it's unnatural," Dara found herself saying, before she could catch her lips, "its *magic*. If it was natural, it would just be *work*." She expected someone to chide her for her impertinence, but to her surprise they all just nodded in agreement.

Dara was shocked. Had her dangerous trip up the mountain and her return with Frightful actually garner her a little respect in the eyes of the adults in her life? She was mystified and gratified at the same time.

"Little Bird is right," her uncle said, amused. "Old Railan can't stop cussing the man. That tells me a lot. He brings a lot of new change to the vale, and that's going to upset a lot of people who grew used to the way things were done. There are . . . *magic lights* up at the castle, now. I've seen them myself. And other things folk aren't used to."

"Lights and lumber are all very well and good," Dara's aunt said, bitingly, "but that still doesn't answer what kind of lord he'll be."

"Then perhaps this will," her uncle said, with a certain amount of satisfaction. "When I was in the village I chanced to talk to the reeve from Gurisham. Lord Minalan has decided to begin his lordship over Sevendor . . . by forgiving the debts owed to the castle by *every yeomanry*."

"What?" her aunt gasped, her eyes wide.

"It's the truth," Kasten admitted. "I heard it myself. Every debt to the castle, wiped clean. The castellan apparently pulled all of the pegs out of his board, and will start over from scratch."

"That must be . . . that has to be . . . *hundreds* of ounces of silver!"

"It is," Kasten agreed, grimly. Why was he acting so taciturn at such good news? Dara wondered. The debt each Yeomanry owed the castle was the leverage old Sir Erantal had used for years to get his way. For the castle to just voluntarily erase that debt was magnificent news! "But the magelord has spent at least that so far, purchasing supplies and labor. He is, apparently, a rich man."

"Apparently," Kamen agreed. "But rich enough to forgive such a large debt?"

"It is said he wants his lordship to be just, and prosperous for all," her uncle reported. "That's what's sticking in Railan's craw. He's dominated Sevendor Village for years, protecting it and its villeins from Erantal's drunken whims. Now there's no one to protect them from. Instead, it's Railan standing in their way, now."

"Well, that's news to hear," chuckled Kamen. "It sounds like I'm going to like this new lord."

"Magelord," corrected her uncle.

"Hmpf!" her aunt grunted. "Let's see what he does about Farant. That's when I'll know what kind of man he is!"

Farant was the yeoman of Farant's Hold, which Dara knew was somewhere at the base of Matten's Helm. It wasn't a proper estate – the people looked half-starved and Farant's stall at the market always featured the very poorest fare. But Farant held power because he ran an illegal distillery, with the tacit permission of Sir Erantal, supplying the illicit needs of the peasants of Sevendor . . . and collecting what little spare coin they had in return. He also supplied other illicit interests, as the dirty, tear-stained cheeks of the women of his holding could attest. An ugly man could always come by a bride from Farant's Hold . . . for the right price.

Dara's aunt despised Farant on general principal, but bore a particular hatred of the slovenly man since last summer, when his idiot son – Korl, Dara thought he was called – had said something crude to her sister at market, and tried to kiss her unwillingly.

Her brother Kyre had been there and had laid Korl out in

the dust with one blow of his fist. The reeves got involved, but both boys were released when the situation had been explained. Nothing really could be done to Korl – as long as Farant had Sir Erantal leashed by his illegal liquor. He should have known better than to try anything with the daughter of the Master of the Wood, but by all accounts Korl was not particularly bright. He didn't need to be. His father protected him.

But now that Erantal was gone, Dara realized that Farant had lost his patron.

If Aunt Anira doubted the virtue of Lord Minalan before, when news came a few days later that he had exiled and outlawed Farant and his sons, and had set up his own man to oversee Farant's Hold, she could think of little bad to say about the man. That stunned Dara. She always thought her aunt could find fault with the sunrise, if she put her mind to it.

But the changes wrought by the arrival of the Magelord started to affect everyone. The demand for labor in the village and the castle was so strong that young men felt compelled to beg off their duties in the Hall and work for the rare opportunity of good coin, instead. Kamen had a hard time restricting the movement – most of the estate's preparations for winter were complete, and the weeks before Yule were usually a time of quiet repose and work on indoor crafts, as the weather outside became cold. The labor wasn't needed here.

And the pay was certainly worth it. Never had Westwood Hall seen silver flow in such abundance. During market days their wares brought twice the usual price. Of course the price of everything else had gone up at market, too, but the Westwood was mostly self-sufficient. Apart from a little barley, oats, and ground flour, there was little the estate required on a regular basis.

Dara paid attention to the stories and news attentively, even as she continued training Frightful. Her falcon was growing quickly and her plumage was starting to come in beautifully. Her dark head had started to produce the bright silver feathers her species was known by, and her wingspan was already more than two feet wide.

Dara bonded closely with the bird. It was hard not to, with her on her fist or her shoulder nearly every waking moment. But Frightful was getting properly manned. She did not even startle when the many dogs of the Westwood suddenly barked, as she did when Dara had first returned from the nutwood.

The days got shorter and the nights got longer, and both got colder as winter progressed. The day came when the news from the village involved the Westwood: the Spellmonger desired all of his Yeomen or their representatives to attend the castle's Yule feast, in celebration of his lordship. And to formally swear oaths of fealty to the new lord. That sent the entire Hall into a tizzy. Kamen's leg was still on the mend, and getting him to the castle would be difficult and painful. Just going to the nutwoods had taxed him. In the end, he begged off, detailing another to go in his place.

But not his brother, Dara's uncle. He insisted that Kyre be the one who spoke for the Master of the Wood.

That was a significant development, Dara knew. Kyre

was only a few years older than she, but he was already a better woodsman than rangers twice his age. He had the self-confidence and athletic ability that made him a natural leader, and he had been groomed for taking over the Wood when his father retired the post, hopefully many, many years from now. While not technically a hereditary post, the customs of the Westwood made the Master's son the expected heir of the position.

"He's ready," her uncle conceded, when the topic came up around the Flame. "He's a firebrand, but he's got a cool head, too, when needed."

"I want you to go, too," Kamen insisted. "You know more about our affairs than anyone, but I want Kyre to be under the Magelord's nose. Take a few of our best lads," he counselled. "And take Dara, too."

"Dara?" her uncle asked, curious and surprised.

"Me?" Dara squeaked, unexpectedly.

"She's very observant," reasoned Kamen. "She's sneaky. And she's socially adept, no matter what her aunt tells her. I trust her reporting more than most rangers, to be honest. We need to know more about this lord. And the new folk he's expecting at Yule." That was news to Dara - she'd always been under the impression that her candid observations were one of the things the adults of the Hall hated about her. *Was her whole universe coming unraveled?*

"Wilderlanders," her uncle noted. "Good folk, from what I've seen. Free men."

"Less inclined to look down their noses on us," agreed Kamen. "And soon they'll outnumber the Vale folk, if I remember how to count properly. But Dara's eye will be able to spot what we need, while your lads are drinking the magelord dry."

Dara was unsure how she felt about the trip. On the one hand she was excited – she'd only been to the castle once in her life, though it lay less than a mile from the Hall. That had been at a rare summer court, where she had been "presented" to Sir Erantal, as was custom, who hadn't given her a second glance. The castle had been a grand old pile of rocks, the same dark stone as the mountain she'd climbed, and even though it had supposedly been "cleaned" it was filthy and smelled of mold and mildew.

But now, with a new lord, she wondered what the place would be like. Not just a new lord, a *mage*lord.

Dara's hesitation to go evaporated when her sister discovered she wasn't included in the party. Any time she could make her sister jealous Dara reveled in it. The resulting tantrum was impressive to behold, as her sister bounced back and forth between her Aunt Anira and her father to beg, whine, and wheedle her way to the feast.

Her aunt was intractable. Her father dismissed her insistence with one volley:

"I will not have this entire Hall beat a boy near to death because you couldn't contain your flirtations," he pronounced. "There is no predicting what will happen there, with all those Wilderlanders arriving, and I know how you get around a bunch of young, strong boys. Don't deny it," he warned. "This is a business meeting, not a ball. And there will be other feasts at the castle in your future, unless I miss my guess."

Dara was secretly pleased until her sister pointed out that Dara, herself, was in just as much danger of an incident as she was.

Her father snorted. "She's got a figure like a boy and hasn't even had her monthlies, yet, Flame knows. I'd be more worried about Kyre attracting attention."

While the explanation stung, Dara couldn't argue with it. Compared to her pretty sister, with her big dark eyes and her gorgeous long dark hair, Dara felt like a weed growing in a flower garden, sometimes. But that was just because she hadn't finished growing yet, she consoled herself. She remembered how scrawny her sister had been just a few years before, and knew that curves and an obsessive interest in the doings of boys was inevitable.

After her sister's tantrum subsided, she appeared at the door of Dara's room and uncharacteristically offered to help her prepare for the event.

"Why would you help me?" Dara demanded, placing Frightful on her block, away from Linta. The bird had a tendency to get protective, when Dara was upset, and the last thing she needed was to explain to her Aunt Anira how her pretty sister's face had been wrecked by her falcon's talons.

"Because they won't let me go, and I want to hear about everything that happens," she admitted, avoiding her usual set of manipulative falsehoods. They wouldn't have worked with Dara, anyway. She was far too used to her ways to fall for flattery and simple persuasion. "Besides, if I don't help you, someone might mistake you for one of the boys."

"Hey!" Dara protested.

"I'm serious! You run around in breaches and tunic all the time – I think I've seen you in a gown once, since you turned ten!"

"Well, I do a lot outside," Dara shot back. "Dresses aren't really helpful for that!"

"Which is why I want to help you," pointed out Lista. "By the Flame, I just want to see you represent the Hall well. And yourself."

Dara couldn't help herself – her mouth seemed to move without thinking. "Since when have you ever cared at all about me?" she demanded, and immediately regretted it. Her sister did not get upset, to Dara's surprise. Instead she looked at her with a very serious aspect.

"I know it may seem that way," she admitted, "but things are . . . different, now. Everything has changed since the Spellmonger came. Our whole lives have changed in the last few months."

Dara glanced at Frightful. She couldn't really argue that.

"So? It's change. It happens. It still doesn't explain—"

Now her sister was irritated. "Flame and ash! You do make things difficult, don't you? I do care about you, Little Bird, and I haven't shown it much in the past, it's because you were a little girl. Well, you're not a little girl anymore, and either am I. You and I want different things, so there's no need to compete.

"Father was right to send you to the castle. Kyre won't notice or remember any of the important things, so he's useless. You will. I need you to tell me who is who and what they were wearing. Who is important and who is not. What our new lady looks like, and what kind of woman she is. The *important* things," she repeated, stressing the word.

"We've got a new lord and lady, an invasion of all these Wilderlanders, the possibility of fighting with West Fleria looming, and you want to know what everyone was *wearing?*"

"And their *hair,*" her sister added, with the utmost gravity. "You must remember *exactly* how everyone's hair looks."

Dara affixed her sister with a steady gaze, and was about to deride her for her shallow and pointless exercise when she stopped herself.

This was the first time – ever, really – that her sister had shown any semblance of kindness or respect toward her. While it was completely self-serving, she realized, the novelty of the appeal felt good. Her sister *needed* her. And had asked her, like an adult.

Things really were changing. First Kyre and now Linta. Dara realized that her sister's world had changed far more than hers, really, and she was scared and excited by it. A few months ago her best hope in life was to marry one of the lads from Sevendor or Gurisham, perhaps as even as far as Southridge Hold or Jurlor's Hold, estates farther away from the castle. She had expected to court and marry sometime soon.

But now, with the Magelord making such impressive changes so quickly, that had changed. The population of marriageable men in the vale had risen, and it was going to rise more. While Dara didn't share her sister's aspirations of a good match and a prosperous holding, she couldn't fault her for trying to adapt to the new conditions, either – and if it helped her to know what kind of dresses Lady Alya liked, or how she wore her hair, or how many boys there were at the party between the ages of fifteen and seventeen, Dara could help with that.

Besides, feasts like this were where being a girl became really important, and Dara had to admit that she had never done well at the grooming and wardrobe, while her pretty sister had excelled in the practical exercise of femininity. Dara could use the help.

"All right," she said, after taking a deep breath and changing her own attitude, "you're going to need your metal comb," she said, fingering the rat's nest of flame-red hair that fell over her shoulder. "And a lot of time . . ."

Chapter Seven

Sevendor Castle

The day of Yule dawned overcast and gloomy, cold and windy, but to Dara it was exciting. She hurriedly fed Frightful and began preparations for her bath. Even with her sister's help, and with the assistance of a dress she had outgrown but which almost fit Dara, it took hours, it seemed, to prepare for the event.

Finally, she was ready to go . . . but had to wait in the Hall on her brother and the other men in the party. They were gathering additional stores from the sheds and holds, at Kamen's orders. Her father had heard how the suddenly-expanded population of the castle had picked the market bare, and now with winter here they were struggling to feed them all. Yet Master Minalan had yet to send out parties to demand additional food from his estates, as most normal lords would do.

Then there was the fact that Sevendor had recently expanded, which had everyone excited. Word had come that the magelord had led a small military expedition against the nearby estate of Brestal, and had taken the small tower there without bloodshed in a nocturnal raid.

That was serious news. Brestal lay to the north and east of the Westwood, beyond Matten's Helm, a separate lobe of the valley that had, until several years ago, been an estate of Sevendor. But a few years back one of Sevendor's neighboring lords, the fearsome Warbird of West Fleria, Sire Gimbal, had coveted it for one of his sons. Though everyone knew it was wrong for the lord to do so, he had raided the estate, burned a village to the ground, and installed his son as its puppet lord. Sir Erantal, who was supposed to defend and protect Sevendor in the name of the Duke, had done nothing about the conquest, partially to punish the people of the Vale who had grown unruly in the face of his increasing demands. Sir Erantal was a hired knight – he did not care about the domain.

But the folk of Sevendor certainly had an opinion about the matter. Being told that a third of the domain was no longer part of Sevendor was an affront to the pride of the whole vale. Westwoodmen and Vale folk alike had been insulted by Erantal's dereliction of his sworn duties, but there was nothing that could be done.

But the Spellmonger, apparently, had wanted his estate back and his domain whole and secure. And he was willing to fight for it.

Dara was amazed at the transformation in her father, brother, uncles, and all the other men of the Hall when they heard the news. They seemed to carry themselves with more pride, and began speaking of their lord – whom few had even laid eyes on – with new respect.

Aunt Anira and the other older women of the manor, on the contrary, were suddenly worried. Military action was always worrisome, and even though Sevendor had not had to muster arms in Dara's lifetime, the prospect of battles ahead concerned her aunt. The armory, in a bay off of the main hall, was filled with old spears and mail coats, iron helms, short swords and bows. And there were rumored to be other caches of arms, deep in the woods or other hidden places, should the Westwoodmen need them.

"That's just the stupidest thing I've heard," Anira admitted, when Dara had wandered into the kitchen while waiting for her brother. "Going and goading a powerful lord like Sire Gimbal is just *asking* for trouble! And in the winter, too! The man has taken several domains in the last few years, and most far more bloody than how he dealt with Brestal. What is he *thinking*, endangering us all like that?"

"But isn't Brestal *supposed* to be part of Sevendor? Wasn't he right to take it back?" Dara asked, confused.

"Right and wise are often strangers," Aunt Anira admitted, citing an old proverb after some lip-chewing consideration. "It may be our lord's *right* to that estate, but when tempers flare and swords are drawn, it will be his *people* who suffer. Do you really want to see your brothers and cousins go off to war and never return again?" she demanded, shaking a spoon under Dara's nose.

"N-no," Dara admitted. She had never really considered such a thing . . . but just as her sister was fated to wed, her brother Kyre, as a future Yeoman of the domain, would indeed be expected to lead troops if the new magelord went to war. Not just her brother, but her father, uncles, cousins and all the other able-bodied men of the Westwood. She tried to imagine the estate without them around, and shook her head. She could not imagine it running at all, much less with the prosperity the Westwoodmen had become accustomed to.

"But Lord Minalan has his own men," Dara pointed out. "They should be arriving any time, now!"

"Those Wilderland men! And do you think he'd risk them when he could compel the lives of strangers?" Anira fumed.

Dara didn't know what to say to that, so she retreated back to the safety of the Flame in the hall. She had never considered that before. The Magelord, for all the good he had done the domain, also had the power to order her brothers and cousins off to war . . . perhaps never to return. The Westwoodmen were canny archers and passable rangers. There were stones in the fireplace memorializing those who had left the Westwood in service to their lord, and had never come back.

That sobered her, as she finished her preparations for the court. While her excitement over the evening was still present, it was tempered by the serious nature of the festival. The Yule Court was, traditionally, where the Yeomen of Sevendor swore their allegiance to the Lord, by proxy or in person, as well as presentation of "gifts" from each estate in the form of tribute, often negotiated in advance. Sir Erantal had only required the symbolic rite every few years (though he was enthusiastic about the tribute), and for the last few occasions her father had sent an emissary rather than go himself.

But this year the Magelord had summoned the Yeomen in person, and only Kamen's bad leg had kept him from attending. Dara knew that was significant. The vale was over six miles long and three wide, and there were several yeomanries: estates, villages, agricultural manors. To gather together all the leaders was a weighty thing. She could see it pained her father not to go in person, but traveling that far, up that steep a grade on his splinted leg could re-injure it, and everyone knew it. He was hobbling around for short periods, now, using a staff for support, but he was still far from recovered from his skirmish with the old castle men.

There was a stir out in the yard in the late afternoon, with dogs yapping and a boys shouting. Dara went outside and saw a great store of food and supplies – including a few freshly-hunted stags, dressed and salted and ready for the fire.

"What . . . is this?" Anira was demanding.

"It's the Master's orders," Kyre explained, as he was overseeing the distribution of the fare. "It's to go to Sevendor Castle for the feast."

"He did not discuss this with *me!*" she said, resolutely. "There's enough there for *two* feasts!" The Westwoodmen had a large store of meat and nuts and other foods secreted away, against the depredations of the – old – castle folk. But part of their wealth in such things came from their thrifty nature . . . and what had been unloaded in the yard was a gracious amount.

"The castle folk are expecting more settlers," Kyre said, patiently, as he faced down the woman who had raised him like a mother. "Their stores are low, and they've spent a fortune at market to procure without *once* asking for more than was their rightful due. The Master of the Wood has decided to voluntarily send more food to them as a demonstration of his compassion and the loyalty of the Westwood."

"We'll see about *that!*" Anira snapped. "Kamen may be Master of the Hall, but *I* am mistress of my kitchen and the stores! If there isn't enough for us—"

"You will *not*," Kyre said, sharply. That was a new tone in her oldest brother's voice, one which commanded respect. "I checked the stores myself. We have enough to go through two winters or more, without even hunting. I will not have good folk go hungry while we hoard food like bandits."

More than his voice, his mannerisms had changed. He seemed to stand straighter than she remembered, and when did he get so tall? Just a few weeks ago she remembered Anira slapping his hand with a wooden spoon in the kitchen over some slight – yet this was not a boy in front of her. He was not attempting to persuade her, or even invoking his father's authority – he was establishing his own.

Anira was not having any of it, though. "And do you think you're old enough now to dictate how I run my kitchens, lad?" she said, challenging, her hands on her hips.

"I am son and heir of the Master of the Wood," Kyre said evenly, his brows fixed as his voice dropped. "When he dies, my word will be law here. Until he dies, *his* word is law, here . . . even in your kitchens. And his word sent this food to the castle. You need not bother him about a command he has already made."

Anira snorted, but there was a note of doubt in her voice, now. "So I just have to contend with the shortfall, should it come, do I?"

"If the kitchens have a lack, you may address that with the Master . . . but until they do, you may rest assured that he has acted with the best interests of the Hall in mind." Kyre's tone was wholly business-like, now, and not at all deferent to Anira's maternal position.

Dara was flabbergasted. She had never heard any of her brothers speak so strongly to their aunt. But Kyre was correct, their father did rule the manor . . . and addressing him about a decision he'd already made was disrespectful. While Anira could and did do it regularly – "speaking her mind" she commonly called it – it was a presumption, and everyone knew it. Only the astute job she did overseeing the work and her position as Uncle Keram's wife kept her from being taken to task over it.

Kyre, apparently, did not have their father's patience with such presumption . . . and had spoken to Anira more sternly and with more rank than anyone had dared.

What astonished Dara more was the reaction. She expected the woman to explode into a rage and lay about the boys (and possibly her – Anira wasn't particularly accurate) with her long wooden spoon.

Instead she stared at Kyre and eventually dropped her eyes. "As the Master has spoken, in front of the Flame," she agreed, reluctantly. "Merry Yule, then," she said, simply, and rushed inside past Dara.

"What . . . was *that?*" she asked herself aloud. She hadn't expected an answer, but her sister Lista was nearby, having seen the whole episode through a window.

"That was Kyre acting as the Heir of the Wood for the first time," she chuckled. "Father and the other men woke him up last night, after all were in bed. Some stupid rite or another. But he's been wearing that sword ever since," she said, pointing toward their oldest brother. Sure enough, hanging from Kyre's belt was a ranger's sword, such as were hanging in the armory in the Hall. Dara's breath caught.

"Are they . . . expecting trouble?"

"No, I don't think so," her sister dismissed. "I think they just want to make a good showing. You know how those vale folk are," she mentioned. "They think we eat our babies and howl at the moon half the time, anyway. It's good relations to remind them of that."

"Flame! We're not barbarians!" Dara moaned.

"We're Westwoodmen, that's worse," she snickered. "But the other Yeomanries need to remember that. Especially with all these half-wild Wilderlands folk Lord Minalan is bringing in."

"Is he old enough for a sword?" she asked doubtfully.

"Plenty," her sister agreed. "We've just not had the need. But the boys sneak off and practice with sticks somewhere, I know. He wears it well, I think," she considered.

"I guess," Dara said, absently. The blade under his mantle seemed so foreign to her brother, somehow . . . but she couldn't deny that he carried himself more proudly while wearing it. "That's it? Father gave him a sword, and suddenly he's all grown up?"

"Boys are strange," her sister agreed. "But it means that they think that Kyre is old enough to lead the Hall, should anything happen to Father."

"Kyre? What could possibly . . ." Dara said, trailing off. Of course something could happen to Kamen. Everyone died and fed the Flame eventually. All the talk of war, with the reconquest of Brestal, made her consider the possibility for the first time. Even her beloved father would die. And when that happened, the Hall would need a new leader. She couldn't imagine anyone seriously taking orders from her brother – he was only seventeen – but she couldn't deny that her other brothers and male cousins were treating him differently.

"He's our brother . . . and he's going to be our boss someday," her sister said, with resignation. "I guess we're lucky. Kobb could have been born first instead of Kyre."

Kobb was their mutually least-favorite brother. A smart-ass with a wickedly cruel sense of humor and a laugh like a concussed llama, he had terrorized each sister in turn over the years. He had messed with Dara often enough . . . before she'd gotten Frightful. Apparently the idea of having his eyes scratched out by a falcon without a sense of humor was what it took to keep Kobb at a safe distance. The idea of their goofy brother as Master of the Wood, instead of Kyre, was troubling. But even Kobb, who was even more defiant and obstinate than Dara, deferred to Kyre now, she noticed.

The party eventually set out, and for one of only a handful of times in her life Dara ventured beyond the chasm that was the eternal border of the Westwood, proper, and entered the wider world. Not that she was going far. Sevendor Castle was about a mile away from Westwood Hall as the falcon flew. The long, circuitous route through the valewood and down into the road to the castle took far longer, of course. Once they arrived at the gate of the castle, the sun had set behind the ridge and all was growing dark.

All but Sevendor Castle, that was. It was lit with a strange, unearthly glow from several bright balls of light that just seemed to float in mid-air.

"Magelights," her brother Kyre explained quietly, when she halted to stare. "The castle uses them all the time, now. No torches, no tapers – well, just a few, I guess; not everyone there is a mage. But the Great Hall is lit by them now."

"Amazing!" Dara grinned. She had never seen anything so wondrous before, save her falcon. The castle seemed to glow and sparkle in the arcane light. "So spells for light, spells for wood . . . what does the magelord even *need* with villeins, then?"

"Someone has to empty the chamber pots," Kobb quipped. "No magic for that, probably."

"You will be respectful and polite to everyone this evening," Kyre ordered his younger brother. "The magelord is expecting a lot of new settlers from the Wilderlands, and everyone is like to be on-edge over Brestal. This could develop into a tense situation, and I won't have it said that the Westwoodmen contributed to it."

Dara was shocked – none of the young men with her gave any of their usual jeers or insults when Kyre spoke, now. Not even Kobb. Uncle Keram looked pleased, nodding as his own sons signaled their obedience.

They walked under the gate along with other folk destined for Sevendor Castle's Yule celebration – not just Vale folk, from Genly and Gurisham, but strangely-dressed people from the Wilderlands, way to the northwest, and good Riverlands tradesmen wearing their festival best under their thick woolen cloaks.

"Most of those now live in Sevendor Village," Kobb whispered to her, when a beefy-looking man in a furry hat stopped ahead of them to greet a friend. "Tradesmen and artisans. Carpenters. Wainwrights. A smith. You won't recognize the place anymore," he promised. "They're building houses there so fast you'd swear they're using magic!"

"They *are* using magic," Uncle Keram reminded them, quietly. "They used it to cure the timber from the valewood, and they're using it to bind the pieces together, I've heard."

"That's very interesting," Dara said. She didn't know much about magic, aside from a few folktales around the Flame, but the lights above the castle intrigued her mightily. She wondered what they would look like from the peak.

The castle was crowded as they went through the second gatehouse and into the inner bailey. The yard was a riot of horses and wagons, carts and donkeys, castle servants yelling to each other and throngs of villeins and villagers drinking merrily in the yard outside of the castle's great doors.

The place seemed far more festive than foreboding, now that there was a proper lord in residence. The shabby-looking exterior Dara remembered from last time she was here had been meticulously scrubbed and the steps swept. A youth (one of the Wilderlands folk, she guessed) just inside the door invited them each to wash their hands in a warm basin, and then dried them with a towel. Dara hadn't had anyone wash and dry her hands for her since she was a child, but she had to admit it made her feel quite noble.

The hall of Sevendor Castle was even more brightly lit with the floating spheres than the exterior. Every corner and rafter in the place seemed to be lit up, and the fresh rushes on the floor had been mixed with evergreen boughs, giving the hall a spicy scent. A gallery above them contained a few village musicians sawing away at a viol, a tabor, and singing some seasonal hymns. Dara looked around at the many trestle tables that had been packed into the room. There had to be a hundred or more folk crammed in, yet there were places for plenty more.

"Where shall we put these?" Kyre asked a tall, important-looking man in a long mantle. A Wilderlord, Dara guessed. He had a darker-complexion and his face was bisected by a bushy mustache, brown hair with just a bit of curl over the top of his large ears. He carried himself with the dignity of an oak tree, she noticed, and when he spoke his voice seemed to fill the hall. Was this the Magelord? She wondered.

The tall man stared at the dressed bucks and the other provisions the boys carried or hauled in a wheelbarrow.

"What . . . what *is* this, may I ask? And who are *you?*"

"I am Kyre, son of Kamen, Master of the Wood," Kyre said, proudly. "And I bring our Yule tribute . . . and a gift from the Master of the Westwood to the Magelord. My father apologizes for being unable to be here himself, but his leg is yet splinted after an accident this autumn."

"And I am Sir Cei, castellan to Sire Minalan, the Magelord of Sevendor," the man – a *real* knight, Dara realized excitedly, and one who looked the part the way Sir Erantal didn't – said, graciously. "To what occasion does the Master of the Wood ascribe this generous bounty?"

"No more than the thoughtful consideration of a yeoman for his rightful lord," Kyre said, boldly, stressing the term "rightful" just a hint.

Dara couldn't believe this was actually her brother speaking. Kyre had always been confident, but he spoke with the tall castellan nearly as he would a peer. "When he heard the Lord was expecting . . . additional guests for Yule," he said, referring to the Wilderlands folk that were arriving at the castle from up the Sevendor Road even now, "he did not want it said that the Castle lacked the hospitality of the season because the Westwood did not provide. By the Flame, he would not have it so."

Sir Cei looked surprised and grateful, and then carefully studied her brother's face. "I think I'm going to like your father, young Kyre of Westwood. Pray introduce me to the rest of your party," he encouraged.

"If it please you," Kyre said. "This is my Uncle Keram, called the Crafty, my father's right-hand man. My brothers Kobb and Kran, my cousins Kapi, Keru and Kitt, and my Uncle Kamal . . . and this is my little sister, Lenodara," he finished. Dara was startled by the introduction, although she had known it was coming, and hurried to give the tall knight a curtsey – only the second time she had ever made the formal gesture in earnest.

"A fine family, and a fine estate you have," Sir Cei boomed, warmly. "I will have the servants take charge of your bounty, and move it to the kitchens and storerooms. It is much appreciated. Please, by the gods come in and warm yourselves, take some wine and food . . . Magelord Minalan will be holding court and receiving pledges of fealty in a while," he assured them.

The Westwoodmen made their way toward the large stone fireplace as if the Flame bade them. Along the way Dara passed some folk she knew but many who she did not. She made sure to keep her eyes open and her ears pricked up to hear the slightest bit of gossip.

Kyre filled his drinking horn from a jug borne by the castle butler, and Dara found herself with a battered but polished tin cup full of wine – the first unwatered wine she'd ever had. She took a sip and immediately regretted it.

She vowed to sip it, slowly. And not much – the flavor did not like her tongue. But sipping gave her an opportunity to observe the rapidly-filling hall and determine who was who among the crowd. That's why her father had sent her, after all.

The Genlymen and the Southridge folk were huddled in one corner of the hall, while the Gurisham folk and a delegation from Caolan's Pass, including old Yeoman Karkan and his children, was near to the folk from suddenly-reunited Brestal. Dara could see these people as regular folk of Sevendor Vale - Sevendori.

Then there was the knot of strangely-dressed Wilderlands folk at the other end of the Great Hall. The *Bovali,* she overheard them call themselves. As opposed to the Sevendori.

We're the Sevendori, she realized. She had never considered herself so before. The Westwood was part of Sevendor, but it wasn't *of* it. To the Wilderlands folk – the Bovali – she and the villein farmer girls from Genly might as well been the same, she realized.

Between the Bovali and the Sevendori were a third knot of people – the new artisans and shopkeepers who had come with the Bovali and the new lord. They looked a little uncomfortable, at first, but the Bovali were no stranger to drink, for all their odd manner of speech and dress, and they were plying the Riverlands artisans with a lot of it. Soon the new residents of Sevendor Village were toasting the health of the Magelord with their new Bovali neighbors. Yeoman Jurlor's folk joined in, soon enough, Dara noted.

The representatives of Genly and Southridge, Dara noted, glared balefully at the merrymaking. Railan the Steady (who had been removed from his position as head of Sevendor Village in favor of a common footwizard, she heard someone mention nearby) was deep in conversation with Yeoman Ylvine, and their faces bore looks of frustration and concern.

Dara had seen the Southridge man at market once, and hadn't liked him then or now. He had always held himself up as a shield between the corruption of the castle and the hardworking folk of the vale, and was respected – if not liked – nearly everywhere for his fair judgment. But he was also a figure of some derision, as well as sympathy, in the Westwood. A man who seemed so passionate about who got the privilege of plowing, sowing, weeding and harvesting a particular piece of dirt, and who ruled his estate with iron control, was the antithesis of a good life in the Wood.

While she watched, her uncle came up behind her. "What do you see, Little Bird?"

"Genly and Southridge are against the Magelord," she reported, quietly. "But Jurlor, Caolan's Pass, and the Westwood stand with the Bovali. The Brestali don't know who to trust, and don't care – they just want to eat. Who are the Bovali?"

"The Wilderlands folk. Like that big knight we met, Sir Cei. The land there is wild and remote, and their folk are as hardy as the Westwoodmen, so it seems. And they're fighters. They lost their lands to the goblins," Keram said, just as quietly. "The Magelord rescued them, and wants to settle them here. The vale folk are not happy about it, as you can see – at least *some* of them," he amended, as squat Yeoman Jurlor began to roar with laughter in the company of three Bovali.

"The Bovali *want* to be friendly," she said, realizing the situation as she spoke the words aloud to her uncle. "The vale folk – *some* of them – are going to try to subvert the new lord! Why would they want to do that? Everyone suffered under Sir Erantal!"

"Not everyone suffered *equally*," Keram pointed out. "Sevendor Village bore the brunt of Erantal's whims, yet Railan the Steady was one of the most important men in the vale. And one of the richest, outside of the castle. Now he isn't even among the top ten most important. Yeoman Ylvine has schemed to position himself near the old lord, yet now his plots are undone and he has to start anew . . . with a lord who won't fancy his wife, I'm guessing."

"So what do you want me to do, Uncle?" Dara blushed, wanting to change the subject.

"Be the Little Bird you are," he chuckled, kindly. "Fly around the room. Keep your ears and eyes open. Say *nothing*. Remember *everything*. We'll speak of it afterwards," he promised.

She nodded and began to slowly circle the room like a falcon over a rabbit.

She was fortunate – no one paid much mind to a scrawny Westwood girl, with all the other distractions available for their eyes and ears. By the time she had made a complete circuit of the room she had a much better idea of the state of the vale, and the opinion of the vale folk of the new lord. The Genlymen, in particular, seemed angry about the wizard who now ruled them . . . though they drank his wine and ate his food freely enough.

Finally, the Magelord himself appeared along with his lady. It was the first time Dara had seen the mage, and she was struck by how young he was. She had expected a long white beard or something, but Magelord Minalan was not much more than twenty-five, by her estimation. He had a beard, but it was close cropped and as brown as his hair.

His wife was close to him in age, a pretty woman with honey-colored hair and a tired expression. Likely, Dara reasoned, because she was so *very* pregnant, and while she seemed determined to put a brave face on the festivities she did not look comfortable in the slightest.

Dara found a spot out-of-the way near her brother when court began. She watched Kyre stand in his turn and swear fealty on behalf of the Westwood estate, and saw him receive twenty new spears from the new lord in return.

Twenty new spears seemed like an odd gift to Dara – you only needed a few to hunt boar, she knew. Then she realized with horror what the gift implied. The new lord had armed the Westwood not to hunt, but to go to war at his command.

Suddenly, the Magelord did not seem so benevolent anymore.

The Westwood was not the only estate to receive a gift of arms – in fact, *every* estate received some spears or other weapons. The implications of the gifts were clear. Yet the recipients seemed to accept the harbingers of death and violence gratefully. Dara desperately wanted to ask Uncle Keram about it, but knew now was not the time.

There was drama at the court, too. Yeoman Ylvine protested the changes the Spellmonger's folk had brought to the vale, and the Magelord stripped him of his title and sent him packing. That shocked everyone, but the strong words and resolute action did paint the new lord as one who expected – *demanded* – loyalty. A Wilderlands man – Bovali, Dara reminded herself – was appointed to run the estate temporarily, and that caused much grumbling among the Genly and Brestal folk.

Lastly, the representatives of the Bovali refugees who had just arrived in Sevendor spoke, and Dara got a much better picture of the plight of those poor people. The tale of their battles, their desperate siege way in the Minden mountains in the west, and their daring, magical escape made a powerful tale. It also made Dara look at the scruffy-looking bunch of travelers with new respect. While there were a few Wilderlands knights among them, they suddenly looked far tougher and resolute than the Sevendori peasants they were mingling among.

Most of all, they looked devoted to their new lord. More than devoted, Dara observed, they looked nearly fanatical. And there were a lot of them – and more on the way, if she believed the rumors she overheard.

No wonder the Genlymen and other peasants of the Vale were unhappy – it was clear now that any restless rebellion, any move on the part of the Sevendori villeins would not be dealt with by guile, posturing, and empty promises, as Sir Erantal had done. It would be met with steel and fire, Dara realized.

The spears the Magelord had distributed, the number of Bovali folk who seemed to be armed – with *swords*, even, though they were forbidden to commoners by the Duke's Law – all of it presaged a virtual invasion of the quiet little valley. An invasion that would stand for no dissent.

Which side would the Westwoodmen come down on, she wondered, if it came to blows? Would they stand with this foreign wizard, or with the folk of the Vale who had lived beside them for generations?

As the Westwoodmen walked back through a light snowfall, late in the night, Dara finally had a chance to put that exact question to her Uncle Keram.

"We shall do whatever the Master of the Wood tells us to, by the Flame," her uncle said, solemnly. "But your brother swore an oath of fealty to this new lord on his behalf, and that oath is as binding as if done before the Flame. If he calls upon us to do our lawful duty and take up arms on his behalf, I cannot foresee why the Master would not respond."

"Do you think the Genlymen will cause trouble?"

Keram considered. "They would be fools to. What did you see tonight, Little Bird?"

"The Vale folk angry at their new lord, and fearful of the Bovali."

"That is one perspective," he agreed. "But I also saw a young, vibrant lord aggressively taking charge of his domain, ordering his estates, and bringing change to those who fear it most of all. Railan the Steady, Ylvine, Farant, they all benefitted from Sir Erantal's rule, one way or another, and now they do not know how to contend with their world changing so quickly.

"Yet not only did the Magelord not announce new taxes, as most newly-seated lords would, but he forgave the debts of the villeins. More, he has been including them in the prosperity he seeks to bring to all in the Vale. Yet they cannot see beyond their own losses to see how all around them are profiting. So yes, Dara, I do expect them to cause trouble, before long. And if they do, then the Westwood will fulfill its oath to the rightful lord of Sevendor."

Dara considered that in silence the rest of the way back to the Hall. It troubled her to think of war and violence, and it made her fearful for her kin who would be involved. But she also had to admit that Sevendor Castle had seemed a symbol of hope and stability, for all of the changes the Magelord had wrought, not a symbol of oppression and despair. The Bovali were kind-hearted and friendly, for all their strange ways, and they seemed eager to work, not to fight.

As they came to the first bend in the road into the forest, at the top of a rise, Dara looked back out over the valley, across the stream toward Sevendor Village and its broad commons, where hundreds of tents and shelters were being erected in the snow by torches and magelights.

For the first time in her life, Dara felt really hopeful about her future. Instead of living in dread of the world outside of the Westwood, she suddenly felt a sense of anticipation.

It almost made up for the exhaustive report of what everyone was wearing that she would have to deliver to her sister.

Chapter Eight

The Blizzard

In the days that followed the magnificent Yule celebration at the castle Dara immersed herself in training Frightful, under her Uncle's supervision. There wasn't much work she could do in the cold, outside, so she worked in her room or in the expanse of the hall. The little bird had more than doubled in size since she'd captured her, and required nearly-constant attention. The weather outside had turned to blustery cold, making hacking Frightful in the meadow problematic, so Dara contented herself with perfecting her calls and encouraging the falcon to fly from block to her gauntleted fist when she gave one.

"She's coming along nicely," her Uncle Keram noted with approval one night, after he had come in from the tanning sheds and watched her at work. "Her feathers are beautiful and well-tended. She's very alert. Just be wary of overfeeding her," he cautioned. "It's natural to want to encourage her to bond with you, but making her complacent will spoil her for hunting. Hunger is the falconer's friend," he reminded.

"I'm paying attention to it," Dara promised. "Unless we're training, she doesn't get anything until she's nearly ravenous, just like you said.

"Keep this up and we can take her for her first real flight this spring, as soon as the weather clears," he nodded as Frightful flew across the Hall to Dara's gauntleted fist again. "One without the lead."

Dara froze at the thought. "Don't some birds fly off, without a lead?"

"They do," he agreed. "That first flight can be a disaster, if a falconer hasn't prepared her bird well enough. But I don't see the kind of skittishness or strong-headedness in Frightful that I recall in birds who did that. It's more of a danger in hawks, particularly the social species, than in the falcons. But I don't think you have to worry. I think you're doing well," he praised her.

Dara was thankful for the praise – without it, she felt as if she was the most useless person in the Hall. Standing there calling to a bird over and over again in the Great Hall while others hurried to their tasks and chores made her feel like she was shirking. But, as her annoying brother Kobb (of *all* people) pointed out, her position as daughter of the Master afforded her the time. As much as she hated to trade on that, she also knew if she let up on her training regimen with Frightful her falcon would not be properly trained.

At last the weather broke enough for Uncle Keram and her father (who had been released from his wooden cast just the day before) to escort her out to the small meadow for Frightful's first flight.

The falcon had been hacked out in the meadow often enough, tied to a board by her jesses. It was familiar territory, from the spruces and hickories that surrounded it to the nests of wild birds in the trees and grasses. This was the outdoor space Frightful knew best as "home," and Dara hoped by the Flame that it would be alluring enough to encourage the falcon to return to it.

"Let's start off with a few practice flights, on the line," Uncle Keram suggested. Dara dutifully tied the long waxed cord – the same cord she had used to ascend the mountain – to Frightful's jesses before moving away from her, the tiny silver bells on her legs jingling merrily in the cold.

Dara gave the call sign, and held out her fist. Frightful took a moment to recognize it, but the bird flapped and made it across the twenty feet of distance, trailing the string behind her.

"Again," encouraged Keram. "A few more times. Let her get used to her wings."

Dara complied, as her father watched proudly, and each time Frightful took to wing at the summons. Dara moved farther and farther away from Frightful's block, until she was nearly forty feet from the falcon. It was as far as she flew indoors, in the hall. Still, the bird flew unerringly to her fist.

"All right," Keram sighed, nervously. "Let's take the lead off and see if she notices."

Dara nodded, and quickly untied the string while Frightful was hooded. She moved a mere twenty feet away and pursed her lips to call.

Unhindered and unbound, the beautiful bird flew directly to her glove.

"*She did it!*" Dara said, excitedly, as she offered the bird a treat. Frightful took it daintily.

"Let's see if she'll fly the length of the meadow," Keram said, taking the bird from her hand. Dara nodded excitedly and ran to the other end of the grassy lawn. She held her fist high, where Frightful could see it, and pursed her lips for the call. Keram unhooded the falcon and flung it into the air. That startled the bird, but in seconds she was flying gracefully on the wind.

Dara pursed her lips and called frantically. Frightful started to veer out of the proper direction for her flight, but another call caused her to correct herself. In moments her horny talons bit into the padded knuckles of the gauntlet.

"Well done!" her father boomed, smiling broadly as he leaned on his staff. "As pretty as any wild hawk!"

"Falcon," Dara and her uncle corrected him, simultaneously.

That made Kamen laugh. "*Falcon*, then. You've done a good job, Little Bird!"

"You have," agreed Keram. "She's healthy, happy, and ready to hunt. As soon as the weather gets warm, we can start *real* fieldwork. Until then we'll have to make her a better lure to start practicing with."

"A better lure?" Dara asked.

"A bit of leather with some feathers and such attached," explained her uncle as he gathered up the falconry gear into the basket Dara had started carrying it in. "I'll show you how to make one. Something that resembles prey enough so she can practice with it. Play with it," he corrected.

"Falcons . . . *play?*" asked her father, amused.

"Not the way a cat or dog would," admitted Keram, "but they do sport with their prey a bit. A lure is essential to help her develop a feel for hunting. And next time we can try a longer flight – a true flight, beyond the meadow."

Dara was even more hesitant about that. Once Frightful was beyond her line of sight, only the tinkle of her tiny bells gave Dara any sense of her presence. She couldn't even imagine what she would feel like if the falcon flew away and never came back.

"That's enough for today, anyway," she sighed, postponing the anxiety that came with the anticipation as she glanced at the cloudy gray sky through her steamy breath. "It looks like snow."

* * *

Sevendor did not get much snow.

Dara could recall only seeing snow twice, and only once had it accumulated to any depth. When it did come in any quantity, Keram explained as they hurried back from the meadow, most of the estate's business shut down. The way he kept looking nervously at the approaching clouds told Dara he was worried about it.

Within the hour flakes started to fall across the vale. Dara delighted in the beautiful, full flakes that dropped gracefully over the wood and hall. They looked absolutely lazy, she decided, and the patterns were beautiful, even if they made her dizzy. Frightful was less impressed with the snow, and kept fluffing her feathers indignantly by the time they had reached the yard.

By nightfall over an inch had gathered, blanketing every surface in sight in a pristine layer of snow. It transformed the manor, making the normally-dirty brown and gray exterior bright and festive. The children of the Hall played in the yard in the novelty until the winds picked up and drove them inside to the warmth of the Flame. There was a note of anxiety and excitement surrounding the snow. How long would it last? How deep would it be? Would regular chores get canceled? Would they be stuck in the hall for days? Weeks? Would they run out of wood and freeze? Would they all starve? Would they have to resort to eating the dogs and cats? To *cannibalism?*

The children's fantasies got richer and more complex as they imagined more and more dire consequences due to the snow. *Had she really been like that?* she asked herself as she overheard their enthusiastic predictions of doom.

As excited as Dara was to tell the tale of Frightful's first unencumbered flight at dinner that night, her news was once-again overshadowed by the lord of the domain. Not even the unexpected snowfall was more important than the news from Sevendor Village. Dinner that night was filled with conversation about a scuffle Magelord Minalan had with one of the neighboring domains.

Dara couldn't help it – as eager as she was to share in front of the Flame her success with her bird, she was just as eager to hear her cousin Keru's account (which he got from a Gurisham girl who was sweet on one of the Magelord's apprentices) of an actual lordly *duel.*

It seemed that the displaced titular lord of the stolen estate of Brestal had been upset with the Magelord re-conquering his illegally-taken lands, and had sought out the mage to settle the matter with a formal duel. Sir Gimbal's son was young, and had just been knighted by his father a few months before. As a knight, he had felt honor-bound to fight for the lands his father had stolen for him.

He had appeared at the far pass with an entourage of unlikely knights – newly-made members of the chivalry, their squirehood barely behind them – and demanded satisfaction from Lord Minalan for his loss.

The Magelord had given him satisfaction . . . by defeating him soundly.

"Sir Ganulan was the instigator, 'tis said," Keru reported in front of the Flame with a grin, "a vassal of his father, Sire Gimbal, the Lord of West Fleria." West Fleria was Sevendor's neighbor to the north, a far richer country, agriculturally speaking, than the mountain vale. But what prosperity the people were able to pull from the land was quickly taken up by the Warbird: the Lord of West Fleria and half a score other domains. Sire Gimbal of West Fleria was a legendary figure to the peasantry of the lands around Sevendor. And it was to his son that the tiny Brestal estate had been carved off of Sevendor and included in his holdings. After the duel, there could be no doubt about its ownership. Now the lad had not just lost his estate, he had lost his dignity, from what Keru said.

While the younger men seemed enthusiastic about the drubbing their new lord had delivered to a hated foe, Dara noticed her uncles and her father exchange concerned looks. Such insults between lords often led to violence that affected the common folk, she knew. She, herself, was thrilled to hear of the Magelord's victory, but she also was starting to appreciate what that pride might end up costing her.

"It really is coming down, out there!" one of her older female cousins called from the window as she peered out of the shutters at the yard. "The whole courtyard is covered, now!" The talk grew lively until Aunt Anira asserted her authority, glancing at the Flame as she sent them back to their tables. There was a delighted murmur in the Hall, as another great log was placed upon the Flame. Calls went up for the Story of the Flame, as tradition demanded, and all eyes looked toward her father, who sighed and lurched to his feet.

"It is a snowfall," he began in a loud tone of voice that cut across everyone else's. The hall immediately quieted down. No one wanted to disrespect the Master of the Wood in front of the Flame. "When the snow covers the ground, then the time comes to retreat to the comfort of the Flame, eat, drink, and tell stories in its light as the wood is enshrouded. And the first story, by tradition, is spoken by the Master of the Wood, and tells of how our folk came to the Westwood, so many generations ago that the count is long lost.

"It is said," her father said, clearing his throat with the help of a mug of ale as the folk of the Hall settled down to listen, "that our forebears were once a people of great learning who lived in a mountain vale far to the south and east of here.

They had knowledge of a secret fire and were charged with protecting and harvesting the fire from the barren land they lived in, for the benefit of many. Why they did this is lost to us, but they were a wise and brave people and for generations they tended their mountain shrine.

"But the day came when they were driven from their home. Their wisdom was valued by evil men, and instead of turning the secret fire to their service they vowed to seal their shrines, bank the secret fire, and take their secrets to a faraway place where they could find refuge and a new life away from the evil men."

He looked around at the faces rapt in attention. Her father did not often tell stories, and usually only at ceremonial occasions, but there were many stories and laws only the Master of the Wood could tell. This one had not been heard in several years. There was no predicting when it might be heard again, so the attention of the hall was focused tightly on her father.

"Their leader was Karl, and his woman was Lissa, and together they led our folk north away from danger. They vowed to live as simple folk of the wood, hidden away in some protected land, and so for months they journeyed seeking a place remote enough to become a refuge. Ever the evil men pursued them. Ever they hid themselves and concealed their retreats. When they were forced to, they fought. They would rather have died than given the knowledge of the secret fire to those unworthy.

"Karl's man Dalias, a ranger of great cunning and a great friend to the chieftain, discovered the vale that became Sevendor, and led Karl and Lissa and all their folk quietly away from their old encampment and to the new, defensible vale.

"But ever the evil men pursued them, desperate for the power of the secret fire and the knowledge to exploit it. The Westwood was remote from the knowledge of men in those days, and all of Sevendor Vale covered in the wood. Dalias and Karl contrived cunning traps along the way, while Lissa fashioned a bridge over the ravine. When she crossed to this very site, which was a great treeless meadow, she prayed for guidance as the sun set over the western ridge. Our folk lit no fire, though it was deep in winter, for though they were cold they did not want to alert their enemies.

"That night Lissa had a dream. The next morning, she awoke with her hair struck red as a new-forged copper. She called her men to her, and that morning they gathered stones from all over the wood and raised a mighty cairn. Within they placed all their knowledge and wisdom of the secret fire, and they closed it up. Lissa built a great fire on the cairn and our folk warmed themselves and cooked for the first time in days.

"Dalias and Karl ranged the vale and harassed their enemies from the protection of the wood. They made a camp on Matten's Helm and concealed their paths with their woodcraft. For days they tormented their pursuers. They shot at them from hidden places. They entrapped them with clever plans and ever hid themselves in the bosom of the wood. As Lissa began to form the first Hall around the fire, her husband and his man kept the evil men at bay.

"One day soon after they arrived here," he continued, taking another mighty pull from his mug, "Dalias and Karl's luck ran out. They were beaten in battle and fell back to the safety of the wood yet again. They did all they could to lead their foes away from their most secret camp, but on that unfortunate day Dalias was slain as a storm loomed over the ridge. Karl fell back across the bridge to the Hall, and begged Lissa to conceal him.

"That brave lady did so, and opened a cavity in the mountain and put her lover within. When the evil men arrived, they were furious. Though they searched everywhere, they did not discover Karl the Rebel, and his lair was no prize. At last they had found the hidden lands of their prize – yet what they saw was not learned sages tending the secrets of the universe, but a band of half-starved rustics huddled around a fire for warmth. Lissa's folk offered no more resistance. But they said only Karl knew where the secret fire was hidden, and they had not seen him in weeks.

"It began to snow. When the evil men finally made it to the ravine, they were tired. Some perished in trying to cross the simple bridge in place there. Those who made it across demanded the secret fire and searched every inch of the encampment . . . while our ancestors huddled around the Flame for warmth. Though they searched desperately, they found naught of either Karl or the secret fire. They did not discover Karl's hiding place, for as they dared cross the chasm the snow fell so thick that it covered Karl's tracks. When they looked for him, they saw only what the snow and the Flame let them see. Only once did they come close to Karl's secret lair, but a pack of wolves appeared, sent by the Flame, and kept the evil men at bay. Karl was gone, Lissa insisted, and eventually they listened.

"Once they left the vale unfulfilled, Lissa ordered the flame to be stoked into a great fire, Karl was brought forth, and a feast was held to mourn the loss of valiant Dalias.

"That night Lissa had another dream, this one promising to secure our folk as long as the Flame was properly tended. The next day she laid upon our folk the sacred charge: to never let the Flame die, to never leave it unattended, and to never let the secrets of our folk be given to those unworthy of them.

"Thus we have endured, all these long years, on this small strip of land. For with the Flame to warm us and the Wood to feed us, the Chasm to guard us and the example of our ancestors to guide us, the Westwood will be secure against all darkness. For in darkness, the Flame abides."

"*In darkness, the Flame abides*," the entire Hall responded, in unison. It was the secret watchword of the Westwood, the central principal of the brave woodmen. It was the ritual words said over a new-born babe, during the private marriage ceremonies within the hall, and over the corpses of the beloved dead before they were burned to ashes.

As long as the Flame endured, it meant that all was well... and that hope yet lived.

* * *

That night, as the snow continued to cover the vale, Dara's sleep was restless. It was a cold night, of course, and in addition to the snow the winds howled wickedly out of the chasm until it sounded like the howls of wolves. Tree limbs clattered and banged, some snapping and falling abruptly under the weight of snow on their boughs. The noise and the chill made Frightful skittish, forcing Dara to hood her before she blew out the taper and tried to sleep herself.

She didn't know why, but she was feeling very anxious as she lay under the great quilt in her bed. The storm did not help her nerves, but that was not the source of her anxiety. Eventually she dismissed the vague feeling of unease as her picking up on Frightful's skittishness – Uncle Keram had often said that a falconer and his bird came to share a bond or affinity like that. Dara's long hours of training and care of the falcon had made her as familiar with her various moods as she was any person in the Hall.

To distract herself, she tried to envision the tale of Karl and Lissa, the founders of the Westwood and the kindlers of the Flame that had burnt continuously for centuries. They had been brave, she reminded herself, fleeing for their lives and protecting the secret of the Flame, whatever that was. They had not submitted to storm, hunger, or evil men. They had established the Flame and built a life for their descendants in the Wood.

That brought great comfort to Dara. But it did not entirely banish her unease. She fell asleep wondering what Karl and Lissa would have thought of the Magelord who now ruled their land.

Dara's dreams were no more soothing than her waking thoughts. They were filled with crazy, haphazard images: memories of her fateful climb up the mountain and her descent, the Yule feast, the endless hours training with

Frightful and . . . other things. There were images and folk she did not know, doing things she did not understand.

At some point, deep in the night, there was a flash, a light that seemed to come from everywhere and nowhere, all at once. Dara was torn from her dream and savagely thrust into consciousness. She woke herself up screaming piteously, her mind in turmoil. The white brightness had been everywhere, a great and sudden wave that had collapsed like a bough of a tree breaking.

Dara opened her eyes in the darkness, the smallest bit of light filtering in from the corridor. Something was wrong, she knew. Something was very wrong.

Not just wrong . . . changed. Something was different.

"Smoke and ashes, girl, what's *wrong* with you?" asked Aunt Anira from the doorway. "What . . . what . . . oh, by the Flame that warms us, what has happened? What have you done?" she demanded, her voice rising in tone and shrillness.

"What have . . . I was . . ." Dara mumbled confusedly, her mouth dry and her stomach churning. Things didn't look right . . . her eyes weren't seeing them properly . . . she struggled . . .

Things became clearer when the thin door was opened and her Uncle Keram pushed inside, carrying a lit taper that seemed much brighter than it should. His eyes were wide with fear.

"What happened?" he demanded.

"I . . . I had a bad dream," Dara said, weakly.

"You screamed?"

"*Dream!*" Dara insisted. "I had a dream. I don't know why I screamed. I was . . . falling, I think, and . . ."

"Are you all right?" he asked, concerned. "Shall I fetch your father?"

"No, no," Dara protested. "I'm . . . I'm fine, it's just . . . why does everything look so . . . different?" Her stomach lurched as she turned her head around. The dark stone of the wall didn't look right . . . it didn't even look dark. As her eyes focused and adjusted to the dim lamination of the taper, it appeared as if someone had snuck into her room and quietly whitewashed the walls.

Only that was impossible.

"What's happening?" someone called sleepily from the corridor. "Why is . . . *why is everything white?*"

Uncle Keram looked at Dara suddenly and sternly. "Dara! *What have you done?*"

"Me? I was *sleeping!*" she protested. "I just had a bad dream, I –" She stopped speaking as her stomach finally came to some decision about its destiny. Dara threw up suddenly.

That sent her aunt into a tizzy as she started barking orders to her daughters and other folk in the vicinity of her voice. Dara felt herself get taken from her bed by her uncle, deposited before the Flame in the hall and stripped while her aunt bathed her with warm water scented with dried lavender.

"There, there," her aunt crooned to her as she wiped the last of the residue from her face. "You poor thing . . . was it something you ate; do you think?"

"Why . . . why is everything white?" Dara demanded, confused, as she looked around. Every stone in the great fire pit, every stone in the wall, even the clay wattle of the walls themselves were bright white. "What happened?"

"No one knows, yet," her aunt said, nervously. "But we'll get to the bottom of it soon enough, don't you worry, Little Bird. You just had a dream," she reminded her. "Nothing to worry about."

"Except for all of *this*," Dara said, helplessly gesturing toward the bright stones of the Flame. "How is this *not* something to worry about?"

"We're still warm, dry and fed," her aunt said, stubbornly as she covered Dara with her mantle. "The Flame is still lit. We'll sort the rest out later."

Dara nodded, and then accepted a sip from a bottle offered to her by her buck-toothed cousin Lanthi. It burned like fire, but it removed the vile taste of vomit from her lips. It also made her sleepy. Before she knew it, Dara was back asleep, the heat of the Flame on her face.

Her dreams continued to be filled with disturbing visions and confusing sensations, but they were more restful under the influence of the drafts her aunt gave her. When she returned to consciousness again, she was back in her bed, her falcon on the block nearby. It was afternoon, if she read the angle of the sun through the shutters right.

And every stone in sight was still bleached white.

"What have I done?" she asked herself in despair. It wasn't just the stones, *she* was feeling differently, now. There seemed to be an unearthly light coming from everywhere and nowhere at once.

"You haven't done anything," came a voice answering her unexpectedly. Dara turned over and saw that her oldest brother, Kyre, was sitting on the stool next to her narrow bed. "Welcome back to the living, Little Bird. Again."

"What happened?" she asked, sitting up slowly. "Am I . . . are we . . . *dead?*"

"You've been out for two days," he chuckled at her confusion. "So no, you are not dead, and neither am I. This was the result of a magic spell, apparently. One of the Magelord's. His son was born a few days ago – the very night that this," he said, gesturing around to the white stone around them, "happened. There were complications, and . . . well, no one really knows what happened. Except that all the stone and rock closest to the castle has all turned white, for some reason."

"But it wasn't *me?*" Dara asked, relief flooding through her.

"No, it wasn't you," he assured her. "But once we sent someone to the castle with word of what had happened, we heard that it had happened to others, too. You weren't the only one that threw up."

"Huh? Why?"

"We don't know," he shrugged. "But the Magelord is investigating it. How do you feel now?"

"Uh . . . better," she admitted, after she evaluated herself. "Less sick to my stomach, at least. But my eyes . . . it's like I'm seeing things differently . . ."

"You aren't the only one. Several people reported getting sick after that . . . that light. Even Sir Cei, the castellan. Some side effect of the magic, they say."

"If that's magic, you can have it!" Dara said emphatically. "That was awful, Kyre! I still feel strange."

"Well, don't be too hasty," Kyre said. "We haven't heard back yet, but when you fell sick our father sent word to the castle. The Magelord hasn't officially responded yet, but . . . well, I spoke to his man, Banamor, who is a kind of wizard, I guess, and he suggested that those who got sick may prove to have the *rajira* talent."

"The *what?*"

"*Rajira*," repeated her brother with a grin. "I hope you weren't too set on a career as a falconer, Little Bird. From everything that I've heard in the last few days you – and everyone else who got sick – may well be talented enough to learn magic."

"I . . . *what?*" Dara demanded, as the words sunk in. "Don't be stupid – I'm no mage!" Dara insisted, desperately.

"Not yet," agreed Kyre. "But it's possible you have the talent to be one. Father sent to the castle for someone to help make that determination, but since the road is still covered with snow as far as Gurisham, that might take a few days."

"Me? A mage?" Dara asked, her mind swimming.

"It's *possible*," her brother stressed. "*Just* possible. But you seem to have recovered from the . . . whatever it was. I need to go tell our aunt – that was my instruction. I'll bring you something to eat, if you like."

Dara realized that she was famished – it had been a couple of days since she had eaten, if what her brother said was correct. "Yes, that would be lovely. Thanks, Kyre," she said, earnestly. Her older brother gave her a smile and a hug and then went to fetch food.

A mage, eh? Dara's mind began considering, after he'd left. She had little idea what that meant, but the dizziness she felt presaged what a great change that would mean to her life. *And here I thought climbing a mountain was the stupidest thing I've ever done.*

Chapter Nine

Wizards Of Sevendor

It was weeks after the snow fell before anyone from the castle came by to check on Dara. During that time the girl continued to recuperate from her strange experience. Though she could not fault her physical condition, after a few days, she still experienced dizziness and disorientation at unexpected times. Dara felt . . . fragile, somehow, though she could not quite put her finger on exactly how.

She was not the only thing that had changed after that fateful night. The white coloration that had affected every bit of stone, rock, sand and dirt – including the mountain that towered overhead – did not melt away with the snow. Rundeval had been nearly-black basalt since the Westwoodmen had come here, centuries ago. Now it was as white as a snowdrift.

The change was startling, and though there was no less amazement at the transformation in the Hall itself, the white mountain's magical coloration inspired true awe among the folk of the estate. The Westwoodmen frequently stared up at the peak and murmured words to the Flame. Everything in a two-mile radius of the castle, it was said, had been magically transformed this way.

Most saw the startling transformation as a sign – of what, no one precisely knew. Mostly it was seen as a good omen. The Westwoodmen were pragmatic folk, and though each of them had seen strange things in the Wood in their lives they were slow to indulge in superstition.

The folk of the vale were less stable in their beliefs. Word came from market, the first day it was clear enough to hold one, that the folk of Genly hamlet were certain that the Snow That Never Melted was a curse sent against Sevendor by the gods for accepting a wizard as a lord. Railan the Steady's yeomanry of Genly was also within the sphere of the spell, and he was not happy with the result. It was a curse. He had led a campaign of dark whispers saying as much. The unexpected blizzard was sent to punish the good folk of Sevendor, he maintained, for the Magelord's temerity to strike against the belligerent West Flerians.

The Wilderlands folk – the Bovali, Dara reminded herself – had angrily dismissed the rumors and took offense, nearly causing a brawl at market. They understood the storm to have been called down upon the folk of West Fleria after the Magelord's victory over the misguided knights who had dueled him.

Dara thought that was just plain silly. How could the gods find fault with Lord Minalan's rule, when everyone – including the Genlymen – had prospered under the Spellmonger's rule? Lord Minalan had banished evil old Sir Erantal, dismissed his wicked men, had forgiven the debts of the people and had spent coin liberally, instead of extorting labor from the people. How could the gods find fault with that?

Dara didn't know much about the gods of the Vale folk, but if they took offense at justice and prosperity, she didn't see the point of them.

Of course, another part of her knew, if she really was talented in the arts of magic, then supporting Lord Minalan was just in her best interest. Yet other than her dizziness and the odd way she saw things now, she didn't seem to be able to manifest any other abilities. No lightning shot out of her fingers, and her sister persisted in talking despite Dara's intense wish that she stop. If Dara was a mage, she decided after a few days considering the matter, she wasn't a very good one. At last she gave up and went back to training Frightful to the lure.

Her falcon was coming through the winter well, her uncle assured her, and once Dara was permitted normal activity again she continued working with her bird over short distances. By the third day back at work she had her flying from her block at one end of the now-spotless white flagged yard to the other . . . without the line.

Dara was in the yard when a call came down from the watchtower overhead – visitors were approaching. That was not unusual, of course, but the nature of the visitor was. A man in a long robe and a floppy old hat who was there to see Dara.

She thought she recognized the man from Yule, and recalled him completely once he introduced himself.

"I'm Banamor," he offered in a Riverlands accent and with a small bow, as her uncle joined the two of them in the yard. "I was asked by the Magelord to inquire after anyone who fell ill the night of the blizzard. I heard that at least one person here did . . ."

"That was me," Dara admitted, nodding in the cold as she hooded Frightful. "Lenodara of Westwood, at your service, my lord," she said, trying to bow. It was difficult with a heavy falcon on her wrist.

"I'm not a lord," grunted the man dismissively, "I'm a *mage*. A footwizard, or at least I was, before I came to Sevendor to take Master Minalan's service. Now I'm . . . well, I guess the term will be decided later, but I am one of the Magelord's retainers, one helping him with magical affairs here. I am at least enough of a wizard to determine whether you have *rajira*, though probably not a good enough one to tell you how much or what variety – not my specialty. But if you don't mind speaking to me for a while . . . preferably somewhere *warm* . . ." he said, as a cold gust blew out of the chasm.

"By the Flame, then, with the Master of the Wood," her Uncle Keram nodded. "You have the hospitality of the Hall, Master Banamor."

"My thanks, Master Keram. And may I say what a magnificent bird that is? A Silver Hooded Raptor, if I'm not mistaken?"

"From yon peak, Rundeval," Dara agreed, nodding toward the mountain. "It's not as easy to climb as it looks."

"As it looks utterly impossible, I'll take that as a testament of your bravery," the mage agreed as they went inside. Uncle Keram called for food and drink for a guest, and her cousins hurried to fetch it and bring it to them before the Flame.

"Now," Banamor said, when mulled cider and a few cakes had been laid at his elbow, "I have been tasked with seeing just who may have reacted to the unexpected spell the other night . . ."

"Just what happened with that? If you don't mind me asking?" Keram asked.

"It was the night of the birth of Minalan, the Magelord's son. There were complications – magical complications, don't ask me for details – and the Magelord intervened. The white rock and the wave of nausea that followed was a side-effect of the spell. But mother and child are doing fine, gods bless them. A fine baby boy, who seems completely unaware that he turned the world white with his birth cries."

"So the Snow That Never Melted happened at the birth of the Lord of Sevendor?" Keram asked, with especial interest.

"Well, his son, at least. A future lord of Sevendor, perhaps. So it seems," Banamor agreed. "It is seen as auspicious, by some—"

"Well, how could it *not* be?" insisted Keram with a grin. "Such an omen is profound enough, but for it to occur during the birth of the lord of the vale? That is clearly a sign of favor!"

"I'm a mage, not a priest," shrugged Banamor. "I'm far more interested in magic than mysticism. Now, Lenodara, let's begin with the night it happened. Tell me what happened that night . . ."

The questions lasted all morning, and often the former footwizard asked unusual things. He cast a few spells (Dara assumed they were spells) and he asked her to do a few strange actions while he watched, but by the time they were done with luncheon Master Banamor was fairly certain Dara possessed at least a little measureable Talent.

"It's hard to say about this sort of thing, exactly," he mused as he prepared to leave. "The onset of magical ability usually manifests in puberty, but the spell seems to have accelerated and accentuated the Talent in those it affected. We have about a dozen cases of vomiting from that night, over-all. Every one of them has tested well for *rajira*, which I find professionally interesting.

"But not all have manifested a discernible Talent, and I theorize that whatever it is that pushed each of you to express your *rajira* may have awakened an incompletely formed talent. In other words, I expect this to be the mere sprouting of your *rajira*; it may develop more in time, much more." The wizard rose and began to depart. "We will check back with you in the spring. But be certain to let the castle know if you begin demonstrating any strange occurrences."

"What *kind* of strange occurrences?" Aunt Anira asked, wiping her hands on her apron as she eyed Dara warily.

Banamor shrugged. "She's a twelve-year-old girl. If she does anything a regular twelve-year-old girl doesn't do, that's noteworthy."

Uncle Keram cleared his throat. "Respectfully, Master, Dara climbs mountains without permission and trained a falcon in secret. I've not known any other twelve-year-old girl to do that."

"A fair point," agreed Banamor with a smirk and an indulgent look at Dara. "Well, then, if something suddenly catches on fire, or if water suddenly overflows, ice, steam or fog appears inexplicably, or if rocks or small objects start shooting around the room without apparent reason to do so . . . that sort of thing."

Dara's eyes were wide. "That could happen? I could set things on fire? With magic?"

"It *can* happen," he agreed, reluctantly. "But it's usually something subtle. In fact, I think your Talent may go dormant for a few months or even years before it manifests. For some the appearance of *rajira* is a gradual thing. For others it is sudden and often disconcerting. For maidens, it often appears soon after their first flowering. For boys, it can go just about any time. And there's no guarantee that it will develop into anything at all. Not all with *rajira* are subject to its whims. It's just too soon to tell." Banamor went on to give her a brief history of magic and wizards, most of which she was unaware of.

He explained how magic had once been common, during the age of the Old Imperial Magocracy, the great human civilization to the east in ages past. When that magic-fueled culture had been destroyed by human barbarians invading from the north, the new folk had been highly suspicious of magic, though they themselves practiced it in a limited form. After those barbarians had conquered the Magocracy, they had settled down and became the Five Duchies.

For four hundred years the Five Duchies of human civilization had limited the power of wizards – magi – by strict statute and ruthless enforcement known as the Bans of Magic. The enforcers of the Bans were a dour, deadly order of warmagi, wizards trained to fight known as the Censorate of Magic.

That, Banamor explained, was where their new lord, Minalan the Spellmonger, came in. He had overturned that old order. He had captured a *witchstone*, the footwizard said with a gleam in his eye, from the hand of a goblin shaman in battle far away in the Minden mountains. A witchstone, he explained, was a tiny sliver of green amber that could magnify a mage's powers dramatically. It was also prohibited by the Bans.

"But our good lord was not going to let a silly law keep him from defending his people, so he not only ignored the Bans, he captured another twenty or so witchstones and gave them out to his friends. Used them to pull off a daring escape right under the noses of an army of goblins, too. He would have been arrested and executed by the bloody Censorate, had he not convinced Duke Rard and Duke Lenguin to let him raise an army and stop an invasion. After he cast a spell to summon a hundred-foot fire elemental and drove off a dragon, the Duke had the good sense to overturn the Bans and knight the Spellmonger on the field. That's how he became your lord: Sevendor is his reward for saving the Duchies."

"So what about these Censor fellows, now?" asked Keram, worriedly.

"They've been asked to leave Castal," Banamor informed them, grimly, "but they are reluctant to go, owing no Duke their master. They hate the Spellmonger with a burning passion, for what he has done and who he is. Our lord has enemies. But he also has powerful friends. He's been asked by the Duke to train more warmagi in using witchstones, for his stone is the only one that can wash away the taint of goblins from them.

"But it's either the very best time to discover you have magical Talent, or the very worst," he shrugged. "And Sevendor is either the very best place to be with magical Talent, or the very worst. It all depends upon your perspective. Either way," he said with a grin for Dara, "Discovering you have *rajira* is right now, there's only one thing I *can* guarantee."

"What's that?" Dara asked

"It will be interesting. It won't be boring. Not that it appears you suffer from a boring life," he said, glancing at Frightful, who was still wary of the strange man around her human. "But for good or ill, my dear, you have had the fortune to learn you are Talented in perhaps the most magically interesting place in the world, at the most interesting time."

* * *

The after-effects of the spell that had turned the mountain white and made Dara ill lingered on in her, fading but not entirely going away. Especially as she was falling asleep or waking up she seemed to feel and see things that other people didn't. It was confusing, but it passed quickly enough when she shook herself into wakefulness. After a few weeks she grew so used to it that her prospective Talent faded from importance. It wasn't as if she had time to dwell on it – Frightful was taking up an awful lot of her time.

Since her successful first free flight Dara and Keram had continued to work on establishing good retrieval training in the bird, encouraging her to return to Dara's gauntleted fist. Dara had developed a special call that meant "come back now!" It worked indoors, to the point where Dara could put Frightful anywhere in the hall or yard and she would stay put until called, then fly to her.

But while the falcon was obedient around the Hall, she proved stubbornly reluctant to return when flying free. The first time Frightful had refused to return to her glove in the meadow had been a terrifying and anxious experience for Dara. She was working alone that day, and the weather was overcast, making it difficult for her to spot the bird in the sky.

She frantically made the retrieval call, over and over, and listened for the bells. But Frightful seemed far more interested in circling the meadow and investigating treetops. Dara got mad – Frightful seemed to be mocking her, the way she dove down into the meadow and then pulled up, her growing wings catching the air as she climbed away from the glove. Dara made the call again and again, and dangled the feathered lure in the air, but Frightful refused to comply until hunger finally drove her to return.

Dara was furious, but Frightful was a *bird*, not a *person*, her uncle explained that night when she told him about it. He cautioned her against taking the training process personally, which no good falconer did. Frightful's reluctance wasn't a failure of training, he told her, but a bird's natural curiosity about its surroundings. Only patient, persistent persuasion could bring her to obedience.

Dara was unconvinced. Frightful seemed to be laughing at her.

Those incidents grew fewer and fewer, as the weather warmed and Dara continued training. But the bird's capacity to be distracted was maddening to the girl. Just when she thought she was making progress towards a well-trained hunter, Frightful would decide that she'd had enough of the routine and go off on her own, her tiny silver bells tinkling mockingly in Dara's ears as she flew away. While she always did — *eventually* – return, the experience was frustrating Dara to no end.

Spring arrived at the Westwood with its usual abruptness. As the new leaves sprouted on the trees and the foliage began to green, the wood came alive with distractions, from chipmunks to badgers, and it seemed like every bird in the world wanted to investigate the tamed falcon that flew over the meadow.

On her uncle's advice, Dara took Frightful across the bridge and into the vale to give her some new territory to practice in. He recommended the cleared land in the valewood, the former forest sacrificed to build the homes of the Bovali settlers. The land was marked by the snow spell as well, the stumps of the felled trees poking out of chalk-like soil, but the plants and animals there didn't seem to notice. The stumpy wasteland bordered on the orderly fields of Sevendor Village, where the peasants were already breaking the ground with their great wooden plows.

The fields seemed perfect for the task of flying her bird. There was little in the way of distraction in the clear-cut land, and it provided an unobstructed view of her falcon as she flew farther and farther from her.

Things seemed to be going well, that morning. Dara had let Frightful fly across the stubbly field half a dozen times, and after every flight the falcon had obediently returned to her glove when she had waved the lure and made the retrieval call.

But then the seventh flight the idiot bird had gotten the idea that there was something interesting in the edges of the field, and refused to respond to the call. In fact, the more frantic Dara called and waved the lure, the more disdainful the falcon became.

Dara started swearing after a half hour of fruitless calling. Frightful studiously ignored her, and continued to fly wide circles overhead. She was soaring impishly toward the northern ridge of hills, toward Caolan's Pass, when Dara's frustration turned to fear. If the bird got over the ridge and lost her bearings, it was possible she would not find her way back.

As dread clung to her heart, Dara repeated the call over and over again, waving the lure over her head. But Frightful continued to ignore her call. Dara focused her eyes on the diminishing speck in the sky, her fear rising higher and higher with each passing second . . .

. . . and then something remarkable happened. For a few moments, Dara *found herself wrenched out of her body*, and seemed to be soaring overhead *with Frightful*.

It was only for a few seconds, but in those seconds Dara became completely disconcerted. The scale and perspective she witnessed from Frightful's point-of-view was so strange and different than what a human saw and felt that dizziness overcame her. The Westwood, the croplands, and the ridge all spread out in a majestic view before her, but the distance to the ground and the far horizon were strange and confusing to a mind used to thinking in two dimensions.

In a panic Dara lashed out with her mind, and felt Frightful's confused and terrified response. The feeling of confusion and dizziness from vertigo were too much. Dara fainted, her face falling into the cool, damp earth.

When she came to wakefulness again, she was not alone. A gawky-looking youth with unkempt hair and a concerned expression on his face loomed over her.

"Are you all right?" he asked, his eyes wide with worry.

"What? I . . . *where's my bird?*" Dara said, sitting bolt upright. That was a mistake, she realized, as the world swam around her. She still felt some residual vertigo from her uncanny experience. Her stomach churned with nausea.

"You mean *this* terrifying-looking creature?" he asked, amused, as he nodded toward a nearby stump. There sat her falcon, looking at her accusingly.

"She came back!" Dara sighed, a wave of relief washing over her.

"You fainted because you were upset your pet falcon didn't come back?" the youth asked, confused.

"No, I . . . wait, who are you?" she demanded, sitting up more carefully this time. She looked at the man more carefully now.

He wasn't a villein, she could tell – he wore a good woolen tunic and wool mantle, and his shoes were sturdy boots made for traveling, not plowing. No, Dara decided, those hands had never touched a plow, or much else involving blisters. There was a dagger and purse on his belt, and he wore an odd little pointed cap.

"Me? I'm Gareth. I'm a warmage. Or, at least, I was *supposed* to be one," he said, discouraged. "I was tried for a witchstone, but I . . . well, it doesn't matter. I'm a mage, even if I'm not a warmage. I did well at thaumaturgy at school, though, so the Magelord asked me to stick around for a while, even if I don't get a witchstone. Yet."

"You don't look like a warmage," she pointed out, though she had never seen one, to her knowledge.

"Yes, I know," Gareth said, patiently. "I'm a hundred pounds too light, I barely have the strength to wear real armor, and I'm kind of clumsy, too. It wasn't really my first choice," he admitted.

"Why would you want to be a *war*mage?" she asked, confused. "Isn't that dangerous?"

"Why do you want to be a falconer?" he replied, a little defensively. "Isn't *that* a little dangerous?"

"Falconry? It's not dangerous!" she insisted.

"... coming from a girl who just fainted dead away in the middle of a field," he pointed out, "you'll excuse me if I find you less than convincing."

"It's not *usually* dangerous," Dara amended, bringing herself slowly to her feet with the youth's help.

"Well, I didn't really want to become a warmage, but I figured if I tried, I might be able to get a witchstone from the Spellmonger. Turns out he's a thaumaturge, too, like me, so he wants me to join him. A witchstone would be very valuable . . . for research," he added, warily. "So why did you faint?"

"I'm new at this, and . . . well, I had a . . ." she didn't know how to describe the experience, she realized.

Then she realized that of all the people who could have found her, the Flame had brought one of the few to her who might lend some insight on the experience.

"You're a mage?" she asked, almost accusatory.

"Licensed and registered," he said, proudly, as he helped her take a seat on a nearby stump, "although after what the Magelord has done to the profession, I'm not sure exactly what that means anymore. But yes, I'm a real mage. Why?"

"Because I've been told I might be Talented," she said, carefully, "because I threw up when the mountain turned white."

"*Really?*" Gareth asked, with renewed interest. "That's fascinating!"

"Not at the time," she corrected. "My sheets were ruined. But a wizard from the castle came by and said I might have . . . ra . . ."

"*Rajira?*" Gareth finished with a grin. "That's looking likely. Several people have reported some strange effects from that spell. Including the revelation of undiscovered *rajira*. I've been helping Master Banamor keep track of them, for the Spellmonger. That's fascinating!" he repeated.

"So you said," Dara replied, a little irritated, as she looked to check on Frightful. The bird's eyes were glaring at her accusingly, but she seemed otherwise undisturbed by the strange incident. "But the reason I fainted was that while I was trying to get this ungrateful, *spiteful* bird back, something happened. Something very strange."

"What?" asked Gareth with intense interest.

"For a brief moment . . . I was *there,*" she said with emphasis, nodding toward Frightful. "It was like I was behind her eyes."

"Behind her eyes," the mage repeated, stroking his chin. There wasn't much that could pass for a beard there, yet, Dara noted, but the way he stroked the few hairs there it was as if Gareth was encouraging them to grow. "That's . . ."

"*Fascinating?*" Dara supplied, wryly. "It also made me faint. So why did that happen, oh great and powerful wizard?"

"Thaumaturgically speaking," Gareth began, ignoring the jibe, "I would have to say you experienced a trans-species bilocation effect."

"Can you repeat that again in language real people use?" Dara asked, mildly irritated with the mage. It didn't seem to bother the man – he grinned instead.

"You slipped into her consciousness," he explained. "It's known as forced rapport, when you do it to a human being, and it's very, *very* difficult. With animals," he continued, "the effect is easier to achieve but harder to control. There are actually magi who specialize in that sort of thing, although I don't know how terribly useful it is. They're known as Beastmasters, some places. Some can work only with one or two kinds of animals, others can eventually inhabit most creatures, with practice."

"With practice? Why would anyone want to practice that?" Dara demanded. "I almost threw up!"

"If it was the first time it happened, it's no wonder that you had a poor reaction," Gareth soothed, taking a seat on another stump. "I've studied this, in Thaumaturgic Theory. It's sometimes known as Brown Magic. Theoretically speaking, forcing a human consciousness into a brain the size of a hazelnut is problematic. It would take a lot of getting used to. The good news is that it gets easier and more manageable with practice. In *theory*," he repeated. "Beastmasters can supposedly do remarkable things with their familiars."

"Familiars?"

"A beastmaster term for their special animal friends," Gareth explained. "If you try to establish that rapport and you both get used to it, eventually you should be able to control her, see through her eyes, and direct her actions. I'd think that would be a handy skill for a falconer to have," he pointed out.

Dara couldn't argue with that . . . but the idea of voluntarily experiencing the massive vertigo and dizziness she'd felt sounded appalling.

"Try to work with her when she's *not* flying," suggested the mage thoughtfully. "If you can establish a rapport when she's at rest, then getting used to it when she's flying will be easier. Eventually it will be as easy as getting dressed in the morning."

"You have no idea how challenging that is for a girl," Dara said, recalling the many, many times her sisters had turned the Hall upside down over their wardrobe choices. "But thank you for your advice. And thank you for your help, Gareth," she said, as she gathered up her supplies.

"It wasn't a problem. I was just exploring the edge of the snowstone effect – that's what we're calling it – when I saw you fall. It's not every day you find pretty redhead maidens just lying around in a field, so I thought it would be unchivalrous of me not to at least stop and see if I could help. Do you live in Sevendor village?"

"Well, thanks," she said. "No, I'm . . . I'm from the Westwood. The Westwood estate. Dara – sorry, Lenodara of Westwood Hall," she introduced herself. "But everyone calls me Dara. I'm the youngest daughter of the Master of the Wood."

"The Yeomanry near the castle," he nodded. "I've seen your folk around, on market days. You keep to yourselves, don't you?"

"We've always been . . . apart," she said, struggling for the right word. "The Wood and the Vale are different places. They require different people."

"Which means you see the vale folk as sod-footed farmers, and they see you as ignorant woodland rustics," he chuckled. "But you've probably intermarried for generations."

"Well . . . yes," Dara said, a little embarrassed that an outsider could so quickly and aptly sum up the complex relationship between the two peoples. "But in all fairness, most of the villeins *are* sod-footed farmers."

"And no doubt you have some ignorant rustics up in the woods, too," he pointed out. Dara was about to object when she thought of her brother Kobb, and kept quiet. She was too impressed with how well Gareth had observed the relationship.

"You must be a pretty good wizard," she finally conceded. "You've been in Sevendor for how long?"

"Only a month," he shrugged. "But I've travelled enough to know how such things work. It's not magic, it's just observation. But learning magic forces you to observe such things. If you don't know how things fit together and influence each other, you can't do magic."

"It sounds complicated," she said, picking up Frightful on her glove. She examined the bird closely, but did not see anything amiss . . . except the accusing look in the bird's eyes. She fed her to soothe her a bit and then turned to go.

"It is. But it beats being a sod-footed farmer. And it really did open up a wider world for me. So, how far is it back to your hall?"

"Just a mile or so," she shrugged. Then she realized that the mage was waiting to escort her back. "I can manage on my own," she said, before he could ask.

"Considering you were out cold when I found you, I'm going to walk you back anyway," Gareth said. "My duties are kind of loosely defined right now, and I don't have anything better to do. The Magelord would be vexed if I let anything happen to one of his most important Yeomen's daughters."

"The Magelord considers father to be important?"

"I've heard him speak with admiration of your folk," Gareth agreed, starting down the path toward the Westwood. Dara was forced to follow, regardless of whether or not she wanted his company. "He sees the Westwood as loyal. Not everyone is considered so," he added, diplomatically.

"You mean Yeoman Railan?" she asked, suddenly interested.

"It would not be prudent to spread such rumors," the mage said with quiet dignity. "To be honest, you probably know more about the situation than I do. But the Westwood is fair in our master's thoughts. And bound to grow fairer, if it produces magically-talented girls like you."

Dara didn't know what to say to that as she walked with Gareth, so she turned the conversation to falconry, and discussed the difficult and demanding art with the man. He took her all the way to the bridge, where the watchman hailed her and allowed her to pass. She considered inviting the mage over the bridge, but he decided to head back to the village instead.

"I'd love to see your Hall, but it's getting late and I do have a few things on my list to complete today," he demurred. "But I'm sure I'll be seeing you around, Lenodara of Westwood." He grinned, waved, and returned down the trail.

"Who was *that?*" Anira asked curiously, when Dara passed her on her way back to the Hall. Her aunt was overseeing the hanging of laundry out in the yard, a task Dara was glad she was exempted from.

"Just a . . . a wizard from the castle I met out in the fields," Dara dismissed, casually. "He saw Frightful and wanted to see her." She did not want to try to explain the unusual event that led to their meeting to her aunt, who would have her in bed under a sick watch if she discovered the fainting.

"He looks . . . nice," Anira said, curiously. It took Dara a moment to figure out what her aunt was suggesting, and when she did she blushed.

"He just wanted to see my falcon," Dara said, defensively.

"That's what they all say!" snorted her aunt as she pulled another wet sheet out of the basket.

"He wasn't—"

"Of course he was," Anira said, shaking her head. "Don't get your feathers ruffled, Little Bird, it's about time that the lads started noticing that you're a girl. That one's no different, wizard or no. Nothing to be ashamed of. Or shocked about. You aren't as fair as Leska, perhaps, but you'll turn a head or two someday, mark my words."

Dara prepared to explain, in *no* uncertain terms, that Gareth had *no* such thoughts about her in his head and was *merely* intrigued with her falconry to her busybody aunt . . .

Then she remembered he had called her *pretty* – the first time a boy had *ever* done that – and she blushed even more furiously. To her horror, she realized that her aunt was correct, and that Dara was wrong. Gareth wasn't properly a boy, either. If he'd his mastership papers, or whatever it was wizards used, then he was nearly a man in his own right. That made Dara even more confused and flustered. She had reached her thirteenth birthday only a few weeks before, and the idea of such attention was deeply disconcerting.

"I'm going to my room," Dara said, darkly, her feelings confused. *To hide for the rest of eternity,* she added to herself. Frightful squawked with annoyance as she jerked suddenly toward the hall doorway, reflecting her own mood.

She was still a child, after all – why would a man be interested in *her?* She was a mere girl, and a scrawny one at that, from a people of "ignorant rustics." Sure, Gareth was no dashing warrior himself – his arms and legs had been thin and spindly, and he had a kind of odd face, but he was polite and friendly and he had a nice smile, and . . .

. . . and he had called her a "pretty redhead".

Compared to the confusion and anxiousness of realizing a boy was interested in her, "trans-species bilocation" seemed a pretty simple and easy to understand thing to Dara.

Chapter Ten

Market Day

After her disconcerting experience with bilocation in the fields, Dara kept close to home for a few days, quietly working over the same routines with Frightful and the lure she always had.

Only now there was something additional in their relationship. Dara was wary of the bird – not of her sharp talons or beak, but of her mind. The more she worked with the bird, the more Dara was aware of the capacity to slip her mind behind Frightful's eyes.

Finally, tired of being scared of her own bird, Dara dared to try to will the bilocation to happen. The first time Dara managed to consciously make the transition was in her room. She stared at Frightful, who was preening on her block. Remembering how she managed it the first time, Dara allowed her mind to wander, unfocused as she stared at Frightful, who was grooming her feathers. She felt the connecting rapport between them, but instead of pushing it away, she welcomed it. Before she realized what was happening it was Dara who was doing the preening.

It was frightening, at first.

The sense of dislocation and the change of perspective and perception was daunting. Falcons see things differently than humans, hear things in different ways. Frightful's eyes saw things very differently than Dara's, and in those seconds the way the room around her warped and twisted as she chased mites in her feathers was strange and thrilling. They noticed the smallest movements while ignoring large objects.

The sensation lasted for a few brief seconds, but during that time Dara experienced Frightful's emotional perspective as well: bored, vain, a little hungry, and feeling a little pressure on her tiny tummy, as a casting prepared itself for ejection. Only when Frightful suddenly looked up at Dara – and Dara got the unique and chilling sensation of seeing herself through her falcon's eyes – did the moment of intense intimacy end. She was startled at how her falcon regarded her. She looked strange and inhuman, her hair and eyes featuring prominently to the bird. It would take time to acclimatize herself to filtering what she saw through Frightful's perceptions, she realized as she withdrew from the rapport.

Sweat poured from her brow and her chest heaved like a bellows as she recovered from the shocking experience. She could feel her pulse in all of her limbs as her mind settled back down.

As frightening as the experience had been, she did not hesitate to repeat it, after she had recovered. From then on, she increased her magical rapport with her falcon a little each day until she could manage to "be" inside Frightful's mind for several minutes at a time. She never did much more than observe the world from her bird's perspective, allowing Frightful to get used to the sensation. For Dara could tell that Frightful was aware of her intrusion, even if the falcon had little idea of its nature.

Dara was reluctant to share the news of her unusual gift with anyone else, though she desperately wanted to discuss it at least with Uncle Keram. He, at least, would be empathetic about her discomfort . . . without the slightest idea of what she was experiencing.

But she was also wary that revealing the talent would result in even more complications to her life. Already she felt like a slave to her falcon, and the knowledge that she might be magically Talented had been both exciting and fearful. Admitting that her talent had manifested through beastmastery felt like inviting yet more trouble into her life. She lost some of her anxiety as she continued to practice and strengthen her rapport with Frightful. Getting used to seeing things from her perspective, sorting out which feelings were Dara's and which were Frightful's, and understanding the nature of the strange sensations involved with flight slowly gave her a growing confidence in their bond. Mentioning it casually over dinner, in front of the Flame, would invite a level of oversight she was not willing to suffer.

Instead she continued to quietly work with Frightful in the little meadow all spring until the bird returned from flight unerringly at the sound of the call. Their lessons went beyond normal falconry, now. Dara had learned how to slip behind Frightful's eyes and "encourage" her a little, after a few weeks of practice, something a regular falconer couldn't do. But she also found that by increasing her will just a little while "riding" Frightful's mind encouraged her to be a more obedient falcon. Perhaps, she reasoned, Frightful was unable to distinguish between her own desires and what her handler wanted. If so, Dara eagerly used the mistake to her advantage. Within four weeks of her first flight, Frightful took her first prey.

Dara slipped away to the meadow in the afternoon, narrowly escaping working hides in the tanning shed. All of the animal hides the Westwood hunters took in the fall had been soaking in tannins all winter, and while cured, they were as stiff as wood and needed to be beaten, folded, and worked until they were pliable enough to be used in leatherwork. It was rough, demanding, brutal work that left your hands chafed and raw, the worst kind of unskilled labor. It also smelled revolting, the acids stinging your nose while they slowly burned your skin. When Dara saw that her brother Kobb had been assigned to lead the party she decided it was a *great* day to work her bird. Kobb wouldn't hesitate to draft her for the task out of simple spite.

That day Frightful was responding obediently to the hunting routine. Dara would toss her into the air, allow her to circle overhead for a few passes, then wave the lure and make the hunting call. Frightful would respond by diving until she took the lure out of Dara's hands and settled a few feet nearby. After pecking out the sliver of raw meat on the feathered lure, the pair repeated the exercise.

On the fourth pass, however, as the falcon dove toward the lure she veered at the last moment and missed it entirely. Dara rolled her eyes and was about to insult the falcon when she saw what had distracted Frightful. Instead of the lure, she had pounced on a baby rabbit that had emerged from its lair at the wrong moment.

It took Dara a few seconds to realize what was going on – Frightful had made her first kill! She watched with fascinated horror as the falcon used its beak to break the little brown rabbit's neck with a twist, then begin to tear the flesh hungrily apart with its talons. She watched with pride and elation until she realized what a mistake she was making.

Her Uncle Keram had been clear about this from the beginning: you *could not* allow a falcon to feed on its own kills and remain a dedicated hunter. If the bird did not see food as coming exclusively from its handler, the falconer would lose his hold on the bird. With a startled squeak Dara ran across the meadow and pulled the baby rabbit's corpse from Frightful's eager rending, earning a scratch on her hand and a baleful look from the startled bird.

Dara started to reach out through the rapport – only to experience the rare pleasure of her bird reveling in the guts of the baby rabbit, bragging with a victorious call. Dara could feel the blood, the viscera, the still-warm body of the animal as her bird devoured it. It was such a primal excitement that it almost overwhelmed the girl – she withdrew from the rapport almost immediately. It was time to be a falconer, not a beastmaster, for a moment. Dara snatched the limp form of the rabbit from the bird.

As Frightful glared at her for stealing her kill, Dara quickly handed her the lure, augmented with a double portion to reward her for the kill. Dara praised Frightful, petting her head with a finger and cooing to her as she tore hungrily into the meat on the lure. Dara felt like throwing up, watching the glee with which she attacked and ate the treat, the memory of the feel of baby rabbit in her mouth still haunting her. Her rapport with the falcon was intimidating. Frightful was still in an aggressive mood, Dara realized, probably from the thrill of her first kill. As sick as she felt, she could not keep her from celebrating such an important development. Only when she had stripped all the meat from the lure did Dara hood her and then take her carefully back to the Hall to report to Uncle Keram.

Her uncle congratulated her on the success and asked a dozen questions, before telling her how proud he was of her accomplishment.

"It's not every falconer who can train a bird to hunt that quickly. A baby coney is hardly a prize to brag about, but she'll do better as she grows. Keep at it – see if she can take a full-grown hare by midsummer," he suggested. "*That* would be something to boast of in a yearling!"

So Dara redoubled her efforts. It was helpful that Frightful was beginning to show her final adult plumage, and her bodyweight was increasing rapidly. It was also helpful that the forest was alive with creatures this time of year as the cold retreated and the green leaves advanced. Within a week Frightful had taken two sparrows, a chipmunk, and a pigeon almost large enough to eat. And all without the benefit of Dara's magical interference.

That didn't mean Dara was not continuing to use her growing mastery of bilocation, but she had yet to develop the confidence to direct Frightful's hunting. It was hard enough, she reflected, to ride Frightful's tiny mind while she was in flight.

There was a difference, the girl noted, in being inside Frightful when she was at rest on the block and when she was soaring overhead. The serenity of flight came with a kind of eternal searching, a businesslike attitude that was very different than Frightful's personality when standing on her block. When Frightful was in the air she was *working*. When she was on the block she was just living. The difference was as pronounced as the attitude of a dog herding sheep versus a dog napping by the fire.

But when Frightful was aloft, and Dara was secure in riding her mind, despite the falcon's focus on prey, Dara enjoyed the feel of flight in a way she didn't think even Frightful was aware of. The elation she felt when the bird beat her wings to gain altitude, for example, or the sweet sensation of speed as she dove out of the sky, wings folded, toward the tiniest dot on the ground below, filled her with awe and delight. The serenity of banking on one wing and turning gracefully in the air was a magic all its own. And the sense of perspective she got with her new aerial point of view made her privy to a world she never knew existed: the world of the air.

Far from being empty sky, as her human self-observed, from Frightful's perspective the air was alive with birds and insects and other flying things, all dancing around the winds like wildflowers in a breeze. The higher you went, she quickly learned, the fewer birds there were, but she could always sense precisely where they were through Frightful's keen perceptions. Her own mother had returned to the cliff-face after the harsh winter to raise another clutch of eggs, and Dara became acutely aware of Frightful's reluctance to return to the spot. Falcons were territorial, she knew, and Uncle Keram had cautioned her repeatedly about invading a wild bird's space.

There was a great allure to being able to rest her back against a tree after tossing the falcon into the air and just let her fly, with Dara quietly making subtle suggestions about where to go and what to do. Under her direction the bird ranged farther away from the woodland meadow, and Dara went with her in spirit.

She spent a morning quietly inspecting Sevendor Castle, through Frightful's eyes, after she had the falcon perch on the rooftop. She got to watch the Magelord and his wife return from Chepstan Fair, the glorious entertainment held in a neighboring barony each spring, their castellan Sir Cei looking both troubled and elated . . . what had the big Wilderlands knight done to warrant such anxiety? Dara couldn't think of a thing in the world that should trouble the man.

Another afternoon she had her bird skip from one new rooftop in Sevendor Village to another. Dara barely recognized the place through Frightful. She hadn't been there since before the Snow That Never Melted, and she could not believe her eyes – Frightful's eyes – at the changes that had occurred. The construction and repairs were the most impressive thing. Gone were most of the simple round pole houses the villeins of the village had lived in – now long homes of planks and stone bearing newly-thatched roofs filled the street.

And there was an *actual* street, as opposed to a mere track between two rows of houses. At least a hundred feet of the center of the village had been cobbled using the white stone that lay under half of the town. There were buildings and people that she didn't recognize, a lot of them, and more buildings going up all the time. At least twenty new houses already stood, and there were twice that many sites where men dug or sawed or hammered. There were still plenty of tents and shelters out on the Commons, but the Bovali refugees were being quickly resettled as housing became available, she could see.

She also sent her familiar (as she had begun thinking of her falcon, thanks to Gareth's advice) to the top of distant Matten's Helm. The small mountain dominated the center of the vale, dividing Brestal Vale from Sevendor Vale proper, and loomed over the entire valley like a benevolent spirit. It was as close to the center point of Sevendor as mattered, and from it she could see into all of the Vale, through her falcon. Dara had never been that far away from home, in person, but she could see the hill from the entrance to the Westwood . . . and from the air. In fact, you could see it from just about everywhere in Sevendor.

She spent the day exploring the empty mountaintop and its environs in Frightful's guise before hunger and a headache forced her to encourage Frightful to return home. Sending Frightful so far away was risky, she knew, especially at this age. But then most falconers did not have the option of using magic to affect their charges. It only took the faintest tug on Frightful's mind through their rapport to convince her to turn back to her owner's hand.

Guiltily she realized after spending a week exploring Sevendor from the air that she had woefully neglected Frightful's practical hunting exercises. She focused back on training for a week, but it seemed pointless, now. It was almost effortless to slip into the bird's mind and direct her to seek, to hunt, and to return with her kill now.

There were other side-effects of the secret practice. Dara noted with a bit of alarm, one morning, when she woke up completely ravenous that she herself was not particularly hungry . . . but the bird at the foot of her bed was starving and making a ruckus in her head. The two beady black eyes looked at her accusingly, a new wave of hunger rolling across her mind like a thunderstorm until Dara got up and gave the bird a morsel to keep her quiet. Only after she fully regained wakefulness – and Frightful was gleefully devouring the bit of chicken - did the gnawing feeling inside her subside.

It was an odd feeling, fielding emotions that did not originate in her own mind, but once she got used to discriminating which feelings were hers and which were her falcon's, Dara found it a useful method of communication. She tested the limits of that control as often as she could. One morning she flew Frightful in a full hunt in the meadow, scoring two small brown rabbits, without once using a call or signal. She just directed the bird with her mind and let her do the rest.

Dara got used to the pressure she felt with the connection, too. But, as Gareth said, maintaining the bond became easier and easier with practice.

When her Uncle Keram finally asked to inspect her hunt to check on her progress, he was amazed at how tame, docile, and obedient Frightful was for Dara – one more good reason not to mention her Talent. She hunted the falcon until she brought back a fat dove for his inspection.

"Well done!" he boomed, proudly, as the dead bird was dropped at their feet. "You really have a knack for this, Little Bird!"

"We've been working really hard, for weeks," she assured him. "I think we're about ready to go after a full-sized hare, now. She's almost big enough to bring one down!"

"I think so, too," Keram agreed, as he inspected the falcon. "You've taken remarkably good care of her, for lacking a proper mews. She's as healthy as any falcon I've seen."

"She's beautiful," Dara nodded, smiling benevolently at her falcon as she slipped the hood back over her eyes. "And getting more clever by the day."

"I was wondering if you'd like to take her to the village when I go next market day. You're old enough to tend the booth and earn a few pennies, and I think you'd like to show off that pretty bird."

Dara's mouth gaped. Outside of festivals, market days were about the most exciting thing a child of the Westwoods could attend. Dara had been six times and each trip had been an adventure. The prospect of going with her falcon on her arm was just too good to pass up.

By right and tradition, Westwood Hall maintained a regular booth at the market to sell the estate's surplus. Each of the young folk of the Westwood got an opportunity to man the booth, and get paid a few pennies for their service, while their elders shopped from the other stalls or discussed business with the vale folk. It was a rite of passage, one reserved for those who were ready to begin bearing the responsibilities of adulthood.

A category to which Dara realized, to her shock, she apparently qualified. She gravely thanked her uncle and then excitedly went to prepare.

Market day dawned warm and clear, and Dara was up with the sun and ready to depart with the rest of the sleepy-eyed group when it was light enough to walk across the bridge without falling into the chasm. Three great wheelbarrows were taken laden with wares: nuts, herbs, some early berries, leatherwork, some smoked venison and ham, and a thick stack of freshly-cured buckskins. When they returned, the carts would contain the things the estate needed that it couldn't produce: cheese, barley, oats, wheat, and maize, perhaps cloth.

Dara was impressed and excited by seeing the changes to Sevendor Village since the last time she'd been, in person. Seeing it from the air had been one thing, but she noticed things on the ground that had completely escaped Frightful's attention.

Once a small collection of round huts clustered around the headman's longhouse, the village had been transformed – as if by magic – by the Magelord and his Bovali immigrants. There was nary a roundhouse left. They had been replaced by sturdy timber longhouses, some with stone foundations – turned white, where they had been affected by the Snow That Never Melted – and thatched with reeds. A few larger structures had been built, great timber buildings that were growing roofs of baked tile. The old yeoman's house, where Railan the Steady had dominated the village since living memory, had been entirely knocked down. It was now the site of a proper manor hall under construction. Another large building was growing across the street – and it *was* a proper street, paved for a hundred feet along its length with gleaming white cobbles. It even had a gutter down the center that drained it into Ketta's Stream. Smaller buildings were being built around them, just as sturdy and expensive. Shops, Dara realized. Like permanent market stalls, where artisans lived and worked and sold their wares. A blacksmith, a carpenter, and other skilled laborers were already in residence.

As many houses and shops as were being built, the village Commons was still covered in tents, lean-tos, and make-shift shelters. Over a thousand Bovali were still living in temporary quarters, she learned as they walked to the market. Dara couldn't see how they could build that many houses in Sevendor Village, but she also learned what was to become of the new arrivals. Most would be moved farther away, to the entrance of the vale, where a new village was being built on the site of the one the Warbird had burned when she was a baby.

Dara didn't know how she felt about that. How could you just *create* a new village? Villages were something that just *were*, not something you built.

Then she decided that was silly – a child's understanding of such things. Villages were just collections of houses, after all. Houses could be built. People could move into them. That's all a village was, she reasoned. The idea of another village in Sevendor Vale was strange, but no less strange than magelights or the other changes the Magelord had contrived.

The sheer number of people packed into the market now was daunting, she felt, as they reached the plaza of hard-packed dirt (now a dirty white). Her fuzzy memories of her previous trips recalled a lively crowd, but not one nearly as large or as densely-packed. Even in the early morning hours, as the other merchants set up their stalls, there were more people in the market than Dara remembered being there at midday.

As the Westwoodmen busied themselves with preparing their own wares for the day, Dara had to calm Frightful, who was easily spooked by the noise. Dara eventually had to hood the bird and tie her to her block to keep her from threatening passers-by. There were a lot of admirers, too. Before the old bronze bell rang to signal the start of trading, dozens of folk had come by the booth to gaze upon Frightful's regal bearing and beautiful plumage.

Dara took a lot of pride in that admiration, particularly when she was asked who had captured and trained her. Dara ended up telling the story a dozen times that day to all sorts of people, many who were skeptical of her truthfulness. Her Uncle Keram came to her defense each time, insisting that Dara alone had been clever and strong and brave enough to make it to the peak, and then back down again with her bird safely in hand.

It wasn't just Dara's pride he was feeding, though, she realized. Frightful's attractive feathers and the tale of her capture and training lured people to the Westwood booth all day, and business was good as a result.

Dara didn't mind helping out the Hall, of course – that was ever a Westwoodman's duty – but she was just as glad to be given leave to wander the grounds midmorning to stretch her legs. Her uncle even gave her a few pennies to spend, his generosity fueled by the boost her bird had given sales. Dara took the tiny coins and eagerly began looking at what wares were available.

She stopped at a few booths to see what they'd brought and was disappointed. Most of the items were common household goods or foodstuffs. The Bovali were hungrily buying up much of what was available, and there were few luxuries available that she desired. Dara soon found herself more entertained by just listening to the conversations of the people at market than shopping.

She soon learned far more about the goings-on in the world beyond the Westwood than she had in the last year. To her surprise she discovered the dour Wilderlands castellan of the Magelord, Sir Cei, had triumphed at the Chepstan Fair tournament, winning not only a domain of his own but the hand of a fair young widow. The champion had declared he would not give up his current post, and his bride would come live in Sevendor Castle with him after they were wed.

More exciting than even that was the news that the Magelord himself had been attacked by some wicked magi, (the Censorate, she overheard) at the Fair, and had to get no less than Baron Arathaniel to intervene. That was terribly scandalous, she knew – *no one* fought at a fair. That was like lying in front of the Flame. Even Dara knew that and she hadn't even been to one.

But the more ominous news concerned the ongoing feud their lord had been suffering with the Warbird – the lord of

West Fleria, Sire Gimbal. Bad old Sir Erantal had been a friend of his, she knew, and she secretly worried the corrupt knight would somehow use his powerful friend to strike back at her home. The Warbird had been a name of quiet dread in her ears for her entire life, as tales of the brutal knight's conquests of his neighbors had become local history. Brestal, the easternmost estate in Sevendor, had been conquered by the Warbird's men before it had been recovered by the Spellmonger.

Dara found it interesting how the opinions she overheard diverged, depending upon who held them. The native Sevendori (who were now a minority at market, she noted, amused, even if you added the Westwoodmen into the sum) were fearful and cautious about the idea of the fearsome Warbird setting his eyes on Sevendor. They saw the Magelord's defiance against him as a reckless taunt against a powerful foe, and they muttered that no good would come of it.

The immigrant Bovali, on the other hand, seemed to encourage their lord's feud. The strangely-dressed, odd-accented mountain people were convinced of the Magelord's righteousness and his ability to defend the domain, should it come to blows. Indeed, they seemed to welcome the chance to go to war against the Warbird, and made no end of jest about it.

The Riverlands folk who had come to Sevendor recently seemed somewhere in the middle. The carpenters and smiths, merchants and artisans who had been attracted to the Magelord's coin had little opinion of the Warbird, specifically, nor of the Magelord. They just wanted to keep making profit and avoid war that would disrupt it – perhaps the most commonsense perspective, in Dara's opinion.

She was trying to casually listen in on a heated conversation between two Genlymen and a Bovali settler when she felt someone come up behind her.

"Oh, it is *you*," a familiar voice said. "I didn't think there could be two redheads your size in the valley."

Dara whirled at the unexpected interruption and saw it was the mage Gareth. He was wearing a pointed cap, his short but gawky body leaning on a plain wooden staff, his mantle flung back. His grin was wide and his eyes were smiling. She started to relax and then got tense again – *why would he want to talk to her?* She wasn't even fainting!

"Gareth!" she said. "What are you . . . ?"

"Me? Master Banamor is overseeing a lot of the market, now, and he hired me to help. He even has a booth of his own, selling magic supplies. Here, come with me and I'll show you."

"*Magic* supplies?" she asked, confused and intrigued. She had no idea what that might be.

"Oh, just some basics, for now: parchment, ink, a few herbs, some stones. He's even created a few trinkets to help spur sales. Not many buyers and not much inventory, yet, but there's more of both on the way."

"What do you mean?" she asked, confused.

"The Magelord has decreed that Sevendor is to host the first-ever magic fair this autumn," he explained, as he walked her to his booth. "He decided it would help encourage magic, now that the Bans are lifted, if the various footwizards and enchanters and such had a place to come and exchange important wares and news and the like. And encourage trade in general. He's already made some promising local discoveries, that could enrich a few folk. There's really a market for that sort of thing, and he'd like to see Sevendor fill it. Come autumn, this whole market and Commons will be filled with wizards from all over the Duchy. And beyond," he promised.

"That's . . . it's going to be *here?*"

"That's his plan," promised Gareth with a grin. "I heard it from Tyndal himself – that's the Magelord's senior apprentice, Sir Tyndal," he boasted. "A knight mage."

"The Magelord has apprentices?"

"Two," Gareth said. "He was a Spellmonger before he was a Magelord, and they were both apprenticed to him before his ennoblement. And they distinguished themselves at the battles, last year, enough to be knighted by the Duke himself. But between you and me," he confided, "they're both a little pigheaded. Especially Tyndal. Rondal's all right – he's supposed to drop by the booth today – but they're restoring the old gate tower, now, by the dike—

"The what?"

"Master Minalan and his apprentices used magic to raise an earthen wall and ditch across the low pass," explained Gareth. Dara understood what he was talking about now – the strange new construction she could see from Matten's Helm. Frightful just didn't have the understanding to know what was going on. "That dike and the new tower will help protect us from men like the Warbird. But Tyndal and Rondal are both working on it and they just about hate the sight of each other," he added, amused. He stopped in front of the booth. It looked rather sparse, compared to its nearby competitors.

"Not much to look at now," admitted Gareth, sheepishly, "but Master Banamor thinks that there's a real possibility Sevendor could become as famed for magic as Gilmora is for cotton. Especially now that the Snow That Never Melted happened. From what I can tell, all this white stone makes it ridiculously easy to do magic here, now. That's going to attract a lot of wizards."

"It is?" Dara asked, curious.

"It already has," nodded the skinny youth, solemnly. "There have been all manner of footwizards and magi who have come to the Castle. Enough so that two new inns are being planned."

"Inns? Here in Sevendor?" That was unheard of. *No one* came to Sevendor. It wasn't on the way to anyplace else, and there was really no reason to come here. Only, now there *was* a reason to come, Dara figured, so she decided an inn or two wasn't a bad idea. From what her father and Uncle Keram had told her, inns were dens of wickedness. She hadn't asked them to elaborate, yet, but she suspected some of the things that went on there, from the hushed tones they took.

"Not just inns, but all sorts of other things," promised Gareth. "Magelord Minalan has invested a lot of money in this valley. Probably more than it's worth — no offense — but he wants to make it better. With magic. He's already starting to build a mill pond so you don't have to go outside of the domain to grind your grain."

"We use our own grinding stone," Dara pointed out. "The boys take turns with the crank. But we don't eat as much bread as the villeins." A mill wasn't that impressive, to a Westwoodman. But Dara did have to admit to herself that it would be a boon for the peasants. "And what does magic have anything to do with a mill, anyway?"

"They're using magic to build it. I'm sure they'll use magic to run it somehow — not really my field of study. But the wizards and magi will be coming. Especially once the Magic Fair is held." He stopped and looked at her searchingly, which startled Dara. "How has the bilocation been going?" he asked, quietly.

"I . . . I've been practicing. I'm getting pretty good at it. I can do it in flight, now."

"That's impressive," Gareth nodded. "Is the change in perspective hard to contend with?"

"It takes getting used to," she said, suddenly grateful at the opportunity to discuss the matter with someone — anyone. Keeping the secret was difficult, but the hardest part was not being able to talk about it to other people. "When you're that far up in the air and you look down, you see the whole world differently. Not just from up high, which is bad enough — believe me, I know — but you see it differently. You see and notice different things. It's . . . strange."

"That's magic," chuckled the mage, picking at his mantle. "Have you been able to manage it with other animals?"

"*Other* . . . animals?" Dara asked, confused. "What do you mean?"

"Few Beastmasters use only one animal. In fact, from what I've read, most of their study involves learning how to inhabit many different kinds of animals. Each one is a different kind of challenge. It's supposed to get easier with practice, but it takes years to learn how to do it well."

"I'd never thought about that," Dara admitted. "Uh, Gareth? Can I beg a boon and ask that you not mention my . . . my bilocation to anyone just yet?" she asked. "Not while I'm still practicing, at least."

"Well, sure," agreed Gareth, reluctantly. "Although I don't know what's so bad about it. Beastmastery is a great Talent to have. And it may lead to more."

"That's why. Right now it's taking everything I can do to train Frightful. The bilocation has helped that, but while I'm learning that *and* falconry, well, it's just easier not to complicate things."

"And that way no one knows you're using your Talent to train your bird," Gareth guessed. "They just think you're a really, *really* good falconer."

Dara blushed. She hadn't thought of it that way. "Something like that. I'm just already the redheaded freak of nature, running around in the Westwood with my pet bird and not doing proper things like needlework and looking at boys. Only a few people even know I have Talent. It's just easier to contend with it without everyone staring at me. Even more."

"Your secret is safe with me, Dara of Westwood," Gareth grinned. "I don't think—"

Dara never learned what Gareth didn't think, because at that moment a ruckus was raised nearby. Angry shouts and snarls, the sound of men arguing. Immediately the crowd parted, as it does when tempers flare and fists might fly, and the heads of all turned toward the noise.

Three men – a Bovali man and two native Sevendori, Dara noted – were having an argument, and it did, indeed, look as if it would come to blows. It was hard to piece together from the shouts, and was made worse by the Bovali man's western accent, but it was clear that the Sevendori felt the Bovali man had cheated them, somehow. A goat was involved.

But the acrimony seemed to spark some resentment among the rest of the crowd. Dara noticed the native Sevendori, particularly those from the hamlets of Genly and Gurisham, seemed eager to find a reason to fight with the Bovali immigrants.

The Bovali in the market, on the other hand, were just as quick to come to the aid of their countryman. Worse, the Bovali seemed to have an awful lot of long knives and other weaponry about them. Sevendori peasants did not carry arms – such a thing was an affront to the nobility – but the Bovali had fought for their lives escaping their homeland, Dara had heard, and the habit of being armed was a hard one for them to break.

As tempers rose and the crowd pressed in, segregating into two sides around the arguing men, Dara realized with horror that she might just be in the middle of the first violent riot in recent Sevendori history.

"Stay behind me," Gareth warned, although how the skinny, failed warmage expected to protect Dara was uncertain. The shouting was getting louder and louder, and another Bovali man jumped in to defend his fellow. The Sevendori pushed. A fist was drawn back. The crowd held its breath, waiting for the inevitable fight to begin.

"HOLD!" came a bellow from the rear of the crowd. The shout was so strong and so commanding that everyone did as they were told – they halted, and looked around.

A large man with a wide face and a new-made mantle strode into the center of the altercation. Railan the Steady, Dara recognized, the former Yeoman of Sevendor Village. Now the Yeoman of Genly Hamlet. He had a fierce look in his eyes as he put a hand on a shoulder of two combatants and pushed them apart.

"Are you mad?" shouted the village leader. "Will you bring the wrath of the Spellmonger down on us all?" he demanded of the Sevendori from his new village. Railan had been one of the leading voices in the vale for years, she knew, and had used his influence to quietly combat Sir Erantal's excesses. Dara would have thought the man would have welcomed his replacement, but as it had led to his dispossession and demotion, she supposed she could see why he might not see the Magelord in an entirely positive light.

"The wrath of the Spellmonger?" one of the Bovali men asked. "We don't need Master Min to settle our affairs for us! It's the wrath of the Bovali you should fear!"

"Enough of that talk!" barked another man, an older Bovali with a dark green mantle and a thick beard. "We're here to trade, not fight. It's no one's wrath you should fear, it's the loss of coin. Is there no proper marketwarden to sort this out?"

"In our time we did not need such things to trade," Railan the Steady shot back. "We could trust that it could be done with decency and fairness."

"We saw what you had to trade when we got here, mate," a Bovali accent called from the crowd. "It don't take much decency to trade a handful of sticks for a handful of rocks!" The jibe sparked a ripple of laughter among the Bovali. The Sevendori peasants took offense to the joke.

"And now we pay thrice the value of a single egg, thanks to you lot!" growled one of the Sevendori combatants, angrily.

"And thrice the value of your labor, you lazy sods!" came another Bovali retort.

"ENOUGH!" shouted Railan, angrily. "Have you no appreciation for the danger we're in? Our land lies under the rule of a wizard and is cursed by the very gods. This Snow That Never Melted is a sign!"

"Yeah, a sign we're all going to be bloody rich," Gareth whispered to Dara. "Doesn't that sodfoot realize that yet?" She was a bit shocked at his temerity, openly criticizing an elder – and a man of rank - that way, but she was also a little thrilled to be taken into his confidence, like an adult. It emboldened Dara to offer her own opinion.

"He's just plowed under because he's now the leader of Genly, and he has to watch his old home turn into a proper village. He was once the third most important man in Sevendor domain," she pointed out, in a whisper. "Now he's just the most important man in Genly."

The insults and japes between the two parties had continued, airing a lot of grievances on both sides along the way. If Dara had to learn about the folk of Sevendor for the first time from hearing the lively voicing of differences, she would have discovered that the Bovali were dirty cow herders, that the Sevendori were lazy villeins, that the Bovali were arrogant heathens from the Wilderlands, that the Sevendori were unmanly dullards too ignorant to realize the sun was shining, that the Bovali were scheming drunkards intent on destroying the vale . . . as the insults flew, they got more personal and more profane.

As frightening as it was to Dara, knowing violence could break out at any time, it was also terribly exciting to witness. As a Westwoodman, she felt a bit neutral in the debate. Indeed, the Westwood folk generally agreed with many of the Bovali's criticisms of the vale folk – they'd been making the same observations for years.

But she had to admit that the Sevendori peasants were just as apt about their descriptions of the newcomers. As a Westwoodman she might agree with the Bovali assessment of the native peasants, but as a Sevendori she also could sympathize with the villeins.

The Bovali had changed the nature of the vale since they'd arrived. The economy, the politics, the language, the food had all transformed within a short time. They had all hated Sir Erantal's corrupt reign and had always looked forward to its inevitable end . . . but they hadn't anticipated the upheaval it brought, and they were scared. A new lord would have been difficult enough for the simple peasants to contend with. A new lord who was also a wizard was disconcerting, and a new wizard lord who came with an army of strangers made the changes terrifying.

"You certainly look better fed now than when I first saw you!" the Bovali man in the green cloak was barking at Railan. The original combatants had faded into the crowd, at this point, as leaders among the two parties took it upon themselves to argue on behalf of their folk. "If this land is cursed, it's cursed with plenty!"

"Honest hunger is better, in the eyes of the gods, than a plenty purchased with sorcery!" Railan countered.

"Sorcery? Master Min paid good coin for that fare," bragged the Bovali man – who Gareth told her was named Rollo, a leader of some importance among the Bovali. "Or beat it out of the Warbird's whelp. But he's not used a spell to conjure it, from the way he complains of the cost!"

"And how long until that resentment turns to spite?" asked Railan, appealing to the crowd as much to Rollo. "How long until the wizard comes down out of his keep and turns his wrath on us?"

"Why would you give him reason to?" demanded Rollo. "Master Min is a fair man, more than most, and a better lord than you lot deserve. First thing he did when he got here was tear up the stocks – I don't recall you being upset by that. He's been nothing but openhanded."

"At what price?" countered Railan. "What have we lost in return for this . . . generosity?"

"Poverty?" suggested Dara, boldly and loudly, before she realized her mouth was moving. Her high, feminine voice cut through the noise of the debate like a knife, and every head turned to stare at her.

She immediately regretted speaking. But once her lips began moving, however, they seemed to take on a life of their own. Ignoring her station, youth, and gender, her lips boldly dragged her into the attention of the entire marketplace.

"Fear? Corruption? Injustice? Starvation? Your old threadbare cloak?" she added, a bit sarcastically, knowing that Railan had considered his sturdy old mantle a badge of his position . . . yet he had tossed it away for the one the Spellmonger had gifted him with quickly enough.

That brought a titter of derisive laughter from both sides of the crowd. And earned Dara a deadly look from Railan the steady.

"Impudent girl!" he spat. "What does a child of the Westwood know about the affairs beyond the chasm?"

Dara realized uncomfortably that she was now part of this debate. And she was forced to speak not just on her behalf, but on behalf of her whole kin. She had an obligation, by the Flame, to bring honor to the Hall. She swallowed. This was easily more terrifying than dangling off of the side of a mountain.

But her father and her uncle would want her to be just as brave. She took a deep breath, chose her words carefully, and let her impudent lips loose upon the debate.

"We woodfolk can see the whole vale, from the heights," she countered, evenly, the same way she would have faced off another child in an argument. "The crops are growing in this 'cursed' ground, the people are fed and at honest labor, we serve a proud and just lord, and we have Brestal Vale back," she counted off on her fingers.

That made Railan blush. From what she understood, he had had something to do with provoking the Warbird into conquering the estate in the first place. But once going, with everyone's attention upon her, Dara found she could not stop speaking. "Seems to this child of the Westwood that the only one whose station has fallen since the Magelord arrived is Railan the Steady's . . . and for some reason you want to convince us all that a kettle full of stew is a chamberpot!"

The metaphor struck the crowd as apt and funny, and the laughter that erupted on both sides made the big village elder's broad face turn red. Angrily he stalked toward Dara until he was mere feet away, standing with his hands on his hips.

"And when that Magelord brings the wrath of the Warbird down on us, and it is your kin going to war and your virtue as the prize, will you think so highly of full bellies and pretty clothes? What will you think of the kettle, then?" he demanded with a snarl.

He was trying to intimidate Dara with his size, his station, and his age. But that just made her mad.

"I'll think that the Westwoodmen haven't forgotten their valor, and we'll serve our rightful lord in the defense of our domain, as we have sworn by oath! I would hope a Yeoman who swore that oath himself would remember that," she added, ignoring his size, station, and age. Railan was just a bully, she decided, and while she knew she was getting deeper and deeper into trouble with every word, she hated bullies of any stripe. Kobb had given her that gift.

That was the fatal blow to his argument, too. There was a loud moan from the crowd – calling out both Railan's valor and his oathkeeping would have instigated a duel, perhaps, if she were a grown man. Coming from a child, it was a doubly sharp barb. It also turned the tenor of the crowd, she realized. No longer were Bovali and Sevendori segregating their opinions by class. Dara's words rang too true in the ears of all to be lightly dismissed. Everyone could see that Railan's ire was mere jealousy, now, and his empty threats of future retribution were mere fear-mongering.

"Impudent girl," he growled, as the crowd began to dissolve, its energies spent. "It's unwise to interfere in affairs you know nothing about!"

"I'm an ignorant girl from the Westwood," Dara admitted, in a more conversational tone. "So go ahead, tell me I'm wrong. Tell my father I'm wrong. Tell anyone I'm wrong. I'm sure they'll believe you over me. But the Magelord is a good lord, and he's far better than Sir Erantal, and some of us have the sense to see that. But what do I know?" she said, tauntingly.

"I'll see you beaten for this!" he snarled.

"You'll do no such thing, Master Railan," Gareth suddenly intervened. "Dara spoke her mind, and said much others would have said. The Magelord doesn't agree with children being beaten for having opinions, I imagine."

"Another cursed wizard!" spat Railan. "You'll bring doom and destruction on us all," he warned Gareth. "And you'll be the ones to help!" he added, jabbing an accusing finger at Dara.

"Doom and destruction?" Dara snorted, looking around at the busy market. There were easily four times more people there than in the markets she remembered. Instead of making her feel intimidated, the audience emboldened her – particularly when she saw several sympathetic faces nodding toward her in the crowd. Both Sevendori and Bovali faces. "You sound like a bad character in a minstrel's story, Master Railan! Look at how full this market is! This looks like prosperity, not doom and destruction. If this is the curse we get for living under a magelord . . . I think we can live with it!"

Chapter Eleven

To Arms!

"Little Bird, why did you have to go open your beak like that?" complained her father sadly, that night after dinner. News of her ugly debate with Railan had spread across the Westwood like fire, and the repercussions of her bold speech were swift. Her father had quickly taken her aside, to his accustomed seat near the Flame, and began chastising her as soon as the trenchers had been cleared away.

She knew she had a lecture coming for her behavior, but Dara wasn't ready to be cowed, yet. She was still angry.

"I didn't say anything that I wouldn't say in front of the Flame," she promised, her eyes automatically glancing to the dancing fire. Lying in front of the Flame was shameful. "And he called me impudent," she added, irritated.

"Proving that even Railan the Steady can recognize that water is wet," her father said, darkly. "Dara, do you realize what you have done? Not only did you challenge a powerful man, you insulted him."

"I just reminded him of the same oath you both took to the Magelord," she said, defiantly.

"And since when is it your place to remind powerful men of such things?" her father countered.

"Isn't that what impudent girls do?" Dara asked, boldly. "Gareth told me that I only got away with it because I'm a cute girl!"

"Who is Gareth?" her father demanded, confused.

"He's a mage I met at market," Dara said, her eyes darting guiltily at the Flame. Technically, she met him in a field, but she reasoned that she wasn't implying, necessarily, that she had met him for the very first time at market . . . unless her father chose to interpret it that way. The Flame, by all accounts, was more forgiving. "He's very nice. He was going to protect me, if things got . . . violent."

"A mage? You're consorting with wizards, now?"

"Aren't you? We are ruled by one!" she challenged, boldly.

Dara fully expected Kamen to explode in rage at the defiance, but to her surprise he caught himself and immediately calmed.

"And that fact alone may spare this Hall some grief you've earned it," he sighed. "Magelord Minalan is a fair man, and Railan the Steady is not an enthusiastic supporter of our lord . . . as you discovered," he said, with a quiet chuckle. "And it seems that every malcontent left in the vale has gathered to hear his whining. Because it serves our lord's purpose, politically, to have Railan cut down a peg in front of everyone, I don't think he'll take seriously any request by the man to have you beaten."

Dara looked up sharply. She hadn't really considered the Yeoman's threat seriously.

"Oh, yes, that would be within his rights," her father agreed to her unasked question. "You are not yet of age. Had old Sir Erantal heard Railan's complaint, he might have you beaten just to spite me. And I mean a beating with a sheaf of willow reeds by the reeve, over the old stocks, in the commons, on market day. The kind you take a few days to recover from," he said, with a look in his eye that told Dara he'd experienced such a state personally. "It is no small thing, Little Bird. What you said was bold, no one would say different. But it was also dangerous."

"There were plenty at market who agreed with me!" she countered.

"That's why it was dangerous," her father replied. "The vales are on edge right now. The Magelord has made enemies of our neighbors, and those, like Railan, who were raised in fear and know nothing but submission are terrified of what may come. War," he said, after a pause, as if speaking the word aloud before the Flame would make it come to pass. "It is a possibility."

Dara's heart sank. Everyone dreaded war. They still told stories of the day, a century before, when the vales were full of men and the fields burst with crops . . . until the Lord of Sevendor marched away with three hundred of the vale's best men, and never returned. And of the night, when she was just a baby, when the Warbird's men burned down a village and took Brestal Vale away in one bloody raid. The Westwoodmen had been safe behind their chasm, but the rest of the estates in the vale had been forced to suffer while the corrupt lord who was supposed to protect them looked on.

"But . . . we have the Magelord," she said, almost in a whisper.

"Mage he might be, but he is still a lord, and lords wage war," her father said, quietly. "His magic won't keep the wolves at bay. We've heard disturbing things at market, and not just from Railan's lips. The Warbird is angry, it is said, over the insults he perceives our lord to have committed against him. He is preparing troops. No one knows when he might strike, but there is also unrest in Sashtalia, to the west of Sevendor, as the Warbird's agents stir up trouble. If the Warbird marches against us, it is likely that we will be assailed from two sides."

Dara swallowed, barely able to breathe. Caolan's Pass was half a day's walk from this very spot, she knew, and beyond that . . . beyond that lie the enemies of Sevendor, from what her father was saying. Worse, in the event of war, the Westwood was pledged to guard that pass. Her family.

"I'm . . . I'm sorry, Father," Dara said, formally. "I should have held my tongue. I knew not what was at stake, and thought I merely spoke my mind."

Kamen looked at his daughter in the light of the Flame with approval. "The Westwoodmen learn early how it is more important to listen to what is said than to be heard. You are learning the beginnings of wisdom, Dara. It looks good on you. But we both know just how spiteful Railan can be. I think it would be best for all concerned if you avoided the market for a few weeks until this matter is behind us. Spend the days hunting and training that splendid bird. By midsummer things should have blown over."

* * *

"Just what will happen at the Magical Fair?" Dara asked Gareth, two weeks later when she again found herself at market. Frightful had been adept at attracting onlookers, and Kamen had not hesitated to capitalize on the beautiful bird. If that meant he had to bring Dara along, too, he was willing to bear it. The row between the Westwood and Genly had blown over, just as her father had suggested it would, replaced in the minds of the marketgoers by the latest gossip from the castle.

She had found Gareth wandering around the stalls, idly gazing at the wares and keeping an eye on the proceedings as a good marketwarden should. As the Bovali and the Sevendori seemed less inclined to fight, this time, that meant he was bored for much of the time – and that gave Dara a few precious minutes to ask him questions.

"Well, it will be like any old fair, I suppose," Gareth shrugged. "Lots of merchants, lots of food, probably a couple of fights. Only it will be all wizards, or mostly wizards so . . . well, no one really knows," he finally admitted. "No one has ever had one before."

"Why not?"

"Such things were actually illegal, under the old Censorate of Magic – or at least strongly discouraged. The Censorate never liked it when too many wizards got together at once and starting talking and trading. So when Master Minalan decided to break the tradition, he figured Sevendor was the best place to hold it. After the Censorate tried to arrest him at Chepstan Fair . . ." he said, shaking his head with a grin, "they should know better than to come to Sevendor."

"But they will be selling . . . magical things?"

"They'll mostly be selling boring old regular things that you can use to make magical things," explained the young mage, "but I'm sure they'll be plenty of demonstrations. And of course there's some sort of tournament or contest."

That got Dara's attention. "What kind of contest?"

"Master Min is being a bit secretive about it, but from what I understand there will be some sort of open competition among all low magi. The winner, it is rumored, will be given . . . a witchstone." He said the word in hushed tones, as if speaking of something sacred.

"A witchstone? What's that?"

Gareth looked at her in surprise. "You really don't know a lot, do you?"

"Hey!" Dara protested. "I've just turned thirteen!"

"I forget, sometimes," Gareth chuckled. "Witchstones are made up of irionite, the mages call it. It's a kind of magical green amber. It has the power to magnify the potency of any mage who uses one. More than tenfold, it is said. It can turn a powerful mage into a great mage, or a mediocre mage into a good one. It's nearly unlimited. And incredibly illegal, according to the Censorate."

"So how did the Magelord get some?"

"Do you jest?" asked Gareth, amused. "That's the whole reason he was given Sevendor. He took a witchstone from a goblin shaman in battle, away in the Minden mountains. He used it to fight the goblins, last year, and he helped other magi get some. The Duke of Castal said he could keep it. In defiance of four hundred years of Censorate laws and ducal tradition."

This was all news to Dara, who had always thought of magi as either great and powerful or weak and tricky vagabonds. "So why did the Duke do that?"

"No one knows," admitted Gareth. "Politics, most likely. But by doing that he broke the power of the Censorate to regulate magic in Castal. And threw them out. They're awful, to ordinary magi. They wear long black and white checkered cloaks and hunt down clandestine magi. Hedgewizards, footwizards, village witches, anyone with Talent who isn't properly registered. And they enforced the Bans on Magic against the registered magi. No one liked them."

"Well, they don't sound very likable!"

"They're not. They arrest and execute magi all the time. They kept a lock on trade in magical materials to discourage any one mage from becoming too powerful. They're warmagi, only they don't answer to anyone but themselves. Even the Dukes fear them – or did, before Master Minalan came along. And the goblin invasion. When the Duke asked the Censorate if they could keep his people safe and they said no, he overturned the Bans and had the Censors ejected from the Duchy."

"That's . . . didn't he get into trouble?"

"With who? His fellow dukes? The Censorate swore allegiance to the king, and there hasn't been a king for over four hundred years, now. So there really isn't anyone who could get him into trouble. Anyway, because he did that now any mage can theoretically use witchstones, now that the Censorate is gone from Castal."

"Are they valuable?"

"One is worth enough to buy a barony," promised the mage. "Or an army. Or a fleet. You don't understand, Dara, they're precious. Far more than gold. Or gems. Or even lands. I came to Sevendor hoping to get one, and even though I failed as a warmagi, I'm still hoping I can convince Master Min . . ."

"So what kind of contest is it?" Dara interrupted, fascinated by the idea.

"I have no idea. I do know that a bunch of Master Min's closest and most powerful wizards are working on it. And that there are witchstones available that he could give away. So it's quite possible he would grant one of the lesser ones to a mage who distinguished himself in the contest. Apart from being a really good warmage, that might be about the only way you could get one."

"Surely they'll reserve that contest for practiced magi?"

"Or maybe Master Min enjoys watching the various wizards compete among themselves. From what Master

Banamor has told me, the contest will be open to anyone. And . . . between you and me," he said, looking around the crowded market with concern, "I think he likes to see how people respond to problems."

"So you're joining?"

"Me? No! I'm good," admitted the awkward young wizard, "but there are going to be warmagi with years of experience competing to keep me at the back of the line. And I'll probably be too busy working the fair to participate in it. Master Banamor has been announced as the Fairwarden, and as I'm already deputy Spellwarden, I'm sure I'll have five times too much to do to consider competing."

"So what kind of contest will it be?"

"I have no idea," sighed the young wizard, philosophically. "But it will be tough. Master Minalan has Lady Pentandra working on it. She's the one organizing all of the magi, now that the Censorate is gone. She's one of the most powerful magi in the duchies. So you can bet that the trial will be tough."

Dara could imagine Lady Pentandra, a dour old matron swathed in robes that concealed everything about her . . . except her piercing eyes. Dara shuddered at the vision – if that was the kind of mage who was designing the contest, and Gareth, a real wizard, was reluctant to try his mettle, Dara didn't think she had much chance. Her bilocation was going splendidly, but she didn't really know any actual magic beyond that.

"That's too bad," Dara agreed. "You deserve one of these witchstones, Gareth. You've been very nice to me."

"Me? It's me who should be thanking you. I don't know anyone in Sevendor, except for a few wizards. You're really the first native who's been . . . welcoming."

"We're really a kind of ignorant lot, aren't we?" she giggled.

"It makes me wonder why Master Minalan was so determined to build his estate here," he agreed. "I mean, you Sevendori are good people, don't mistake me. But . . . well, I suppose I'm just used to being around people who know how to read. Everyone at the academy did. Here . . . outside of the wizards, there probably aren't ten books in the domain."

"You are probably right," conceded Dara. "Maybe I'll learn, someday."

"You will if your Talent erupts," he assured her. "You can't really become an Imperially trained mage without knowing how to read. A wild mage, maybe . . . but why would you want to do that if you didn't have to?"

"Wild mage?"

"Someone who figures out magic on their own," Gareth explained. "Usually wrong. Or just wrong enough to be dangerous. There are a lot of natural, wild magi out there, and some of them even learn how to use their powers, after a fashion. If they aren't killed by the Censorate first. But Imperial training is what turns Talent into progress," he said, confidently.

"Who would want to train me?" snorted Dara. "Besides, I have a vocation. I'm a falconer," she said, smugly.

"A falconer who can ride behind the eyes of her falcon," Gareth said, softly. "You've still told no one?"

"Just you," she shrugged. "I don't think anyone else would believe me. Besides, I'm getting pretty good at it."

"Really? You're using it to hunt?"

"More than that," she assured him, grinning. To demonstrate, she stopped their walk and closed her eyes. In a moment she made contact with Frightful, thankful that she wasn't hooded. Or tied. The bird had gotten used to the people at the market very quickly, and was unlikely to stray from her perch. Until called.

A moment later, Dara thrust her wrist into the sky, her thick leather gauntlet donned for the occasion. In seconds a shadow streamed over them, and then Frightful was landing gracefully on her arm.

"See?" she smiled, feeding the bird a morsel as a reward, "it's a lot easier. I could even have told you what everyone's hats looked like, if you asked," she added, proudly.

"A deep and mysterious arcane skill, indeed," he said with false gravity. "But keep practicing. It will make you an adept . . . falconer."

She knew the young man was just teasing her, but she was grateful for the praise anyway. She had struggled mightily to train her falcon, and yet was barely respected for her efforts, back at the hall. Only Uncle Kamen, her father, and a few of her brothers were impressed with her. And none of them knew about her abilities – just that she had the potential to be a mage someday. Hearing from Gareth that she was doing well, developing her powers on her own, gave her the renewed motivation she needed to complete Frightful's training.

Dara hunted the bird relentlessly after that. All summer she beat to the high meadows as soon as the sun was up, working for rabbits and ermine one day, doves and partridges the next. At first she returned empty-handed, as often as not. Even with her magical abilities, Frightful was still inexperienced at the hunt and Dara was an inexperienced falconer.

But they got better, together. Later, as the summer waxed full, Dara would come home at night with one very tired falcon and a string of dead animals to leave for the tanners to clean and skin.

She never kept track of her kills – she was far more concerned with making a clean kill and then rewarding Frightful for her work than worrying about her haul – but near to midsummer her uncle approached her at breakfast, one rainy day when she and Frightful were confined to the manor, and dropped a small purse in front of her.

It clinked.

"What's this?" she asked, curious.

"Your pay," he said, expectantly. "From what Kobb says, you've brought in thirty-eight rabbit skins, twenty-one ermine, and Flame-only-knows how many other creatures in the last few weeks. The market has been selling well. There's nearly four ounces of silver in there," he said, respectfully.

Dara's eyes bulged. "Four OUNCES of silver?" she asked, incredulously.

"That's after the Hall takes its share," he reminded her as she started counting out the thin coins on the table. "Half, as is fair, to pay the tanners. But the rest is yours."

Four ounces of silver was a lot of money, even for the daughter of the Master of the Wood. While her father and Uncle Kamen handled a lot of money on behalf of the estate, she knew that most of her brothers, sisters, and cousins were constantly seeking coin. Four ounces of silver could purchase quite a bit: a full-grown goat, for instance, or a dozen chickens. It was rent on a hovel in the vale for half a year, or the cost of one quarter of a cow.

Dara couldn't even contemplate having that kind of fortune. A few pennies, sure, even a silver penny she'd gotten for her thirteenth birthday. But four ounces of silver was real money. The kind of money that adults made for their labor. She had no idea what to do with it – she wanted for little, and coveted few of the ornaments that she'd seen in the market. Her sisters could spend money like words, and seemed to desire everything they came across, but Dara was far more conservative in her tastes. In the end, she put the money with the rest of her savings in the base of the new block her cousin had built to keep her falcon in her room.

After that, Dara focused on hunting the falcon for rabbits and ermines, more than game birds, as the mammals were worth more for skins as well as meat. The day before the next market day she took five rabbits from the high meadows, which could be sold immediately at a higher price.

And she returned to the market to oversee how well her trade was doing.

She wandered the market and idly examined the booths, her money jingling in her pocket as she considered and rejected many of the wares on display. As was becoming habit, she found Gareth the Mage wandering around the square with his staff-of-office in hand, examining the well-behaved patrons. The two of them fell into an easy conversation, with Gareth inquiring about the health of her falcon and her family while Dara asked about the exciting life of a Deputy Spellwarden and part-time Marketwarden.

It turned out that such a life was not particularly exciting.

"It's been boring as a temple service, since the Magelord left for the capital," complained the mage, good-naturedly. "Sir Cei is keeping things well in hand, and Lady Alya is in charge, but really there's not much to do in this bloody valley in the summer but stand around and watch the wheat grow!"

"Hey! That's a revered local pastime!" giggled Dara. "If the vale folk didn't have their crops to dote on like children, they might take up hunting or something. Put my people out of business."

"It is, in its defense, some of the more exciting wheat I've seen," admitted Gareth with a chuckle. "And I'm mostly lying about being bored. Every week it seems Master Banamor has more work for me to do. Different work," he added. "He has great vision for Sevendor village. Unfortunately, that vision seems to require an awful lot of footwork from me, too."

"So why did the Magelord go to the capital?" Dara asked in a friendly way.

"The Duke called him to speak at the Coronet Council – that's the meeting between all five Dukes. They only happen every few years. But Duke Rard wanted him to speak before the council about the goblin invasion. And he's having some sort of convention among the top-level magi, while he's there. Court wizards and warmagi and such. He even took his apprentices . . . meanwhile I'm stuck here!"

"I'm sure they're having a horrible time," Dara suggested to the funny-looking mage with another giggle.

"Yes, choking on all of that rich food, being tortured by the finest musicians in the land, forced to dance with the fairest maids in the Duchy and make merry until all hours of the night . . ." grumbled Gareth. "I hope Tyndal and Rondal are miserable!"

Dara barely knew the Spellmonger's apprentices by sight, but apparently Gareth had a relationship with them that included a small bit of resentment and good-natured jealousy.

"Well, look at all of the fun they miss out on by not planning the Magic Fair," she said, taking his arm the way she'd seen her sister do to young men she walked with. It felt awkward, but it made her feel a bit more grown up. Gareth seemed surprised, but did not shy away from walking that way.

"Yes, not overseeing the sanitation requirements of an additional few thousand people is certain to gnaw at their souls," Gareth said, sarcastically. "I've been toiling for weeks on the fair, and do you know what responsibilities those two layabouts got? Building warding spells on the slopes of Matten's Helm for the contest! I have half a mind to—"

The wizard was interrupted as a commotion broke out near the center of the market when a horseman entered the dirt square at full gallop. Before the dust had even begun to settle around the man he was off his horse and shouting.

"The Warbird approaches!" the man managed, between heaving breaths. "To arms! I was riding south from Sendaria town when my way was blocked by a party barring me from Sevendor. They wore the Warbird's livery, and said that no traffic would pass until the valley was once again under the Warbird's control! I slipped by them, but they gave chase in a most warlike fashion. Worse, when I was coming through the low pass, Master Olmeg was being set upon by warriors – bandits, by their clothing, but they moved with assuredness of soldiers, not thieves! He slew two of them before he fell under their blows and would have died, had not our guards driven them off. The captain of the gate bid me deliver the message to arm to Sevendor!"

A thousand questions were volleyed at the poor rider in the next few seconds, and several men of importance beat their way through the crowd to hear a more complete tale. Important men, Dara noted: Yeoman Jurlor, her uncle, the yeoman from Gurisham, and – to her dismay – the tall form of Railan the Steady, Yeoman of Genly, was also crowded around the messenger. The man did his best to answer as best he could, but the cacophony was too much for him.

Suddenly a loud voice pierced the noise.

"BIDE!" it bellowed . . . and Railan the Steady was no longer the tallest man in the crowd. The impressive form of Sir Cei, Sevendor castle's Castellan, strode through the press of humanity wearing a long chain hauberk and his sword belted at his side. The tall man surveyed the crowd with his steely eyes, bidding them all to be silent with a glance, and then bent to hear the messenger's tale for himself.

Dara could not hear what was being said, but she and Gareth exchanged several worried glances.

"Do you think it's real?"

"They beat Master Olmeg!" the young mage snarled. "He's the nicest mage I know! It's real now!"

Dara was surprised at how upset the young man was getting – Gareth seemed like the gentlest of souls. It was hard for her to imagine him ever wanting to be a warmage . . . until now. The look on his face was pure hatred and contempt. It shocked Dara that her friend could change his visage so easily.

Sir Cei listened with rapt attention to the messenger's story before he straightened. "We have been attacked," he pronounced.

"Just as I said we would be, if we continued this madness!" Railan the Steady insisted loudly, as he looked to Jurlor and his fellow yeomen for support. They were the ones responsible for organizing the common folk in the defense of the domain. If Sevendor did not have the support of its Yeomen it would be hard to mount a defense, Dara realized.

"It is not your place to dictate policy to the Magelord," Sir Cei said, smoothly. "The crisis has found us; it is our lot to contend with it. Right or wrong the domain is under threat. I shall bear news of this to our lady and learn her mind on it," he said, grimly.

"You would allow the defense of the domain to be determined by a woman?" Railan asked, scornfully.

"The defense of the domain will be determined by its rightful lord – and Lady Alya is seated in that position, at the moment. I serve her faithfully," he added, darkly. "I would take offense at any sworn man who did not share my devotion."

"We sit on the edge of ruin and you—" Railan continued, again looking to Jurlor for assistance.

"Oh, shut up, Railan!" Jurlor, the ugly old yeoman of Jurlor's Hold, spat. "Olmeg's been beat and our folk attacked. Just like the last time he started trouble. You want to give Brestal back to him, do you, and hope he'll leave us alone?" demanded the man.

"Uh, oh!" Dara whispered.

"What?" Gareth whispered back.

"Railan is well-respected in Sevendor," admitted Dara of the Yeoman, "but not nearly as respected as Jurlor. Especially now that Railan was sent to run Genly, and Jurlor has prospered so much. Jurlor is known for his good sense, just as Railan is known for his stubbornness. If Jurlor is in favor of arming . . ."

"Why wouldn't he be?" Gareth asked, confused. "Aren't they obligated to by oath?"

"It happens, I hear," Dara said, repeating news she'd heard from her more-traveled cousins and uncles. "In fact, it happened here, the last time the Warbird raided the vales. Sevendor and Genly and Gurisham rose to the defense, but Farant's Hold and Southridge both barred their gates and did not. Usually the victors will be more inclined to bargain with holdouts like that, instead of punishing them."

"Wouldn't they only do that if they were certain which side will win?"

"Which Farant and Southridge apparently did, last time around. Far too cozy with Sir Erantal. But—"

"Wait!" Gareth said, harshly. "Sir Cei is speaking!"

The big knight took a single step up on top of a trestle table, and while the thing did not look happy about the weight of the armored knight, it did not collapse. Sir Cei cleared his throat and addressed the few hundred people in the market.

"It appears that Sire Gimbal, the Warbird of West Fleria, has taken affront to the justice of losing Brestal. He has mustered troops and sent raiders against us. I can only guess that further indignities will follow. While I have yet to learn Our Lady's mind on this matter, in my experience of her it is unlikely she will allow such a blow to go unanswered.

"Therefore I invite each of you to make whatever purchases you have left and return home – for on the morrow it is likely we will face a banner call. Remain calm. Go home, then, and take up your arms and your station."

The cry "To arms!" and "Sevendor!" was quickly taken up and spread like a wild fire through the crowd. Soon the market was emptying as folk hurried off with the news, or to find their family or neighbors to tell before the rush to the manor hall armories.

Dara felt dizzy as she stumbled her way through the crowd. She was fortunate that Gareth was escorting her, for a few times she nearly fell. But soon the young mage was depositing back in front of the Westwood's booth, a grim expression on his face.

"I need to go see to Master Olmeg," he explained through gritted teeth. Apparently Sir Cei's instruction to stay calm had little effect on Gareth. "And then I need to talk to some . . . people. I may not be a warmage, but I'm not going to let them hurt my friend like that and get away with it!" he said, adamantly, as he turned and pushed his way back through the crowd.

Dara's mind raced as she helped her family pack up their goods prematurely. No one was buying rabbit furs, now, or summer berries. They were buying bacon and sausage and cheese and wheat, all staples that could last a long time. Like if the valley was under siege for a long time.

As Dara and the other Westwoodmen trudged wearily back to their hall, she could still hear the cries all around her in the distance: "To arms! For Sevendor, *to arms!*"

HAWKMAIDEN

Chapter Twelve

Under Siege

The news came sporadically, after that, but the announcement was ordered by Lady Alya to be made to each manor in Sevendor, in the Magelord's absence: Sevendor would arm and defend itself against the aggression of the Warbird. From the highest tower in Sevendor Castle, the green banner with the white snowflake the Magelord had chosen as his device flapped in the breeze, a red ribbon flying from its tail. The war banner was flying. The men of the vale were called to muster.

The Westwood had been abuzz with activity ever since. The young men had been excused from their duties, the armory was opened, and they were issued spears, helmets, and arrows for their quivers. They drilled out in the yard, practicing marching and holding formations. Her father was busy, of course, mustering the menfolk of the manor together. He wore his armor constantly, even at meals. Dara was fascinated with watching them, at first, but then realized that all of the boys and men she saw marching so proudly may not return when the fighting was done.

After that she lost interest in watching their practicing.

The day after market day, news reached the Westwood about a successful raid the Sevendori had conducted – without orders – against a village in West Fleria. A lot of damage had been done, even if few enemy soldiers had been slain. That made her father look grim, but made her brothers grin.

"About time Sevendor struck a blow against the Warbird!" Kobb cackled. "They even used magic against the poor sods! Some of our sparks had a grudge for Master Olmeg, it seems!"

Dara was amused, until she remembered the look on Gareth's face when they'd parted. She could guess that he'd been involved with the raid. She hoped he'd not been injured.

Her concern for her friend was secondary after her concern for her family, however. Seeing her brothers and cousins and uncles drill and practice in the yard made her anxious, and she wasn't the only one. Her aunt couldn't concentrate, several of the girls in the kitchen were weepy, and the optimistic mood that Dara had gotten used to around Westwood Hall was gone, replaced with grim purpose.

Dara didn't know what to do with herself. So she went hunting.

Alone with Frightful in the high meadows to the north of the Westwood usually would have given her some peace. It was so remote and quiet up on that ridge that it was easy to forget there were any other people at all in Sevendor. Yet Dara couldn't concentrate on even basic drills while her brothers were marching. She felt helpless. But there was little she could do, despite her strong desire to do something.

It was frustrating. At the same time, she wanted to pick up a bow and join her brothers she also wanted to keep them in the Westwood, safe behind the chasm, and protect them. She could do neither she knew – which only added to her frustration. It infuriated her to think of enemy soldiers – old Sir Erantal's allies – skulking around outside of Sevendor's frontiers.

The valley had many natural defenses, particularly the strong ridges that bordered it on the north and south. No man could easily scale those. Sevendor could only be entered through the low pass at the mouth of the valley to the east – which the Magelord and his apprentices has strongly fortified since they had taken possession of the domain – or through the high pass to the north.

Caolan's Pass, it was called, a long, steep, narrow trail that wound up to the high pass into Sashtalia. At the top of it, at the ridgeline, was a single stone cottage and a simple wooden barricade. As the winding trail was difficult to climb, the pass was not impossible to defend. Traditionally Caolan's Pass was where the Westwoodmen were stationed in a time of emergency. Dara had only seen it from afar, as it was little used except by messengers or tradesmen from Sashtalia.

That pass was *so* close . . . particularly as the falcon flew.

When it was clear that Frightful wasn't particularly interested in hunting that day either, Dara allowed the bird to slip away over the ridge. She rationalized that she was just letting her bird get a little exercise, but there was no denying that she had higher purpose in what she did.

Seeing through Frightful's eyes, she guided the falcon over the ridge and down into the vale on the other side. It looked similar to Sevendor, but from Frightful's perspective the landforms were strange and unfamiliar.

Dara had her falcon glide slowly over the land, looking down as if she were hunting the far side of the ridge. Dara could see the long winding road up to Caolan's Pass from the other side of the ridge, with the forest it traveled through stretching out for miles. There were isolated farmsteads and manors, and not a few tiny cottages, but like Sevendor the land here was marginal for farming at best. The folk here, as in Sevendor, barely managed to keep food on the table.

Dara could see through Frightful's eyes the towers and castles of the Sashtalian lords in the distance. They stood out, from this height, even miles away. The nearest was a squat square tower behind a wooden palisade, but it appeared to be unprepared for war. That was good, Dara reasoned.

But less than a mile from the tower was a clearing, an old sheep's meadow between hills. That was where Dara saw the threat to Sevendor. It was covered with people, soldiers mostly, armed warriors and horses. It was hard to count through Frightful's perspective, but Dara estimated there were at least three or four hundred men-at-arms here. There were no other castles around that seemed to be the target of their ire.

And the banner they flew bore a large, bellicose-looking bird. The Warbird's standard.

Dara knew that the path up to Caolan's Pass wasn't terribly difficult, but it was steep. If the pass was defended it would be difficult for any of the invaders to take it, without suffering mightily in return.

Yet there seemed to be an awful lot of men down there, Dara realized worriedly. If they were, indeed, bound for Sevendor through Caolan's Pass, they seemed determined about it. And that did not bode well for her people.

She had to warn them, she realized. No one knew about the raiders prepared to take the pass. No one knew how close they were. There was an old man in charge of the pass, the one who took the infrequent tolls from travelers coming in Sevendor's "back door," but he was hardly able to stop an assault from a force that size. By custom it was the Westwoodmen and the Genlymen who guarded the pass in times of emergency.

Just as Dara was about to steer her falcon home and break contact, Frightful got a glimpse of something else as she circled high overhead from the encampment. A flash, but a distinct image of someone coming out of an arming tent.

Someone wearing a long black and white checkered cloak.

She had to warn her people. They didn't know about the Warbird's soldiers. If they did not find out, the pass could be overcome before they even got there. They certainly didn't know about the Censor who was with them. Dara knew little about magic, but from what Gareth had told her the Censors who hated Magelord Minalan were highly skilled warmagi. If they were helping the Warbird, that couldn't be a good thing for Sevendor.

Abandoning her gear in the meadow, Dara started down the rugged path. As soon as it evened out a bit, she started running. And she didn't stop until her legs carried her all the way to Westwood Hall.

The men and boys were still drilling, of course, although now they had progressed from simple marching to using spears and shields as defensive positions. Another squadron of Westwoodmen was practicing archery at the butts, dozens of arrows sailing down the range and into the thick wooden target. Dara brushed past them all and burst inside, where she found her father deep in conversation with her brother, who wore his new wolfshead sword proudly.

"Father!" she interrupted. "I have news!"

"Dara!" he reproved, as soon as he saw her sweaty, dusty face. "Look at you! You must—"

"Not now, Father!" she groaned. "I've been training, up in the high meadows, and—"

Her father heaved a sigh, making the broad plates of his armor swell. "Dara, I've been called to a war council by the castellan, and Sir Cei does not approve of being—"

"Father! This *is important!*" she insisted, her voice nearly squeaking she spoke so loudly. Kamen glanced at her, and then focused his full attention on her. Dara was gratified – she knew how indulgent her father was, compared to others.

But he had not raised her to be silent when she saw something that required his attention.

"What is it, Dara?" he asked in a voice that told her that it had better, indeed, be important.

"I . . . there is a small army nearby, just over the ridge, three miles west and a little south. They're encamped in a pasture beyond the closest castle. About three hundred strong, well-armed. Knights, even."

"Dara, don't be foolish," her father said, shaking his head. "You've been gone for maybe three hours. You did *not* climb all the way to the ridge top and back in that time, and I know you cannot even see the next tower from there. Flame burn me, there's no way you could—"

"Father, I'm a *beastmaster*," Dara explained, abandoning subtlety in her moment of desperation. Kamen's eyes stared at her blankly, uncomprehending. Dara's mind raced. "I . . . do you remember last winter; the night the Snow That Never Melted fell? The night I threw up? Remember how Master Banamor said I might have magic Talent?" she said, quickly, without taking a breath. "Well, I did, and I do, and I'm particularly Talented at being able to . . . to see out of Frightful's eyes," she said, looking for the simplest way to explain a complicated phenomenon she, herself, didn't really understand.

Her father looked at her with a mix of suspicion and doubt. "Dara, now is *not* the time—"

"It's called 'bilocation' by the magi, and it's not uncommon, according to my sources," she continued, even more quickly. Dara figured if she could say enough before her father really stopped her, she might say enough to convince him. "That's why I sought out Gareth to begin with, after I started having strange things happen between me and Frightful during training. I wanted to know if it was magic or if I was going mad. He assures me it's the former," she added, when she earned a quick look. "That's how I've been able to hunt so well with her, I get . . . I get 'behind her eyes' and direct her hunt. I can see through them, and I can tell her where to go. I got worried about . . . about things and had her take a quick trip over the ridge. It really isn't that far, as the falcon flies," she added.

Dara watched her father's face go from skeptical to thoughtful. "You haven't been one to lie," he admitted, "even when you aren't in the presence of the Flame. And Master Banamor did say . . . but Dara, why didn't you tell me about this before?"

"You had enough to contend with," she said with a shrug, "and I really didn't think it was that important. And I . . . I may have been enjoying my success a bit much," she added, guiltily thinking about her uncle Keram's praise for her good falconry. And the silver. "But now it *is* important and I *am* telling you. More, I'm telling you that I think that army is going to come against Sevendor. Soon. Please listen to me, Father!" she pleaded.

Kamen looked at her more thoughtfully and then nodded. "I will pass along this bit of intelligence to the castellan and our lady," he agreed. "Though I will also tell them of the source. If any would believe your wild tale, it is they who have lived with magic. Gareth knows of this, you say? The deputy Spellwarden?"

"Banamor's assistant," nodded Dara. "He was there the first time . . . the first time it happened," she said, remembering how disconcerting the experience had been. "He's been coaching me, a little. He's not a beastmaster himself, he's a thaumaturge, but . . . that's not really important. He knows."

"Then you go get cleaned up and see what you can do to put the Hall in order," her father said, quietly. "We weren't supposed to be deployed until tomorrow morning, but if what you say is true . . ."

"It is," Dara reassured him. "I saw it, Father. Through Frightful's eyes."

"Then that is what I will tell them."

Dara did go and get cleaned up, sneaking a venison pie from the kitchen on her way up to her room after calling Frightful back from the sky. Her bird wasn't sure why they weren't hunting on such a lovely day, but a few slivers of meat and she didn't care anymore. Dara hooded the falcon and then went to help with the preparations.

She was not happy with the work, as it implied gloomy things: cutting and rolling bandages, preparing space in the hall for wounded, taking inventory of stores and supplies, they all were harbingers of suffering ahead. The Westwood had never been taken in a battle, but there were tales of times when danger had kept the Westwoodmen behind their chasm, subsisting on the bounty of the forest for months at a time.

Dara wondered if the bandages she rolled would ever be used, and if so, whether they would be used on any of her kin. The thought disturbed her greatly, but she worked with new purpose.

Her father and his party returned from the castle just before dinner time, a grim expression on his face and a set to his jaw Dara had only seen a few times in her life. None of them had been pleasant.

"We are to take control of the high pass," Kamen announced to everyone at dinner. "We march after this meal. The Westwood is to hold and reinforce Caolan's Pass until we're relieved. That was expected. But we're to go tonight and march in the darkness. Certain . . . intelligence has passed our way that leads us to believe that the pass will be assaulted. Perhaps soon. We want to be there first, and in strength. Otherwise we'll be having a lot of fun shooting at the invaders who come down that hill."

There was some grim laughter at that – the Westwoodmen had concealed blinds for hunting and defense all along the ridgelines and the edge of their territory. Many could cover the long trail down from the pass, shooting from cover and inaccessible places.

After dinner Kamen took her aside again, near the Flame, as her brothers and cousins donned their armor and the kitchen prepared food for them to take.

"I told Sir Cei what you reported," he said, quietly, so no one else could overhear. "He accepted it as good reporting. That's why we're leaving tonight, instead of at dawn. He suspects that the only reason that they would encamp so close to the pass is if they expected to press a surprise attack."

"And dawn would be the perfect time to attack an undefended pass," agreed Dara. Her father nodded approvingly. Even though she didn't have the rudimentary military training her brothers had been forced to endure, she understood basic tactics.

"Which is why the Westwood will be there in force," he nodded. "I'll lead the lads up myself. If they try to come up that trail they'll do it sprouting arrows like spring plumage!"

Despite his brave words Dara could see that her father was afraid. Not of his own life, as much, she realized, as for what the potential of battle could do to his family. Those weren't just soldiers he was leading up that ridge. Those were his sons and nephews. Dara developed a new appreciation for the supposed "power" of the Master of the Wood. If that was power, she wanted none of it.

Still, she felt somewhat responsible herself, for what she had done: gotten her family deployed into danger earlier than they had expected. As the boys marched across the rope bridge, singing a simple hymn to the Flame, Dara felt her heart sink. How many would return, she wondered.

News came before the dawn the next morning. Dara had barely been able to sleep, worrying about her father, uncles, brothers and cousins atop the ridge. When the shouts from one of the younger boys raised the sentry at the chasm, most of the Hall woke up to hear the report.

Dara's intelligence had been correct, as had Sir Cei's analysis of it. The West Flerians had tried to take the high pass in an early morning raid. Had old Carkan, the Yeoman of the pass, been alone the foe would be marching on

Sevendor Castle past the very door of the Westwood. But with the Westwoodmen able to respond so quickly and by surprise, the West Flerian men had been driven halfway back down the ridge in disarray. Now the ridge was held under the Westwood's small wolfshead banner.

The messenger who brought the news was jubilant – there had been almost no injuries in the fighting, and the West Flerians had clearly not expected the pass to be held in such force. That was welcome news for the community.

But Dara was still frightened of what might happen if the West Flerians continued to push. She was forbidden to go out ranging, even in the Westwood, now that the war banner flew from the castle's highest tower, but as soon as it was light enough she took Frightful out to the yard and flung her into the air. Then she returned to her room, took to her bed, and fell into rapport with her falcon. She had to know what was happening at the ridge.

Frightful's perspective swam crazily for Dara in her mind's eye until she settled in behind the bird's eyes. Below the land was waking up, the fields and meadows were alive with creatures stirring for the day's first meal. Ordinarily that was what Frightful herself would be doing, if Dara hadn't had other plans for her.

The gap in the ridge to the north that made up Caolan's Pass was narrow, and the road up to it was twisty and steep, but it took the falcon almost no time to reach it. Dara noted how attentively the dark-clad figures of her folk manned the log barricade they had thrown up at the ridgeline. A few bodies lay still below the ridge on the other side, testament to the Westwood's skill with archery.

Still further down the trail on the other side of the ridge, just a few dozen feet out of bowshot, gathered thirty or forty more soldiers bearing the Warbird's livery, regrouping and scheming. No doubt they were considering other plans, now that their first had been so quickly upset. Dara was no soldier, but she saw little hope of the West Flerians taking the ridge. The path up the hill was well-exposed to the arrows of the Sevendori, and it was far too steep for a war horse to be used to any effect.

Satisfied that the enemy was, indeed, at bay, Dara had Frightful wheel back around and return to circle the pass. She was almost startled when she saw the strangely small figure of her father notice the falcon and wave up to her, recognizing her for what she was.

The thought of him waving up into the sky at his daughter amused her so much she almost lost he rapport with her bird. Instead, she commanded Frightful to glide to a landing on the barricade.

It was odd – she could hear everything that Frightful could, but that did not mean she understood. Her father was speaking to the bird, she knew, but it took tremendous concentration for her to ferret out the actual words. To Frightful such human speech was largely unintelligible. But after some effort Dara was able to understand that her father was reporting that all was well, and that he would be returning to the Hall soon enough.

Satisfied, Dara had Frightful return to Westwood Hall for a well-deserved treat. She spent the rest of the day rolling bandages and helping prepare more medicines, until her father returned alone at dusk.

"We had a right fun day," he told his half-empty hall. The place seemed abandoned, almost, without the usual noise from all of her male relations to fill it. "Three sorties they made up that slope, since dawn. Three times we drove them back with arrows before they came half-way. The last time they left a half-dozen men behind," he boasted. "I left Kyre in charge of the men."

"Kyre?" asked Aunt Anira, a little alarmed. "Should not Keram be—?"

"Kyre will be master of this Hall in his own right, some day," Kamen observed to his sister-in-law. "He has the respect of our folk and the courage to lead. It is well and right that the boy should command his own men."

"That's . . . but in time of war?" she asked, skeptically.

"Particularly in a time of war," Kamen said, darkly. "He is my oldest son. I cherish him above all else as the hope for our people. Yet I would not deny him the opportunity to take his position as a man, even though it is at risk of his life."

"He's just . . . so *young,*" Anira said.

Dara was astute enough to realize what she was really saying: *Why did you not leave my husband, your brother, in charge of such an important assignment?* Her aunt was as loyal as anyone in the Hall, but Anira had always harbored some resentment over her brother-in-law's position. Keram the Crafty was adept at much, Dara knew, and the Hall wouldn't work without his diligence . . . but he was not Master of the Hall, nor would he be.

Unless her father and all of her brothers died.

"I've a duty to report to the castellan and our lady at the castle," Kamen continued, "let them know what forces we face at the ridge. I had to leave someone in charge while I did so. We heard that a raid was staged on the Diketower, too," he added. That was the main entrance to the vale of Sevendor, at the far eastern end of the valley, where many of the Bovali immigrants had settled. "Sir Roncil rode by to inspect us and brought the news. We drove them back. The Diketower stands well-defended. If the Warbird wants Sevendor, he'll pay dearly for it!" he declared, with more fervor than Dara had suspected he had.

"Do you think they'll just . . . go away, now that they see we're defended?" Dara asked, knowing how silly the question was as soon as she asked it. The Warbird had a reputation across the vales as a man of great power and vengeance. He ran the neighboring domains with an iron fist. As poor as the people of Sevendor had been, as neglectful as Sir Erantal had been, the prospect of Sire Gimbal the Warbird as overlord of Sevendor sounded appalling. There was no way his honor would allow him to retreat, once battle had been engaged.

"Nay, Little Bird," her father sighed. "They've been preparing for weeks, awaiting the Magelord's journey away from here with his apprentices. They won't back down now, not when they have an advantage. They hoped to conquer us quickly, though. Thanks to your intelligence, we denied them that at Caolan's Pass," he said, gratefully. "I'll be mentioning that to Sir Cei and Lady Alya, when I make my report."

Dara continued to fret as she prepared for bed. She didn't know how she could possibly sleep while her brothers and cousins faced danger only a mile or so from her bed. She tossed and turned in her sheets, the heat of the night feeling oppressive to her. When sleep did finally come, it was a restless sleep full of dread and anxiety.

She found herself being shaken awake in the middle of the night. Terrified, she bolted upright, her eyes wide with fear. Her father, still in his armor, was standing in front of her with a taper. Frightful started to wake up, her tiny eyes shining in the light at the foot of Dara's bed.

"What is it? What's wrong?" Dara demanded, fearing the worse.

"Calm yourself, Little Bird," Kamen said, soothingly. "There's nothing amiss. Last word I got from the Pass said all was well, and there's no beacon fire on the ridge. I just got back from the war council at the castle," he explained. "I thought I would tell you what came of it, as you were so helpful yesterday."

"What happened?" Dara asked, as she composed herself. No one was hurt, she reminded herself. Her dreams had not been real.

"I gave my report in turn, as all the Yeomen did," her father said, taking a seat on her creaking old bed. "I told them how you suggested we deploy up the ridge early . . . and why. And how our being there kept the West Flerians at bay. Sir Cei was mightily impressed," he smiled. "Both with our boys' initiative and bravery, and with my daughter's cleverness."

"I wasn't being clever," Dara dismissed.

"You were clever enough to bring it to my attention, and spare us a bloody battle in our vale. You may never be Master of the Wood, Little Bird, but you've certainly the wit and wisdom for it."

The unexpected praise made Dara blush – and change the subject. "What happens now?"

"We continue to guard the pass," Kamen replied. "The domain is under siege, now. The folk of Gurisham, Genly, and Sevendor Village have already been moved into the outer bailey of the castle as a precaution. We will be safe enough behind our chasm. But if either the Diketower or the Pass falls, then we will see a different type of war," he said, darkly.

Dara suppressed a shudder. "We won't let that happen," she promised, encouragingly. "The Magelord will learn of this and return in time."

"Aye, that's the hope," sighed her father. "Though what one man, even a mage, can do against an entire army is beyond my ken. You needn't worry yourself. Sir Cei and Lady Alya have things well in-hand. The castle is provisioned, defended, and manned – far more than Sir Erantal ever did. And there are plenty of brave men willing to fight for Sevendor. The Bovali seem to be spoiling for a fight. A stout castle and brave men can withstand a siege of hundreds of days, if need be." Despite his assuredness, Dara could tell her father had some doubts. "The biggest problem, they say, is magical."

"Magical?" Dara asked, confused.

"Aye. Many of the defenses the Magelord put into place before he left were magical. Without him or his fellow wizards around, they're useless. Or something like that. I confess, I knew but half of what was said at council when they spoke of magic and spellcraft. Thing is," he continued, "they want every mage in the domain to go to the castle and help."

"Well, they should!" Dara agreed. Gareth had pointed out several of the footwizards and other itinerate magi who had made their way to Sevendor, at market. They were generally odd-looking fellows, looking more like vagabonds than tradesmen, but there had been several. Surely they could be put to use. "We're at war! Everyone should be willing to do their part! Are some of the other wizards not—"

"Oh, the castle is full of wizards," chuckled Kamen. "Master Banamor is there, fretting over his enterprises. That young man Gareth you spoke of is there. Master Olmeg the Greenward is there, though he is still hurt. And a few others from the village. None of them are warmagi. Fighting wizards," he explained.

"I know what warmagi are!" Dara said, rolling her eyes. Gareth had explained that to her *weeks* ago.

"Then you know how valuable they are in war," Kamen said. "And why the Magelord needs to return. But that's not why I mentioned it, Dara. When I spoke of your help in the battle yesterday, Sir Cei and Lady Alya were very intrigued."

"I was glad to help," she said, uncomfortably.

"That is good to hear," nodded Kamen. "Because an order has been issued that all wizard folk are to report to the castle for service. *All* wizard folk." He paused, and looked at her meaningfully. "Including Talented, untrained beastmasters who figured out how to . . . *bilocate*," he said, his mouth having difficulty with the strange word. "Sir Cei wants to see you and Frightful at the castle, first thing in the morning."

"Me? Why *me?*" Dara asked, her eyes wide.

"Because they want you to use your powers to help the war effort," he explained. "They want you to use Frightful to spy on the enemy. They want you, Dara, to join the other wizard folk at the castle in the Magical Corps . . . and try to defend and preserve our domain until the Magelord returns."

Chapter Thirteen

Sevendor At War

Sevendor Castle looked different since she had been there at Yule.

The festive greenery was absent now, replaced with hastily-erected woodworks and platforms upon which archers patrolled. The outer bailey, the vast empty space behind the castle's first wall, was no longer deserted and barren. Wagons and tents now filled the road on either side with more rumbling in behind her. Livestock was herded into a fenced enclosure near the wall, while makeshift shelters were built on the cliffward side. Dozens of campfires began cooking the breakfast of the displaced folk. Dara tried not to stare too hard at their worried faces.

The castle was bustling inside the inner gate, even at this early hour. Soldiers drilled in the yard in front of the castle while Bovali archers practiced shooting their great Wilderland bows in volleys. Men shouted to each other across the yard, and horses were being saddled and readied to move. There was a sense of urgency in the air that took Dara's breath away. She had wisely hooded Frightful, worried that she'd be startled by the noise. She was glad she had taken the precaution.

The door of the castle's great hall was guarded by a pair of burly-looking soldiers in mail coats, each bearing a spear and shield. They checked the face and story of everyone entering into the hall, and Dara had to explain twice why she and her falcon needed to be admitted. If it had been any other guards of any other castle, they might have sent her away as mad. But in Sevendor, now, the idea of a girl magically seeing through the eyes of a falcon was almost mundane. They let her pass with little question.

The interior of the hall was busy, as the night shift of guards came off duty and the morning shift was leaving breakfast to take their place. The white walls and stonework were brightened even further by a few scattered magelights in important areas.

One hung over the far end of the hall, near the great white stone table near the great fireplace. Dara could see that was where Sir Cei and Lady Alya were seated, overseeing the defense of the vale. There was a line of people who urgently needed to speak to one or both of them. Dara stood at the back of it, when she asked a guard what to do, then patiently waited to present herself.

It didn't take as long as she feared. Those ahead of her gave their reports or asked their questions quickly and were ushered away by a stubby-looking Tal Alon.

It was the first time that Dara had seen one of the strange nonhumans up close and in the light. She had heard of them, of course, from tales and stories, but no one in

Sevendor had seen a living Tal Alon – called River Folk in polite company, or "spuds" by those who disparaged them – until Master Olmeg the Green, the wizard the Magelord had appointed his Greenward, had brought a tribe of them to the vales. They had begun building a settlement in what was left of Farant's Hold, with the Spellmonger's permission.

The Tal servant who worked with Lady Alya and Sir Cei looked nearly human, save for his low height and its thick coat of shaggy brown fur. It was portly, by human standards, but the way it moved made Dara think that this was a normal state of affairs for the Tal, not an exception. The River Folk's reputation for both industrious cultivation and degenerate vice made many people wary of them, but the castle servant seemed quite level-headed, from what Dara could tell. He wore a broad green vest and short pants, as well as a perky cap that seemed far too small for his head, all originally intended for human wear but adopted by the Tal.

He spoke Narasi, Dara's language, fairly enough to be understood – indeed, he seemed more polite and articulate than most of the vale folk, if she had to swear before the Flame. He knew his business, ushering people along out of the way of the leaders before they could slow down the line with the same efficiency she imagined a human servant might show.

Dara found herself daydreaming when it was finally her turn in front of the table. She realized she didn't have any idea what to say to the lady of the domain. Luckily she was spared the embarrassment she felt when Sir Cei recognized her.

The castellan stood and smiled grimly when he saw her approach.

"Ah! The Westwood girl! Kamen said he would send her along, last night. True to his word," he said, approvingly. Dara didn't know what to make of that – as if a Westwoodman would be untrue!

Before she could get offended, the big knight motioned her to approach more closely, so that both he and Lady Alya could hear her. "This is the girl that Master Kamen spoke of," he reminded their lady, who nodded in recognition. "The one who espied the enemy in the field and kept us from losing the pass prematurely."

"The hawk girl!" Lady Alya nodded. "Sir Cei was telling me about you. Good work, that. Do you think you can do it again?"

"Yes, my lady," Dara agreed, swallowing hard. "It's easy enough to see from behind Frightful's eyes," she offered. "Although understanding what she's seeing is hard, sometimes."

"I can imagine," Lady Alya agreed. She looked tired, Dara decided, though she was a young, pretty woman, perhaps just a few years older than Dara's oldest sister. "But it would be invaluable if we could keep up to date on what our enemies are plotting. Your father suggests you can be trusted on to give reliable accounts – is that true? And what is your name, girl?"

"Uh, yes, my lady," Dara nodded, swallowing hard. "My name is Dara. Short for 'Lenodara'. This is my falcon, Frightful."

"She's utterly gorgeous!" Alya said, admirably. "I used to watch them for hours, back home in the Mindens. I grew up at a place called Hawk's Reach." Lady Alya paused from looking at Frightful and regarded her mistress, instead. "You look scared, Dara – why?" she suddenly asked, in a very direct manner.

"Me?" Dara squeaked. "Maybe because there's an army coming against us? And I'm just thirteen? And I'm suddenly . . . involved?"

"And you never pictured yourself a warrior," nodded Lady Alya. "I understand. Six months ago, I'd never had pictured myself leading the defense of our home. Yet here I am sending men to go stand on the walls and defend us. I may do more before all is said and done. We all take up challenges in such a situation. Give us your best against the Warbird, and we'll keep the valley defended."

"We will do our best," she added, apologetically.

"That's all we're accepting today," Alya grinned at her. "Welcome to our little army."

"I'll take her up to the rest of the Magical Corps in a moment," Sir Cei suggested. "I have some dispatches they need to see, anyway. Just pull up a stool for a moment, girl," the big knight ordered in a kindly voice. "I'll be ready for a break anon."

Dara found a small wooden stool against the wall next to the fireplace and pulled it up near to the castellan, who was already addressing the next person in line – a guardsman with a report from Southridge Hold.

Dara ended up waiting for three more messengers while she soothed Frightful on her wrist. The fire on the hearth was small, a mere token in the summer heat, and the hypnotic crackle and pop was soon lulling her into lethargy

. . . until the great wooden doors banged open and a commotion began at the far end of the hall. Dara had to stand to see what was happening, and ended up standing on top of her stool to see, but what she saw was worth the effort. A somewhat familiar figure was being dragged before the Lady of Sevendor and her servants by soldiers – and not just any soldiers, but her brother Kyre and two of her cousins!

Dara was speechless. She hadn't expected to see many Westwoodmen at Sevendor Castle, much less her oldest brother. What struck her about him was how adult he appeared as he pushed his prisoner down the aisle between tables toward the dais. He didn't move with the cocky self-assuredness of her adolescent brother, he moved like a very angry young man.

With a sword.

"My lady!" he called as he and his kin pushed their prisoner forward. "Caolan's Pass was attacked again at dawn!"

"Casualties?" inquired Sir Cei, coolly, as he stood and assessed the situation.

"Four wounded," Kyre reported promptly. He did not see Dara, from where she was standing, but she could see him well enough. His eyes were flashing hotly as he spoke the words. "Two of our cottagers were fetching water from the spring and were shot in the attack. Two others were wounded when they swarmed our position. They sent forty men up the slope this time. Only thirty-two returned when we drove them off. We took four prisoners, including this . . . *gentleman*."

The disgust and disdain Kyre felt for his prisoner was clear in his tone, and Dara wondered just what the enemy soldier had done to deserve it from the usually fair-minded Kyre. The man was older, somewhat rotund, and wore a rustic-looking coat-of-plates. That had to be the lucky part of his body, Dara reasoned, as his face was battered, bloody, and muddy. His hands had been tied behind his back and a rope was looped around his neck. Then Dara's breath caught as she realized just who the prisoner was.

"Sir Erantal," Sir Cei said, identifying the prisoner. Dara held her breath. Sir Erantal had presided over Sevendor's slow death from neglect. His name alone had been used as a means of scaring young children in the Westwood, and for as long as she could remember Dara could not recall ever hearing someone saying something kind about the man. "And here I thought we had seen the last of you."

"I have taken service with Sire Gimbal," the man said, simply, as he looked around his old castle in wonder. "What have you done with this place? What sorcery is this?"

"The very best sort," Lady Alya dismissed. Dara decided she liked her, from the contemptuous way she treated the valley's old oppressor. "Sir Erantal, I believe at our last meeting you were instructed to leave Sevendor and never return. Yet now you are here, bearing arms against us."

"When my lord rides to war, I follow, or I am no knight," he said, haughtily – earning a contemptuous snort from Sir Cei and a derisive chuckle from the Westwoodmen . . . and a fair number of other native Sevendori. Not many who had acquaintance of him took the statement seriously.

Sir Cei eyed the man intently – he really was a knight, compared to Erantal. He had fought in a war and even won a wife and a domain of his own with his jousting. Sir Erantal had never drawn his sword, from what Dara knew of the man. Yet he was clearly trying to impress his captors with his importance. "I was given the honor of leading the attack on the pass."

"A high honor," Lady Alya nodded. "And one that injured four of my subjects. Yet your puissance was not so great as to keep you from getting captured yourself," she noted.

"He tripped and fell over his own feet," Kyre said, loudly. "As he was running away from our counterattack."

"He seems rather bruised for one little fall," observed Sir Cei, looking at her brother meaningfully.

"He fell down again as we were descending from the pass," Kyre offered in a tone that Dara was certain he'd never use in front of the Flame.

"Fell down?" Lady Alya asked, as she looked closely at Sevendor's former lord.

"A *lot*," Kyre assured her, lying to her face in a shameful manner. "He's *quite* clumsy."

"I would say so," the lady agreed, evenly. "Yet no worse for wear—"

"No worse?" asked Erantal in disbelief. "I was thrown to the ground repeatedly by these ignorant wretch—*umph!*" he finished, as Kyre slapped the back of his right knee with the flat of his new sword.

"Outrageous!" the old knight howled. "When I am ransomed back to Sire Gimbal, you can be certain I will speak of my treatment at your hands!" he said, threateningly.

"You mistake yourself, Sir Erantal," Lady Alya said, softly. "You assume we will seek to ransom you back to your master."

"What?" Erantal asked, eyes wide.

"Ransom is a courtesy," explained Sir Cei, taking Lady Alya's lead. "A courtesy among fighting gentleman. While your little raid technically places you within that category, the codes do not mandate that ransom be sought for a valuable prisoner . . . they merely encourage it."

"In this case, what we could fetch for you is dependent upon your ability to command the loyalty of your new master," Lady Alya continued, picking up from Cei. "More importantly, it is dependent upon our willingness to make such an exchange."

"What?" asked Sir Erantal again, confused.

"While ransom is a courtesy, it need not be one which we choose to exercise," explained Sir Cei. "In your case, Sir Erantal, as much as Sire Gimbal no doubt values your counsel and capabilities as a war leader," he said, managing to keep a straight face, "I'm afraid you are far more valuable to the people of Sevendor. I do not think we will be negotiating for your release. With *anyone*," he added.

"That's outrageous!" declared Erantal, desperately. "You can't do that to me!"

"Do you never tire of being wrong?" Alya asked, amused. "Indeed, we can. Sir Roncil, please escort Sir Erantal to the very largest cell in our dungeon, as befits a noble prisoner of his high station," she ordered another burly Wilderlands knight who stood nearby, his arms folded over his chest. "There you will await not a negotiated release, but capital judgment from my husband, upon his return."

"Your husband?" snorted Erantal. "He'll never return! We've made sure of that. He'll never break through our defenses, warmage or no!"

"Then you will be enjoying your former dungeon for a very long time," Lady Alya said, sweetly. "But there you will stay until he can hear your case."

"Surely some more expedient method could be considered," Erantal said, his face pale at the mention of the dungeon he'd thrown so many Sevendori into over the years. It appeared as if the old knight wanted Lady Alya to sit in judgment on him. Perhaps he considered her more merciful than her fierce lord.

"I could, indeed, try you myself, here and now," agreed Alya. "I'm tempted. If you insist, I will. But I advise you to await my husband," she continued. "Of the two of us, it is my guess he is less inclined to have you summarily executed."

Erantal's face went even paler.

"Of course, he'd do it nice and clean. I would have a set of stocks commissioned to replace the ones we destroyed, when we arrived here last autumn, for the express purpose of allowing the folk of Sevendor vale to show you their gratitude and devotion for your management of the domain over the years. From what I understand, there are many in the vale who would relish such an opportunity. For *days*. Take him away," she commanded Sir Roncil.

"As for you, Kyre of Westwood, for taking this important prisoner I reward you with an ounce of silver," she continued. Sir Cei did not argue – he dug into a purse on the table and threw the boy a heavy silver coin.

"That's very welcome, my lady," Kyre said as he caught the coin, noticing Dara for the first time behind the table, "but what we really need is some relief. My men have been on watch for two days, now, and have borne two dawn attacks. We can keep at it another day or two, but . . ."

"Fear not," Sir Cei said, nodding. "We've mustered the village militias. They are preparing to march in support of the Diketower, Caolan's Pass, and other strategically important areas. By dusk you should stand relieved, and can retire and get some rest. You've done admirably," he added. "What kind of force do you need to relieve you?"

"It's not a hard job, standing at the top of a hill and keeping folk off it," Kyre acknowledged. "A few bowmen and you can sweep the trail for a hundred feet down. A score, two if you can spare them, can hold that pass."

"We do need the hardier troops for defense of the Diketower," agreed Lady Alya. "Sir Forondo is preparing the garrison to engage in a charge to break through the besiegers," she added, hopefully. "We'd like as many infantries to support them as possible. But if a few score bowmen and spearmen can hold that pass, we can spare them."

"It would be a gracious respite, my lady," Kyre said, bowing with his hand on his chest. Dara felt proud of how well he comported himself. He had been in an actual battle – two, if you counted yesterday's raid – and he had survived. More, he had taken a valuable prisoner. That brought honor to the Westwood. Dara hoped she could add to that.

Kyre gave her a wink and a smile before he departed, as Sir Roncil – one of the few Bovali knights who had come with the settlers – dragged Sir Erantal down to the dungeon. Dara made a point of watching every step the man took. She knew she would be asked about it over and over, once she got back home, and she didn't want to miss a single detail. Sir Erantal was hated in Sevendor. His capture almost made the war worth it.

"That man is a disgrace to the chivalry," Dara overheard Sir Cei tell Lady Alya. The young noblewoman nodded grimly.

"Disgrace to the chivalry?" Dara felt her mouth say before she could catch it. "He's a disgrace as a human being. My entire life I've lived in fear of the mean old knight in this castle. I'm just happy I got to see him get stuck under it."

* * *

Dara had no idea what a "magical corps" was when Sir Cei escorted her to the Magelord's private workshop, pointed her to the right door, and then hurried off on important castle business. But she soon discovered that it was merely what the group of warmagi attached to an army was called.

Of course, at the moment Sevendor's "magical corps" consisted of only one mage with any formal training in warmagic – her friend Gareth, who looked like he was made of sticks and straw. He was waving his hands in the air over a table of sand while his employer, Master Banamor, looked on.

She had met Master Banamor before, when Sevendor's Spellwarden had come to visit the Westwood after the Snow That Never Melted. He was a man of middle age who wore a simple peaked cap and a burgher's robe. Gareth had mentioned to her that he was a former footwizard – an unregistered mage who illegally pedaled his spells from village to village, often one step ahead of the feared Censorate. Now that he had taken service with the Magelord, the former vagabond had prospered in Sevendor. . . and if Dara was any judge, he seemed like a man unwilling to allow his fortunes to vanish without a fight.

Olmeg the Green was present, looking like he was slowly recovering from the savage beating by the hated West Flerians. His long, wide face still bore the signs of his resistance. There were bruises on his face and fresh bandages wrapped around his head. As the domain's Greenwarden, Master Olmeg had been put in charge of all of the plants in Sevendor, and that included the Westwood. He had made several trips to the estate since he'd arrived. He was hard to miss, as he was not only taller than Sir Cei, but he wore an even taller pointed green hat and a green tunic or smock. He also went everywhere barefoot.

Her father spoke highly of the man for his wood-lore and wisdom. Dara could tell immediately why. Master Olmeg never seemed to hurry. He always considered everything he said before he spoke, and then he spoke slowly. He was staring at a parchment map of the domain and muttering under his breath as he fingered something in a tiny wooden box.

The last member of the "magical corps" was a mage Dara had never met, one of the Bovali immigrants, by his dress. He was a funny-looking fellow, a bit like Master Olmeg in some ways, but instead of a simple tunic or robe he wore a shaggy sheepskin vest over a dark maroon tunic. His bushy beard hung down almost as low as Master Olmeg's, and his eyes were two kindly lamps in a well-weathered face. He seemed to be engaged in a staring contest with a bowl of water. Unless Dara was mistaken, the bowl was winning.

Master Banamor was looking frustrated with Gareth, who had his eyes closed and was waving his hands slowly in the air in front of him. Dara could almost see something there, she thought for a moment – a kind of distortion in the air, like the heat over a fire. But then it was gone. So was Gareth's concentration, when he realized that she had arrived.

"Dara!" he said, excitedly, when his eyes fluttered open.

"Damn!" barked Banamor. "Concentrate, boy! Didn't they teach you that at that fancy academy?"

"Sorry, Master, but it wasn't working anyway," the young mage said to his employer. "That's the fourth time I've tried.

Someone has blocked traditional scrying in the vales beyond the frontier. I can't get anything beyond the Enchanted Forest."

"Enchanted forest?" Dara blurted out. She had heard rumors that Master Olmeg was planting something out beyond the Diketower, but Dara had never been that far from home to see it.

"A bit of nastiness that Master Olmeg is growing," Gareth supplied, helpfully. "Gallows Oaks, deadly plants, briars, enchantments . . . it's actually pretty impressive," he said, admiringly.

"More impressive in a few years," admitted Olmeg, thoughtfully. "Most of my obstacles will not be fully grown for several seasons, even with magical assistance. But they cannot dispute my control over it," he added, proudly. "They can stop me from scrying, but there are other ways to see through the Green."

"They must have a warmage aiding them," Gareth agreed. "That's the only reason our scrying is blocked."

"My sightings, too, are obscured," the strange mage reported with a shrug. "I am Zagor, hedgemage of Boval Village," he said, giving her a curt but polite little bow.

"What's scrying?" Dara asked, feeling foolish for not knowing. "And where is Boval Village?"

"Boval Village is what they're calling the new settler's new village," explained Gareth, standing and stretching. "It's near the sight of the old Brestal Farms village, the one that the Warbird burned down when he took Brestal Vale. Zagor came here with the Bovali, and he's set up shop there in Boval Village as a spellmonger."

"Hedgemage," corrected the man with the thick accent. "I do not sell my spells. I sing an enchantment for folk I find worthy. Then they give me a gift, sometimes," he shrugged again.

"It's still commerce, and it's still getting taxed as such," Master Banamor insisted, gruffly. "I don't care if you try to pretty it up with your folksy ways! As long as I'm Spellwarden, that's how it will be seen. And scrying?" he added, as he pulled out his long pipe and leaf pouch and began packing it. "That's when a mage uses magic to see someplace that's not right in front of him. Lots of ways to do it. Unfortunately, there are an equal number of ways to *keep* it from happening. If they have a warmage . . ."

"They do," Dara said, realizing that she had valuable information that only these men would know what to do with. "When I was scouting over the northern ridge with my falcon, I had her fly over their encampment. She only saw it for a moment, but . . . I believe there was a black and white checkered cloak among them."

The face of every mage in the room went pale. Master Banamor stopped packing his pipe.

"The bloody Censors!" Banamor cursed. "How I hate that order! Even after they've been sacked, they still won't leave me alone!"

"Are you certain, Dara?" asked Gareth, concerned. "I only mentioned them that one time, and—"

"Black and white checks are fairly distinctive," Dara said, defensively. "And while I might just be a girl, unused to weapons and war, I think I know what a cloak looks like. It was there," she said, with certainty.

"That would explain a lot," Master Olmeg nodded, sagely. "Our inability to scry, the failure of my defensive spells . . . a warmage is involved. And the Censorate's antipathy towards our lord is well-known."

"Would they actively assist in a small, private war like this?" asked Zagor. The rustic hedgemage had had little experience with the regulators of magic, Dara figured, if he had come from way off in the Mindens.

"You'd better believe it," grunted Banamor. "Despite their pretensions of neutrality, the Censorate will use whatever means it needs to in order to achieve its goals. Toppling the Spellmonger while he's off in the capital is, apparently, a high priority."

"Lucky us," Gareth said, shaking his head darkly. "If they're rendering magical assistance, I imagine that they may be lending material assistance as well."

"You think?" Banamor asked, lighting his pipe with a flame that just appeared on his finger. "That would be very bad, then. If we face the might of West Fleria alone, we're going to be outnumbered. If Sire Gimbal has managed to hire mercenaries on someone else's coin . . ."

"That would be very bad," agreed Zagor, conversationally. "But what can we do?"

"Precious little," Gareth said, starkly. "We can't scry. And we can't see beyond the Enchanted Forest. And that's where Dara comes in."

"The falcon," smiled Olmeg. It was a very big smile on a very big face. In other circumstances she might have found it intimidating, but Dara could tell it was genuine. "Your beautiful falcon."

"Her name is Frightful," Dara said, stroking the back of the bird's neck with a finger.

"And you can bilocate with this animal?" Banamor asked.

"I can," she nodded. "I've been practicing."

"Good," Banamor nodded, smoke trickling from his nostrils. "We have a sortie ready to go forth against our besiegers. At least thirty heavy lancers. We have no idea what they're going to be facing. If there's any way you could remedy that . . ."

"Can you open a window?" Dara asked, looking for a place to launch her falcon. "And find a comfortable place for me to sit? I get a little stiff, if I'm with her too long. And if you don't mind sending to the kitchens for a little raw meat, kidney or liver if you have it, she's going to be hungry when she gets back."

Chapter Fourteen

The Magical Corps

All morning Dara sent Frightful soaring across the valley investigating the movements of the West Flerians from the sky. The work was mostly beyond Sevendor's enclosed valley, out beyond the ridges to the north and west.

It was farther than either Frightful or Dara had ever gone before, and both bird and trainer were uneasy at first. But with patient direction from Gareth and Banamor she managed to get the bird to the top of Matten's Helm, to get her bearings, and thence across to the large earthen dike and small fortress known as the Diketower. There the bulk of Sevendor's defenders were concentrated.

Though it was difficult to gauge exact numbers through Frightful's eyes, Dara could see hundreds of Sevendori – natives and Bovali immigrants alike – patrolling with bow and spear the great earthen wall that now guarded the pass. More peered out from the top of the three-story tower that overlooked the pass, their arrows ready to fire. Yet more waited behind the dike, ready to defend it.

Beyond the wall, Frightful found most of Sevendor's few mounted troops assembling for a sortie against the West Flerian enemy. Sir Forondo, the man who served the Magelord as Captain of the Guard, had formed up a line of thirty brave lancers to take the field. Frightful saw the long line of horses, felt their excitement and smelled their rider's dread. It took Dara's mind to see the men in glittering armor, their long lances tipped with sharp steel held high. From many of the points a small green-and-white banner fluttered.

The Snowflake of Sevendor. Dara had barely known of it, before she came to the castle, but the Magelord's new device for the small domain was starting to appear in banners and tokens everywhere around the place. It was a wild-looking six-pointed star in white, on a green field, said to be what a snowflake looked like up close. It was the device adopted by the Magelord, in honor of the Snow That Never Melted.

It was pretty, if odd, especially through the eyes of a falcon. Dara had no idea how one would perceive such a thing, but the spider-web like device had been eagerly adopted by the fighting men in this little war. At least it was simpler to stitch, than, say, a holly leaf. That exercise had been what had convinced Dara that needlework was not her strong point. But the Snowflake would be easy to copy, she decided. A larger example hung defiantly from the top of the Diketower, she noted, when Frightful circled back once over the horsemen.

The road to Sevendor below the dike descended through a rocky wasteland that had recently been planted with trees – that was Master Olmeg's new Enchanted Forest, Dara guessed, as Frightful winged over it. She saw men moving below, hiding behind boulders or saplings. She couldn't guess which ones were fighting for Sevendor and which were against it from this height. She pushed her falcon to move on.

Less than a mile down the road she saw the first band of foes on the road. She had Frightful land in the top of a tall elm tree within sight of the road. Thankfully, the men ignored her. But she could easily see them from her vantage: a score of men bearing the device of the Warbird on their sashes and tabards. Only a quarter of them were mounted.

It didn't take long for Frightful to become aware of other noises and smells from her vantage point, however. She cocked her head when she heard more horses in the distance. Dara urged her to take wing again and wheel in the direction of the noise.

Off the road, to the east, lay a much, much larger company. More than four times the number of Sir Forondo's brave men had mustered in a barren pasture, ready to ride to the defense of their foes. While the distances meant little to the falcon, Dara realized that the larger army was ready to pounce on any defenders Sevendor might send forth, should they chase the lure of the smaller force in the road. That could be devastating to Sevendor.

Frightful flew on. Beyond the mounted men by another half-mile was a fallow field sprawling with tents, canopies, and wagons. Far, far more men than Dara had ever seen together at one time. It was dizzying for her to see from that high in the air, and even more dizzying to contemplate.

There had to be over a thousand, she reasoned, as she tried to gauge exactly how many.

Periodically in her flying she would land Frightful somewhere, or give her some basic but firm direction, and then break her trance long enough to report back to Gareth or Banamor. When she reported the larger force lying in wait for Sir Forondo, he raced from the room with impressive speed.

"How will he get there in time?" she asked, her eyes wide. If he didn't, she realized, thirty men and their horses would be dead or captured.

"He's rushing to get Sir Cei," Gareth explained. "He has a device – a magical device – called a Mirror. It uses magic to allow the castellan to speak with the commander of the Diketower, for just this sort of thing. As soon as he can get to Sir Cei, a messenger can be dispatched to reach Sir Forondo in time . . . I hope," he added.

Dara immediately went back into contact with Frightful. It was difficult, at this great distance, but long practice and familiarity soon brought her back over the besieging army. She had Frightful circle the twenty men being used as a lure by the West Flerians, and saw as Sevendor's small force advanced down the road, two by two.

The vanguard of the company spread out as much as the road allowed and advanced. The West Flerians feigned surprise and began a ragged retreat down the road, drawing the Sevendori into the trap. Just as the first of the lancers reached the point where their foes had awaited them, however, a swift horse came up from behind and found Sir

Forondo before the company was committed . . . and ensnared.

With a sigh of relief Dara slipped back out of her trance and told the other magi the good news.

"That's the second time you've saved the domain, you and Frightful," Gareth pointed out, as Zagor and Olmeg went down to the Great Hall to relay the news to the rest of the castle. "That was about the only mounted force the domain has, and it would have been tragic if it had been taken . . . or slaughtered."

"I was just trying to help," Dara said, dazedly.

"That's the kind of help we need more of," Gareth assured her. "With the Magelord gone . . ."

"Has no one sent a messenger?" Dara asked in disbelief. That would seem like the first thing she would have done . . .

"We tried," nodded Gareth, as he stifled a yawn. "But they were intercepted by the West Flerians. Zagor tried to contact him through the Otherworld, last night, but—"

"The . . . *Otherworld?*" Dara asked in confusion.

Gareth shook his shaggy head in irritation. "Sorry. I'm used to having this sort of discussion with fellow magi. The Otherworld . . . well, you know that place you go when you dream? That's the gateway to the Otherworld. It's like . . . like our world, only it exists in the magosphere, not here in reality."

"You know, as explanations go, that was a particularly poor one. It made no sense to me at all," Dara decided.

"Of course not," Gareth sighed. "You just don't have the education. Maybe if your Talent really emerges someone will see to training you properly."

"I'm a *falconer*," Dara reminded him, a little defiantly.

"And I'm a *thaumaturge*," Gareth replied, "only now I'm a *warmage*. When I'm not being a *junior assistant bureaucrat*. We do what the gods want us to do, Dara, not what we *think* we should do," he said, sadly.

"Anyway, the Otherworld is a way that one mage can communicate with another, only it's hard. Not everyone can do it. You have to be very familiar with the person you're trying to contact, and I don't think any of us really know Master Minalan well enough to be able to get his attention in the Otherworld. *If* we could even find him."

"So what *are* you doing?" Dara asked, frustrated by her ignorance.

"Master Minalan has another magic Mirror that Master Banamor had made for him. We've been trying to speak to him through it, day and night. The problem is he has to actually be *using* it. And he has to remember he even has it – it's likely still packed away in his luggage. But we have someone trying. We may have gotten a message to Minalan's friend, Baron Arathaniel. But I don't know if he wants to risk a war over a man he's known for half a year."

"So we're . . . alone," Dara said, frowning.

"Don't worry," Gareth urged, with concern. "I may not be a real warmage, but I did study a lot of it back at the War

College. Private wars like this often sputter out for all sorts of reasons without much of anything really happening."

"The two attacks on the pass certainly happened!" Dara pointed out. "My brothers were almost killed!"

"I didn't say it would turn out that way, just that it might," Gareth said, a little discouraged. "We aren't defenseless, here. It's not like it was, before the Spellmonger arrived. The Bovali are strong, and with war leaders like Sir Cei and Sir Forondo around we should be able to hold out for weeks, here. Maybe even drive them off, if we're clever."

"I'm clever," Dara blurted. "At least . . . that's what I'm told," she added, blushing a bit.

"Yes, you're clever," Gareth agreed. "And you are a falconer. And you are Talented. So let's bring all of that wealth to bear on our problems, and see just *how* clever you are."

Dara returned to her work with new purpose. If she could help, she wanted to. For the rest of the morning she sent Frightful crisscrossing the enemy encampment, spying on where their sentries were stationed, where their supplies were kept, and where their forces were deployed. Gareth made notes on a sheaf of parchment and placed counters on the large map of the domain.

A little after midday Zagor returned to the tower and bade them join the company in the Great Hall for luncheon. Dara realized that she was famished – not only had she not eaten since dawn, her falcon had expended a lot of energy flying under her direction. She recalled the bird with a gentle command and skipped down the stairs after the other magi.

The magical corps was afforded high status in the castle, eating at the trestle table closest to the dais where Lady Alya ate with her new baby. Below them in order sat the garrison soldiers, some of whom had returned from duty at the Diketower. Dara enjoyed listening to their rough talk and frank discussion of the work being done there. They expected an attack to come at any time, but seemed almost enthusiastic about the idea.

Her attention was returned to the magi at her table when Gareth and Zagor began discussing how scrying worked, magically. She found it fascinating, the idea of a simple human mind commanding the very elements by magic. Dara did her best to absorb every word.

Most of the language was far above her, but it was helpful that Gareth was what he called "formally Imperially trained" and Zagor was a rustic mountain wild mage who had learned much of his craft from the mysterious Tree Folk – nonhumans who were acknowledged as the masters of magic. The two colleagues frequently had to stop each other and explain something or define a term, and Dara greedily absorbed as much as she could from the conversation.

She was tempted to ask questions . . . but she remembered how difficult it had been for Gareth to explain the Otherworld, without her understanding simpler concepts. Dara might have magical Talent, but she actually knew very little about what that meant. She kept quiet and focused on listening. By the end of the meal, she actually had a pretty good idea of what the Otherworld was, and how it functioned, just from the context of their conversation.

Frightful was waiting at the window for her, when she got back, and she spent some time feeding and praising the bird for her good service. Someone had left a bowl full of chicken innards for her, and she rewarded Frightful with the liver, which she ate greedily. The falcon was confused over Dara's praise. From her perspective she had been flying all day long, and had not caught as much as a sparrow. Dara was reluctant to send her out again so soon, but she wanted to check on her brothers at Caolan's pass, and the enemy they faced on the other side of the ridge.

There was a skirmish of sorts going on when she climbed back behind Frightful's eyes as she circled over the pass. A half-dozen West Flerians were attempting to flank the Westwoodmen's strong position by going off the trail – but that was of little value, Dara figured, based on the number of still bodies lying about with arrows in them. The last fifty feet of the road sloped up to the pass in a way that allowed the defenders an excellent opportunity to shoot at the attackers from behind the barricade at the top of the hill. And the folk of the Westwood were excellent shots.

At the bottom of the slope, safely around a bend to the south and out of bowshot, a larger group of fifty men waited impatiently for an opportunity to do something, while effectively keeping the Sevendori from escaping. As there was no simple way around the barricade at the pass, there was no simple way off of the trail that could avoid the besiegers.

The smaller of the attacking armies was still in the same place as a few days ago, Dara reported, and gave a more accurate picture of their disposition and arrangement to the magical corps, who in turn reported them to Sir Cei. While the Sevendori could do little about the armies that besieged them, at least they were aware of where and who they were.

"It looks like most of the troops facing the Diketower to the north are from West Flerian domains, by their heraldry," Banamor observed, when he read their report that afternoon. "A thousand peasant militia, and three dozen knights and their households. With two small companies of mercenary archers and a company of mercenary lancers. The army in Sashtalia seems to be mostly mercenaries, from the look of it. Light infantry and cavalry, probably locals getting paid by the day. One large company of professional crossbowman – that red rose and spear device you described fits the description of a mercenary unit known as the Gardener's Men, from Lanteel. Less than a quarter of the army is actually Sire Gimbal's sworn men."

"But that's where I saw the checkered cloaks!" Dara pointed out.

"So you did," agreed the Spellwarden, pursing his lips. "They've warded the bottom of the trail and kept us from scrying. It's possible that they've laid other traps along the way, too. If the Censorate is who is paying for those mercenaries, you can bet that they'll want to keep a pretty close eye on how they're used."

"So what help is that to us?" Dara demanded. She had worked so hard, gathering that information, she wanted someone to look at the map and yell "Aha!" and realize a way to win the war. But Master Banamor merely shrugged.

"We don't know yet," he admitted. "This is just one part of the puzzle, my dear. And one I'm not very good at, I'm afraid. But it's always a good idea to know who you are facing in a conflict. And where they are. The Censorate has gone to a great deal of trouble and expense to conceal their armies' movements, and with an afternoon's worth of work you managed to ruin that for them. That, my dear, is a serious boon, even if we don't know yet how it will prove useful."

Dara had to be satisfied with that. She was exhausted, after so much mentally-challenging work guiding Frightful's path and helping the magical corps. After Master Banamor thanked her for her assistance and dismissed her for the day, she had Frightful make one final circuit around the pass before heading back to the castle. Once she was certain her kin were faring well, she felt like she could go back to Westwood Hall and rest.

Thankfully the Westwoodmen still had control of the pass. The attackers had retreated their archers back down the mountain, and a column of Sevendori militia was marching up the other side of the ridge to relieve her tired brothers.

Dara's relief was cut short, however, as Frightful passed overhead. Something caught the bird's eye, if not its attention, and Dara had to exert herself to get her tired falcon to wing back around for another look. She mollified the falcon by letting her rest on a tall branch overlooking the trail . . . and the soldiers.

As the small line of men climbed up the shadowed hill like a troop of determined ants, Dara caught sight of the small banner they bore in addition to the snowflake emblem of Sevendor. A haystack: the symbol of the hamlet of Genly.

The Genlymen were relieving the Westwoodmen in defense of the pass. Just to be certain, Dara held Frightful still until she sighted the leader of the company. Sure enough, the tall form of Railan the Steady plodded into view. The man ignored the bird, as most vale folk ignored wildlife, but Dara did see him turn back and gaze at the castle and villages below him, a strange look on his face.

With a feeling of foreboding in her heart, Dara summoned Frightful back to the castle and broke contact.

"What's the matter?" Gareth asked, tiredly. "Did something happen?"

"No, the attackers have withdrawn," she said, mimicking a term she had picked up from the military folk. It wasn't that hard, once you knew what the words really meant. "The militia marches to relieve the pass now."

"But that's *good* news," Gareth said, his mouth askew with concern.

"Well, yes . . . only the ones who got sent to relieve them are the Genlymen. The villein militia of Genly Hamlet, under Railan the Steady."

"But . . . Railan is a sworn yeoman of Sevendor," Gareth pointed out.

"Who doesn't like magi, Bovali, or the Magelord," reminded Dara, uneasily.

"To betray Sevendor would make him an oathbreaker," Gareth said, shaking his head. "He could lose his head for that. Or worse. He wouldn't risk that, Dara. It just wouldn't be . . . sane."

"You don't know the vale folk like we do," Dara said, shaking her head. "They've been kept down for so long that Railan has them convinced that that's the only thing that they deserve. Look at them: most of them have never eaten so well or lived better in their lives, yet they're always the ones complaining at the market. They call us woodfolk superstitious, because we hold the Flame in reverence, but the fact is they listen to Railan far more than they do their proper gods. For years he told them that he was their only shield against Sir Erantal. Now he's telling them that he's their only hope against the Magelord. Putting him in charge of that pass is a mistake," Dara warned.

Gareth shook his head. "Sir Cei knows what he's doing," he insisted. "He's been to war, before, and he's a good judge of men. He wouldn't send Railan and the Genlymen up there unless he was certain of their loyalty."

"He wouldn't send Railan and the Genlymen up there if he was better acquainted with them," Dara sniffed. "I only hope that I'm wrong."

"So do I," agreed Gareth, seriously. "If we lose that pass, our enemies will be able to march right over it and to the gates of the castle."

"And right past the Westwood," Dara nodded, gravely.

That evening Dara joined a long line of folk risking leaving the castle before the great gates were shut and locked for the night. The guardsmen recognized her, apparently, from the falcon on her arm and let her pass without questioning. Dara was just as glad that they hadn't – she was exhausted. She had considered lingering at the castle for supper, at

Gareth's shy invitation, but she wanted to see her brothers and ensure that they were really alive. Each of them, even Kobb.

Thankfully the Hall was glowing with light and merriment, though there were three men guarding the bridge. The fighting men had returned home to a generous dinner, and everyone wanted to hear stories of battle . . . particularly the capture of the hated Sir Erantal.

Usually it would be Kobb who dominated the conversation with bragging and boasting, but even he deferred to Kyre with respect Dara had never seen before. Her uncle and her father looked on proudly as her oldest brother quietly recounted the second dawn attack, and how he and two of his brothers had tackled the knight as he tried to turn and flee. They had wrestled his sword away from him, demanding his surrender in the name of the Magelord. The old knight had been frightened and had promised him a great reward if he let him go . . . but the *Westwoodmen knew their duty*, as Kyre said, quoting a popular proverb.

"Then the clumsy ox kept tripping over his feet all the way down the mountain," Kyre shrugged with a rare grin. "As hard as I tried to keep him on his feet, he kept falling into briars, and brambles, and the occasional tree or shrub . . ."

That brought a roar of laughter from the Hall. Everyone hated Erantal for his years of neglect and abuse. Kamen's unfortunate injury last winter had been only the last of the insults the knight had given the entire domain over the years. That laugh seemed to release the long-held tension everyone had always felt about Sir Erantal. Only now, with him sitting in a dank cell below his former castle, did everyone feel safe.

Kyre had little good to say about his relief at the pass, however.

"Don't misunderstand me," he said, glancing at the Flame, "we're *tired!* Two solid days and nights was hard. We would have been happy to see a company of Tal Alon with wooden spoons, if they were there to relieve us. But to see that . . . that brigade of peasants standing there, holding their spears like hoes and their bows like snakes . . . by the Flame, I hope they don't face anything tougher than a stiff breeze! Yeoman Railan was just as glad to see us go, the way he dismissed us. Like we had bungled the whole thing up . . ." he growled.

"He's just jealous that he wasn't the one who captured Erantal!" called one of her cousins, which inspired more laughter. Railan had long been Erantal's chief opponent, in the valley. He had hated Sir Erantal longer and with better reason than most. Personally, Dara was glad that it had been her brother, and a Westwoodman, who had taken the prize. He might not be worth much in ransom, perhaps, but just having him under lock and key made everyone feel better.

Dara kept quiet about her own role in the war effort. She didn't want the attention – she barely understood what she had done for Sevendor, and it didn't seem nearly as important or glorious as Kyre's contribution. He and their kin had risked their lives, after all. She had just flown her falcon a lot.

The older men had broken out a bottle of spirits to toast Kyre's victory and everyone's service, and perhaps because everyone was anxious and some of them just needed a snort before bed. But Dara found herself yawning in front of the Flame. Custom said that meant it was time for bed, and no arguments. While Dara was now old enough to decide such things as when to go to bed on her own, she could feel her body getting heavier and her eyelids drooping.

She quietly excused herself and went upstairs, checking on Frightful's perch before stripping off her clothes and putting on her sleeping gown. She rarely bothered with the thing, usually, but suddenly sleeping in soft linen in a comfortable bed sounded extremely appealing. With thoughts of the Otherworld and armies spinning in her head, Dara fell asleep.

The next morning she awoke late, the sun already in the sky. She didn't know why or how she knew, but something was wrong, she felt. The Hall didn't sound different, from her room, but something was . . . *off*.

Not even bothering to dress she bounded down the creaky stairway barefooted, expecting to see the Hall packed for breakfast before everyone went to their duties for the day. Instead it was mostly empty, with only a few women bustling about the kitchen. But their voices weren't their usual calm, chattering tones. There was a note of anxiety in them that disturbed Dara before she even heard their words.

When she entered the kitchen she was surprised to see her aunt – not working at kneading bread or stirring soup or directing the making of the porridge, but standing before a little-used cabinet door. The spice jars and preserves stored inside had been pushed aside, and her aunt was handing out short bows and quivers of arrows to her cousins and kinswomen. The looks on their faces were stark.

"What's wrong?" Dara demanded. "What's happened?"

"Little Bird!" her aunt scolded her. "Go put some clothes on! The sun is long up!"

Dara ignored her. "What is happening? Why . . .?"

Dara's aunt looked troubled. "Word came before dawn this morning – a young knight from the castle and his men. They went up to inspect the pass. Only they were greeted with arrows, not passwords."

"What?" Dara asked, her eyes wide in disbelief.

"That damn fool Railan has gone and *turned his colors* on us!" spat her aunt, furiously. "He and his idiots waited until all the responsible folk were gone, and then they sent word down to the enemy. Sometime after midnight they laid down their arms and surrendered. *Without a fight.* The West Flerians hold the pass now – I guess Sir Erantal will have the last laugh, Flame burn his bones!"

Dara didn't know what to say – her worst fears had come to pass! The road from Caolan's Pass led straight to the gates of Sevendor Castle, bypassing the strength the domain had gathered at the Diketower. This was a disaster!

"So where is everyone?" Dara finally managed.

"That young knight collected all the menfolk at the manor to hold the bottom of the trail – if we can't hold the pass, at least we can deny them the use of the road. They're up at the second landing, I expect, keeping them at bay."

"So . . . why are you . . .?"

Dara's aunt grunted. "The chasm protects us and the Westwood from ruffians, girl, but it also overlooks that road almost half way down. There are places that can be held, where invaders can be shot at across the chasm without worry of them coming after you."

"So why aren't the men out there?" Dara asked, confused. If that was a safer position, then . . .

"Because they're needed on the road," her aunt explained, with diminishing patience. "All of them! Your father, your uncles, your cousins, your brothers, all of them!" She sounded desperately worried.

But then she picked up the last bow from the secret cache and strung it with surprising familiarity. Then the dumpy middle-aged woman slipped a quiver over her back and drew an arrow in a smooth motion. "They're needed on the road, but it doesn't take a man's arm to hold a bow. Every woman here has learned how to nock and fire, and if we can help snipe at the foe then that will discourage them from harming our kin!"

Dara looked around at her female cousins, and even saw her sister among them, a bow in her hand. None of them looked particularly enthusiastic, but they all looked determined. They knew what was at stake, and they knew their duty as well as any in the Westwood. Westwoodmen could shoot . . . that was true regardless if they wore skirts or leggings.

"No bow for you, Little Bird," her cousin Linta said, shaking her head sadly. "But if you want to fetch us shafts while we wait . . ."

"No," Dara said, quietly, almost to herself. Then she said it louder. "No, I don't need a bow!" She turned to head back to her room.

"You can't expect to use that toy crossbow of yours!" her aunt called to her back. "That won't even shoot across the chasm!"

"I'm not getting my bow!" Dara promised. "I'm getting my *bird!* And when I'm done with them, every West Flerian in that pass is going to be sorry they ever *heard* the name Sevendor!"

Chapter Fifteen

The Lifting Of The Siege

The road down from the captured pass lay for much of its length along the eastern side of the great chasm that separated the Westwood from the rest of Sevendor. Along much of that length, concealed on the protected western side of the great gash in the earth, were places where archers could stand and shoot, harassing any attackers from behind the great natural defense. Hundreds of years before the strategic value of the chasm had been recognized by the Westwoodmen, and they had long established ideal positions on the western side to protect the road.

Chief among these were the Seven Steps: seven particular positions, all of them great stones or natural landings, from which the Westwoodmen could cover nearly the entire run of the road. While most of the armed men of the estate were now clustered at the bottom of the steep slope, the womenfolk of the Westwood quickly took up positions on the Seven Steps. At every position four or five women set up their quivers and prepared their bows, nervously awaiting the chance at a target.

They didn't wait long.

Dara surveyed the defenses from Frightful's eyes as she flew the length of the road. With the sun at her back in the early morning, the falcon's eyes were particularly sharp – she could easily see the individual archers taking up their positions behind stones and embankments on the other side. While they were just "people" to Frightful's mind, when Dara exerted herself and exercised her will, she could identify individuals, like her aunt and her sister.

The base of the slope was barricaded by the Sevendori against the West Flerians. Two large wagons had been pulled to block the way, while men with pikes and spears stood behind. Flanking the position on either side were pockets of four or five Westwoodmen or archers from the castle. More than seventy men stood to defend the road.

Their leader was not, she saw, her father, though Kamen was certainly there. It was a young knight from the castle, bearing a dirty white cloak and a shock of unruly hair, when he took off his helmet. He was no older than Kyre (who was paying rapt attention to the man as he discussed his plans with them), but he was directing the defense with the kind of confidence only a knight could command.

Dara didn't spare much time watching her kin – she wanted to see what the enemy was up to.

Frightful glided up the slope, catching a small thermal over the chasm for lift. As she soared to a hemlock tree fifty feet from the pass, she saw the other side of the battle forming up. Nearly a hundred men now swarmed over the small frontier station of Caolan's Pass, and a slow trickle of reinforcements was hiking up behind them.

These were not the lightly-armored archers who had harassed the pass the last few days. These men bore long swords, large shields, and well-crafted chain armor or coats of plates. Twenty crossbowmen were setting up defensive positions, using the same advantages in height and angle that had been used against them the day before.

Unfortunately, there was no sign of Railan the Steady or his treacherous Genlymen. Dara's heart burned with hatred over the Yeoman's betrayal. His fear and resentment had put every soul in Sevendor at risk – especially her family. As she watched the big, ugly-looking mercenary soldiers file in behind each other, preparing to descend the slope two-abreast, her fear for her father and brothers overtook her hatred of Railan. She had to do something to help. But what?

Convinced that she understood the nature of the forces about to come down, she directed Frightful back to her room and then went looking for her father. The guards at the bridge almost stopped her, citing the danger. A cousin and two second cousins tried to keep her safe in the hall, but when she threatened to make them bird food, they allowed her to pass. Dara didn't usually joke about such things, they knew.

She ran for almost half a mile through the outer forest until she got to the fork in the road. She took the left-hand way, and within moments she was standing breathlessly at the blockade she had just seen from the air.

"Dara!" her father shouted across the field, his voice heavy with concern. "What are *you* doing here? What's wrong?"

"I . . . I . . ." Dara panted, until someone handed her a waterskin. She gulped it gratefully before continuing. "I used Frightful to scout up ahead. They have almost a hundred men up there, now. Twenty with arbalests. Mostly sword-and-shield men. They're preparing a sortie now!"

"What?" the young knight asked, as he came to see what the commotion was about. "How came you to know this, girl?"

"My sister is a beastmaster, Sir Festaran," Kyre explained, helpfully. "She can ride inside her falcon's head."

Dara expected the young knight to be skeptical and dismiss her, but instead his eyebrows shot up.

"This is true?" he merely asked. The young man was tall and thin, and had a face full of freckles inside his steel helmet. Nor was he a Bovali – Dara had become used to their strange accent, since the Magelord had come, but this man spoke like a proper Riverlord.

"Yes, my lord," Dara said, her eyes downcast. "I'm a . . . a falconer. But I'm also Talented. I, uh, I was flying the bird one day and saw a batfox raiding a chicken coop for eggs one morning," she lied, thinking up a plausible story. For some reason she was reluctant to mention Gareth's role in her discovery to the young knight. "Before I knew it, I was inside my bird's head, seeing it as it attacked. It was scary," she said, truthfully.

"Amazing!" the knight nodded, his eyes wide in wonder.

"Since then, I helped scout out the enemy positions for the Magical Corps all day yesterday," she admitted. "When I heard what that . . . rat Railan did, I knew you'd want to know what you were fighting against as soon as possible."

"Outstanding initiative!" praised the young knight. "That's more help than I was looking for, but no less welcome. What is your name, girl?"

"Lenodara – Dara, that is," Dara answered, self-consciously. "Of Westwood Hall."

"Well, Dara of Westwood, I am Sir Festaran of Hosly. Technically I'm a prisoner of Sevendor awaiting ransom – a long tale for another time – but as my loyalties seem to be more with my captors than my father's liege at the moment, I have accepted a temporary position as assistant to Sir Cei. Who has tasked me to hold this road," he added, glancing nervously at the end of the mountain trail. "That is what I aim to do. Further, I think it would be a lovely wedding gift to the man if we could re-capture the pass and secure it."

"I can think of few finer, my lord," agreed Dara, allowing the young knight's enthusiasm to lift her spirits. He didn't sound discouraged at all – this was simply a task he was assigned, and he would do it with full devotion to duty, she suspected. There was no gloom or fear, here. That made her feel better.

"Then, if you please, employ your falcon to spy on our foes. Let us know when they advance, for as you can see we cannot sight the top of the pass from here. In truth I cannot see up to the second landing. I have archers covering the entire eastern side of the road," he said, pointing out to a few scattered knots of archers in the fields and scrublands around the trail."

"You also have archers covering the western side," Dara pointed out. "My aunt led all of the Westwood's womenfolk up to the Seven Steps. They're ready to fire."

"The Seven Steps?" the freckled knight asked, confused. "The womenfolk?"

Kamen stepped forward to explain the nature of the defense, assuring that the women would not even be seen by the attackers, thanks to the concealing rocks of the Steps, and that they would be competent enough at their archery to be effective. Sir Festaran looked thoughtful, studying the winding path with his lips pursed.

"We will be best served if we can lure our foe into advancing, then, attacking him from an unexpected direction," he decided. "Send a runner to these Steps, of yours," he ordered Kamen, "have them hold their fire until they hear the signal: a loud pop."

"A loud pop?" her father asked, skeptically.

"I am," Sir Festaran informed them all, proudly, "not *just* a simple country knight; thanks to the Spellmonger's magical snowstorm, and the capricious whims of the gods, I seem to have possession of the smallest amount of *rajira* – magical Talent," he explained.

"A knight . . . who is a wizard?" Kamen asked, amused.

"No worse than a lord who's a wizard," considered Kyre.

"I believe the accepted term is 'knight mage' – or at least it will be if Lord Minalan gets his way. Alas, the gods gave me only a small measure of *rajira*. Even with some schooling in the arcane arts by the Spellmonger, I'm unable to do most of the spellwork ordinary wizards do. Instead I have been given the ability to . . . well, *estimate*."

"Estimate?" Dara asked.

"Ask me how much ale is left in a mug, how many sheep are in a field, how many pins in a cushion, and I can tell you the number almost instantly . . . or at least very, *very* close to the proper number. It's what the magi call a 'sport talent'."

"So . . . how is that useful here?" asked Kamen, confused.

"It isn't," shrugged the knight. "At least, not as far as I can see. But I have been studying with the Spellmonger's apprentices, a little, and when I haven't been beating them soundly in swordplay they've been teaching me a few of their smaller spells. The few I have the Talent to manage. One of which is a cantrip that does nothing more than make a loud pop. And as pointless as it seems, that spell may, indeed, prove useful here."

"So it may," conceded Kamen. "Very well, Kyre, send Kibi back to the first of the Steps; tell them to hold fire until they hear a loud noise, then fire at will. Pass it on up until they all know," he ordered. Kibi, a second cousin not much older than Dara, sprinted off to do so.

"Now, Dara of Westwood," Sir Festaran asked in a friendly voice, "can you climb back inside of your bird and tell us what our foes are up to?"

* * *

The first attack down the road came midmorning, when thirty heavily-armored infantry men marched down the hill, two-by-two. They bore their shields in front of them, their spears on their shoulders, and walked with an arrogance and cockiness that angered Dara. She was about to see that cockiness put to the test.

Sir Festaran allowed the invaders to advance unchallenged until they were half-way down the long slope. When the first of them came within range of his farthest-set archers, all of the Westwoodmen on the eastern side of the road opened fire. From her tree-top vantage point, Dara could see the shafts quietly let fly in a ragged volley, from positions all over the eastern side.

The West Flerians quickly moved to defend themselves from the surprise attack. Unfortunately for them, the shallow ditch on the eastern side of the trail gave them little cover from the arrows, and their attackers were spread out enough so that they only way they could defend themselves was to collect all in one place, using their great wooden shields to cover each other. Men fell by ones and twos as arrows found their marks, and the shouts and screams from the road were pitiful.

Just when the West Flerians were preparing for a counter-attack, to leap across the ditch and give chase to the lightly-armored Westwoodmen, the women of the wood let fly with their own attack – directly into the unprotected backs of the invaders. The sound of bowstrings twanging was unheard as the men tried to defend themselves from the front. By the time the first shafts fell among them, it was too late.

The leader of the sortie was wise enough to know when he'd been beat. He called the retreat and the remaining West Flerians scrambled back up the hill to the pass, leaving twelve men on the ground behind them.

"That's the spirit!" the young knight cheered, when the report came back down the trail. "That will teach them that they can't just walk into Sevendor!"

Dara continued scouting by falcon for the rest of the morning. Near noon, she saw the West Flerians preparing another sortie. This time the Westwoodmen prepared a more aggressive response. Sir Festaran took twenty men – including her father, uncle, and brothers – up the trail to the first switchback, where a blind landing gave them some cover from above. There they waited until, once again, the Warbird's troops began marching down the mountain, albeit with more caution this time.

Shields held carefully to their sides, against the scattered sniping, the West Flerians descended in force to halfway down the trail. The hail of arrows from the western side of the chasm was more relentless, so they favored that side, but whoever was in command of the sortie had figured out that running the gauntlet of arrows would be easier if the invaders began running, instead of walking slowly and presenting easier targets.

Dara couldn't fault the logic of the enemy commander, but she watched with grim amusement as the West Flerians broke into a run. While that did, indeed, make it more difficult for the defenders to hit their targets, it also scattered the West Flerians. It also gave them ample opportunity to stumble and fall down the trail, which they began doing with increasing regularity. By the time the force was near to the final quarter of the run, a third of their number had been wounded or slain.

Then Sir Festaran sprang his trap, and for a few hot, heart-stopping minutes Dara watched her family in battle through Frightful's eyes.

Her father swung his sword with efficiency, picking his targets and carefully but decisively thrusting and cutting as needed. Her uncle had chosen a battle axe from the manor's armory, and he was hacking away with it like he was cutting firewood for the winter. Her brothers Kobb and Kasdan danced on the edges of the battle and struck from the flanks with their spears, while her cousin Kinden, a keen-eyed lad who spent more time ranging the woods than in the hall, was slashing away at the disoriented foes with a long hunting knife.

But Dara had trouble sparing any attention for anyone but Kyre. Her oldest brother strode commandingly into the middle of the battle, where his uncles and father fought shoulder-to-shoulder, and he began making fast, hard strikes in support of everyone he saw. His new sword whirled in the air, and he wielded it as if he had been fighting since boyhood, not a few short days. Dara was morbidly fascinated to see him not just fight, but use his enemies against themselves. He was nimble and sure in his movements, his arms constantly in motion and his feet never still for long.

The sudden and unexpected attack by the defenders pushed the remainder of the attackers back up the hill, and they faced sniping from the sides the entire way. Sir Festaran did what he could to press the attack all the way to the top of the ridge . . . but when he made the third landing, thirty men behind him, a volley of crossbow bolts from the pass stopped him.

"Those are war bows, not hunting bows," Sir Festaran said, panting, when they returned to the first landing. "They've got a longer range and they penetrate armor like hot tea in the snow. They can put an iron quarrel clean through an oaken shield, at range. And with that height advantage we're going to have a hard time getting up there." Only two men had been hit by the insidious things, but that was enough. Both men had to be carried back down the mountain and all the way to the castle.

"They keep getting reinforced," Dara reported, dutifully. "Frightful sees another score marching up the northern side of the slope."

"Once they have enough," counseled one of the other soldiers from the castle, as he gazed at the pass above, "they won't hesitate to send a hundred men down that trail. We couldn't stop a hundred men, not if they have crossbows."

"Sure we could," Uncle Keram dismissed. "They have to get through the gauntlet from the Seven Steps, first. Then they'd have to meet us on the trail, where they can't put more than two men abreast, or at one of the landings, where we can bottleneck the trail."

The argument went on for some time, as everyone caught their breath – too long, as it turned out. Another sortie tried to descend the trail a few hours after noon, and Sir Festaran elected to meet them on the second landing. That had the advantage of forcing one half of the line to hold a shield wall against the women of the Westwood's withering fire while the other half fought. A few strategically-placed snipers and

Sir Festaran were prepared when the West Flerians fell on the second landing.

The battle was heated, Dara knew, for she had remained back at the base of the mountain and was flying overhead with Frightful. She witnessed the relentless attack, the desperate defense, and the methodical archery of her folk. While only a third of the arrows fired found their marks, the ever-present whiz of shafts among them kept the West Flerians too distracted to press their assault.

Sir Festaran bravely led a countercharge, once the foe closed with them. The lanky young knight threw himself into the battle with bravery and enthusiasm, Dara noted. Though he was not nearly as graceful or deadly as her brother Kyre seemed (when she saw him shoot a man trying to flank the landing, then drop his bow and draw his dagger in time to stab the arm of another opportunistic West Flerian, Dara began to suspect that her oldest brother had a talent for battle), Sir Festaran was undoubtedly leading the effort.

He gave orders that made sense and were followed; he called encouragement to his men as they beat their swords and spears against the shields of the West Flerians, and then he yelled curses at the foe as he pushed his shoulder between their shields and struck at them with his own blade.

The work was hard and hot, and the field quickly became bloody as more men fell; mostly, Dara noted with relief, among the attackers. When the West Flerians finally sounded a retreat and limped back up the mountain, another ten men lay dead along the trail to Caolan's Pass. Eight of them were West Flerians.

But none had stepped foot on the floor of the valley, yet. That, Sir Festaran assured them, was a victory in itself.

When Dara reported that a large contingent had broken off from the main group at the pass and was seeking a way down through the high trails, Sir Festaran took the initiative and pressed a surprise attack that afternoon. There was no easy way down from the ridge that way, everyone in Sevendor knew – the cottages in the high meadows along the ridge were tiny and isolated, almost another world altogether from either the farmers of the vales or the woodsmen of the forest. Most of the residents of the ridges had been evacuated to Sevendor Castle days ago. Their cots and fields would be empty, up there, and the men sent to investigate them were too far out to be of use to their comrades.

Only twenty men held the pass when Sir Festaran launched his attack. A few of the Westwoodmen (including her brother Kobb, she realized) had volunteered to climb the steep and unforgiving slopes outside of the trail, a difficult task even for those who knew it well. When the bowmen were in place, they began firing on the sentries, allowing Sir Festaran and Keram and Kyre to lead half of their force to attack the pass.

That had been another hot battle and longer than the first two skirmishes. The West Flerians who held the pass were well dug into the site, and only surprise and a quick advance kept them from clearing the trail with their crossbows. As it was the ten-minute battle ended in defeat for the Sevendori when more reinforcements from the other side of the ridge arrived.

Sir Festaran was loath to give even an inch to the foes, but enthusiasm and valor were not protection against arrows. Though they had made impressive gains at the top of the ridge, the West Flerians drove them back again. Realizing he was overmatched, the young knight led his men in a strategic retreat down to the third landing. The West Flerians saw the momentum change in the fight, and they pursued to the landing. Sir Festaran had hidden several of the Westwoodmen there to cover a retreat, if necessary.

They fired adeptly at the mercenaries who followed, and for a few moments it looked as though the momentum had changed again. But then some crossbowmen sent down the rugged slopes found a spot from which to shoot, and between them and the mercenaries, the fate of the Sevendori defenders was in doubt. Sir Festaran himself fought bravely next to Dara's brother Kyre and her cousin Kinder for awhile, each incapacitating a man before falling back, while she watched from Frightful's eyes.

A particularly large mercenary bearing a wide blade and a shield the size of a barn door broke through the line of Sevendori with a powerful bellow. He turned to strike at them from behind, and Dara realized that none of her friends could even see where he was, much less defend against him.

Without even realizing it, Dara's anger and fright at her brother's life welled up inside her, and she began directing Frightful almost automatically. She flew the bird into the big mercenary's face, pecking madly at his eyes through his helmet with her sharp beak, while her talons raked across his armor. Dara felt united with Frightful in a terrifying new way: their anger had joined together, and that anger transformed into violence. To Dara's surprise and horror, that violence felt good to express in defense of her friends.

Even though she did little damage, Frightful's unexpected attack kept the big mercenary from hitting anyone. He swung around wildly, clawing at the air with his sword while he ducked his head to avoid the manic pecking at his eyes.

A horn suddenly sounded at the far end of the landing. Dara sent Frightful skyward to recover, circling over the battle. That's when she saw the large form of Sir Cei, in full armor. The big Wilderlands knight lead a party of soldiers into the fray in support of the Sevendori, his Wilderlands greatsword slashing relentlessly against the enemy. He blocked the mercenary's next attack, pivoted around on one foot, and drove his sword against the man's helm, hard. Though the blade's edge failed to connect, the blow was hard enough to send the man sailing off into the rough next to the landing, his sword and shield flung wide.

The unexpected reinforcements allowed Sir Festaran to withdraw his forces without losing a life – though the Westwoodmen's archery took a few. Sir Cei and his men, arriving so forcefully, pushed the mercenaries up the trail . . . those who did not fall before his blade. When Dara was certain that Sir Festaran and the Westwoodmen had made it safely out of range of the crossbowmen still lingering along the trail, she sent Frightful back to her and then withdrew her consciousness. She waited impatiently for the defenders to arrive in the lowest landing, and didn't properly breathe until she saw all of her brothers and uncles- and especially her father - in the flesh.

"We'll stop here, for today," Sir Festaran said, panting through his helmet once he'd seen the survivors (her brother Kobb had been stabbed in the arm, she saw, but it didn't appear to be serious) safely back down the mountain. The young knight was himself nursing a wrist sprained in the battle, and now carried his sword in his left hand. "They won't try to descend at night – actually, I hope they do – and we can see about some reinforcements ourselves on the morrow."

"A unit of militia from Southridge is already preparing to march," assured Sir Cei, as he left the trail, pulling off his helmet. "You did good work here, today, Sir Festaran. You led your men well, and got them down alive without losing a one. Perhaps when this is over," the big knight said in his thick accent, "I can speak to the Magelord about lifting your ransom and offering you a post as deputy castellan."

"That . . . that would be a generous offer, my lord," Sir Festaran said, bowing uncomfortably. "But I fear it is poor precedence to reward failure."

"Failure is in the eye," Sir Cei countered. "Thanks to your attacks, the West Flerians will be far more hesitant to come down that slope. They know that it is held, enthusiastically and in force. They won't try again until they have far superior numbers, or are relieved from this side of the ridge. We can set some scouts up above to make certain. And tomorrow we can re-assess their strength and consider how we might dislodge them.

"But for now," the castellan said, gazing up the trail, "we'll just hold here and make sure none of those . . . *gentlemen*," he said, choosing his words carefully, "make their way into Sevendor tonight. That, at least, we can do."

* * *

The Flerians did not attack that night, nor did they try to come down the mountain at dawn, just as Sir Cei predicted. Dara encamped all night with her brothers, though it would have been easy enough to return to the manor, because she did not want to miss anything – and she thought she might be of use. Not that she could fly Frightful at night, but she could not imagine not being there with them as they stood guard.

But the expected dawn attack did not come. At dawn there was no attack. The scouts reported that the West Flerians merely made breakfast and guarded the pass. Indeed, they seemed content to hold the site and wait, a fact that irritated Sir Festaran to no end.

"If they would attack, we can whittle them away by attrition," he griped, as the day wore on. "But if they just sit up there . . ."

"I don't see as we have a choice, my lord," Uncle Keram pointed out to the younger man. "We've shown them that we can deny them the trail – but if we cannot retake the pass, then they are likely ordered to hold it against us while their fellows work against the Diketower. Any weakness on our part will be exploited, to Sevendor's defeat."

"You may be right," muttered Sir Festaran. "While we've been fiddling with this lot, the Diketower has been attacked thrice – and held," he added, proudly. "As many as five hundred men have attacked it, and it's held. Surely we can do as much here."

The West Flerians were content to stay up on the ridge, Dara reasoned, so there was no real need of her falcon hanging around them. Intrigued by the story of the other battles, Dara convinced Frightful to veer away from Caolan's Pass and seek out the main entrance to the vale.

The devastation was impressive and sickening, once she realized those cast-off-looking dolls on the ground were grown men who had fallen. Just beyond the Enchanted Forest there was a large gathering, hundreds of men and horses, and there seemed to be places farther back where construction had begun on various things. Dara thought it odd that the West Flerians would be building anything, so she landed Frightful unobtrusively in a nearby tree and looked over the busy workmen.

It was hard to say with certainty, but Dara became convinced that they were building some sort of siege engine. She'd heard of the things, of course: a huge machine capable of hurling boulders or other missiles against a fortified wall – or over it. Though the West Flerians looked as if they were in the early stages of construction, they seemed to know their business. She told Sir Festaran, who understood the gravity of the information and had her make a report to Sir Cei.

After that, Dara reported to the Castle every morning to help scout. The West Flerians occupying Caolan's Pass weren't attacking, Sir Festaran and the Westwoodmen were unable to re-take the position, so there was really little she could do of value there.

But scouting the much larger army was helpful. Their attacks on the Diketower became insistent, and preparing the garrison for whatever Sire Gimbal felt like throwing at the Sevendori that day gave them an edge. Gareth was there, these days, lending what little magical assistance he could. The young mage was entirely dedicated to defending his adopted home, Dara could see when she spied him through Frightful's eyes. But his powers and abilities seemed inadequate to the task. Though he knew some warmagic, as he had bragged, his spells were not highly regarded by the folk he was ostensibly protecting. He looked more and more dejected about that.

Dara pitied him – Gareth was so earnest, so smart, and so friendly it pained her to see him try and fail at things his colleagues could do easily, thanks to their witchstones. He was very smart, but without that power he wasn't very effective. The most he had been able to do was deduce which tents the Censorate warmagi were in.

Dara was about to say something to him - one day a week into the siege - after a spell he'd hoped would discover the exact location of the Warbird failed. He looked distraught, his thin face contorted in anger at himself. Zagor was there, and Dara witnessed how adept the hedgemage was at talking to Gareth, but it was clear that the young wizard was frustrated. Gareth had thrown a book across the room, after his spell collapsed. Zagor was beginning to sooth him with a tale when the door to the tower room burst open.

"We've made contact with the Spellmonger over the Mirror!" came the news from Banamor, excitedly. "He's heading home at once! Hopefully he can handle this whole mess and let me get back to planning the fair!"

"And . . . save all of our lives," Gareth said to his master's back. Banamor was already spreading the news to others, and in a few moments various parts of the castle began to cheer. Zagor smiled, nodded to the two young people, and headed toward the chamber where the magic Mirror was kept.

"Just in time," Gareth said, dejectedly, but with some relief. "Any longer and we would have cocked up the entire war, and likely lost the domain for the Spellmonger."

"We did all right," Dara countered. "We've been under attack for a week, and we're still here. That's important," she reminded him.

"You always know the right thing to say," sighed Gareth. "Maybe the Spellmonger won't be quite so mad, now."

"He won't be mad at you – at *us*," she corrected. "He'll be mad at the West Flerians."

"You're right – and I don't envy them. I know Master Minalan only a little, but I would never want him mad at me. He has . . . creative ways to express himself. Thanks," Gareth said, catching her hand. He stared at her intently. "I really appreciate all the help you've been," he said with a shy smile.

"It's my duty," she said, off-handedly. But she was suddenly uncomfortable at the intensity of his notice. "And I have learned a lot about magi," she added, quickly. "And magic!"

"Good," Gareth nodded, realizing he was being too intense. "You really do have a lot of Talent, Dara. No matter what, you should develop it. You're smart enough to be a really good mage, someday."

"I can't even read," dismissed Dara. If she'd learned anything about magi in the last week, it was how important books and words were to their practice. To her, they were just incomprehensible marks on the parchment, but Gareth, Olmeg, and even Banamor referred to the books in the workshop frequently.

"You can learn," Gareth shrugged. "It's not that hard. I've even seen children learn. And life as a mage isn't so bad."

"I'm a *falconer*," reminded Dara, nervously. "I don't need to be a mage."

"Dara, you *are* a mage," he said, standing. "You're a beastmaster. A novice beastmaster, but you've developed very quickly, and I think you have a lot of native Talent. You could go a long way, if you had the right resources and training. And encouragement," he added.

"Maybe," she shrugged, pretending that the lad's sudden intense interest didn't bother her. "But while this is fun, it isn't as much fun as hunting Frightful. *That's* what I really want to do," she assured him.

"You can do both," he replied. "And more. Magic informs, it doesn't limit. Not anymore," he said, earnestly.

"I . . . I'll think about it," Dara said, more lightly than she felt.

After that she avoided Gareth as much as she could for a few days. Instead she worked with Zagor, or sometimes Olmeg. Eventually she noted that Gareth wasn't showing up at the Magelord's workshop in the castle anymore, and she got worried. He had volunteered to be at the front, at the Diketower, Master Zagor told her when she asked. That made Dara worry about him, because it was dangerous at the Diketower. But at least he wasn't here, looking at her.

It wasn't that she didn't like the young mage – she did. Gareth was always friendly and talkative, always polite. He treated her like a noblewoman and a colleague of sorts, not a dimwitted, ignorant drudge born in the woods. In fact, that was part of the problem. He treated her . . . *too* well. With too much deference. She had seen her brothers and cousins do that, occasionally . . . but only when they *liked* a girl.

Dara couldn't face the idea that Gareth liked her. She didn't know why, but it made her uncomfortable. The mage was only a few years older than she, and he was odd-looking, even a bit homely. But while working with him in the Spellmonger's workshop, she had sensed his interest in her. For whatever reason, Dara could not face that – or him – without feeling terribly confused. Instead she buried herself in spying on the movements of the West Flerians, scouting the frontiers and even checking on their far-flung outposts with her bird's eyes.

That's what allowed her to be the first to spot the column of troops approaching the vale from the east. She was using her bird to examine the road that ran to Sevendor's vale from the east, toward the heart of West Fleria. While the flow of reinforcements from the Warbird's lands had slowed to a trickle, Sevendor had to be on guard against more foes. That's what threw her, when she first saw the banner at the head of the column.

At first Dara thought it was yet more reinforcements for the attackers, but then the vanguard of the army got closer, and she saw that they bore a banner, green and white. A white snowflake on a green field. Behind it was a long column of fighting men, armored, marching, or mounted. Many bore tabards or sashes with the same device.

The Spellmonger had arrived, finally, to save them all.

Chapter Sixteen

The Spellmonger's Trial

After Magelord Minalan returned life nearly returned to normal in Sevendor. The barricades were hauled away and the bodies were buried. The wounded were healed and the harvest was begun. Dara returned to her room at Westwood Hall, her services no longer needed by the Magical Corps, now that the Magelord was back and the war was over. The Magelord had not just returned to save Sevendor, he had taken the opportunity of the Warbird's deployment to hire a mercenary army and conquer the Warbird's entire unguarded domain. Sire Gimbal had been sent packing back to his brother's court.

Everyone else just tried to get back to normal.

Dara helped out at the castle until her help was no longer needed. Then she resigned herself to finishing out the summer by perfecting Frightful's hunting. The high meadows of the Westwood would only be active for a few more weeks, she knew, before the creatures there began settling in for the winter. Already the birds had begun to change, as the migratory ducks and geese made their stop in Sevendor's small ponds and single lake on their way from the Kuline mountains in the north to warmer climes along the coast or beyond.

Dara hunted Frightful in peaceful solitude – at first. By the second day she was already bored with simply hunting and killing. So was Frightful. Most falconers had to guess what their birds were feeling, but Dara inescapably *knew* when Frightful was bored, thanks to their bond, and after the third rabbit of the day the falcon was finding the exercise tedious.

The one day she spared herself from hunting was a week after the siege was broken. Most of the wounded men had returned to the Hall from the castle already, as the place stood down from a condition of war. There were friendly soldiers everywhere, Dara saw as she followed her family, dressed in finery, as they crossed the bridge and made their way to the Sevendor Village commons.

Master Minalan had summoned all of the Yeomen and their families for a special court, held in conjunction with no less prestigious persons than Sire Sigalan of Trestendor and Baron Arathaniel. Dara had heard of neither man before her brief service in the Magical Corps, but the experience during the siege had introduced her to the politics of the greater world beyond Sevendor's ridges. Now Dara knew who they were, and what their presence meant.

Both men were neighbors and firm allies of the Magelord. Both had lent him troops in his conquest of the Warbird's unguarded domains, while his men and armies were occupied besieging Sevendor. The Magelord had hired mercenaries, used his powerful magic, and gotten the aid of his fellow warmagi. The tale was being told that he had confronted Sire Gimbal on the field with the sight of his captured wife and children, and those of his lords and castellans, that the Magelord and his allies had taken as they had rampaged through West Fleria.

Now the Magelord sat in judgment. Dara watched with a mixture of horror and fascination as the man wisely dealt with those who had aided his domain in its time of need . . . and those who had betrayed it.

First, the criminals. Dara watched as Railan the Steady, Sir Erantal, and a bunch of Genlymen who had been captured in battle by the Spellmonger's forces were tried and convicted for treason by the Spellmonger. With harsh words and contempt in his voice, Magelord Minalan sentenced both men to die by magic . . . and then had their heads off on the spot faster than a man could draw a sword.

To the others he banished or punished with magemarks – large red splotches across their faces that told them out as criminals. More than a dozen Genlymen were sentenced that way, and to the Westwoodmen it seemed like an overabundance of mercy. While none of their folk had died in the siege, plenty had been injured. The sense of betrayal was worst of all – a man who went back on his oath, in front of the Flame or not, was not a man to be trusted with anything of value.

But then came the rewards.

To her father he granted the Yeomanry of Caolan's Pass. That was a shock and surprise to Dara – she knew the post was lucrative, as the keeper of the pass collected part of the toll every traveler paid him. But the reward also entailed guardianship of the pass – no small thing, considering how strategic it was. To Dara, Caolan's Pass had always seemed like the end of the world, she mused as she watched her brothers and uncles and father be rewarded for their service. Now that she had seen beyond it, through

Frightful's eyes, she knew that it was merely the gateway to a wider world.

A gateway her father now owned a piece of. She smiled when the Spellmonger praised her kin for their steadfast defense of the domain. Honor to the Hall was honor to all, went the saying. When the Magelord presented her brother with a beautiful brown charger, taken as spoils of war, as a token of his esteem for the Westwoodmen, Dara joined her family in cheering wildly.

"He's beautiful!" Dara agreed, when she got the chance to see the horse after court had adjourned. "What will you call him?"

"Autumn," decided Kyre, stroking the horse's black mane lovingly. "I'll have to keep him at the castle stables, but . . ."

"He's a magnificent animal," agreed her Uncle Keram, as he and her father joined them. "One of the Lord of Northwood's finest. That was a rich gift!"

"And one with expectation of greater service," agreed her father. "Caolan's Pass is to be ours, but it will be a lot of work to maintain, in addition to the Westwood. Our fortunes are rising, but the price is our toil."

"I can get used to the price," bragged Kyre, grinning. "Father, the Magelord is an honorable man. A cunning man. A worthy lord," he said, meaningfully. Dara wasn't exactly certain what he was talking about – wasn't all of that obvious?

"I have eyes, my son," Kamen reproved, gently. "But the moods of magi are fickle. He has done well by us, to be sure." There was more being unspoken than spoken, in front of her, and Dara didn't like it one bit. Clearly her father and brother were continuing a conversation she wasn't privy to, and it was irritating. Why was this important?

"Time will tell, as well as deeds," Keram added, wisely. "I think—"

"Excuse me, gentle people!" Dara never learned what her uncle, known for his craftiness, was thinking, because Master Banamor chose that moment to interrupt.

The Spellwarden was dressed in a long, dark brown robe of richly dyed wool. He wore a sash of office and a sword uncomfortably at his side. He pushed his way into the knot around Kyre's horse, searching around.

"Has anyone seen – oh, there you are!" he said, finally laying his eyes on Dara. "The hawkmaiden! Excellent, excellent . . . the Magelord directed Sir Cei to reward the loyal defenders of the castle and domain, before he scurried off to visit his bride-to-be before the wedding . . . but that's not why I sought you out. Before he left, the castellan directed me to bestow a small gift to the . . . well, let's be charitable and call ourselves a Magical Corps. That includes you, my dear," he added, when Dara's face did not seem to recognize what he was saying.

"M-me?"

"You were instrumental in field observations," he pointed out. "Not to mention saving our pass from being overwhelmed quite as quickly as they planned. So . . . please accept this token of a grateful lord and domain," he said, laying a small purse in her hand. It was heavy, she realized. "And don't be afraid to stop by my shop with that lovely bird, sometime," he reminded her. "When your Talent finally emerges fully, you'll be wanting some advice," he warned.

"Thank you, Master Banamor!" she said, giving the man the closest thing to a curtsey she could muster. As the Spellwarden wandered off in search of his assistant, Dara opened the purse . . . and took out five heavy pieces of silver.

"Five pennies?" asked Kyre, excitedly. The small silver coins were highly valued in the Westwood, where silver was rare.

"Five ounces!" corrected her father, grinning. "Dara, you could buy quite a lot with that!"

"Five ounces of silver?" Kyre asked in disbelief. "Flame! That makes you nearly rich!"

"Hardly rich," her uncle said, shaking his head. "But it would buy you cloth for a dozen dresses—"

"As if I need more dresses!" snorted Dara. She preferred a legging and tunic to dresses, one reason she enjoyed hawking so much. She had three dresses – one of which she was wearing – and she found them a bit of a bother. She was not the kind of girl for whom staying clean was a priority.

"Well, think of something to do with it," advised Keram. "That kind of money can be powerfully tempting."

"Oh, I'm sure I will," Dara said, absently. "For now, I'll save it. The magical fair is in a few weeks. I'm sure there will be something interesting to spend it on, there."

* * *

As the days of summer drew to a close and the leaves began changing color, the valley began filling with people – strangers – who were arriving for the famous Spellmonger's magical fair. Dara found herself skipping training and going across the bridge into the village more and more, as the day of the fair grew nearer.

Sevendor Village was being transformed yet again by the fair. Strange-looking merchants and oddly-dressed men from foreign parts arrived with pack horses, wagons, and on foot. Some had skin darker than basalt, others were as fair as a puffy cloud on a sunny day. Most were magi, Gareth explained to her, while walking through the High Street one day before the festivities started.

Dara had renewed her acquaintance of the wizard finally when he confronted her on the High Street in Sevendor Village. He looked a bit older and more serious, since the siege, but he had thankfully also stopped being so obviously interested in Dara. That allowed her to get past her own discomfort and talk to him as a friend.

Still, the young wizard seemed a bit withdrawn and distant from Dara. When she looked at him, he'd nervously cut his eyes away and mumble a response. Or he would stumble over his words unbearably. It was only when she discussed the upcoming Magic Fair that Gareth seemed to come out of his mask of reserved propriety.

"I have registered and collected fees from nearly all of them," he boasted, as they passed by a group of magi lingering in front of the new tavern that had sprung up on the Commons – one of the many things the late Railan the Steady had been upset by. Had he seen the wild folk arriving for the Fair, reasoned Dara, his head would have exploded before the Spellmonger could have taken it. "Many are footwizards, some are spellmongers, some are real High Magi – they have witchstones, like the Spellmonger."

"There seem to be a lot of them," she said, warily, as a tall, dark, handsome man with a big green stone in his ear and a bow on his back pushed his way inside the tavern.

"There are," agreed Gareth. "And you'll be seeing more warmagi arriving, too – tough customers, those. But they aren't about to pass up a chance at a prize like that. Master Minalan has declared that the mage who passes the Spellmonger's Trial will get a witchstone. A real piece of irionite. Only . . . I'm disqualified, since I'm helping to run the contest," he added, sadly. "Probably the only way I could get a witchstone, too . . ."

"What will the trial be like?" she asked, curiously.

"No one knows, for sure," Gareth shrugged. "I know parts of it, but . . . well, Master Minalan has called in some favors from very powerful wizards – High Magi all. They've used their witchstones to build the . . . whatever for the trial, but I have no idea what it might entail. It will be very, very hard, though," he admitted.

"Do you have to be a registered mage to do it?" she asked. Only Imperially trained magi could become registered, she knew; most of the footwizards who were haunting the village couldn't possibly be registered.

"Oh, no, Master Minalan wants everyone to have an equal chance at it. Anyone with Talent can participate. Even wild magi. That's . . . well, this whole event is unprecedented, but that's particularly bold. Most Imperially trained magi don't think footwizards and hedgewitches are potent enough to do more than remove warts or sell fake love spells. Master Min wants to include all magi in the way things are, now that the Censorate is gone."

"They aren't gone," Dara said, shaking her head. "I heard that they left here and went east."

"That's what I heard, too," Gareth agreed, quietly. "One would hope they would not stop at the ocean." Regardless of their station and class, Dara had come to understand *no* mage liked the Censorate. Some were particularly aggressive in their dislike. "We've been looking for anyone trying to sneak in. That's just the sort of thing they like to do. It would be like them to try to disrupt the Magical Fair the way they did Master Minalan's wedding, or the Chepstan Fair last spring."

"Oh, they wouldn't *dare!* Not with the Magelord back!" Dara protested.

"I hope he keeps them at bay. They're putting a lot of work into the Trial. If anyone messes it up . . ."

Finally, the opening day of the Magical Fair arrived, after the excitement of the formal state wedding of Sir Cei and Lady Estret. Dara waited until the initial festivities were over before she took Frightful and her purse – much heavier, once she'd been paid again for the skins she and Frightful had taken in late summer – across the bridge and quickly found herself in a whirlwind of excitement.

She had never seen so many outlandish folk! Men in long, colorful robes, ladies of noble bearing wearing long, elegant gowns, enchanters from Remere and peddlers from southern Alshar, spellmongers, hedgemagi, witches and sorcerers of all descriptions were eagerly crowding the Commons, where the fairgrounds had been set up. Dara paid her admission price to the keen-eyed fairwarden, swore her oath (the first time she had ever been required to do so) and entered the fairgrounds.

Most of the wares on display seemed as normal as any other market, with stacks and bundles of merchandise piled up behind fast-talking merchants. But the nature of that merchandise was intriguing – Dara had no idea what most of it was for. A lot of merchants seemed to be selling various rocks, or sticks, or coral, or mud, dust, dirt, sand, little bits of glass, twigs, berries, nuts, oddly-shaped pots . . . it was a bewildering array of junk to her untrained eye.

When she saw a man pay three ounces of silver for a box of sand that could fit in her palm, Dara realized that there were valuable commodities, here, for those who knew how to use them. And from the hungry look of anticipation she witnessed on face after face, she reasoned that this fair was a welcome release from the scourge of the Censorate.

There were some actual displays of magic at the fair, as different merchants demonstrated the efficacy of their wares. One vendor bearing master Banamor's device on his baldric was selling twigs that lit up at the end with a tiny magelight at a word. Another was selling stones that radiated heat all winter long. Another was showing off a smooth stick's ability to shoot gouts of flame into the air. Dara had to hood Frightful at that display. She could soar thousands of feet in the air, viciously dismember prey her own size, and even attack a grown man in the heat of battle . . . but no animal appreciated the sudden appearance of a column of fire.

Dara saw a few folk she knew from the castle and some others she'd met during the siege, but most of the Sevendori were hugging the edge of the fairgrounds and just watching the spectacle.

"That's a lot of wizards," a familiar voice from behind her tiredly observed. Gareth, wearing a wide straw hat to keep the sun out of his eyes, was leaning on a staff, a weary look on his face. "Over four hundred, give or take, by the Spellwarden's rolls. But they seem to be having a good time," he noted with an air of satisfaction. Dara knew he had been working night and day, since the siege, to help Master Banamor organize the event. He looked much older, for some reason.

"You did an excellent job," she smiled. "I've never seen so many people in Sevendor . . . well, I suppose I have, but . . ."

"I know," grinned Gareth. "Completely mad, isn't it? And this is just the beginning . . . this afternoon is the Spellmonger's Trial, then a special feast for the champion tonight, and then tomorrow a special court. That's after we held the wedding of Lady Estret of Cargwenyn to Sir Cei of Bov—of Sevendor, yesterday. *Sire* Cei, now," he amended.

Dara had learned during her brief time in the Magical Corps that the difference between "sir" and "sire," when it came to knights, was land ownership. The form of address "sire" denoted that a man was a landholding knight. Sir Festaran, for example, was a knight by birth and training, but he would not become *Sire* Festaran unless he was given title to a domain of his own, someday. Sir Cei, the castellan knight, became Sire Cei, landowning noble, with his wedding to the fair Lady Estret.

Dara knew the story well: a young widow in the nearby Barony of Sendaria, she had petitioned her lord, Baron Arathaniel, to find her a husband and her tiny domain a lord, after her husband died. The Baron had offered the prize at last spring's Chepstan Fair tournament. Sir Cei had been so enraptured by the sight of the widow that he had soundly defeated every knight he faced, breaking lances on the jousting field until they lay around like kindling . . . or at least that was the tale that was told.

The wedding had been the consummation of that victory, and cemented ties between Sevendor and Sendaria. Dara had come to understand politics enough lately to realize why that was important. Sevendor needed allies, she knew, and the Baron of Sendaria was a powerful one. He was here, she knew, specifically for the wedding. Her Hall had been in a tizzy all week – she had narrowly escaped getting caught up in the preparations – as her brother presented the castellan with a wedding gift of a bearskin cloak – the bear he had hunted last winter, and then cured the fur himself. He had been proud to present the important man with it. Dara thought he was crazy to give up such a noble item, but Kyre insisted that Sire Cei was worthy of such a gift.

The ceremony had been glorious, and the feast had been magnificent, she had heard. She had been invited, but after the excitement of the last several months she had decided against it. It was a bit overwhelming, and she didn't quite feel adult enough to contend with dancing, flirting, and meeting important people whose names she wouldn't remember. She adored Sire Cei, after his daring rescue on the trail to Caolan's Pass, and she admired what she'd heard of Lady Estret . . . but she just didn't feel up to it.

As enchanting a story as that was, however, Dara's attention was focused on something more dear to her curious nature.

"But what about the Spellmonger's Trial?" Dara asked, as much to keep Gareth from asking why she hadn't attended as any other reason.

"Well," Gareth said, conspiratorially, after looking around to make sure he wasn't overheard, "all I can tell you is that it involves Matten's Helm," he said, gesturing over his shoulder at the big hill you could see from just about everywhere in Sevendor. "You may have heard, there was a bit of commotion there, the other night—"

"Commotion? Another attack?" Dara asked, alarmed. Frightful flapped her wings, picking up on her trainer's emotions.

"Not that kind of commotion," Gareth continued, slyly. "There was a delegation from the Tree Folk. The Alka Alon, masters of magic and song. They apparently want to live here."

"What?!" Dara asked, shocked. If the Tal Alon were buffoonish characters from fable, the Alka Alon were mysterious figures out of legend. The Tree Folk, as they were commonly called, were creatures of myth, magical beings who lived deep in forests or caverns or mystical palaces, or something . . . not new neighbors.

"It will be kind of like an embassy," he continued, calmly. "They want to study snowstone and be close at hand to the Spellmonger. But that's not the best part," he said, with a certain amount of relish.

"What's the best part?" Dara asked.

"They've adopted human forms," he confided. "I saw them. And they are *beautiful!*"

Dara rolled her eyes. The greatest magicians in the world had stepped out of legend and wanted to move to Sevendor, and Gareth was most impressed by how comely they looked.

"The Spellmonger's Trial?" she reminded him.

"Eh? Oh! Because of that, Matten's Helm will be off-limits. Master Minalan essentially gave it to the Alka Alon. But before they take possession, it's going to be used in the Trial."

"How?"

"I can't say," Gareth said, his eyes twinkling.

"Gareth!" Dara exclaimed, irritated.

"I can't, I swore an oath!" he protested. "Do you know how many cutthroat warmagi are in town right now? Any one of them would torture me to death for what I knew," he assured her.

"I can see the appeal of that idea," she said, her eyes narrowing.

"See?" he pointed out, alarmed. "When irionite is the prize, even friends can turn on each other! The Spellmonger will be sharing the details at the start of the Trial. If you want to know more, you have to go register."

"Register? For what?" Dara asked.

"To compete," Gareth said, meaningfully. "Dara, this contest is open to all with Talent. Even you."

"I'm going to compete against a bunch of real wizards?" she scoffed.

"No one knows what challenges the Trial holds," he said, cryptically. "Master Minalan is encouraging everyone to participate. He wouldn't do that if there wasn't a chance you could win. And considering how low the entry fee is . . ." Gareth looked a little uncomfortable. "I, uh, could loan you the money, if you need to. I get paid pretty well . . ."

"I have my own coin, thank you very much!" Dara said, bridling at the offer. Gareth looked taken aback, and she realized she may have been more forceful than she intended. "I got some money from Master Banamor, from helping out with the siege. And I make some from pelts we sell at market," she said, nodding toward her bird.

"Then you should really consider competing," Gareth said, tight lipped. "Now, if you'll excuse me, there are about a thousand things that I need to be doing. See you at the Trials," he said, and wandered off.

Dara debated with herself mightily as she continued wandering through the fairgrounds. Entering the contest seemed a waste of good money – she had little hope of winning. Or even competing properly against real magi. But as she looked at the mysterious, intriguing wares for sale, she also realized that there wasn't anything else she could really spend her money on, here. She had no idea what any of the stuff did, or why it was important, or why she should buy it.

She found herself near the booth where magi were continuing to register for the Trial. A barker out front spoke in a loud, clear tone of the contest, repeating the magnificent prize for the champion, over and over: a witchstone, a shard of irionite, stone of magic and mystery, a prize above all others . . . Dara listened to the man's market pitch three times while she watched magi of all descriptions come forward, pay their fee, and add their names to the list.

Dara was next in line without even realizing that she had gotten in line.

"Name?" the officious little clerk asked, looking up from his roll of parchment.

"Lenodara of Westwood," she answered promptly. She knew her name. That was the easy part.

"Discipline?" the clerk continued.

"I beg your pardon?" Dara asked, confused.

"What kind of magic do you practice?" the man asked, patiently. "Spellmonger, Resident Adept in general practice, footwizard, hedgewitch, arcane academic, enchanter, thaumaturge, warmage, that sort of thing," he explained.

"Oh," Dara answered. She supposed she knew this one, too. "Beastmaster."

"Really?" the clerk asked, his eyebrows rising. "How intriguing. Class?"

"Huh?"

"How far advanced in your field of pursuit?" he asked, smoothly.

"I, uh, just figured it out this last spring," she admitted.

"Uh, *novice*," he decided, making a note. "Good of you to participate. It should be an educational experience, if nothing else. We're hoping for few fatalities, at least. The Spellmonger wants a good, clean, fair contest."

"And there really is a witchstone for the winner?" she asked. She had no idea what she would do with one, but for some reason Dara felt she wanted that stone more than she'd wanted anything except Frightful.

"There really is," he assured her. "I've seen it with my own eyes. For the victor," he reminded her, "whomever that is. You have your fee, young lady?"

Dara pushed her coins at the man, and he returned her the change. She had no idea how much was appropriate, and she had to trust him, but to cheat her would violate the fair's oath. She stumbled out of line in a daze, only partially realizing what she had done. She had entered a contest, with real magi.

"I'll never win," Dara told Frightful, after she purchased a tiny meat pie from a vendor and found a spot on the commons. It was a pretty day, and even if she was doomed to lose her money, it was exciting just to be included, she decided. She watched the other contestants prepare themselves as the time for the Trial grew closer.

If Dara wasn't intimidated by her competition before, she was now. Warmagi appeared in full armor, whirling their swords – "mageblades," Gareth had told her when she'd asked about the distinctive blades, part weapon and part magic wand – and doing strange exercises. Remeran magi in flowing robes were chanting and burning incense. Ragged-looking footwizards were muttering over their staves, and keen-eyed young student wizards leafed through their books searching for helpful spells.

Finally, the bell tolled, summoning the contestants to the tent in the middle of the fair, and Dara followed everyone else over to hear the instruction.

The Magelord looked quite lordly, Dara decided from her vantage at the back of the crowd. He had trimmed his whiskers and hair, and his garments were rich and colorful. He looked older, she noted, than the first time she'd seen him. She supposed she might look older, too, with a new baby, a troubled domain, and a war. Still, he smiled a lot and seemed quite enthusiastic about his Trial. He explained who could compete, why he was doing it, and a lot of other stuff, only half of which Dara heard.

Then came the important part: where Magelord Minalan revealed the nature of the Trial.

"A few nights ago I chanced to stroll across the peak of Matten's Helm," he said, gesturing to the tall, steep hill in the distance. "I was enjoying the evening, and smoking a pipe with my new Alka friends," he said, casually, as if he supped with legends and gods daily. "I suppose in my reverie I laid my pipe down on a stone and forgot about it. I would dearly love to have it back, but . . . it is such a long way from here. I have scryed the site, and am sure it is still there . . . but it may be guarded," he said, mischievously. "Your trial is simple. The mage who lays my pipe in my hands first will win the stone."

There was a great stir of excitement in the crowd. Dara watched as the magi around her reacted – some with surprise (particularly the warmagi, who had thought that combat would enter into the trial) some with delight. Merely fetching the Magelord's pipe seemed like a small thing, an achievable thing. After all, what could stop someone from fetching a pipe?

It couldn't be that easy, Dara figured. Not from the smile on Magelord Minalan's face. The crafty wizard lord had powerful friends, and he had toiled for days over the Trial – there had to be many obstacles in the path of the contestants. That was the assessment of many of the magi, too, as they sprinted away at the sound of the opening bell. Magelord Minalan and his retinue laughed merrily at the scramble toward the road to Matten's Helm, and walked off to the central pavilion to await the result.

The top of Matten's Helm, Dara thought, *that's . . . that's someplace we've been! Frightful lands there all the time,* she reasoned. *Surely . . . surely it can't be that easy!*

She thought about it. Clearly the Magelord had placed challenges in the path of those making their way up the mountain . . . but what about those who came in from above?

It couldn't hurt to try, she reasoned. Dara quickly found a spot behind a canopied tent selling long sticks of wood at really high prices, and she took off Frightful's hood.

"Just a quick trip to Matten's Helm," she promised. "It will give you a chance to stretch your wings and get away from all of these people."

Frightful didn't answer back, not in words. But the falcon was always eager to fly. And when Dara made contact with her mind and visualized the familiar hilltop. It was wide and flattish, dotted with rocks, with a small valley descending the crest to drain away the rain. Frightful recognized the place at once, and chirped a response.

"Go *there*," Dara directed, forcefully. "Let's see if we can see this pipe!" With that she flung her bird into the air, and watched her beat the wind with her wings to gain altitude. In seconds she was hundreds of feet overhead, quickly overtaking the magi streaming toward the hill. Dara closed her eyes, leaned back on a pile of magical sticks, and allowed her mind to sink behind the eyes of the falcon in flight.

Soon she was winging away with the bird, seeing things the way she did. They were in strong rapport as they surveyed the growing peak of the hill, and Dara convinced the falcon to circle the entire mound before considering landing. As she did, the girl noticed several places along the trail where people were waiting. With some concentration, she was able to recognize one of the Magelord's two apprentices – which one, she wasn't certain of. As he was holding a sword, she was just as glad she wasn't taking the long way to the top.

There didn't seem to be anything obscuring Frightful's flight to the top of the hill, so Dara gently guided her into the wide meadow there. It looked just as it did the many other times the two had visited it in tandem, with two exceptions.

One was a magnificent tree that had grown there, suddenly, where Dara was certain there had been no tree before. Work of the Tree Folk, she reasoned – if they had been here, and the Magelord had met them up here, then they were probably responsible for the pretty tree.

The other was a long pipe sitting on a large boulder nearby the tree.

Frightful hopped toward the rock, cocking her head as she observed it. Dara could tell the bird had no idea why the thing was so important – a falcon's curiosity was usually limited to dining prospects – but she cooperated with Dara's guidance and got closer.

The pipe wasn't unprotected, she realized. There was . . . *something* whirling around the great stone in the middle of the hilltop. Something magical, of course. Some trap or spell. Or both. She was familiar with the effect the wizards called 'magesight' – Gareth said nearly all Talented magi developed the capacity to see magical forces. She'd started to feel it herself, especially when she was at the castle, and she knew that some animals were sensitive to it. Whatever this spell was, Frightful could sense it.

The Spellmonger had assured everyone that there were no intentionally lethal spells in the Trial, but that didn't mean accidents didn't happen. As Frightful watched the vague disturbance in the air around the pipe Dara tried to appraise the potential harm in the spell.

She didn't want to hurt Frightful. But she was so close to the prize, when all the others were so far away. With a flash of impulse, she compelled Frightful to take wing again. Circling the meadow once, she brought the bird down to grab the pipe in her talons.

Victory seemed on the brink, as the pipe got tantalizingly closer . . . but then Frightful hit the outer limits of the spell, and all was chaos.

Dara wasn't quite thrown out of Frightful's head, but it almost felt like it. She clung desperately to the connection as the bird tumbled wildly off course. As she righted herself, next to the stone, Dara's conscious clawed its way back into control.

All right, not the most graceful attempt, she chided herself. The wave of feeling and emotion that had overtaken her mind when the spell was active had been potent. She had been infused with the strongest desire not to disturb the pipe in any way – just the sort of deterrent a wizard would use, she guessed. She had thought of a thousand excellent reasons why doing so would lead to disaster, all occurring to her mind at once, and the effect was so profound she felt nauseated.

Frightful, thankfully, did not seem to have been affected by the spell. Had Dara's mind not been so firmly in control, she barely would have felt it.

Perhaps it just doesn't work as well on animals, Dara considered. *Could that be the answer?*

She knew from her short acquaintance with wizards – Gareth and Master Banamor, mostly, but also Olmeg and Zagor – that they liked to trick with their magics. Gareth had explained once that sometimes the best way to accomplish magic was by convincing everyone not to do something, for instance – and he had been in the process of crafting spells to suggest that visitors to Sevendor Village not litter or relieve themselves in public, so he knew his business. Yet clearly those spells had not affected the canine population of the growing village, as they seemed content to poop wherever they desired.

Perhaps the Spellmonger's enchantment was similarly targeted toward human minds, Dara reasoned. In that case, she would have to depend upon Frightful to complete the task without her direct guidance.

It was difficult to prepare her bird for the mission – Frightful had grown used to sharing her mind with Dara as she soared along, and had eventually accepted Dara's firm guidance, and its attendant rewards. Dara visualized her desperate need to get the pipe to her bird as they circled overhead. Get the pipe, bring it back to me, she commanded her, until the poor bird's tiny brain understood.

Dara held on to her control of the falcon as she lined up for her run at the boulder, keeping her on task and reminding her of the vital importance of her mission . . . and then moments before the bird flew through the spell, Dara forced her eyes open and broke contact.

She was breathing hard, and sweat poured off of her at the effort. She waited ten full, agonizingly long heartbeats before she closed her eyes, calmed her mind, and sunk back into her falcon's mind . . .

As soon as she was in contact, she saw Frightful was again gaining altitude . . . and that she bore a comfortably heavy weight in her talons. Easier to grip than a rabbit or sparrow, the pipe was nonetheless heavier, and Frightful's wings strained at the burden.

"Oh, good girl!" Dara breathed to her bird, as she began the journey back to the fairgrounds. She spared a moment to witness the arrival of the leaders of the race at the new Tal Alon settlement at the base of the hill. The furry little Tals were delighting in throwing vegetables and clods of dirt at the magi, who had been cautioned about retaliating. The young warmage in the lead proceeded past the flung tomatoes with his jaw locked, a determined expression on his face.

Of course, he was running toward a contest he had already lost. Frightful spread her wings and began the long glide down to the fairgrounds, the fields and pastures of Jurlor's Hold underneath. As the falcon approached the mass of canopies and pavilions in the Commons, Dara broke contact again. Seconds later, as she was brushing magical wood shavings off of her butt, Frightful landed next to her.

"Took you long enough," Dara teased her bird. Frightful didn't understand it as anything but praise, as her trainer fed her a particularly large piece of dried venison liver. Frightful was ecstatic over the treat, and ate it hungrily.

Dara stared at the long, elegant pipe, turning it over in her hands three times before she self-consciously hid it under her mantle. When Frightful was done with her treat, Dara hooded her and put her on her shoulder.

She walked to the main pavilion in a daze. There were no guards, exactly, though there were servants (both human and Tal Alon) working to serve the Magelord and a group of his professional colleagues.

It was a full table full of wizards, Dara realized. Not only was the Magelord sitting there, drinking from a silver cup in splendor, but there were other magi of power there. Master Banamor was present, as were several warmagi or magelords or whatever else a powerful wizard was called. One was a young woman, not much older than her oldest sister, who sat next to the Magelord. She treated the Spellmonger with strong familiarity, something which made Dara's heart surge – that was not proper, she decided. Lady Alya could hardly be happy with that!

The Magelord himself was speaking as Dara stumbled up to the table, avoiding the messengers that darted to and fro into the canopy, mostly to speak with the Fairwarden. Dara quietly made her way as close as she could to the Magelord, until she was standing just behind him, and to his right.

". . . or, conversely, protect us from. We have time to do it properly. Right now, let's turn our attention to the base of the peak – the contestants are arriving, if you'd like to use your magesight to see, and the River Folk are happily pelting them with rotten vegetables. If you look closely you can see the very first of them struggling with the Barrier – yes?" he asked, when he finally noticed Dara at his elbow.

Dara didn't know what to say. Her hand dug under her patched mantle for the pipe while her mouth struggled with the right words. How did you announce victory when the contest had not, strictly speaking, even begun yet?

"Yes?" the Magelord repeated, more sternly, clearly not happy about the interruption. That's when Dara's fingers found the prize.

"I believe you wanted this, Magelord," she finally managed, as her hands pulled the pipe from beneath her cloak.

Magelord Minalan's eyes were wide with surprise – shock, even. He stared at the object as if he didn't quite recognize it. Dara pushed it at him, ready to be rid of it.

"Isn't this your pipe?" she asked, suddenly concerned that she had fetched some sort of decoy. Only that's not what the Magelord's face told her. She swallowed nervously. "Wasn't that what we were supposed to get from the mountain?" she asked, uncertainly. "Sorry it took me so long."

Chapter Seventeen

The Witchstone

The next few hours made the last few months, siege and all, seem like a pleasant diversion to Dara. When she revealed her prize to the Spellmonger, arguments immediately broke out all over the fair. And just as it had when she had plucked Frightful from her nest, Dara's life changed forever.

Gareth and Banamor valiantly tried to control the crowd, as the rumor of her victory spread, and the Spellmonger directed two burly warmagi to protect Dara until her uncle or father could be summoned. Luckily Keram had been at the fairgrounds conducting business, unaware of his niece's intrepid experiment in magical competition.

He learned soon enough. Once the Magelord explained what had happened to him, Keram collected Dara and her falcon and followed the female mage – Lady Pentandra, she introduced herself as – to a wagon. Soon they were being carried up to the castle, a groom proceeding the carriage to clear the way.

"So *this* is how you spend your free time, Dara?" Uncle Keram asked, his voice betraying the gravity of the situation though his tone was light.

"You and father *did* tell me to spend my money at the Fair," she reminded him, just as casually. "I figured sixpence was a reasonable fee for the chance at a witchstone."

Lady Pentandra looked amused. She was young and pretty, not at all like Dara had pictured her, when Gareth had first mentioned her. She was a good friend of the Magelord, it was said, a Remeran mage, who was one of the Magelord's oldest friends and colleagues. It was also whispered, scandalously, that they had once been lovers. But Lady Pentandra was trusted by Magelord Minalan like no other mage, it was also said, thanks to her loyalty and her devotion to him.

Pentandra examined Dara carefully with her eyes as they rode. Dara acted casually, but she could tell that every movement and every glance was being noted by those intelligent, pretty eyes.

"You have earned yourself quite a reputation, in a short period of time," Pentandra said, her lips in a tight smile. "It's not often that one girl and one hawk can cause so much commotion."

"Frightful is a falcon," corrected Dara. "Milady," she added, as an afterthought.

"Don't bother with titles in private, my dear," the lady mage replied. "It becomes tiresome. But I must commend you. It is rare that one can manage such a sophisticated expression of *rajira* as beastmastery, particularly in one so young. May I ask . . . have you seen your bloodmoon, yet?"

Dara blushed. "Only twice," she admitted. It had been one reason why she had avoided Sire Cei's wedding – she had felt poorly that evening.

"Then your Talent is likely emerging," the mage nodded. "Perfectly natural. Especially being so close to this much snowstone . . . tell me, where were you on that fateful night?" she asked, interrupting herself.

"The night the Snow That Never Melted came? At home in Westwood Hall," Dara answered. "It woke me up. I threw up," she added. It wasn't a pleasant memory.

"Of course. Would you allow me cast a few little spells on you, my dear? Nothing . . . invasive. I just want to take a basic measure of your emerging abilities."

Dara looked at Uncle Keram for support. Her uncle's face was solemn, and he nodded once in permission.

"Go ahead," Dara agreed, swallowing.

Lady Pentandra smiled indulgently and took Dara's hands, after she had passed her falcon to her uncle. If the spells were powerful, Dara barely felt a thing. For the remainder of the ride to the castle Pentandra conducted a few magical tests, she explained, nothing more. When they finally arrived in the courtyard Dara was taken to Sire Cei's quarters with her uncle to await the Spellmonger's decision. Lady Pentandra made sure she was cared for before she left.

"Whatever you do, keep your bird by your side," warned the mage, as she departed. "She's beautiful, but there are a lot of hotheads out there that would take a shot at her out of spite for losing."

That was a sobering thought. Dara paced the neat, tidy room that the castellan called home. He was off with his new bride somewhere, Dara figured, so his room was vacant. The trophies on the walls and the banners hanging from the rafters gave her something to look at for a while, as did the massive wooden pegboard that kept track of the domain's expenses, but she was soon bored. Her uncle wasn't much help. He was content to nap in the castellan's new bed.

An hour after they arrived, a human servant brought up ale and cakes for them, then closed the door firmly behind him. Dara could hear the commotion from the fair from the window of the keep. There were a lot of people upset about this, she realized. Really upset. Not just agitators like Railan the Steady had been, but warmagi and adepts of great power.

What were we thinking, Frightful? she silently asked her bird. The falcon had no answer.

As she was finishing off her second cake and wondering if she would be imprisoned in the white castle forever, the door opened again . . . and Magelord Minalan himself stepped in.

Her uncle immediately got to his feet, with far more speed than Dara thought possible, and he had a dagger half-drawn in his hand. When he saw who the visitor was he sheathed it and stood respectfully, but the Magelord motioned for him to sit.

"I don't have a lot of time," he said, apologetically. "So I have to make this interview brief. How, exactly, did you retrieve the pipe, Dara?" he asked.

Dara took a deep breath, glanced at Frightful, and told the entire tale, as concisely as she could. The Magelord stroked his beard absently while he listened, nodding his head in places. When she finished, the wizard lord nodded his head.

"I see," he said, beginning to pace the room much as Dara had. "This is my fault, I'm afraid. I honestly hadn't thought of anyone going for the pipe from the air – certainly not with a hawk."

"Falcon," Dara corrected, automatically.

"Whatever," dismissed the nobleman. "In a way, you did me a great favor by exposing the weakness in the Trial so early in its history. Next year, he said, chuckling, "that sort of thing will not be possible."

"But it was this year," her uncle pointed out. "And though we suspected it not, she entered, paid her fee, and then won the contest."

"So she did," admitted the mage. "And such ingenuity should not go unrewarded."

"I believe a witchstone was the prize offered, Magelord," Uncle Keram said, respectfully. His meaning was clear, however: if the Spellmonger went back on his word and Dara did not receive the piece of irionite that was promised, that would affect how the Westwoodmen viewed their lord. The Magelord was a wise man – he got the implication immediately, as well as the subtle, respectful way in which it was delivered. Dara was surprised – she didn't think her uncle would stand up to a lord as good as Minalan over one little girl.

"I appreciate the complexities of the situation, I assure you," Minalan said, a little discouraged. "Tell me, Dara, if you could do anything in the world, *be* anyone in the world, who would it be? *What* would it be?"

Dara considered – it was the *last* question she'd expected anyone to ask her, and the one she was least prepared to answer. It irritated her to have it sprung on her like that . . . but she also guessed that displaying indecision, or worse still, mumbling in confusion, would not be the best course of action.

She took a deep breath. "With respect, Magelord, I've only finished my thirteenth summer. I love falconry. I love the Westwood. I . . . I'm starting to like magic," she admitted, shyly. "So if you're waiting for me to blurt out that I want to be a chandler's wife and have a lot of fat babies . . ."

"I understand," chuckled the mage. "Perhaps that was the wrong question, but you answered it smartly enough. You love birds, you love the forest, you like magic. I think that is something I can work with." He gave her uncle a meaningful glance. "In truth, I spoke at length about you to both your father and your oldest brother. They say good things about your character, even though they're family. Particularly your bravery and intelligence. Those are rare qualities, I'm learning, and they should be nourished where I can find them.

"I'm going to discuss this issue with my advisors, now," he said, after a moment's pause. "I honestly do not know what decision I will make. But whatever it is, it will be one that sees that your courage and ingenuity are properly honored. I could do the Westwood no less, after the service it has done for Sevendor."

"Well, that sounded encouraging," Uncle Keram said, when the wizard had left.

"Uncle! You didn't have to insist that I get the stone!" Dara nearly exploded. "Do you realize what kind of position I have put him in?"

"The fact that *you* realize it, and aren't merely greedy for your prize, says much about you, Little Bird," he said, quietly. "So much has changed in the last year, and you most of all. And not just the fit of your tunics," he teased. "You've had to grow up more quickly than I like, even if it was through better times than I'd hoped. I figured your father and I would be starting to entertain proposals for your hand by now – the daughter of the Master of the Wood is a high position. *Not* negotiating with wizards over your future."

"It's just a silly rock," Dara dismissed.

"It is *not*, Dara, and you know it," Keram said, warningly. "Don't discredit my admiration with false humility. You should understand, by now, just what being in a mageland means for the folk. We live under the rule of wizards, and you've seen proof of how mighty they can be. Master Minalan destroyed three of the Warbird's castles, while he was harassing us here – without besieging them. He destroyed them by *magic*. With his witchstone."

"I'm not a mage—"

"You're just a thirteen-year-old girl with a pet bird," Keram finished. "I *know*. But the chance at a witchstone, even the least of witchstones, grants enormous power to these magi. That's an offer of position no one in their right mind should shy away from. Far above what your father could offer you."

"But I don't *deserve* a stone!" Dara complained. "I . . . I *cheated!*"

"You won the contest fair, by the rules," Keram said, sternly. "The Spellmonger said as much. Don't worry, everything will work out fine."

"Then why did you wake up with a dagger in your hand?" Dara accused.

"Because while I'm confident in the Spellmonger's wisdom," Keram said, chuckling, "I'm less so about that of the warmagi. I've listened to these men drinking, in the taverns. They have the strength of soldiers and the power of magi . . . and the patience of a toddler. The lad who came in second place, Jendaran, I think his name is, seems a good sort . . . but some of his friends . . ." he shrugged. "Your father and I – and the Spellmonger – thought it best if you had some protection from the hotheads until this gets sorted out, is all."

"I never meant to cause any trouble," Dara said, her shoulders sagging. "I was just . . ."

"You were just being Dara," he chuckled. "What did we expect you to do? We didn't tell you not to go and become a powerful wizard, any more than we told you not to scale an obscenely dangerous mountain to get a falcon to train. I suppose we should have been more thorough in our instruction," he said, diplomatically.

"That would have been surprisingly helpful," Dara said, dully.

"Then while I'm thinking about it, don't slay any dragons," he said, giving her a hug. "Does that help?"

She was glad she had such stalwart, understanding family. Though she loved and revered her father, her Uncle Keram had been the one to whom she felt closest to. She was glad he was here with her, while the rest of the domain considered rioting over her stunt.

"By the Flame, I will keep it under advisement," Dara assured him, hugging him more tightly.

* * *

That afternoon, Dara and her uncle were led to another part of the castle, the very familiar room of the Spellmonger's workshop, where she and the other members of the Magical Corps had worked during the siege. It looked different, now. Sloppier, somehow. There were bags and baskets and such all over the room. Many seemed to be samples from the Magic Fair, or gifts, or books. Others looked like parcels delivered after a long journey, bundled in crates or large sacks. A Tal Alon servant brought them bread, cheese, and fruit for their luncheon while they waited, and poured them each a glass of wine.

Dara was feeling better, now. She had taken strength in her uncle's confidence, and Minalan's affable manner. He wasn't angry with Dara for her victory, she realized, he was just attempting to contend with the difficult result. That did make her feel better . . . and willing to accept whatever decision her lord made.

There was plenty of noise still rolling out of the encampments on the Commons as the wizards reacted to rumors and news about the contest. Below, in the Great Hall, the decorations left over from the wedding were replaced with more arcane ornaments, as the servants prepared for the great awards banquet the champion was supposed to attend. Who would that be, she wondered?

Eventually the Spellmonger returned. The Magelord was not alone, however – a large man, almost as tall as Sire Cei and broader by a span across the shoulders, followed Minalan into the workshop. He stood straight up, his plaited hair neatly arrayed down his back, and he wore a shining hauberk of polished steel. In his gauntleted hands he carried a staff of dark wood, and a sword – a mageblade, Dara corrected herself – hung from his belt.

"Lenodara of Westwood, this is Jendaran the Trusty, a warmage. The warmage who made it to the top of the hill first," he added. "He wanted to come talk to you, before I announced my decision."

"So you're the little squirt who stole my prize," the big man boomed. Dara felt her uncle stiffen behind her, but she didn't blink. This was a man, she decided, who used his size to intimidate people, just like Railan the Steady used to. The fact that he was armored and well-muscled, not to mention a deadly warmage, probably added to the effect, she decided, but when she had given up her fear and confronted Railan, she had decided she disliked being intimidated like that.

"I'm the mage who won the Trial," Dara agreed. "I hear you did pretty well yourself," she added, boldly.

She didn't know if Jendaran would be angry or not at her impudent retort – but she didn't care. Either she would win the witchstone, or she wouldn't. Either way, she would not back away from her accomplishments.

"So you're a beastmaster," he said, snorting a bit over the title. "And that's the bird that took it?"

"Frightful," Dara agreed, evenly. "A falcon. I captured her and trained her myself."

Jendaran folded his arms over his chest and stared at her. "And you think training a pet bird entitles you to a witchstone?" he asked, warningly. "I charged a company of Remeran knights single-handedly, and slew *nine* of them," he boasted.

Dara refused to be intimidated. "I scaled an eighty-foot sheer basalt cliff, lowered myself down the other side on a rope, and dangled over a seven-hundred-foot drop to certain death to get that bird," Dara said, calmly. "By myself. Without armor." Jendaran still looked skeptical. "When I was *twelve*," Dara pointed out. That, at least, made the warmage think.

"I cannot fault your bravery," he admitted. "Nor your ingenuity. But to think that you're entitled to—"

"What I fairly won? According to the rules of the contest, as announced and certified by the Coinbrothers?" Dara snorted. "With all respect to your abilities, powers, and position, Master Jendaran, what would you do in my position? What would you have done? Not used the one bit of magic you had to win the contest, when you saw the chance?"

"Well, when you put it like that," the mage said, his face starting to break a little, "I suppose I can see your perspective. I suppose all we can do is trust in this Spellmonger to do what is fair."

"It has been our experience that Magelord Minalan is quite attentive to fairness, in his administration," her uncle said, for the first time. "I trust his judgment implicitly. I encourage you to likewise."

"So if he decides to give me the witchstone, and not you?" Jendaran asked, a hint of challenge in his voice.

"I will respect the judgment of my lord," Dara pledged. "Regardless of the outcome. Will you do the same?"

"By Duin's . . . axe," swore the warmage, choosing the god of war to invoke, "I will. If it is decided I was bested by you, I can at least admit it was done out of quickness and intelligence, not strength or deceit."

"I appreciate your understanding," Dara said, graciously. "Honestly, I never thought it would work. When it did . . ."

Master Minalan smiled weakly. "Fascinating, isn't it?" he asked. "Success very rarely comes to us without attendant problems. Even when you think you're doing the right thing, it can cause problems. Well, if I can count on the two of you not to contest the outcome and kill each other, I will announce my decision at the banquet. I think we have a little time for you to prepare yourselves. But I'd like to keep you here, under guard at the castle, until the decision is reached. We've already had a few, ah, altercations over the result. The Coinbrethren refuse to pay on the day's wagers until a winner is chosen, so a lot of people are feeling emotional over this."

When Jendaran and the Magelord left, Dara was surprised to see her sister Linta appear, bearing her very best dress that didn't quite fit anymore. She looked shocked and surprised, as if Dara had been replaced by someone else bearing her name and face.

"You . . . you *won* the Spellmonger's Trial?" she asked without bothering to greet her youngest sister.

"It was kind of an accident," Dara said, apologetically.

"I knew that hawk was trouble," she accused, as she laid out the dress on a worktable. Uncle Keram smiled and excused himself, leaving the sisters alone.

"*Falcon*," corrected Dara. "Frightful is a falcon."

"Whatever," she said. "All I know is I was enjoying a really interesting conversation with a handsome young spellmonger from Rikken when Father appears . . . not to assault the man, like I suspected, but to order me to run home and get *your* festival finery up to the castle. Like I was a common servant!" she fumed, her nostrils flaring.

"It is hard to believe you've survived so long under such dire conditions," Dara agreed, pulling her plain woolen tunic over her head.

"Isn't it?" Linta said, without realizing Dara was being sarcastic. She helped strip off her leggings, stained by the mud and straw and magical sawdust of the fairgrounds. "I brought you slippers, too – mine, because yours look like they belong to a doll, now," she said, rolling her eyes as she handed them to her.

Dara took them. They did look bigger . . . but then she hadn't worn her slippers since . . . she couldn't remember the last time. Falconers wore boots, after all. She pushed her feet into them and was surprised at how comfortable they were. Perhaps her feet had grown.

So had other parts of her – Linta had to whip out scissors, needle, and thread and hurriedly let out the top of the simple festival dress that was Dara's best. She was very appreciative of it – considering her appalling skills with a needle, if it had been left up to her she would have likely sewn herself to the dress. Linta adeptly tacked the pieces together, then joined them with a running stitch.

"I can't believe you pulled this off, Little Bird," Linta said, wistfully. "I knew you were trouble, but did you have to go and involve the entire domain? Everyone is talking about this, now. How some freckle-faced girl snuck in and stole the contest from two hundred real wizards. The boys are all expecting fights to break out. Father had the guards doubled at the bridge, and . . . well, everyone knows who you are, now," she admitted, expediently snapping the thread in two with her teeth.

"Sorry," Dara said, trying her best to hold still.

"Don't be," Linta said, shrugging again. "Let me do the other side, now. It was strange, having boys ask me if . . . if I was 'Dara's sister' . . . certainly not something I'm used to . . . but . . ."

". . . but at least they were asking you," Dara pointed out.

"Right," Linta nodded, absently, as her fingers got to work. "Of course I said I was – I have to support the Hall – but now everyone really does know who you are. The maid with the hawk."

"Falcon!" Dara insisted. Linta ignored her.

"The point is, Little Bird, that you, Flame alone knows why, have become very important, all of a sudden. And that's not what anyone was expecting."

"What were they expecting?"

"Well, that wouldn't be polite to speculate upon," Linta said, with a hint of the meanness every older sister is capable of. "But this? You almost getting us in a fight with two hundred angry wizards? In *one day*? That's exceeding everyone's expectations. There. Your dress is done," she said, snipping the thread with the shears, this time. "Let me comb your hair and . . . oh, you need a belt," Linta said.

"My belt is right there," Dara said, nodding to the plain brown leather belt she used to carry her falconry supplies around.

"That won't do," Linta said, shaking her head, "there's going to be a *baron* at dinner, not to mention knights, lords, and a whole bunch of wizards. We can't have you representing the Hall looking like the pig girl," she japed.

Before Dara could come up with a witty response, Linta had reached behind her and unclasped the brass belt with the silver bells she wore almost religiously when she went to the Village these days. The same one Dara had repaired for her. "Here, wear this," she said, helping Dara strap it on over the gown. "It looks nice on you . . . if a bit loose," she added, tightening the knot as much as she could.

Dara was speechless – this was an unprecedented act of sisterly benevolence by Linta.

"But . . . but how will you attract attention without . . .?"

"Oh, the belt does all right at that," Linta shrugged, "but having a famous sister does it a whole lot better." Dara felt better. Had Linta not had a selfish ulterior motive, she might have suspected she'd been replaced by some magical double herself. "Good luck, tonight, Dara," she said, as she began brushing her hair. "I have a feeling your life is about to change. A lot."

* * *

The Great Hall at Sevendor Castle looked every bit as splendid as it had at Yule, if not more so. There were, after all, far more magi here now than there had been then, so there were magelights of all description everywhere. The temperate weather allowed the yard outside the hall to be used to extend the banquet space. Trestle tables had been prepared to seat hundreds of guests, and the kitchens had been working since the previous evening to supply so much food.

Dara was inside the Great Hall, of course – more, she was at the Great Table, the huge white stone slab of a table the

Magelord had built himself on the dais in front of the great white fireplace. She was at the same table as the Magelord, Lady Alya, Baron Arathaniel and his wife, the Lord of Trestendor, Lady Pentandra, and a few other magi Dara was unfamiliar with. Her kin were seated nearby, only three or four tables away, so any time she was nervous all she had to do was look up to see her father Kamen, her uncle Keram, her brothers Kyre, Kure, and Kobb, and several of her cousins there. And her sister Linta, with whom she exchanged a shy wave.

Before the porridge course was served, the Magelord stood, silenced the musicians playing in the gallery, and spoke. He must have used magic, Dara guessed, because everyone in the castle seemed to be able to hear him speak without him raising his voice overmuch.

"My friends, neighbors, and colleagues," he announced, after he introduced himself. "It is my pleasure to welcome you to the first-ever Champion's Banquet. Today we celebrate those who met the challenge of the Spellmonger's Trial and triumphed!" There were cheers, encouraged by many in the audience. Some only applauded reluctantly, but Minalan's enthusiasm was contagious.

"As you may have heard, this first Spellmonger's Trial was eventful," he continued. "Master Jendaran bested every challenge along the way, gave a few bruises to my apprentice Tyndal, and pushed his way to the summit . . . only to find himself beaten out by a girl with a hawk. A beastmaster," he continued, as the audience murmured, "and one familiar with the vale because she was born here.

"While some have cried foul over this, suspecting treachery of some sort designed to deny the proper prize to the first man to the top, the fact is that this was my error. I had not considered the possibility when I designed my challenge.

"But the rules are the rules, and I must live up to them, even though I made them. I cannot fairly change them after the fact. But I also have the power to augment them. So I am awarding – just this once – a powerful witchstone to Jendaran, upon the condition that he take his oath to me and then spend half a year fighting the goblin hordes in the Penumbralands, in the service of the military order of his choice."

There was a lot of applause for that, and at the Spellmonger's urging Jendaran stood and received the acclaim of his peers. The big man looked satisfied with the arrangement, Dara decided as he accepted the small, ornate wooden box containing his prize from his host.

"But the fact is, as well as Jendaran defeated the challenges, Lenodara of Westwood was the victor, because she was wise enough to use her strengths to circumvent those challenges. Some have called this cheating. I disagree. I see it as an ingenious use of magical resources . . . something I think many of our colleagues could stand to concern themselves with," he added, earning a ripple of laughter. Dara supposed it was some inside-joke among wizards.

"As adept as she was, however, the fact remains that this youthful contestant is not, currently, in training to master her emerging Talent. Therefore, while I do hereby award the victor at the Trial to Lenodara of Westwood," he said, loudly...immediately causing a rush of folk toward the Coinbrothers, the monks who oversaw wagering at such events, to claim their winnings.

"I also award her the least of witchstones, a small shard of irionite provided from the recently-seized storehouses of the Censorate. In addition," he continued, "as Dara is a subject of mine, and her father is my Yeoman, I must take additional action. I can't very well call myself a Magelord and let such superb magical Talent lie fallow. Therefore, after discussing it with her father, it has been decided that Lenodara of Westwood will henceforth be apprenticed to me to be trained in Imperial-style magic."

Dara's jaw dropped. Even though she was sitting three seats down from the Magelord, she had no idea he had considered such a thing. She searched the room wildly until she found the face of her father, who nodded with resignation. But the Magelord wasn't finished.

"It has been noted that I already have two apprentices, and it has been whispered that I'm not particularly good at controlling them as it is . . . but the fact is that I must look not just to the prosperity of my domain – my domains," he corrected himself, remembering he had just conquered five additional provinces, "but also to their security. As this is a mageland, I need good magi who can be counted upon to defend it. And while I can hire plenty of them – probably everyone here would be willing, I think – I also think that the best defenders are those we grow ourselves.

"Dara will become my apprentice, learn magic, and she will become one of Sevendor's defenders, in my absence –

gods willing," he added with a smile. "She captured and trained that hawk of hers herself. She assisted her Hall with the defense of the domain during the siege. And she outsmarted all of you lot," he added with a snicker, "overcoming the best minds in magic to win the Trial.

"She's intelligent, she's brave, and she's Talented. It is my hope that as soon as we are settled she will come live with us here, at Sevendor Castle, and begin her magical training with me in earnest. So may I present to you, my friends and neighbors, the victor of the Spellmonger's Trial . . . and my newest apprentice . . . Dara of Westwood . . . the Hawkmaiden!" he announced.

Dara was overwhelmed by the thunderous applause that filled the castle to the rafters when the Magelord said her name. Everyone seemed to be clapping wildly, and it was quite overwhelming. Then her kin got on their feet and cheered, and some of the others did, and then the entire castle was cheering loudly enough to be heard all the way back to Westwood Hall . . . perhaps by the Flame, itself.

Dara stood slowly and bowed to everyone, earning yet more cheers, and then accepted the small box that Master Minalan handed her. She opened it, briefly, to see the tiny glowing gemstone inside. It was milky green and plain . . . yet when she opened the box she could feel the witchstone as much as she could see it. It was like the rapport she shared with Frightful, only more intense, somehow.

She snapped the box shut and bowed to her lord. Master Minalan bowed in return, then pulled her in for a triumphant embrace.

"Smile!" he urged her, quietly. "You just kept everyone from fighting over you!"

She smiled, even if her mind was still awash in confusion.

"Sorry about springing the apprenticeship on you," the Magelord continued to whisper, "but your father and I agreed that, under the circumstances, that might be best for you, right now. Are you agreeable to the idea? If not, we can—"

Dara spoke before she knew what she would say. This time her mouth did not betray her. "It's perfect!" she assured him. "At least for now. Does that mean I'll have to learn how to read?"

"Yes," the Magelord agreed, still waving at the cheering crowd. "It's not as hard as it looks. Actually, it's about the easiest thing you'll learn. The hard part will be dealing with my other two apprentices," he said, gesturing over to the two Wilderland boys, Rondal and Tyndal, who sat at a nearby table. Neither one of them looked particularly pleased with their new junior apprentice.

"They're just boys," Dara dismissed. "Believe me, I can handle them. But . . . can I bring my falcon?"

"Frightful? Of course!" Minalan agreed, finally taking his seat. "You're a beastmaster, after all. In fact, we'll probably start exploring that immediately. See if you can bilocate with other animals, that sort of thing. All in good time, Dara. For now, just enjoy the glory," he said, gesturing to the crowd, where many still were applauding her. "It only lasts for a moment. Like childhood," he added, wistfully.

Dara did. For one, magically indulgent moment, she basked in the approval and adulation from the wizards who had competed. Her *fellow* wizards, she corrected herself.

Westwood girl, falconer, and now mage . . . it had been a pretty eventful year, she decided, looking down at the wooden box that contained her precious prize.

Just what would the next year hold? she wondered.

The End

Thank you for reading! You may always email the author at tmancour@gmail.com!

Look out for forthcoming Spellmonger Cadet novels, including the sequel to Hawkmaiden: ***Hawklady!***

The Spellmonger Novels

Spellmonger

Warmage

Magelord

Knights Magi

High Mage

(forthcoming)

Journeymage

Anthologies and Novellas

The Road To Sevendor

The Spellmonger's Honeymoon

CPSIA information can be obtained
at www.ICGtesting.com
Printed in the USA
LVHW020055310323
743121LV00015B/1102